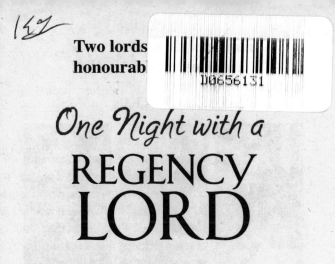

Two lords
honourab

One Night with a REGENCY LORD

ISABELLE GODDARD
LUCY ASHFORD

One Night with

COLLECTION

February 2015

February 2015

February 2015

February 2015

March 2015

March 2015

One Night with a REGENCY LORD

ISABELLE GODDARD

LUCY ASHFORD

Published in Great Britain 2015
by Mills & Boon, an imprint of Harlequin (UK) Limited,
Eton House, 18-24 Paradise Road, Richmond, Surrey, TW9 1SR

ISBN: 978-0-263-25363-4

009-0215

Harlequin (UK) Limited's policy is to use papers that are natural, renewable and recyclable products and made from wood grown in sustainable forests.The logging and manufacturing processes conform to the legalenvironmental regulations of the country of origin.

Printed and bound in Spain
by CPI, Barcelona

REPROBATE LORD, RUNAWAY LADY

ISABELLE GODDARD

Isabelle Goddard was born into an army family and spent her childhood moving around the UK and abroad. Unsurprisingly, it gave her itchy feet and in her twenties she escaped from an unloved secretarial career to work as cabin crew and see the world.

The arrival of marriage, children and cats meant a more settled life in the south of England, where she's lived ever since. It also gave her the opportunity to go back to 'school' and eventually teach at university. Isabelle loves the nineteenth century and grew up reading Georgette Heyer, so when she plucked up the courage to begin writing herself the novels had to be Regency romances.

To the friends who listened

Chapter One

London, 1817

'Amelie, you will do this for me, for the family.' It was a command rather than a question.

The young woman held her head high and blinked back the tears. Despite her resolution, there was a stricken look in the soft brown eyes.

'Papa, I cannot. Ask anything else of me, but I cannot marry that man.'

Her father, pacing agitatedly back and forth across the worn library carpet, stopped suddenly opposite her and raked her with a piercing glare. 'Sir Rufus Glyde is a respected nobleman, one who will give you an elegant home and a secure future. And one who will save this family from disaster.'

She looked past her father to the open window, but

hardly saw the mass of roses filling the garden with a riot of colour in the late afternoon sun.

'Surely, Papa,' she pleaded, 'the situation cannot be that desperate.'

Lord Silverdale was silent. His face, though still handsome, appeared haggard and drawn. He carefully brushed the snuff from a velvet sleeve and spoke quietly but insistently.

'The family is virtually ruined. Over the past few months I have had to sell my entire stable of horses and rent out Nethercott Place to a wealthy cit. Generations of Silverdales dishonoured by the taint of city money! And now Robert's addiction to gambling is likely to lose us our last piece of security—our house here in Grosvenor Square.'

'In that case,' she responded sharply, 'why doesn't Robert find a way of repaying what he owes?' Her brother's decadent lifestyle was something she could not forgive. 'Why doesn't *he* marry for money?'

Lord Silverdale looked at his daughter, breathtakingly lovely even in simple sprig muslin, and said gently, 'Amelie, you know that it isn't possible. What does he have to offer except debt and unsteadiness? Certainly nothing the matchmaking mamas at Almack's want. You, on the other hand, have youth, beauty and a steadfast character. Rufus Glyde admires you and wants to make you his wife.'

'But he is nearly twice my age.'

'He is no more than fourteen years older than you. That is no great age. It is well for a husband to be more experienced than his wife. Then he may teach her how to go on in society.'

An image of Rufus Glyde's dissolute eyes and thin, sneering lips swam into her vision and made her shudder. She would not wish to be taught anything by such a man. In her revulsion she twisted the cambric handkerchief she held into a vicious knot.

'I can never care for him,' she declared hotly.

'But do you care for anyone else? You have had an entire Season to find someone to your taste, a Season I could ill afford. And look what has happened. You have been distant and unapproachable to the young men you've met. Only one was willing to brave your coldness and actually offer for you, and you dismissed his proposal out of hand. So what do you want?'

'I want to remain single, Papa. I'm grateful for my introduction to society, but the men I've met have been either shallow or profligate. I shall never marry unless I find a man I truly love and respect—and that seems unlikely.'

'You will be lucky to find any man in the future. There will be no more Seasons—and no home, either, if Sir Rufus forecloses on our mortgage,' her father added bitterly.

She caught her breath. 'What do you mean?'

'I had not meant to tell you, but you should know the truth of the situation. Your brother has lost this house to Rufus Glyde. In a fit of madness he used it as a stake for his gambling. Either you marry Sir Rufus or we are homeless.'

'How can you allow him to threaten us like this?'

'Come, come, child, the man is willing to make a generous settlement on you, apart from returning the mortgage. He will, I am sure, always treat you with respect and you will have ample money and time to pursue your own interests. Such marriages of convenience are common among our class. You know that.' Lord Silverdale paused, thinking of his own love marriage, its first intoxicating passion barely surviving a year. 'They can often work far better than marrying for love.'

Amelie turned away, unwilling to show the disgust she felt.

'I have no choice,' her father said heavily. 'This is a debt of honour and must be paid, one way or another.'

'And I am to pay the debt,' she cried, her anger bursting forth. 'I am to be the family sacrifice, am I?' She strode furiously up and down the room between the dusty book-filled shelves, chestnut curls tumbling free and framing her lovely face.

With an exasperated mutter, Lord Silverdale walked swiftly towards her and grasped her hands. 'Enough. You forget yourself. You are beautiful and clever, my dear, but you are far too independent. It puts men off and those it doesn't, you will not have. Think yourself lucky that Sir Rufus values high spirits as well as being a connoisseur of beauty. He has very properly asked me for permission to pay his addresses to you, and I have agreed.'

'No, no, I cannot do it,' she uttered a strangled cry.

'Anything but that! I'll go out and earn my own bread rather.'

'Earn your own bread? What is this? Your taste for the dramatic is regrettable and too reminiscent of your French relations,' he said disdainfully, walking away from her towards the tall windows.

When he turned again, his face wore an implacable expression and he spoke in a voice that brooked no further disagreement.

'You have been made a highly advantageous offer, Amelie, which will secure this family's future and your own. You will go to your room immediately and stay there. In the morning you will make yourself presentable. Sir Rufus will be with us at noon and you will accept his offer. Do I make myself clear?'

The interview was at an end. Lord Silverdale sank wearily down at his desk, and began listlessly to leaf through his scattered papers. His daughter, overcome with angry tears, turned on her heel and noisily banged the oak-panelled door behind her.

Once in her room, she cast herself down on to the damask bedspread and wept. Her grief was intense and though her tears soon subsided, her fury remained. To be forced into a repugnant marriage because of her brother's stupidity! And by her own father! She knew him to be autocratic, but never so unfeeling that he would contemplate selling her to the highest bidder. He might try to wrap it up in clean linen, but that's what it came down to. When she was a child he'd been an indulgent parent, reading with her, schooling her on her first pony, bringing surprises each birthday. Yet, if crossed, he could be unrelenting.

Until now she'd been spared this side of his character, but she knew the suffering it had caused his wife. Her heart ached for her dead mother. Louise St Clair's life had not been a happy one: an *émigrée* from France, an unhappy marriage to an English aristocrat and then an early death.

Lord Miles Silverdale must have seemed like a white knight when Louise first met him, just months after her dangerous journey from the outskirts of Paris to exile in England. The Bastille would not be stormed for another year, but revolution was already in the air. Signs of dissent and rebellion were everywhere and when the St Clair family home was ransacked without any attempt by the servants to prevent it, Brielle St Clair had decided it was no longer safe for the family to stay. She and her eighteen-year-old daughter, disguised as servants themselves, were forced to steal away under cover of darkness and embark on a slow and tortuous journey to the Channel coast. They had travelled by night, resting beneath hedges in the daytime, and ever fearful of discovery.

To a refugee in a foreign land, Lord Silverdale's offer of marriage must have seemed like a miracle. He promised happiness and security, a new future for the young, homeless girl. Happiness, though, had lasted only a year until the birth of Robert. Louise was sickly for months afterwards, needing constant nursing, and unable to share in the social flurry of her husband's life. Miles

Silverdale, having fallen violently in love with a youthful form and a beautiful face, found himself without either as a companion.

The constant miscarriages that followed year after year pushed them yet further apart. Amelie's birth and her unexpected survival had brought a brief reconciliation only. Even as a child she'd understood the pain written on her mother's face, as her husband left for yet another lengthy stay at a friend's country house, knowing that most of his time would be spent enjoying the company of other women.

But that was not going to happen to her! She had her mother's beauty, certainly, but also her grandmother's spirit. Louise might have been scared half out of her wits by that flight across France, but Brielle St Clair had exalted in it. Her tales of their adventures had enthralled Amelie as a child. Brielle's subsequent life would always be a shadow of the excitement she'd known. Understanding this, it seemed, she had deliberately made her new home amid the dull gentility of Bath. Amelie smiled wryly as she imagined her mettlesome grandmother exchanging vapid gossip at the Pump Room every day. She'd visited Bath as a young child, but the last time she'd seen Brielle was five years ago at her mother's funeral, a sombre and painful affair.

She stiffened. That was it. She would go to her grandmother. Brielle would be her refuge and would be sure to defend her from the man she blamed for her own daughter's decline and early death. She had warned

Louise not to marry Lord Silverdale, but, desperate for stability, her daughter had not listened.

Amelie got to her feet and straightened the green satin ribbons that encircled her waist. Her grandmother would be her champion, she was certain. But how to get to her, how to get to Bath? Deep in thought, she didn't hear the bedroom door open until a tentative voice disturbed her meditations. Her maidservant, pale and concerned, white cap slightly askew, hovered in the doorway.

'Oh, miss, is it true? Are you really going to marry Sir Rufus Glyde?'

'No, Fanny, it's not true.' Her voice was sharp but adamant. 'I've no intention of marrying. And I detest Rufus Glyde. He's twice my age and not a fit husband.'

'But, miss, he's very wealthy, or so Cook says, and moves in the best circles.'

Amelie shook her head in frustration. 'He may be invited everywhere, but there are whispers that he is a vicious and degenerate man. He repels me.'

Fanny shut the door carefully behind her and said in a conspiratorial voice, 'Mr Simmonds told Cook that Sir Rufus was coming here tomorrow to make you an offer of marriage.'

'You shouldn't listen to gossip,' Amelie chided her. 'He may be coming to the house, but I shan't be meeting him.'

'But, Miss Amelie, how can this be?' In her abstraction the maid picked up a stray hairbrush and began to rearrange her mistress's locks.

'I'm going to escape—I'm going to Bath to my grandmother. But mind, not a word to anyone.'

Her maid, brushing Amelie's chestnut curls in long, rhythmic strokes, gaped at her open-mouthed. 'However will you get there?'

'I'm not sure at the moment. How would *you* get there, Fanny?'

'On the stage, I suppose, miss, though I wouldn't want to travel all that way on my own. It's sure to take a whole day. Master's old valet used to visit his daughter in Bath sometimes and there was always a fuss about how long he was away.'

'Do you know where he caught the stagecoach?'

'It was an inn in Fetter Lane. The White Horse, I believe. He used to leave first thing in the morning.'

'Then that's what I shall do. You'll need to call me early.'

'You're never thinking of taking the common stage, Miss Amelie?'

'Why ever not, it's a public conveyance. What harm can I come to?'

'But it's not right. All sorts of vulgar people take the stage—you'll be squashed in with the likes of clerks and pedlars and I don't know what. And I've heard it's dangerous. There are highwaymen on Hounslow Heath and they'll slit your throat for a necklace. And if *they* don't get you, then the coachman will get drunk and land you in a ditch.' Fanny shook her head ominously.

'Nonsense. If other people travel on the stage, I can, too.'

'But, miss, you're Quality,' Fanny maintained stubbornly. 'Quality don't travel on the stage. And you mustn't go alone.'

'I have to, and no one must know where I've gone. I need time to reach Lady St Clair and explain the situation to her before my father realises where I am.'

'But you can't have thought.' Fanny's voice sank low. 'You'll be unchaperoned, you'll receive Unwanted Attentions,' she whispered in a horrified voice, emphasising the last two words.

'Well then, I must do something to blend into my surroundings,' her mistress said practically.

She was thoughtful for a moment. 'Who wouldn't be noticed on a stagecoach, I wonder? A maidservant such as yourself? I'll go as a maidservant and you can lend me the clothes.'

'No, miss, that I won't.'

'Fanny, you're the only friend I have in this house. You must help me. No one will know and once I'm established at my grandmother's, I'll send for you. Now, we must plan. First we need a ticket.'

She went to the bottom drawer of the walnut chest that had been her mother's and brought out a small tin box. How lucky it was she still had most of her quarterly allowance. She pulled out a roll of bills and thrust them into Fanny's reluctant hand.

'Here, use this to buy a ticket for the stage tomorrow.'

'But, miss, even if I can buy a ticket, how will you find your way to Fetter Lane?'

'I'm sure I'll manage. I'll walk until I find a hackney carriage. That can take me to the inn, and once there I'll take care to stay concealed until the coach is ready to leave. There's bound to be crowds of people and a lot of activity—I imagine the Bath stage isn't the only one leaving the White Horse in the morning. It should be easy to find a hiding place.'

Her maid still looked unconvinced and Amelie put her arms around her and sought to soothe her worries. 'Don't fret, it's going to work. When you return, get some suitable clothes ready for me, but keep them in your own room. And then stay away from me for the rest of the day so that no one will suspect anything.'

Fanny seemed rooted to the spot. 'Go on,' her mistress urged, 'do it quickly before supper and then you won't be missed. Bring me the clothes and ticket at dawn tomorrow. I wouldn't ask you to do this for me, Fanny, if I were not truly desperate. But I must escape this nightmare.'

In the City some miles from Grosvenor Square, Gareth Denville was also contemplating escape. He sat uncomfortably in the shabby offices which housed Messrs Harben, Wrigley and Spence, solicitors, and wished himself elsewhere. But his demeanour betrayed nothing of his emotions. His straight black brows and hard blue eyes kept the world at bay. He could be accounted a handsome man, thought Mr Spence, who sat opposite him, but for the harshness of that gaze. And the decided lack of fashion he exhibited. He was a well-built man slightly above average height with good shoulders and an excellent form for the prevailing fashion of skin-tight pantaloons. But instead he wore buckskins, his coat fitted far too easily across his broad shoulders to be modish and his necktie was negligently arranged. Rather than the gleaming Hessians of *ton*nish fashion, he wore topboots, still dusty from his long journey.

Mr Spence gathered together the papers scattered across the huge oak desk and sighed inwardly. The new Lord Denville was likely to find it difficult to adjust to life in the capital. He looked up and encountered Gareth's austere gaze and quickly began the task at hand. Over the next quarter of an hour, Mr Spence carefully enumerated the full extent of Gareth Denville's inheritance while the beneficiary remained unnervingly silent.

The news of his grandfather's death several weeks ago had been accompanied by a polite request from the solicitors for his immediate return to England. His first reaction to their letter had been to shrug indifferently and carry on with his life, but his grandfather's man of business was nothing if not persistent, and after several summons of increasing urgency, he had bowed to the inevitable. He had been travelling a night and a day now without pause, but his powerful frame appeared not greatly fatigued and his air of cool detachment never left him.

The situation was not without its humour, of course, but that did not prevent a slow burning anger eating him from within. He'd known as he travelled to England after seven years' absence that he was now the Earl of Denville whether he wished it or not. But as Mr Spence drily read the pages of his grandfather's will, the size of his inheritance astounded him. Infuriated him, too, when he recalled the shifts he'd been forced to adopt simply to maintain the appearance of a gentleman. Charles Denville had husbanded his estate well. How ironic that such care and duty should ultimately benefit him, the black sheep, the grandson who could never be spoken of again. His grandfather could not deny him the title, but he must have tried and failed to leave his estate elsewhere. Gareth could imagine the old man's fury that such an unworthy successor was about to be crowned.

'Are you sure, Mr Spence, that there are no other legitimate heirs to the estate?' he asked crisply.

'None whatsoever, Lord Denville. We have done our searches very carefully, particularly…' and here he coughed delicately '…in the light of the peculiar circumstances surrounding your lordship's inheritance.'

The solicitor was far too circumspect to mention details, but Gareth knew well that Mr Spence referred to his banishment as a young man for the gravest of sins in *ton* circles. He had cheated at cards, or so it was alleged, a transgression that had brought instant shame to him and to his family. His grandfather had bundled him out of the country overnight, refusing to listen to his version of events.

'Like father, like son,' Lord Denville had said grimly. 'I was stupid enough to let your father stay in the hope that he would reform his way of life, but he died in the gutter where he belonged. I'll make sure that you at least cannot disgrace the family name further.' And what, thought Gareth, had the family name come to after all?

It had all once been so different. He'd been everything to his grandfather, an unexpected light after the black years of his own father's ruin. He remembered his childhood at Wendover Hall, his grandfather teaching him to ride and to shoot, watching over his progress to manhood with pleasure and anticipation. And then disaster, just three months on the town and accused of marking his cards.

That night was etched on his brain. The heat of the room, the guttering candles, the disarray of empty glasses. And the four other men who sat round the table: his dearest friend, Lucas Avery, General Tilney, an old ally of his grandfather's, the languid form of Lord Petersham, whose customary lethargy belied a sharp intelligence, and Rufus Glyde, playing recklessly that night, his spiteful tongue unusually stilled. It was the General who had first seen the mark on the card and raised the alarm. He remembered the incredulous stares of his companions as it became obvious to all who had cheated.

But he hadn't cheated. Someone there had done so, but why and how remained impenetrable. The men he played with were wealthy and had no need to cheat. But he was on a tight allowance and awaiting the next quarter's in some desperation. It was common knowledge that he was short of money. He had vehemently protested his innocence, but his grandfather had been deaf to him and to Lucas's staunch pleas that his friend was an honourable man; Lord Denville had listened in stiff silence and remained unmoved. General Tilney's embarrassed account of the evening was the only one his grandfather was willing to countenance. Gareth's disgrace was instant and so was banishment.

'My lord, if you would be so kind, we will need to go through a number of documents for which I need signatures.'

The solicitor was trying to regain his attention. His mind left that shadowed room in Watier's, and returned to the attorney's untidy office. He felt he was suffocating, yet the window was wide open.

'I need to take a walk,' he said. 'I need to clear my head.'

'Of course, your lordship.' The solicitor rose and bowed politely. 'I will await your lordship's pleasure.'

'I'm staying at Crillon's. I'll send from there when I'm ready to go through the papers.'

'Certainly, my lord.'

He walked quickly out of the room and down the stairs. The fresh air hit him with welcome relief. Waving away the proffered services of a jarvey, he began to make his way towards the West End of the city. He walked swiftly, street after street, hardly heeding where he went. Inside, he was seething with anger. His fortunes had changed, but his sense of betrayal remained acute. He had no wish to inherit anything that had belonged to his grandfather. Pride made it impossible that he would ever accustom himself to being the Earl of Denville or ever seek to become part of a society he deemed rotten to the core.

Without a glance, he passed the turning for St James's, a thoroughfare housing some of the most famous gentlemen's clubs in London, and continued as if by instinct towards Piccadilly. He came to a halt outside No. 81, Watier's, the Great-Go as it was fondly known to its members. Somehow he'd returned to the scene of his disgrace. He walked slowly up the stairs and prepared to confront his demons.

The doorman, resplendent in black grosgrain and scarlet silk sash, bowed low.

'Good evening, Lord Denville,' he intoned, 'on behalf of Watier's, may I offer you sincere condolences on your grandfather's death, and say how very glad we are to see you again.'

Gareth made no reply, reflecting cynically that commerce knew no moral shades. The doorman handed him on to a footman hovering by the doorway of the salon. He remembered the room immediately. The Aubusson carpet, the straw-coloured silk hangings and the endless line of chandeliers blazing light had not changed.

A group of men nearest the door looked up. They were engaged in a companionable game of faro, but at the sight of him the game stopped and for an instant their conversation withered. A man he did not know, and who was evidently in charge of the day's bank, said something in an undervoice which caused a ripple of amusement around the table. Lord Petersham, looking a little thinner and older now, hushed the man and play continued. The incident was over in a moment, but to Gareth it was as though time had stood still. His newly acquired title and wealth might open the doors of society to him, but he would never be allowed to forget the scandal. His grim reluctance to return to England, even for a few weeks, had been prescient. He had no place here and wanted none.

He blundered down the steps and headed towards the river. The grey waters flowed bleakly by the embankment, an echo of his harsh mood. Defiantly, he decided to drink to the day he would shake the soil of England from his feet for ever and sought out a boozing-ken in a poor area of Vauxhall, known to him from his days of youthful indiscretion. He ordered a brandy and the drink was rough but fiery. He ordered another and tossed it back quickly. He wanted to sink into oblivion. Over the next hours he drank steadily, as though each drink took him one step further from a hated homeland. It was just short of dawn when he finally lurched to his feet and sought his hotel room. His brain, befuddled by brandy, was treacherous and led him in the wrong direction. Very soon he was lost in a labyrinth of unknown streets.

Fanny woke her mistress at four in the morning. She carried in her arms a set of her own clothes and clutched the stagecoach ticket tightly. She appeared nervous, her hands trembling as she gently shook her mistress awake. Her agitation was soon explained.

'Miss Amelie, I don't think you can go. Mr Simmonds is in the hall and he's been sitting there all night. I was so worried I'd oversleep that I woke really early and crept downstairs to see the time. And there he was. You'll have to stay, miss, you'll have to meet Sir Rufus. But maybe it won't be too bad. You'll be rich and have your own house to manage and plenty of fine clothes and carriages and—'

'Do you mean my father has actually set the butler to spy on me?' Amelie was now sitting bolt upright.

'Not exactly spy, miss. But he's there in the hall as right as ninepence and there's no way you're going to get past him unseen.'

'I have to get that coach, Fanny. I must find another way out—the back door?'

'The scullery maids are already up and working in the kitchen. They would be bound to report it to Cook and she'll carry it to Mr Simmonds. You'd have to get over the garden wall into the alley behind and they would know of your escape before you'd even got halfway.'

'Then I must go out of the front—maybe you can distract Simmonds?'

Fanny looked doubtful.

'I have it, I'll go out of the window—we're only on the first floor and we should be able to fashion a ladder from the sheets, long enough for me to reach the ground.'

'You'll never climb out of the window on sheets, Miss

Amelie. It's too dangerous. They could give way at any moment.'

'Not if we knot them very carefully. In any case, it's far more dangerous for me to stay. Quick, let's hurry.'

With that she hastily dressed herself in the clothes Fanny had brought. Then, sweeping the sheets from the bed, she began to knot them urgently, calling on the maid to help. More sheets were pulled from the large linen chest, which lined the bedroom wall, and very soon they had put together an impressive rope.

'We must make sure we've knotted the sheets as tightly as possible. I don't weigh much, but it's quite a way down.'

'It's as safe as I can make it…' Fanny paused in her labours and looked anxiously at her mistress '… safer than for you to be travelling alone all the way to Bath.'

'I don't have a choice. I have to get to my grandmother's. I promise I'll take care. Don't forget,' Amelie tried to reassure her, 'I'll be travelling in disguise and nobody will think of looking twice at a maidservant.'

'But you'll still be a very beautiful maidservant, miss, and people are bound to look at you. You must wear my cloak and make sure you pull the hood over your head whenever you're in public.'

Her mistress fingered the black velvet robe. 'This is your best cloak, Fanny, I can't take it.'

'You must, it will make people think you're a very superior lady's maid and they won't bother you! And it will keep you warm. You've never travelled in a stagecoach before, Miss Amelie, but I'm told they're the draughtiest vehicles out and you'll be travelling for hours.'

'Fanny, you're the best friend anyone ever had.' The maid blushed with pleasure. 'As soon as I get to Lady St Clair's, I'll make sure she sends for you. Then we'll both be safe. My father will never dare to follow us there.'

She quickly slipped the cloak over the borrowed dress, pulling the hood well down over her tangled curls. A small cloak bag lay ready with just a few of her most treasured possessions. She could take hardly anything with her, but she had no regrets. Once this room had been a beloved haven, but now it was a prison, a prison leading only to betrothal with a detested man. Sir Rufus Glyde would arrive at noon, but by then she would be miles away and her family confounded. She knew that Fanny would keep her secret, even on pain of dismissal.

She turned quickly to her. 'I must be gone. Give me the ticket for the stage.'

'When you get to the inn, miss, be sure to hide yourself away until it's time for the coach to leave.'

'I will. Once I've gone, you must go back to your room immediately and don't discover my absence until the last possible moment. Please God they won't find out that it was you who helped me.'

'You're not to worry, Miss Amelie. I'll make sure they won't know from me where you've gone.' Fanny was suffused with tears, her voice cracking. 'Now go, quickly, miss.'

She deftly tied one end of the sheet ladder to the bedpost and opened the window wide. The sash cord groaned ominously and they both held their breath. But the house was silent except for the distant sounds from the kitchen. They breathed again. Fanny played out the sheets over the window sill and helped her mistress on to the ledge. The dawn was spreading a grey light over the quiet streets. A fresh breeze fanned Amelie's cheeks as she climbed nimbly over the ledge and began lowering herself down the improvised ladder. The descent wasn't easy. She had to lower herself one movement at a time and the cloak bag, though light, impeded her progress. She wondered if she dared to throw it down into the cellar area below the railings. But Simmonds might well hear the noise and come to see what had caused it. So she continued to edge her way carefully downwards, the bag slung over one arm.

Fanny's pale face was at the open window, whispering encouragement. 'You're doing fine, miss. Don't look down, not far to go now.'

But her estimation proved to be optimistic. The sheets, which had seemed so prolific in the bedroom, suddenly appeared scanty and far too short. They had both forgotten the deep well below the front door steps and had calculated only to the pavement. Amelie was now at the bottom of the ladder, but still at least fifteen feet above solid ground.

She looked up at the imposing Georgian facade and then down to the terrifying black-and-gold railings that marched along the pavement. What a horrible fate that would be. She suddenly felt very sick. How on earth was she going to reach the ground? She could jump into the well, but she was more than likely to break a leg or worse. Then all chance of escape would be gone. She would have to endure her father's fierce recriminations. She could see him now, his brow creased in red furrows and his prominent eyes glowering.

As she hung there, her light form bracing itself against the cream stucco of the house, the noise of whistling broke the stillness. Tuneless and somewhat melancholy, the whistling was coming nearer. A late reveller, perhaps, on his way home? He was almost sure to see her. Fanny had heard the noise too and began desperately to try to haul in the sheets.

'It's no good,' Amelie whispered hoarsely, 'you'll never have the strength to get me back.'

She could only hope that the unknown figure meandering towards her would be too inebriated to notice a young female hanging from a window. That was wishful thinking. The reveller drew near and stood gazing at her for some time, seemingly trying to work out just what he was viewing.

Amelie looked down and pulled her cloak tighter. She didn't recognise him and he didn't look like any of the fashionable bloods who often ended a riotous evening by staggering home at dawn. But he had an indefinable air of authority about him and she worried that by chance he might remember seeing her at one of the many gatherings of the *ton* this Season. She must avoid discovery at all costs.

Despite having drunk far too much, he seemed alert. His face slowly broke into a derisive smile.

'What have we here then? A mystery indeed. Plainly an escape, but what are you escaping from? What do maidservants escape from before the household is awake? Have you been stealing and now you're trying to make off with your ill-gotten gains? Should I knock and instantly let your employers know of your wickedness?'

'No, sir, indeed I am no thief.'

'Well, if you're not a thief, what are you doing climbing out of the window? The house has a door, you know.'

She answered with as much dignity as she could muster, 'There are circumstances that make it vital for me to escape in this manner. I must not be seen.'

She hoped that he would ask no more questions and be on his way. But the brandy fumes still wreathed around Gareth Denville's brain. He was indifferent to the fact that he was miles from his hotel and had no idea in which direction it lay. He felt reckless and pleasurably detached from a world he hated. He had no intention of walking away—he was in the mood to enjoy this ridiculous imbroglio.

'But why must you leave unseen? It seems unnecessarily dramatic,' he offered provocatively.

'I have my reasons,' she replied stiffly. 'Please leave me.'

'By all means, but is that wise? It might be more

sensible to ask for a little help. Of course I would need to know just who I'm aiding and why.'

'My name is Amelie and I'm maid to the young mistress of this house. I'm escaping to avoid the attentions of her brother.'

Gareth caught sight of a chestnut curl and looked intently at the heart-shaped face trying to cower deeper into the enveloping cloak. 'He has good taste,' he admitted. 'But then so do I.'

He swayed slightly on his heels and finally pronounced, 'We'll make a bargain, shall we? I'll rescue you on one condition.'

'Anything, sir,' she said recklessly. Her arms felt as if they were being torn from their sockets and she knew she would not be able to hold on much longer. The sharp sword points of the railings seemed already to be coming nearer.

'A rather rash promise, but one I shall keep you to. I'll help you to the ground, but in exchange you'll come with me—as entertainment, shall we say.'

'Dear sir, I cannot. I have a journey to make. I'm on my way to—Bristol,' she amended, thinking it best not to reveal her plans in their entirety. 'I have to get to the White Horse Inn in Fetter Lane to catch the stage.'

'Excellent. Bristol, why not? There are boats aplenty there,' he added obscurely. 'We'll go together.'

He needed to get away and he was intrigued by the glimpse of the beautiful face beneath the cloak. Mr Spence would have to wait for his papers to be signed. Perhaps he would never sign them, never avail himself of his newfound wealth. If so, he would manage—he had for the last seven years.

'A perfect solution, then,' he said swiftly. 'I extricate you from your difficulties and we travel to Bristol together.'

He saw her dismayed face. 'You won't have to know me very long—a few hours only. You might even get to like me,' he added harshly. 'I'll bespeak a private parlour when we get to the inn. You can have a good breakfast and I can have—well, let's say, I can have the pleasure of your company.'

Amelie heard her maid moan. Fanny had her head below the window sill, but could hear all that was being said. This was her worst fear come true, but she was powerless to intervene. If she made herself known, the man, whoever he was, would discover Amelie's deception. He might spread rumours about her mistress and Amelie would be shunned by society. Then she would never find a husband, not even a degenerate twice her age. As Fanny fidgeted in despair, the decision was made for her.

Her arms breaking, Amelie gasped out, 'Yes, I'll come with you. Just get me down from here, please, immediately!'

'At your service, madam.' Her knight errant leapt over the railings and down the stairs to the cellar area. Amelie, her hands now nerveless, fell into his arms. He held her to his chest, enjoying for a moment the softness of her young body.

'Let me introduce myself,' he said, putting her down abruptly, and quickly casting around in his mind for a name. 'I am Gareth Wendover.'

Chapter Two

She allowed herself to be led up the area steps and away from the house. Instead of letting her go once they reached the pavement, her rescuer kept a tight grip on her arm as if to prevent any flight. She noticed that his hands were strong and shapely, but tanned as though they were used to outdoor work. He appeared an enigma, a gentleman, presumably, but one acquainted with manual labour. His earlier nonchalance had disappeared and with it his good humour. Glancing up at him from beneath her eyelashes, she saw that his expression had grown forbidding. A black mood seemed to have descended on him as he strode rapidly along the street, pulling her along in his wake. His chin jutted aggressively and his black hair fell across his brow. When he finally turned to her, his eyes were blue steel.

'Why are you dawdling?' he demanded brusquely. 'I thought you were desperate to escape.'

'I am,' she countered indignantly. 'I'm walking as fast as I can and you're hurting my arm. I'm not a sack to be dragged along the street.'

Ignoring her complaint, he continued to tow her along the road at breakneck speed. 'Come on, Amelia—that *was* your name?—try harder. We need to move more quickly.'

He must be drunker than I supposed, she thought ruefully. His voice was cultured and his clothes, though shabby, were genteel. But his conduct was erratic. One minute he appeared to find her situation a source of laughter, the next he behaved in this surly fashion. He thought she was a maidservant and had doubtless helped her to escape because of her pretty face. But he'd hardly glanced at her since that unfortunate moment when she'd landed in his arms and now he was sweeping her away from the house as if his life depended on it, propelling her along the pavement until she was breathless.

Incensed by this treatment, she came to an abrupt halt, almost tripping him up. 'Perhaps you didn't hear what I said. I cannot walk any faster than I'm doing already. And,' she added coldly, 'my name is Amelie, *not* Amelia.'

'However fancy your name, you're still a fugitive,' he responded drily, 'and a fugitive under my command. And my command is to make haste.'

'I will certainly make haste, but at a more seemly rate.'

'Seemly—that's a strange word for a girl who escapes through windows.'

She looked mutinous, but was too tired to argue any further and submitted again to being led at a spanking pace through a maze of streets until they came across a hackney carriage waiting for business.

'In you go,' her persecutor said shortly and pushed her into the ill-smelling interior. He uttered a few words to the jarvey and they were off.

Keeping company with a drunken man, who looked as though he'd known better days, was not part of her plans, but she decided that she would not try to escape just yet. She would stay with this Mr Wendover while it suited her purpose. He'd been useful so far and if he could deliver her to the White Horse Inn, then she would be set for her journey to Bath. Once in the inn's courtyard, it should be easy to give him the slip and hide away until the stage departed.

They sat opposite in the dingy cab, silently weighing each other up. It was the first time she'd been able fully to see her rescuer. He was a powerfully built man, carelessly dressed, but exuding strength. She was acutely conscious of his form as he lay back against the worn swabs. She had no idea who he was, other than the name he'd given, and he was evidently not going to volunteer further information. Instead, he sat silently, gazing at her, assessing her almost as though she were a piece of merchandise he'd just purchased, she thought wrathfully. But he would discover that she had other plans; she would leave him as soon as she was able. Doubtless he would start to drink again at the inn and, once fuddled, would not care what happened to her.

In this she was wrong. Despite his dazed state, Gareth had been watching her closely and had seen her recoil as she sat down on the stained seat of the cab. A trifle fastidious for a maidservant, he thought. The hood of her cloak obscured much of her face, but what he could see was very beautiful, from the glinting chestnut curls to the fine cheekbones and flawless complexion. A strange maidservant, indeed, and a strange situation.

As the brandy fumes began to dissolve, he was left with an aching head and a confused mind. What on earth was he doing miles from his hotel, his solicitor and legal papers all but forgotten? How had he embarked on this mad adventure with a woman he didn't know and one who could well be a thief? Perhaps the hue and cry to apprehend her had already started. And he'd been the one to make sure she escaped pursuit, rushing her along the streets away from any possible danger. He must be very drunk. He would need to keep her close until he worked out what to do. In the meantime there must be a few hours before the Bristol stage left, and he would remind her of her promise. She'd provide a pleasant interlude.

The hackney bounced over the cobbles at considerable speed. There was little traffic at this time of the morning and they were soon at the White Horse. He helped her down with one hand while paying the jarvey with the other. No escape, she reflected. Never mind, her opportunity would come, she would just have to be a little cleverer.

'I suggest we repair indoors and find some breakfast.

A private parlour should give us some respite from this din.'

He had to bend down and speak directly into her ear, the noise coming from the inn courtyard was so great. She could hardly believe how many people were gathered into such a small space. There was luggage scattered everywhere: trunks, cloak bags, sacks of produce, bird cages heaped up pell-mell. Ostlers ran back and forth leading out teams of fresh horses, coachmen took final draughts of their beer before blowing the horn for departure. Everywhere people shouted instructions and were not heard. It was bedlam, and the relative quiet of the inn taproom seemed like sanctuary.

The landlord came bustling out, rubbing his hands with pleasure as there was normally little hope of trade at this time of the morning. All anyone usually bought was a quick cup of scalding coffee. But here was a gentleman and his companion, surely more substantial customers, even if the man did look a little the worse for wear and the woman kept her face shrouded.

'A beautiful morning.' The landlord beamed ingratiatingly. 'And how can I help you, sir?'

Gareth frowned. 'Prepare a private parlour for myself and the lady,' he said curtly. 'We leave on the Bristol coach, but wish to take some breakfast first.'

'Of course, sir. Right away. If you would care to come with me.'

The room the landlord led them to was small and poky with a low window that looked out over the back garden, but it was mercifully quiet. The curtains were grimy and the furniture looked faded and uninviting. Amelie plumped one of the chair cushions and sent up a cloud of dust. Her rescuer glanced across at her, his expression mocking. 'The housekeeping can wait.'

She glared at him. 'If you don't mind, Mr Wendover, I would prefer to be outside.'

'I'm sure you would, but here we'll stay. I can keep an eye on you and we can eat breakfast together. Won't that be companionable?'

His voice was light and his tone ironic, but somehow he made the phrase sound like a caress. Yet the look on his face was calculating. *Weighing me up again*, she thought, *deciding whether or not he made a good bargain when he rescued me*. She was beginning to feel unusually vulnerable, confined to this isolated room with an unknown and unpredictable man. But indignation at her imprisonment gave her courage.

'I'm unsure what you mean by companionable, Mr Wendover. I certainly thank you for the service you've rendered me this morning, but I've no need of food and would prefer to wait for my coach in the courtyard. If you allow me to pass, you may enjoy your meal undisturbed.'

'Not so fast. I have no wish to be left undisturbed. On the contrary, I very much desire to be disturbed.'

He smiled derisively as he spoke, but his eyes were hard and measuring. 'You are mighty proud for a maidservant, are you not?' he asked. 'But then a challenge is always welcome.'

She made no reply, for the first time conscious of

a shadowy fear. The ancient clock in the corner of the room ticked out the minutes loudly in the gulf of silence that stretched between them. She felt bruised by his scrutiny. Then, without warning, he began to walk slowly towards her, his dark blue eyes intent. He no longer seemed a harmless reveller. She was very aware of his close physical presence and the way he was looking at her was disquieting. His hard gaze seemed to drink her in. She was angry that he dared to stare at her so, but at the same time the pit of her stomach fluttered uncomfortably.

Desperately she strove to exert control over the situation. 'I don't understand what exactly you want of me.' Even to her ears, she sounded faint and foolish.

'Really? I'm surprised. Do they make maidservants that innocent these days? Perhaps I should remind you that we had a bargain. I helped you from your predicament and you promised to stay with me until your—sorry, our—coach left the inn.'

'But why?'

'Come, you can't be that naive. Why would any man want a beautiful young woman to stay with him?'

She stepped back hurriedly and collided with the threadbare sofa. 'You surely cannot pretend any feelings for me.' Her voice was hoarse with alarm. 'You know nothing of me.'

'True, but do I have to? You'll be a charming diversion just when I need one. Here, pull your hood back.'

Before she could stop him, Gareth had flung her cloak back to reveal her face fully. He looked at her wonderingly. A tangle of silken curls tumbled down around her shoulders. Her eyes, the colour of autumn, were wide and frightened and the soft cream of her cheeks delicately flushed. It seemed an age that he stood looking at her.

When he finally spoke, his voice was thick with desire. 'You *are* beautiful,' he said. She flinched and wrapped her cloak more tightly around her body.

'There's no need to be scared,' he murmured smoothly. 'I'm sure we'll deal well together.'

'Indeed, no, sir, we will not,' she protested. 'I'm an honest woman and you shall not touch me.'

'Honest,' he mused. 'An interesting word. Honest women hardly choose to escape from their homes at four in the morning. Nor do they come away with men they don't know. Don't play your tricks off on me. Instead, let's be truthful with each other. I'm in need of amusement and you, I imagine, are a little adventuress who will take whatever comes her way.'

He grabbed her hand and pulled her towards him. In a moment his arms were round her waist, a gesture shocking in its intimacy. She shrank from him, but his nearness was making her senses falter. He pressed closer and she felt her body begin to tingle. For a moment they stayed body to body, then quickly she sprang away.

Her face was pink with vexation. 'How dare you touch me!'

'Very easily, I'll think you'll find. Women are made for pleasure and you'll provide it amply.'

He made as if to recapture her in his arms, but was

interrupted by the door opening. The landlord arrived bearing a ham, eggs, some devilled kidneys and toast. A servant followed with a large pot of steaming coffee.

'There we are, sir,' the innkeeper sang out, determinedly ignoring what he had seen as he came in the door. 'Just the job for a chilly May morning. But good travelling weather, I'll be bound.' He continued to spill out words while Amelie retreated to a corner of the room, trying hard to quell her jumping heart.

When the landlord had left, Gareth sat down at the table and began calmly to carve slices of ham and place them carefully on the two plates.

'Come to the table, Amelie, you must eat,' he coaxed. 'No point in starving yourself—you have a long road ahead.'

The glorious sense of irresponsibility that he'd known earlier had gone, but he was still enjoying himself. He had no idea who he was with or what would happen. But this beautiful girl had felt warm and tremulous when he pulled her close and he looked forward to repeating the sensation. It was escape that he needed right now and she had literally dropped into his arms, ready to furnish it.

Amelie resolutely refused even to look at the food.

'Come to the table!' His tone was now peremptory.

She remained sitting in the corner of the room. 'I'm not hungry,' she said in a freezing voice.

'Don't be silly. Of course you're hungry. Come, I wish to eat the ham, not you. Sit down—or I'll make you.'

Alarmed at any further physical contact, she

abandoned her station and went with as much dignity as she could muster towards the table. Perching at the corner, as far away as possible, she nibbled at the ham and a slice of bread. The coffee was mercifully strong and hot and she gratefully downed two cups. He ate more leisurely as though he had the entire morning to finish his breakfast. *And when he's eaten his fill*, she thought, *I'll be next on the menu.*

She was going to have to make her getaway fast if she were to avoid another dreadful scene. She couldn't rely on the landlord to come in so opportunely again. Indeed, he'd had an unpleasantly knowing look in his eye as he'd laid the food down in front of his patron. He would do nothing to help her; she would have to save herself.

She cleared her throat. 'Why do you wish to go to Bristol, Mr Wendover?'

'Why should that concern you?'

'If we are to be travelling companions today, it might be sensible to get to know each other a little.' She wondered anxiously if he would take the bait and relax his guard.

'A change of tune? When I tried to get to know *you*, you weren't too keen,' Gareth said caustically.

'I'm sorry for that, but I find this room a little overheated and when you pulled me towards you…' her voice wavered at the thought '…I felt faint.'

'Ah, that's how it was. Well, I certainly don't want a fainting woman on my hands, so I'll open this window a little and then we can be comfortable. Come here, Amelie, and let me look at my prize.'

Steeling herself, she walked slowly towards him. He stood up, facing her, and smiled. She realised with a jolt that when he smiled, his whole face was transformed from a threatening harshness to engaging warmth. His blue eyes had lost their steeliness and smiled, too, suggesting humour and good nature. His white teeth were even and his lips full. She stared at him, enjoying the picture he presented.

'I'm not surprised you've had trouble from your employers,' he broke into her rapt contemplation. 'You're far too lovely ever to be let near the average young man.' He laughed softly. 'But I'm hardly the average man, so we need have no fears on that score.'

She woke abruptly from her dreamlike state and realised the danger she was in. Picking up her reticule, she fanned herself energetically. 'I'm sorry, sir, but I'm still very warm in here. And I wonder if the ham was all it should be?'

'And what exactly do you mean by that?' he exploded. The moment was gone.

'Just that the ham had a slight taint, I thought. But ham never really agrees with me, so perhaps it was fine.'

'If it doesn't agree with you, what the devil do you mean by eating it?'

'You insisted, Mr Wendover. I was scared of you, so I ate it. But now I don't feel at all well.' She pressed her handkerchief artistically to her mouth and closed her eyes. 'I think I might really faint this time.'

Gareth cursed under his breath and shouted for the landlord, who came suspiciously quickly. She was sure the salacious old man had been lurking outside the door, waiting to see what would occur.

'My companion is unwell, landlord, your ham seems to be to blame,' Gareth said tersely.

'That can't be right, sir, the ham was freshly cured. Mrs Fawley would be very upset to think that aspersions had been cast on her ham. It's the best in the city. You won't get better anywhere.'

'Yes, yes,' said Gareth irascibly, 'that's as may be. My friend here is feeling ill and needs to lie down. Do you have a bedchamber where she can be accommodated?'

'Yes, sir, of course, I'll call my wife immediately.'

Mrs Fawley soon appeared on the doorstep with a martial look in her eyes. It was obvious she had overheard the conversation and was ready to defend her ham. But when she saw Amelie, small and white, and looking decidedly unwell, she took pity on her.

'I've got my own opinion as to what's made the young miss faint,' she sniffed, and escorted Amelie to a small but clean bedchamber on the next floor, overlooking the courtyard.

Once on her own, she locked the door and laid herself on the bed. She was exhausted by the morning's adventures. It seemed that she'd thwarted one persecutor only to fall into the hands of another; she'd only very narrowly eluded her would-be ravisher. It was second nature for her to mistrust any man and she wondered at her stupidity in imagining that Gareth Wendover would be no threat to her.

When she'd first seen him he'd appeared no more harmful than a lively reveller returning from a night of pleasure—untidy and unfashionable and probably a little the worse for drink—but for some reason she'd trusted him. Only after he'd used her so roughly, dragging her along the street, throwing her into the hackney and then—certainly best forgotten—pulling her into his arms, had she realised what a foolish mistake she'd made.

And yet even then, she admitted shamefacedly, there'd been temptation to remain in his embrace, to let those strong arms encircle her. Of course that was simply a reaction to the alarms of the last few days, but thank goodness the landlord had come in when he had. And now her pretence of illness had saved her again, although for a short while only. She was sure that Gareth would be knocking on the door very soon and demanding admittance. And a bedchamber was an even worse place to meet him than the parlour downstairs. She had to be gone by the time he arrived.

She quickly washed her hands and face and tidied her hair in the tarnished mirror, which hung lopsidedly on one wall. She'd noticed as the landlady escorted her up to this floor that there was a second stairway leading downwards. It was much smaller and far less grand, obviously the stair used by the servants. She was sure it would lead out to the garden; if she could reach that, she would easily be able to creep unnoticed to the front courtyard.

She glanced at the clock and could hardly believe the time. The coach for Bath left in just five minutes. Carefully, she unlocked the door and peered out. All was quiet and she tiptoed as swiftly as she could to the head of the small staircase and listened again. The only noise wafting up to her was the convivial banter from the taproom. No strong footsteps mounted towards her door. Gareth Wendover thought she was travelling to Bristol and would not know the Bath stage was about to leave. This was her chance.

Regretfully, she would have to leave her cloak bag behind in the parlour below, but at least she had her reticule and in it the precious ticket. In a minute she was down the stairs and lifting the latch on the door leading to the garden. A woman servant suddenly appeared from the kitchen quarters and stared at her uncomprehendingly. Amelie whisked through the door and quickly took the path to the front of the inn.

The scene was a little less chaotic than when she'd arrived in the hackney as many of the morning coaches had already departed. She was easily able to identify the coach to Bath, and once she'd shown her ticket to the guard, she was helped aboard. She chose one of the middle seats of the bank of four that lined either side. It was likely to be the most uncomfortable, but it would shield her from anyone looking in from outside. A large burly farmer sat to one side and a rotund country woman with an enormous basket on her lap on the other. There was very little room, but she could almost disappear between them.

It seemed a lifetime before the guard blew the signal to leave and the coach was pulling out of the yard. There was no sign of her tormentor. By now he was sure to have begun drinking again and would hardly miss her absence. Strangely, she didn't feel as elated at her escape as she should. It was ridiculous, but she almost fancied that she'd let him down in some way. After all, he'd shown some care for her. If it weren't for him, she would still be dangling on the rope of sheets or, even worse, impaled on the front railings. He'd helped her down, found a cab and escorted her to the inn. He'd offered her shelter and refreshment. He'd pulled her into his arms. He'd held her in a crushing embrace. Her mind stopped. That was an image she must be sure to leave behind.

They were already passing through Belgravia and turning out on to the highway that ran westwards. She hoped her family had no idea yet that she was gone. Fanny would be worrying frantically and the sooner she could let her maidservant know that all was well, the better. And all was well, she convinced herself. She'd had a gruelling experience, but she'd achieved her aim. She would not be there to greet Rufus Glyde this morning. Instead, she was on her way to her grandmother's and to safety.

Gareth drained the last of the coffee pot and decided to go in search of his reluctant travelling companion.

He'd been unsure whether she was telling the truth about the ham, but she'd certainly begun to look very white and he'd not wanted to risk any unpleasantness. Truth to tell, she'd looked so small and vulnerable he'd felt a wish to protect her rather than pursue her. He shook his head at his stupidity. She was as mercenary as the rest of the world, no doubt. Her story about escaping from an importuning son probably had a grain of truth in it, given her undeniable beauty, but he was quite sure there was another tale to tell. Perhaps she really was a thief. Perhaps she'd allowed the son too much licence and was now scared to tell her mistress of the inevitable result.

Thanks to the very strong coffee, he'd sobered up completely in the hour that she'd been gone. He still didn't know what had possessed him to get involved with the girl. A sense of the ridiculous, perhaps? Or a whiff of intrigue—a maid with a French name, finicky manners and a keenness to hide her face. He felt too weary to puzzle any further. Two sleepless nights had begun to take their toll and he was now eager to wash his hands of her. He would simply put her on the Bristol coach and go back to his hotel. It had been stupid of him to think that he could flee his obligations. Tomorrow he would send a message to the solicitor and sign whatever papers that worthy presented.

He glanced at the cloak bag Amelie had left on the bench. He'd better restore it to its owner and assure her that she had nothing further to fear from him. He made his way upstairs to the front bedchamber, but it was empty. Thinking he'd got the wrong room, he looked into another and surprised the chambermaid who was making up the bed.

'I'm looking for a young lady,' he excused himself, 'she was feeling unwell and came up to rest.'

The maid looked at him blankly. 'She's not 'ere.'

'I can see she's not here,' Gareth returned shortly, 'but have you seen her?'

'I shouldn't think so.' The maid continued smoothing out the bedspread with a bored expression on her face. 'Not many people come up 'ere.' She paused and looked vacantly out of the window. 'There wus a stranger on the stairs a while ago.'

'A young woman?'

'I couldn't rightly say.'

'Why ever not?' he asked impatiently.

''Cos of the cloak.'

'A black velvet cloak?' The maid nodded absently.

'That's her. Where is she?'

'How would I know? She went down the stairs and out the door.'

'What door?' Gareth was suddenly alert.

'The back door, of course.' The maid shook her head at his obtuseness. ''Appen she's in the garden taking the air,' she said helpfully.

He swore softly to himself and ran down the stairs two at a time. The garden was empty as he knew it would be, but he saw the path that led around the inn and followed it into the courtyard. The yard was also nearly empty. The last coach of the morning had departed and the inn servants were clearing up the mess the passengers and drivers had left behind.

He accosted a thin, gangling youth who was mournfully sweeping the last of the straw from the cobbles.

'The stage to Bristol?' he enquired curtly.

'There ain't no stages to Bristol today,' the boy confided happily, leaning on his broom and glad for an excuse to stop work. 'Bath now, mebbe. And you can allus go on from Bath.'

'Where's the stage to Bath?'

'Where? Somewhere near 'Ounslow, I reckon.' The boy grinned cheekily. 'What d'you think, Jem?'

Jem staggered to a halt, bent double under the weight of the saddle he was carrying. 'With ole Tranter driving, probably not yet clear of Kensington,' he jeered.

The other men stopped their work and joined in a chorus of raucous laughter. An elderly ostler leaned lazily against the inn wall and chewed a straw. He smiled widely, enjoying Gareth's discomfort.

'Next one's tomorrow, sir. That's if you don't mind a little wait,' he sniggered.

'Move yourself and get me a horse immediately,' Gareth snapped in response and ran back into the inn. He threw money onto the table in payment and snatched up Amelie's cloak bag. He'd been willing to let her go when he could play the benefactor. But how dare she play him false? A bargain was a bargain and he was going to make her pay.

He stormed back into the inn courtyard and tapped his foot impatiently.

* * *

It took nearly fifteen minutes to make the horse ready and by that time he was in a towering rage. He threw the cloak bag across the saddle, then leapt onto the horse's back and wheeled her round to face the courtyard entrance.

''Appen you might catch 'em up,' opined the old ostler, still chewing his straw vigorously, 'but I ain't anyways too sure on it.'

Gareth's reply was to spur his mount forwards and out of the courtyard in one bound.

Chapter Three

Wedged uncomfortably between her fellow passengers, Amelie endured the miles as they rolled wearily on. By now her escape must have been discovered. Her father would be spreading tempest through the house; he would find it impossible to explain her absence to Rufus Glyde when the latter came calling. For a moment the thought of Glyde's likely retribution made her feel a little sick, but she resolutely pushed it from her mind. Lord Silverdale would have to find another way of saving the family.

She had no clear idea of the time, but it had to be around noon. Any moment now Sir Rufus would be stepping up to the front door of the house in Grosvenor Square, expecting to have acquired a bride before he left again. A wave of revulsion passed through her. Anything was better than that, even the harassment she'd suffered from Mr Gareth Wendover.

She was glad to be free of him, too, yet she couldn't quite subdue a twinge of regret. He'd behaved abominably, but then her conduct had hardly been that of a delicately raised young woman. If he'd realised her true situation, he wouldn't have attempted to make love to her. But that was a nonsense. It would have made no difference to him if she were maid or mistress. From the outset he'd shown a predilection for seizing her in as close an embrace as possible. Whether she was the daughter of Lord Silverdale or the daughter's maid would be immaterial.

And shamefully, it hadn't mattered to her either whether he was Mr Wendover, gentleman, or a choice spirit of dubious origins. She'd enjoyed the feeling of being held against his powerful frame. Eyes closed, she thought reminiscently of the strength that had encompassed her, the masculine warmth that promised as much excitement as security. But how foolish! She had no intention of being at the mercy of any man—ever. She'd just escaped from one threatened entanglement and she must preserve herself from any other, particularly with a man who by the look of him could bring her nothing but trouble.

She shifted her position, trying to get more comfortable, but in such a crowded carriage it was difficult. Her feet were already numb from inactivity and her left arm ached with the weight of the portly farmer bunched in beside her. A thin-faced clerk in the corner scowled at her attempts to move, but the country woman smiled in motherly sympathy.

'There ain't much room in these coaches, miss, and we large 'uns don't make it any easier.'

The farmer snorted at this and shifted his bulk again, trapping Amelie's arm even more heavily than before. As well as aching from head to toe, she was beginning to feel very hungry. She'd hardly eaten a crumb at the inn, so intent had she been on eluding Gareth. The motherly lady, sensing her thoughts, reached down to the basket, which now nestled on the floor between her feet. She drew out some slices of pie and cheese and apples and smilingly offered to share her fare. Natural politeness would normally have made Amelie refuse, but her hunger was tormenting and the morning's events had somehow dispensed with normality. She plunged her teeth into the succulent pie just as they left Hounslow Heath.

Her benefactor adjusted her white cotton cap and sighed with relief. 'I'm certain glad we've left that Heath. Terrible things happen there. Just last week my neighbour told me her son was held up in broad daylight and robbed of everything, including his horse. He'd to walk all the way to the City and never a chance of catching the man who robbed him.'

Amelie, too, was relieved, for Fanny's words still echoed in her mind; that at least was one danger she'd evaded. Once replete with food, it was easy to slip into a doze. She knew it must be another eight hours or so before she reached her destination and if she could catnap at least some of the time, the journey would not be so wearisome. She started to rehearse what she would say to her grandmother when she finally reached her and was in the middle of a masterly speech in which she painted a frightening picture of what her life would be like with Rufus Glyde, when her head began to droop and she drifted gently into a deep sleep. The red-faced farmer beside her also slept, his snores keeping time with the rhythm of the coach, but Amelie heard nothing. Even when the stage came to rest at its designated stops, she remained undisturbed.

She slept on, mile after mile, until suddenly just past the Chippenham turn-off the coach lurched to an abrupt halt. She was jolted awake and thought at first that they must have reached the small town of Wroxhall, which she'd noticed was just twenty miles short of Bath. Hopefully some of the passengers would alight there and leave those remaining a little more room. Craning her neck round the still-sleeping farmer to look out of the window, she received a shock that sent her senses spinning.

Gareth Wendover wrenched open the doorway of the coach. He was smiling grimly and in his hand was her forlorn cloak bag. 'You seem to have forgotten something, Amelie.'

The coachman at that moment appeared at his shoulder. ''Ere, 'ere, you can't stop a coach on the King's 'ighway to give back a bag,' he blustered.

'Oh, but indeed I can,' Gareth said smoothly. 'You see, this isn't any old cloak bag and I'm not giving it back. In fact, I have every intention of keeping it—it is evidence!'

Her fellow passengers were now all wide awake and taking interested note of the proceedings. She heard the word *evidence* being bandied around between them and turned to face her pursuer.

Gareth's smile turned positively fiendish. 'It contains some very expensive trinkets filched by this young woman from her employers. In her haste to escape justice, she left the bag behind. But I'll make sure that she answers for her crime. I intend to deliver her immediately to the local magistrate. He is sure to have strong views on dishonest servants.'

There was a gasp from the stout woman who had befriended Amelie. 'Surely not, sir. This young woman can't be a thief.'

'One would not think so, I confess, but appearances can be deceptive. Unfortunately, the young and supposedly innocent may harbour evil impulses.'

'How dare you,' spluttered Amelie. 'You know you're telling a pack of lies. That bag is certainly mine, but it contains only a few personal items.'

'Is that so?' Gareth was maddeningly calm. 'Then I suggest, ladies and gentlemen,' addressing the inhabitants of the coach who were now all craning forward, intent on the play being enacted before them, 'that you decide whether or not a maid is likely to be carrying these particular personal items.'

And with a flourish he emptied the contents of the bag onto the ground. To her embarrassment a few of her garments spilled out, but her consternation was vastly increased when she spied along with them a diamond brooch, a jewelled tiepin and a battered but expensive gentleman's timepiece.

'Now what do you think of that?' her tormentor goaded. 'Do they look the sort of things a lady's maid would own? I really don't think so. They do, however, look the sort of items she might purloin from her employer's bedroom.'

Amelie found her voice at last. 'This is all lies. I've never seen these things before in my life,' she cried indignantly.

'And yet somehow they are in your bag. You did say it was your bag, didn't you?'

Her fellow passengers were muttering to themselves, the motherly lady still swearing that she was sure there was some mistake, but the acidic clerk in the corner talked darkly about the falling morals of servants these days. Even the farmer had woken up and was giving his pointed opinion that they were wasting time, and if they didn't get moving soon it would be dark before they could get anywhere near their homes. The rest of the coach nodded in agreement and seemed to lose interest in Amelie's plight.

Gareth reached into the carriage and grasped her arm. 'Now, my dear, I think you will come with me.'

He pulled her down from the coach as the driver started to put his horses into motion once more. Smiling, he waved the stage on its way. 'Don't worry, I'll make sure this young woman gets her just deserts.'

It was all over in seconds. One minute the coach was still there, the next she was standing in the middle of a deserted country road, Gareth Wendover at her arm and his horse placidly grazing by the roadside.

'You are abominable!' she exploded. 'What have I ever done to you to serve me so ill?'

'Desertion, perhaps,' he queried. 'Have you never been told it's dishonourable to make a bargain and not keep it? I thought you needed a lesson.'

'I need no lesson on how to conduct myself, particularly from you,' she raged. 'The last time I had the misfortune to be in your company, you behaved intolerably even for someone who was clearly not in their right senses.'

His smile faded. 'I may have been a trifle disguised,' he conceded, 'but my senses were working fine. You're a very beautiful young woman, Amelie, but too spirited by far. As a maidservant, you're in need of some schooling.'

She ignored the implied threat. 'How dare you make me out to be a thief? Every feeling is offended.'

'Who's to say you're not a thief? You've behaved most suspiciously.'

She stood erect and looked him squarely in the eyes. 'I have never stolen in my life and I have never seen those articles you tipped out of my cloak bag.'

'No, of course you haven't,' he agreed amiably. 'The watch and tiepin are mine and the brooch is one that belonged to my mother and that happened to be in my pocket.'

She gaped at him. 'Then why did you make up such a wicked story?'

'To get you off the coach, of course,' he replied blandly. 'What else? I could hardly hold the stage up and request you to dismount. You would have refused and your fellow passengers would have supported you, but thinking you might be a thief, they just wanted to get on their way.'

'You are insufferable. You've stranded me in the middle of nowhere because I didn't keep some shameful bargain. Rest assured that I still won't be keeping it.'

'Now that's where we might disagree.' His tone was unyielding. 'After all, what else can you do? As you so rightly point out, you're stranded in the middle of nowhere, and the only possible transport looks to be that horse over there, and that horse belongs to me. So I think perhaps you might be persuaded to keep your bargain after all.'

'Then you think wrongly. I would rather walk for the rest of the day than be anywhere near you.' With that, she stuffed her few belongings back into her bag and began marching rapidly along the road.

'It's at least six miles to the nearest village,' he called after her.

'Then I'll walk six miles,' she responded angrily.

He swung himself into the saddle and sidled his horse up to her. 'I always get my way, you know. You might as well give in gracefully and enjoy our splendid isolation together. The shoes you're wearing hardly seem to be made for rural walking.' The steel had given way to wry mockery.

She looked down at the dainty pumps she still wore, annoyed that she'd not thought to change them for some of Fanny's much stouter shoes. With compressed lips, she marched onwards, Gareth Wendover walking his horse just a pace behind. *We must look like a carnival show*, she reflected bitterly.

'Come, Amelie, this is stupid. Get up on the horse and I'll engage to take you to the nearest inn.'

'Thank you, sir, but your offer is declined. I'm well aware of my likely fate there. I've had experience of what you consider fitting conduct for an inn.'

'You're an obstinate young woman, but I shall win. You might as well resign yourself to accompanying me and be saved a good deal of discomfort.'

His manner was relaxed and he seemed to have all the time in the world, confident that she would eventually capitulate. Her feet were already pinching badly and she knew that the soles of her shoes would hardly stand up to six miles of rough road, but her anger drove her on. The earlier vision of his smile and the remembered pleasure of his embrace had evaporated without trace. He was a persecutor, there was no doubt. He was as bad in his own way as Rufus Glyde and, just as she'd defeated Glyde, she would defeat him, too.

Still incensed, she trudged on and now both were silent. Gareth saved his breath. He could see it was pointless trying to persuade her otherwise. He'd been seized by fury when he discovered she'd disappeared without a word and had made a snap decision to go after her and wreak his revenge. It was a stupid thing to do, but he was unused to a female besting him. From the moment he'd met her, he'd behaved irrationally; she'd somehow got under his skin and it was a new sensation. Women were for dalliance, passing fancies to be enjoyed lightly before moving on. They were not to be taken seriously. Now he was landed with this ridiculous situation.

He was willing to concede that she had cause to be angry. He'd behaved badly, but *her* conduct was hardly blameless. She'd been lying to him ever since they met, he was certain. And she'd made use of him when it suited her. He would show her that no one, least of all a chit of a girl, treated him in that way and emerged unscathed. Let her walk off her temper and destroy her shoes. She would be all the more acquiescent when he made his next move.

Musing in this way, he was unaware of the sounds of an approaching coach. Amelie, far more alert, heard in the distance the clatter of wheels before a curricle and four swept round the corner at breakneck speed. She had a terrifying vision of four magnificent greys thundering down on her before she made a dive for cover. Lost in his thoughts, Gareth could only take avoiding action when it was too late. His startled mount reared into the air, and he was flung over the horse's head, landing heavily in the ditch. The curricle swept by, its driver, clad in a caped overcoat, according them not a glance.

Cowering in the shelter of the grassy bank, Amelie

thought she spied a crest on the side of the coach panel. Surely it could not be Rufus Glyde. But she knew that it was. She was all too familiar with that crest. Her flight must have been discovered earlier than she'd hoped and he'd been sent for, or most probably had taken it on himself to hunt her down. Fanny would never have given her away; her father must have guessed that she'd fled to Bath and her grandmother. Terrified that Glyde might turn the coach and come back to inspect his handiwork, she remained in hiding. There she stayed silent and unmoving for a long time before finding the courage to crawl up the bank to the roadside.

Gareth Wendover was nowhere to be seen. His mount was once more quietly cropping the grass, but there was no sign of the master. A perfect opportunity to escape. The horse was close by and looked biddable. If she led him to the nearest field gate she could manage to clamber into the saddle, then ride to Wroxall, and from there catch the next stagecoach westwards wherever it was going. The sooner she was out of this part of the country, the better. She knew Glyde was not travelling here for his own enjoyment. He was searching for her and he would be back.

A groan sounded from the ditch a few yards away. Tiptoeing to the grass edge, she peered downwards. Gareth was lying on his back, but his foot was at a sickening angle. He had his eyes closed and his face was ashen.

'Are you all right?' She knew it to be an ill-advised question even as she asked.

He opened his eyes and looked directly up into hers. 'Does it look like it? No, I'm not all right, but it's hardly your problem.'

'What's happened to your foot?'

'It appears I may have broken my ankle—I'm not sure. In any case, I can't move more than a few inches. There's no way I'll be able to walk on it.'

She remained silent and he rasped out, 'Don't mind me, rejoice all you wish. You're free to go now. Take the horse and make your escape while you can.'

'But what will you do?'

'Do you really care? I can't imagine so. I shall stay here—I don't have much choice. Someone will come by sooner or later.'

'Let me try to help you up.' She half clambered down the ditch and put her hand under the shoulder that was nearest. At the same time he tried to raise himself to a standing position with his other hand, but the effort was too great. His face turned even whiter.

'I can't do it,' he said, sinking back onto the damp bed of grass once more, 'but thank you for trying. I probably don't deserve your help.'

'No, you don't,' she said shortly, 'and this could be just punishment for your behaviour.'

'Spare me the lecture on my morals and go.'

She hesitated, but then walked down the road and led the horse forwards to the nearby gate. Gareth's last glimpse of her was a mass of chestnut curls flying in the breeze as she disappeared into the distance.

She was an accomplished rider and the few miles

to the nearest inn took her only a short time to cover. She rode into the deserted courtyard of the George and called out for help. No one came. She had to dismount and walk into the taproom before she found anyone. An angular woman with a sharp-featured countenance confronted her. Her worn pinafore and rolled-up sleeves suggested that this was the landlord's wife.

She barred Amelie's passage, her arms folded pugnaciously, and her eyes snapping. 'And what do you want, missy?' she asked in an ill-tempered voice as she looked Amelie up and down with a thinly veiled disgust. 'We ain't that sort of place. Off with you. The Cross Keys is where you need to be.'

Amelie was startled. She'd never before been spoken to in that fashion. She supposed she must look a fright; she was certainly dishevelled from the long coach journey and her tumble down the bank. The hem of her dress was muddy and her shoes practically falling apart. She rather thought her face was smudged, too. It was true she looked an unlikely member of the *ton*, but to judge her a lightskirt!

However, she couldn't afford to alienate the woman further and so pinned on her most appealing smile. 'Dear, ma'am, I'm sorry to disturb you. I'm afraid there's been a riding accident and my present state is due to having been thrown from my horse.'

The landlady's wife looked unimpressed. Her arms stayed folded and her expression was grim.

'We, my brother and I, were on a pleasure ride, you see,' Amelie extemporised wildly, 'and my horse went lame, so we had to leave her behind at a farm we passed and we decided to continue home on Gareth's horse. Only then a coach came along at a tremendous speed and the horse reared up and flung us both into the ditch.'

That, at least, was partly truthful. The woman began to look a little more interested, but her arms remained in their fixed position.

'Gareth, my brother, has hurt his ankle—I fear he may have broken it—and I've had to leave him lying in the ditch. I said I would ride to seek help.' She gave a nervous laugh and finished lamely, 'And here I am. Yours was the first inn I came to.'

The landlady continued to maintain her unnerving silence and Amelie cast round for something that would penetrate the woman's iron reserve. Her eye caught the garish design of what looked to be new curtains.

'Oh, how wonderful!' she exclaimed. 'Such beautiful curtains. I know my mother has been looking everywhere for colours like these, but hasn't been able to find just the right shades.'

She prayed fervently for her dead mother's forgiveness. The praise seemed to be welcome and Mrs Skinner unbent slightly, but it was the thought that she had stolen a march on Amelie's unknown mother that really sealed the matter.

'Where d'you say your brother wus?' she enquired roughly.

'Just a few miles along the road going west,' Amelie

said hopefully. 'If we could send an able-bodied man with a horse and cart, we could carry him back here.'

'*We,*' said the landlady with emphasis, 'can't do nuthin'. You'll 'ave to wait till Mr Skinner gets back from Wroxhall, then we'll see.'

'Yes, of course,' Amelie said placatingly, wondering with anxiety just how long that would be.

In the event it was two very long hours before she heard the horse and cart pull up in the yard. Two hours of nervously keeping watch at the parlour window, ready to run should Rufus Glyde reappear. And two hours of thinking of Gareth, alone and cold, lying in that ditch. He might be spotted by a labourer returning home from work, but it was unlikely that a passer-by would search the gully without reason. And by now he probably lacked the strength to attract attention. Perhaps she shouldn't have left him? What if he caught a fever or, even worse, died? It would be all her fault. No, that isn't fair, she countered angrily—it would be *his* fault. If he hadn't stopped the coach, told such appalling lies about her and forced her to go with him, the accident would never have happened. He wouldn't be lying badly injured and she'd be safe with her grandmother instead of stranded in this dreary inn.

'I heerd you had an accident.' Mr Skinner was as stout as his wife was thin and by good fortune lacked her chronic ill temper. He smiled pleasantly at Amelie, 'I'm sorry I weren't home to help, but I've told Will to pack up the cart with blankets and brandy and then go arsk the doctor to come quickly. When the horse is fed, Will and me will be off sharp to look for your brother.'

'Thank you truly, Mr Skinner. I'm very worried about him.' And to her own astonishment, she shed genuine tears.

'Don't you fret, miss. It'll be all right. It's May and the weather ain't too bad. Happen he'll be a little cold and mebbe in pain, but he'll come off fine.'

'Can I come with you?'

'No, m'dear—best stay here. It's getting dark and we don't want another accident.'

She had docilely to agree. But now that dusk had fallen, she thought it would prove difficult to locate the injured man by lantern light. If she'd been allowed to accompany the rescuers, she was sure she would have found the place easily. Instead she was forced to remain at her post by the window, scanning the darkness with such intensity that it seemed she might cut a path to Gareth through the gloom and herself bring help.

In the first hour after Amelie left, Gareth remained cheerful. She'd had the chance to break free and he'd expected her to desert him. He was surprised that she'd even hesitated. He thought of her attempts to help him. It had been excruciatingly painful, but he'd borne with it because she'd cared enough to try and because she was near. What was it about this girl that led him to behave so rashly? She seemed to exercise a malignant charm over him. By rights he should be at ease in his London hotel, sending a message to his lawyer and planning his escape to the Continent. He supposed wryly that this was a kind of escape although hardly one he would have chosen.

The minutes ticked slowly by and he grew colder as the sun waned and the chill of dusk settled around him. He began to fall into a troubled dream in which a card table and a chandelier swam around the periphery of his vision while a beautiful, chestnut-haired girl danced in front of him. Gradually, he lapsed into a feverish state, the dreams becoming more vivid and frightening. The girl had disappeared and the chandelier was burning his eyes. The cards rose from the table and smacked him hard around the face. Blearily he swam back into consciousness as a hand gently slapped his cheek and a homely country voice encouraged him. 'Come on, sir, time to go. We'll have you in the cart in a twinkling and get you back to a warm bed.'

Mr Skinner's plump build belied a strength that was needed to raise Gareth from the depths of the gully. Only then could Will reach down to help them both up the steep bank. Gareth was now as weak as a kitten; though he tried manfully to aid their struggle, he had to allow himself to be pulled, pushed and finally lifted from his mossy bed onto the rough boards of the cart. A twinkling had been an exaggeration, he thought, in the throes of extreme pain. At some point he must have passed out. He came to, choking on the brandy that Mr Skinner trickled down his throat. The blankets wrapping him smelt slightly fetid and the jolting of the cart sent shock pains through his leg. At last when he felt he could bear it no longer, they turned into the yard of the George Inn.

The first face he saw was Amelie's. He could hardly believe she was there. He'd been too dazed to think how his rescuers had found him, but now he saw he had her to thank.

'You've found my *brother*,' cried Amelie, running forwards and gratefully squeezing Mr Skinner by the hand. She hoped that Gareth was alert enough to grasp his supposed relationship. The innkeeper lifted him carefully down from the cart and, with Will's help, carried him up to the spare room. Gareth was no lightweight and Will could only gasp between breaths that the doctor would be with them presently. Once in the room, Gareth sank, pallid-faced, onto the bed.

With difficulty, he turned to Mr Skinner, and murmured in a faint voice, 'My sister and I are most grateful for your kindness in coming to our aid.'

She was thankful for his quick thinking. If he'd repudiated the relationship, she was sure that Mrs Skinner would have instantly ejected her from the inn, darkness or no darkness.

After the doctor had visited his new patient and made his examination, she crept quietly back into Gareth's room.

'What's the verdict?' she asked anxiously.

He looked up slowly and smiled. It was the warm smile she'd seen in the London inn. That seemed a million miles away now.

'I haven't broken the ankle, thank the lord, but I've sprained it badly and I'm likely to be laid up for a good few days. The doctor's left me a draught for the pain and he'll come back the day after tomorrow to change the bandages.'

She could only smile in response. She felt tongue tied, badly shaken by how intense her relief had been when Gareth was carried into the inn courtyard and how sharp her distress at seeing him in pain. Powerful feelings had surfaced despite her effort to control them. There was an awkward silence. The painkilling draught was already having its effects and Gareth lay dozing. She was about to tiptoe out of the room, when his voice stopped her in her tracks.

'I should say thank-you.'

'There's no need,' she said quickly.

'You could have taken your revenge by leaving me to my fate.'

'I am not dishonest,' she said squarely, 'and neither am I heartless. You'd suffered a misfortune and needed help. I would have done the same for anyone.'

'You could have told them here of the accident and then gone on your way. You need not have stayed.'

His smile had vanished and his voice was almost brusque. It was as if he resented her help, resented being put in a situation where he was beholden.

'Don't worry, I won't be staying long,' she said in a cool voice, 'just tonight and then I'll be gone.'

'Where will you sleep? This seems to be the only spare room.'

'I'm to share a chamber with Betsy—the kitchen maid.'

'Good,' he said mysteriously.

She couldn't see anything good about it. She'd never shared a bedroom in her life and a kitchen maid would not have been her chosen companion. A more worldly-wise Gareth was satisfied. If she were indeed the innocent young woman she claimed to be, then Betsy's chaperonage would be invaluable.

'No doubt I'll see you in the morning before you leave?' His tone was indifferent; it was clear that he was dismissing her and preferred to be alone.

'If you wish,' she replied distantly.

He closed his eyes in weariness, looking so ill and worn that she instantly regretted her coldness. She would have to leave on the morrow as she'd promised, but a small inner voice was urging her to stay and make sure that he recovered fully. The thought was dismissed even as it occurred. It was impossible to remain at the inn; she'd spent the entire day evading his unwelcome attentions, so what on earth would he think if she continued by his bedside?

Chapter Four

She stirred restlessly as the bedroom door shut. There was a thin streak of daylight showing between the badly hung curtain and the window sill, but otherwise the attic room remained dark. Narrowing her eyes, she tried to read the battered clock face on the table beside her and saw that it was only five-thirty. She must have been woken by the maid, leaving for her unenviable duties downstairs. She supposed she ought to rise herself and be on the road to Wroxall as early as possible. There'd be no way of getting to the town at this time of day other than by walking and it would take many hours. She'd have to beg a strong pair of shoes from Betsy.

She tried to work out what time she would reach Wroxhall and if it would be possible to board a coach that afternoon for Bath. It might be that mail coaches also stopped in the town. They were much faster than the lumbering stage and would get her to Bath before nightfall. But the cost of a ticket was also much higher and her remaining funds were modest. She might even miss whatever coaches were passing through the town and be forced to spend a night there. That was something she dared not contemplate.

She'd embarked on this adventure nervous, but confident, that she would succeed in reaching her grandmother within hours. Complications such as Gareth Wendover had never entered her head. And he was a complication. By any measure he'd treated her callously and yet she felt a strong thread connecting them, a thread she was finding difficult to break. But there was no doubt he'd brought added danger into her life and she was well advised to be leaving him. Between them, the landlord and the doctor would do all that was necessary to guarantee his well-being; such a vigorous man would not be laid low for long. And if she left the inn this early in the morning, she could forgo a farewell visit. It would be unmannerly, but much easier to walk out of the door right now. If she saw him again, she might be tempted to stay. Her thoughts went round and round in circles until her tired brain gave up the struggle and she once more slept.

'Miss Wendover, can you hear me?' The landlord's voice penetrated her slumbers. It had a note of urgency and she wondered for an instant who he was calling and why, when she realised it must be herself. She was the mysterious Miss Wendover!

'Miss Wendover, can you come quickly, please?'

She hurried out of bed and hastily donned her travelling clothes from yesterday. At the door Mr Skinner looked apologetic, but very worried.

'Sorry to wake you betimes, miss, but Mr Wendover do seem bad. He's feverish for sure and don't respond. Will and me have tried to give him the doctor's medicine, but he won't let us near.'

She forgot her resolution to leave the inn as soon as possible and ran down the stairs to Gareth's bedroom. The scene before her struck her with dismay. A smoky candle still spluttered on the bedside table, but the curtains remained drawn. In the half-light she could see the bedcovers in disarray, half of them trailing on the floor and the other half heaped untidily on the bed. As for the patient, he was tossing and turning constantly, unable to get comfortable, first throwing off the sheets and then grabbing at them with hot dry hands while all the time muttering incoherently. She went forwards to the bed and laid her hand fleetingly on his forehead. It was burning to the touch and his eyes, glancing unrecognisingly at her, were blurred with fever.

'Have you sent for the doctor?' Amelie questioned, thoroughly alarmed.

'Not yet, miss, we weren't sure to do it, without your say so.'

'Why ever didn't you call me earlier?'

'We did think to,' Mr Skinner conceded, 'but he weren't too bad seemingly.'

'He's certainly bad now.' Her voice was sharp with anxiety.

'Ah, mortal bad.' The landlord looked gloomily down at the threshing figure and shook his head.

She tried to keep the irritation out of her voice. It looked as though she would need all the help she could get.

'Please send Will for the doctor immediately and ask Mrs Skinner to bring a sponge and some lavender water.'

'T'would be best if I get it for you, miss.'

'I really don't care who gets it, just bring it please,' she snapped, her nerves frayed by this frightening turn of events.

There was no help for it—she would have to stay. The Skinners believed her to be Gareth's sister and there was no way she could simply up and leave. And seeing him lying ill and alone, she knew that she wouldn't abandon him. When Mr Skinner returned with the bowl of lavender water, she asked him to raise the patient up while she attempted to plump the lumpy pillows into a more comfortable resting place. Then she sat down by the bedside and gently sponged his face. This seemed to soothe the fretting man and for a while he became calmer. But when she rose to move away from the bed, his hand, which had been aimlessly brushing the sheet, shot out and grasped her wrist.

'Don't leave me,' he muttered fiercely.

The doctor was not long in coming and did not seem overly surprised that his patient had developed a fever. He had, after all, been lying in a wet ditch for a number of hours and, by the look of him, Dr Fennimore thought, he'd probably already travelled a considerable distance and spent much of his strength. But his agitation appeared extreme.

The doctor rose from the bedside and looked thoughtfully at Amelie, his face shrewd and enquiring. 'His fever is unusually severe. Apart from his physical ills, he seems unquiet in his mind. You wouldn't know, I suppose, if there is something disturbing him?'

She avoided his question. She could not imagine that the events of the previous day had seriously bothered such a cool, audacious man. But Gareth Wendover was certainly a mystery and she sensed that there were dark shadows in his life which might complicate his recovery. She sat down by the rickety table, troubled and very pale.

The doctor clasped her hand warmly. 'Don't worry, Miss Wendover. I'm sure this fever is only temporary. Your brother looks a tough man, certainly not one that a few hours in a ditch will finish off.'

He continued bluffly, 'I'll leave you with a stronger remedy. Give it to him every three hours. If his condition worsens, send for me immediately. Hopefully, he should be back to his normal strength within a few days. His ankle is already showing signs of improvement.'

As Gareth's supposed sister, Amelie had also to be his nurse. Pitchforked into intimacy with a man she hardly knew, she could not protest without drawing attention to their false relationship. Fanny's horror would know no bounds, she reflected, but this was no time to be missish. Gareth needed her constant attention.

Throughout the next two days she bathed his forehead, administered medicine and kept his bedclothes as comfortable as possible. All the time his fevered ramblings punctuated the endless routine. He seemed greatly exercised about escaping from a room and needing to find a boat, but none of it made any sense to Amelie and she was too busy to worry over his words.

Mrs Skinner was invariably difficult, grumbling incessantly about the additional work Gareth occasioned. At times Amelie nearly came to blows with her. Fortunately, her husband was of a different disposition. He took Amelie's place by the bedside at nuncheon and dinner to allow her to eat and to stretch her limbs; at night he insisted on taking over Gareth's care and sent her to bed in the early hours of each morning. By then she was too tired to protest and retired gratefully to her little attic room, not caring that Betsy beside her was snoring heavily. She was so weary that she could have slept in Gareth's ditch.

On the third morning Mr Skinner reported that the fever had broken around dawn and that the patient was at last sleeping peacefully. After a hasty breakfast, she tiptoed quietly into Gareth's room with a bowl of chicken broth that the formidable Mrs Skinner had been persuaded to make. He lay supine, a still-powerful figure, but the days fighting fever had taken their toll. She felt a sudden surge of tenderness as she saw the leanness of his face and the pallor beneath the tanned skin.

At her approach, he opened his eyes and a puzzled

look flitted across his face. He appeared to be in a bedroom, but it was certainly nowhere he recognised. He felt amazingly tired and cursed himself for his weakness. The events of recent days slowly began to filter through his brain—a nightmarish ride, exquisite pain and a pair of gentle, soothing hands in the midst of the threatened inferno. He recalled some kind of accident an age ago, or so it seemed; this ravishing girl had been there, she'd ridden away on his horse. So what was she doing in this room? For a while he considered the matter dispassionately but it remained inexplicable.

'You're still here,' he murmured.

She bent over him, gently arranging the pillows to support his shoulders. He was sharply aware of her soft warmth so close to him and her fragrance drifting on the air.

'Take some of this excellent broth Mrs Skinner has made for you. You haven't eaten for days.'

He gave up the challenge of trying to make sense of the world and meekly sipped from the spoon she held out to him.

A few days later he was well enough to leave the stuffy bedchamber and make his way with Will's help down the stairs to the inn garden. Amelie brought up the rear of the procession with a stool and blankets in case it was chilly. But the sun shone blithely from a cloudless blue sky and Gareth, his ankle supported by the stool, lay back in his chair and gratefully soaked up the warmth. Beside him Amelie savoured the perfume of apple blossom and the rich smell of new grass.

He looked disparagingly at the glass she handed him.

'The doctor said you should drink as much milk as you can,' she chided. 'It will help you regain your strength.'

'You need strength to drink the stuff,' he protested. 'I think I'll settle for my present state of health.'

'You're a stubborn man.'

'And you're a stubborn woman. Why are you still here? I seem to remember sending you on your way.'

'You did and more than once—but it would be strange behaviour for a sister to abandon her brother.'

'Ah, yes, I'd forgotten that I'd acquired a new relative. Quite a surprise for me—though entirely beneficial.'

His blue eyes held the warm glow that she found so unsettling, but instinctively she returned his smile.

'It can't have been pleasant for you, forced to tend a sick man you barely knew and with no help from that bracket-faced termagant.'

She wanted to say that she knew him a great deal better now, but instead limited herself to murmuring neutrally, 'Even less pleasant for you, I fear. But Mr Skinner has been so very helpful. He's watched over you constantly and even persuaded his wife to cook for us.'

'Has she been very tiresome?'

'Shall we say she's not best pleased to be entertaining two vagrants.' Amelie grinned, remembering the skirmishes she'd endured while Gareth lay helpless above.

'One thing does occur to me,' he said thoughtfully. 'The Skinners must be wondering why no one has come from our supposed home to look for us.'

'I told them that I'd sent the local carrier with a message when he passed here the day before yesterday.'

'And they believed you?'

'Mrs Skinner probably didn't, but then she wouldn't believe anything. She decided from the outset that we were impostors, and of course she's right.'

For a moment he was startled, wondering how she could possibly have guessed that he was not the man he appeared.

'I mean,' she explained seeing the surprise on his face, 'that we're playing this charade of being brother and sister.' She looked at him enquiringly. 'Do you have a sister, in fact?'

'No.'

'Do you have any family—won't they be wondering where you are?'

'No and no,' he said shortly, then added in a more conciliatory tone, 'My only relation was my grandfather and he's now dead.'

'I'm sorry.' The compassion in her voice touched him on the raw.

'Don't be,' he said roughly, 'it's a matter of indifference to me.'

But she was not to be deterred. 'If you have no family in Bristol, why do you want to go there?'

He shifted his position, but remained sitting in silence.

'While you were suffering from the fever you mentioned taking a boat and escaping,' she persevered. 'What did you mean?'

'I've no idea. When people are feverish, they talk a lot of nonsense,' he retorted.

She had the distinct impression of an iron gate being swiftly clanged shut; she would learn no more. And in a trice he'd deftly turned the tables on her and begun to probe her own story.

'And why were *you* determined on travelling to Bristol?'

He must know that she'd been less than honest with him, at the very least that she'd lied about her destination.

'A family there are advertising for a lady's maid and I intended to apply for the position.'

'They must have advertised days ago. The situation might already be filled.' He'd evidently decided to maintain the pretence.

'I daresay you're right,' she replied airily. 'They're sure to have hired another girl by now.'

'So when you get to Bristol, what will you do?'

'I think,' she said carefully, 'I shall try my luck in Bath. There's any number of retired dowagers living there and one of them is bound to need assistance.'

'I wish you luck. Would you like a testimonial from me?' he joked. Then his face took on a more serious air.

'Without a reference from your previous family, you'll find it difficult to get work.'

'I shall manage. I've no reason to feel ashamed. I shall tell the truth about why I had to leave.'

'Will they believe you, though? As an employer I might find it difficult to accept your situation was so desperate that you had to climb out of the window on knotted sheets. Things like that only happen in novels. If you'd simply told your mistress what her son was up to, she would have intervened.'

'No, she wouldn't. He's spoilt and pampered and no one gainsays him, least of all his adoring mother. She'd never have believed me. She'd have accused me of plotting to ensnare him and I'd have been turned off without notice.'

'How has your situation improved? You're still without a job and still without references.'

'But I haven't had to endure lies and false accusations.'

He looked a little conscious at this. 'Until you met me, I suppose.'

'Yes, until I met you.'

She was looking directly at him and he was caught by her gaze. How could a pair of eyes sparkle with such militancy and yet drown a man in their allure?

'Was there nobody else in the family that you could turn to?' he said quickly. 'What about your young mistress?'

'She was a good friend to me,' Amelie admitted, happily weaving her fantasy, 'but she's to be married to a wealthy man against her wishes. She's powerless to offer me protection.'

'*You* could always marry. You'd receive ample protection then. You must have enjoyed plenty of attention from your fellows—beautiful and intelligent maidservants aren't two a penny.'

'I will never marry,' she declared resolutely.

Gareth smiled indulgently. 'You're not much more than a child—far too young to know how you'll feel in the future.'

Nettled by his mocking tone, her response was sharp. 'On the contrary, I shall feel in the future just as I do now. I intend to stay a single woman if I can.'

'Then you are vastly unlike the rest of your sex. Why so definite?'

'I don't wish to be subject to any man.'

'The right man can be a powerful defender.'

'Not those I've known—they've been either dissolute or vain and shallow.'

'There are men who are none of those things.'

She raised her eyebrows sceptically. 'You, for instance?'

Damn her, he thought, why was she forever putting him in the wrong? He'd behaved appallingly, he knew, and for no other reason than a desire to master her, to ruffle that beautiful surface. She was just too lovely.

Aloud he admitted to his offence. 'I behaved stupidly when we first met, more than stupidly.' He shook his head at his folly. 'I made a bad situation worse by getting extremely drunk.'

She looked enquiringly at him, but it was evident he had no intention of disclosing the cause of his erratic behaviour. She wondered if it had anything to do with the grandfather for whom he'd just professed the utmost indifference.

Trying another tack, she said quietly, 'You may not have relatives in England, but what about friends?'

'None of those, either,' he muttered roughly. 'I'm a wanderer, Amelie, and friends and family play no part in my life.'

She sensed that beneath his grim detachment, there lurked a vulnerability he would not admit. Her eyes clouded with sympathy and without thinking she reached out towards him, gently stroking the tanned forearm that showed beneath his rolled-up sleeves.

His hand closed over hers and held it tightly. He looked directly into her concerned face, hard blue eyes meeting soft brown, his gaze intent, wondering. For a long moment they sat thus. Then he reached out and slowly caressed her cheek. Her pulse began an erratic dance as his touch warmed her face. He let his hand slide from her cheek to tangle itself in the glossy curls which tumbled to her shoulders. Turning his body towards her, he cupped her face in both his hands and tilted it upwards. She watched as his mouth came closer and without thinking offered up her lips. His kiss was hard and warm and lingered long.

How long they would have kissed she had no idea, if Mr Skinner had not suddenly appeared from the depths of the inn leading the doctor behind him. She jumped back, flushed. Gareth looked annoyed. If Mr Skinner had seen that embrace, they would be in trouble. How to explain now that they were brother and sister! Jumping up from her seat, she nodded briefly to Dr Fennimore and quickly ran up the stairs to her bedroom in the eaves. She poured water from the jug into the chipped white basin and bathed her heated cheeks. She must truly have run mad. What on earth was she doing kissing a man of whom she knew nothing or at least nothing creditable? She sat down on her bed and stayed there for a very long time, trying hard to still her racing heart and erase the feeling of Gareth's hard, warm mouth on hers.

The doctor's visit was brief. He was evidently well satisfied with his patient and needed to come no more. She heard him call out his farewells followed by the sound of Will helping Gareth up the stairs from the garden to his room. Until she could leave the inn, she must make sure that they were rarely alone together. He could not be trusted; she'd allowed herself to show sympathy and his response had been immediate—an assault, an assault that she'd made no attempt to escape. She could not trust herself either. His gaze had sent her heart racing, a simple touch had left her breathless. And that kiss. No, she would not think of that kiss.

As the sun slipped from the sky, Mr Skinner appeared at her door with a message. 'Your brother would like to know if you will dine with him tonight. He's feeling a good deal better and would like to celebrate his recovery.' The landlord enunciated the phrases painstakingly, relieved that he'd remembered Gareth's precise words.

I'm sure he would, she thought crossly, *and I can imagine the kind of celebration he intends.*

'Tell my brother that I regret I have the headache and I will not be dining tonight,' she said, adding diffidently, 'It would be very kind of you, Mr Skinner, if you could bring a bowl of soup to my room.'

For the first time since she'd come to the George, she found it difficult to sleep that night, her mind endlessly roaming the day's events, but finding no peace. She could not banish the attraction she felt for Gareth Wendover. Her heart was forever pulling her towards a man with whom it was madness to embroil herself. He was arrogant and capricious. He was reserved and unforthcoming and she strongly suspected that unfortunate secrets lay hidden in the depths of his past. Yet she, too, was equally guilty of dissembling. From the outset she'd told him a pack of lies and ever since had spent considerable effort in embroidering them.

What was certain was that she must leave for Bath as soon as she could. She must not become any further entangled; she must not fall in love with him. If ever she were forced to marry, Lord Silverdale's daughter would be expected to look a great deal higher than a mere Mr Wendover of unknown and possibly disreputable lineage. And she *wasn't* going to be forced to marry. She would not emulate her mother's sad fate; her security and peace of mind lay in an unmarried life and that meant eschewing dalliance, no matter how attractive the man.

After breakfast she repaired to Gareth's bedroom to tell him she was leaving. It was another beautiful May morning and the leaded windows were flung wide to welcome the sun. A warm breeze gently lifted the curtains. He was sitting by the window fully dressed and smiled mockingly as she came through the door.

'I hope I find you recovered?'

She looked blank for a moment.

'The headache? I understand it was so painful that you could manage only a bowl of soup for dinner.' His tone was ironic.

'I'm well, thank you,' she replied, not meeting his eyes. 'And you?'

'I'm well, too—my old self, in fact. Does that strike terror into your heart?'

'Indeed no, why should it? I'm well able to take care of myself.'

He shook his head in some irritation. 'Let's stop sparring, Amelie. Come and sit with me instead.'

She moved towards the window and the empty chair. For the first time she met his eyes directly and her body warmed instantly beneath his gaze. But she ignored the answering pull and disregarded his welcoming hand; she was still on dangerous territory and must step carefully.

'When do you intend to leave for Bristol?' she asked. 'I presume you're still going there.'

'Maybe,' he uttered shortly. 'I haven't yet made up my mind.'

'If you don't continue to Bristol, where else will you go? Back to London?'

'Possibly.'

'So you're as free as a bird?'

'It would appear so.'

Frustrated at his stonewalling, she went on the offensive. 'Are you saying that nobody in the entire world will miss you, if you don't soon put in an appearance?'

'That about sums it up.'

She didn't understand him. Her questions were innocent enough and his bald refusal to answer demonstrated clearly that he didn't trust her. She was good enough to kiss but not to confide in. Sensing her anger, he smiled that warm, entrancing smile.

'Why don't we just enjoy this morning? I imagine you've come to tell me you're leaving soon.'

'Now that your ankle's better, I must be on my way.' She was annoyed with herself that she sounded almost apologetic.

'Of course you must, and I can't detain you. You've kept your bargain, after all.'

For a moment she looked uncomprehending; she'd completely forgotten their old quarrel. Then she gave a half smile. 'Yes, I've kept it—but not quite as you planned.'

'Better, in fact. You've seen me through some very

trying days, so don't let's spend our last few hours arguing.'

She remained mute and stared fixedly through the window at the untended orchard beyond. When he spoke again his voice was tender and caught at her heart.

'I have you to thank for the good shape I'm in. You must know that I'm deeply grateful.'

'I don't want your gratitude.'

'What do you want?' he asked quizzically and once again reached out for her hand.

Mindful of her overnight resolution, she jumped up quickly and said, 'What I want is to leave tomorrow. But in the meantime I'm sure the George can supply us with some entertainment. I'll go downstairs and see what they have to offer.'

And with that she disappeared rapidly from view. Gareth looked after her, a slight flush creeping into his lean cheek. Tendering his hand in friendship to a woman was a new experience for him and being rejected was equally novel.

She returned half an hour later, having searched high and low for dominoes or Chinese chequers. Will had helped her for a while until Mrs Skinner, catching sight of the two of them, had ordered him angrily to fetch water from the pump. Then she'd stood coldly over Amelie and demanded just what Miss Wendover might be wanting. Her attitude was one of unconcealed hostility. Amelie was sure now that the landlord had seen her spring back from Gareth's kiss yesterday and had confided this unsettling news to his wife. She blushed deeply at the thought of their conversation.

'I'm looking for dominoes or chequers,' she said as calmly as she could. 'My brother is feeling a good deal better and it will be a way of passing the hours.'

Mrs Skinner snorted as though she knew well enough how they intended to pass the hours, but reluctantly led the way into an inner sanctum, opened a tall oak dresser in the corner of the room and shuffled around inside. The reek of mothballs floated out into the already malodorous room.

'There's some cards and a game of spillikins.' The landlady thrust the items roughly at Amelie and stood glaring at her.

Understanding that she was dismissed, Amelie made to leave. She couldn't picture Gareth playing the child's game, but she could always leave the spillikins in her bedroom. With hurried thanks, she gathered up the games and ran up the stairs.

'I've found something,' she called out gaily. 'A pack of cards! Or rather Mrs Skinner found them, tucked at the back of an enormous dresser, which I don't think has been opened for at least thirty years. Unfortunately, they smell of mothballs, but then this room isn't exactly fresh, even with the window wide open.'

As she was speaking, she cleared the small table between them of empty glasses and medicine bottles. 'There, a perfect card table. What shall we play? I know very few games, but I imagine you can teach me.'

'No.' The brusque monosyllable startled her.

'I beg your pardon?'

'I said no. I can't teach you any card games, nor do I wish to play.'

She looked puzzled. 'How difficult am I to understand?' he said sharply. 'I don't wish to play.'

'But it's only a game of cards—an amusing diversion,' she protested.

'For the last time, I don't wish to play.'

The familiar bleak expression had returned to Gareth's face. His eyes were once more stony and the straight night-black brows threatening. He leaned back in his chair, detaching himself from the proceedings and refusing to meet her earnest look.

'That's all right,' she said a little uncertainly. 'I didn't mean to upset you.'

'You didn't. Just learn to take a refusal when it's given.'

She bit back a retort. After tomorrow she would never see Gareth Wendover again. It was hardly worth quarrelling with him despite his extraordinary rudeness. But it was difficult to accept that he was the same man who had kissed her with such ardour only yesterday. He was transformed and she felt deeply wounded by the change.

'I'll find something else to play,' she stammered a little shakily.

Minutes later she returned with the spillikins. The hard look on Gareth's face had disappeared and when he saw the spillikins he laughed out loud.

'I know you've been my nursemaid these past few

days, but have I regressed that badly that you need to play a child's game with me?'

'That's all they have downstairs, and we must make the best of it.'

She held upright the bunch of thin sticks and allowed them to fall at will. They scattered wildly across the table top.

'The sticks coloured blue score most highly, red next, then yellow, and green are the most lowly,' she explained.

'I shall be lucky to pick up one stick cleanly, never mind its colour. I've suffered an accident, after all.'

'You've sprained your ankle, not your wrist.'

'But women are so much more dextrous, it's hardly fair.'

'Surely, Mr Wendover, you're not saying that a woman can outdo you.'

'Gareth, please. If we're to be serious competitors, we must use first names. That way our insults, when they start flying, will be nicely personal.'

'I've no intention of trading insults. It's just a game, not a competition,' she said carelessly.

Nevertheless, she tried very hard to win. When it came to her turn she took minutes to weigh up the arrangement of sticks before deciding which one she would try to extricate from its place without dislodging the others. Gareth had gone first and could begin with the easiest stick to lift, but once into the thick of the game, they were both forced to concentrate intently when their several turns came round. At one point, he appeared to disturb one of the sticks he was trying to avoid and she called foul.

'I merely breathed on the stick and it moved of its own accord,' he disputed, shaking his head in bewilderment.

She burst out laughing. 'That's certainly original. I'll give you the excuse if only for sheer invention.'

He laughed back at her, his heart filled with a strange happiness. So the game went on until there was just a small pile of sticks left in the middle of the table, all thickly entangled. They were neck and neck in the number they'd managed to acquire and, faced now with the most difficult moves, they both studied the table keenly, trying to decide their best approach. In the event it was Gareth who managed to extricate his last spill without disturbing the one other that was left.

'Voilà!' he exclaimed.

'Magnifique,' she unconsciously rejoined, responding spontaneously to his skilful play.

'A maidservant who speaks French as well as having a French name! It becomes more and more intriguing.' He looked searchingly at her.

'I'd hardly say that I spoke French,' she said, desperately seeking a way of moving the conversation on to less dangerous ground.

'Still, it's an unusual maid who knows any French. And you *are* an unusual maid, aren't you? You're proud and independent, you speak genteelly and hold yourself like a lady. If it weren't for your clothes, I would take you for a lady.'

From the bottom of her heart, she thanked the absent Fanny for donating her wardrobe, then set about allaying his suspicions.

'My young mistress made a great friend of me and I learned from her how to go on.'

He considered this for a while. 'You may have learned conduct from her but not, I think, your courage.'

'What do you mean?' She was disconcerted.

'Didn't you say that your mistress was being married off against her will?'

'She is, but courage won't help her. Her brother has gambled away the family's fortune and marriage is the only way to restore it. She's expected to make this sacrifice for her family.'

'Quite a sacrifice! Would you make it, I wonder?'

'I would not,' she declared ringingly and with a vehemence that surprised him.

He looked at her as she sat across the table. Her creamy skin glowed translucent in the shadowed sunlight that filled the room and the velvet brown of her eyes blazed a fiery spirit. She had never looked more enchanting.

'Nor should you,' he said, his voice husky with feeling.

The atmosphere was suddenly charged with tension, their bantering mood dissipated. He should defuse the moment, he thought, make a joke, turn away. She'd already chosen to put distance between them and she was right. Instead, he rose quickly from his chair, taking no heed of the damaged ankle, and took both her hands in his. Slowly he raised her up and encircled her in his arms.

Crushed against his hard frame, she felt the same foolish impulse to melt into him; she began to tremble beneath his hands. He touched her face, her arms, and brushed across the warm silk of her breast. He gently kissed her hair, her ears, her cheek. In a moment his tongue had parted her lips and was slowly exploring the softness of her mouth. His body moved against her and she groaned softly with pleasure. She wanted to dissolve into this nameless delight, yet some voice of wisdom pulled her back to consciousness. This was a man who had come from nowhere and would go to nowhere. She would never see him again once they parted. He'd made her vulnerable, created a desire in her that she'd never before known. And desire meant weakness; she had only to think of her mother's fate to know that. Impelled by a new urgency, she hastily pushed him away and began to tidy the scattered sticks, barely able to see them for the emotions churning within her.

'That shouldn't have happened.'

He was still standing close to her, his breathing ragged and his voice rough. He seemed furious with himself.

'After yesterday I vowed I'd never again touch you.'

Distractedly, she smoothed her tumbled hair and then began to pack the last of the spillikins in their box.

'Forgive me if I've distressed you.' His harsh tones grated, breaking through her silence.

'It's of no importance. I don't wish to talk of it,' she managed. Her outward calm belied the turmoil within. 'It must be time for nuncheon,' she continued smoothly. 'I'll fetch some refreshment from the kitchen.'

She glanced fleetingly out of the window, as she turned to leave. A carriage had pulled up outside. In itself this was unusual but this was not any carriage. It was a lightly built curricle drawn by four high-stepping greys and the curricle door had a well-known crest on its panel. It had to be Rufus Glyde. He had traced her after all. He was here. She turned sheet-white and the box dropped from her suddenly lifeless hand.

'Excuse me,' she gasped, 'I have to go.'

And with that she dashed from the room, leaving Gareth baffled and infuriated.

Chapter Five

Rufus Glyde was in no pleasant mood. He'd been driving almost continuously for days without once ever sighting his quarry. In addition he'd had to endure the sharp tongue of Brielle St Clair when he'd dared to enquire for her granddaughter at the Bath house. It had been a terse encounter on both sides, but he'd definitely come off worse, told in no uncertain terms that his intervention in family affairs was not welcome. It had been the first intimation for Brielle that all was not well with her granddaughter. She was furious that Lord Silverdale had not come himself to tell her of Amelie's flight, but instead left it to this sneering and patronising stranger to break the news. Most of all she was desperately worried. She felt sick when she thought of what might have befallen the young girl. Her dread fuelled a naturally acerbic tongue and Glyde was still smarting from his dismissal.

As he entered the George the idea that he was on a wild goose chase became insistent. For a while he'd thought that he might be on Amelie's trail. At Reading where he'd stopped for the night, he'd overheard a conversation between two travellers that gave him pause. One of them had told the strange story of a stage held up on the Bath road, not for jewellery or money, but for a young woman travelling in the coach. It had caused something of a sensation when the passengers had disembarked at Bath and begun to tell their tale.

He'd been sufficiently intrigued by the news to abandon his return to London and head once more in the direction of Bath. By dint of questioning everyone he met—and most of these he castigated as ignorant bumpkins—he'd managed to discover the district in which the hold-up had occurred and then begun to cast around at various inns for news of the errant Amelie. So far it had proved a fruitless task and the George looked no more promising.

Entering the taproom, he was greeted by drab, outmoded furnishings and the stale odour of old beer and tobacco. He turned round full circle. The afternoon sunlight in its attempt to pierce the dirty windows only served to emphasise the dilapidation within. Surely Amelie Silverdale would not be residing here. The inhabitants, if there were any, were either dead or asleep. Nothing stirred. Irritably, he rang the bell on the counter and when there was no response, rang it again more loudly. Mrs Skinner appeared from the top of the cellar steps and scowled at him.

'Did you want somethin'?'

Her voice was not encouraging. Glyde looked the woman up and down. She was gaunt, badly dressed and with a face marked by ill temper.

'It would appear so since I rang the bell,' he countered acidly.

'Well, what is it, then? I'm busy.'

He tried to keep the rising anger from his voice; he needed this woman's help. He told the same story as he'd told at the other dozen inns he'd visited. He'd been travelling with a friend, but they'd become separated. He carefully avoided mentioning the sex of his companion. His friend had not appeared at the rendezvous they'd agreed on and he, Glyde, feared that his comrade had met with an accident. Did the good lady have anyone staying at the inn who might be his friend?

'Nobody you'd know,' she sniffed.

'But you do have someone staying?' he persisted.

Mrs Skinner grudgingly admitted the fact but added, ''E ain't your friend, 'e ain't a top-lofty gent like you.'

'My friend is hardly top-lofty. May I ask who this person is?'

'You can arsk, but mebbe I ain't of a mind to tell you.'

Again he had visibly to control his anger. 'I'm sure we can remedy your lack of memory.'

A sneer slashed his thin white face as he took out his bill folder and extracted a note of some considerable value. Mrs Skinner blinked at this unexpected largesse and thought of extending her prize curtains to the rooms above.

''Is name's Wendover and I've told you 'e ain't a gent, not with 'is scruffy clothes.'

Glyde's hopes withered. For a moment he'd thought he might finally be close to success, but a male resident who wore scruffy clothes and wasn't a 'gent' as Mrs Skinner put it, was not someone who could be of any interest.

'And he is your only guest?'

'You're a nosy one, ain't you?' Mrs Skinner's hand closed over the tantalising money bill. 'As it 'appens, 'is sister's staying with him. They 'ad an accident, too. Funny, the number of accidents round 'ere these days.'

Glyde ignored the witticism, but his mind was working rapidly. A sister of Mr Wendover might mean a young woman, and this young woman could just be the prey he sought. It was a chance in a thousand, but he had to know. He cast around for a way of distracting Mrs Skinner, who appeared to have taken root in front of her benefactor. His luck suddenly took a turn for the better. Will, who had been working in the cellar alongside his mistress, appeared at that moment at the top of the stairs.

'Mrs Skinner, ma'am, where d'you want the new barrels put?'

'Where d'you think, you numbskull?' was Mrs Skinner's pleasant reply.

'There's not enough room behind the old barrels,' Will bravely continued.

'Dratted men,' she muttered, 'can't be relied on to do anythin'.' Giving Glyde a last withering glance, she disappeared back down the cellar steps.

Her head had hardly faded from view before he made his move. In a few seconds he'd reached the stairway leading to the top of the house and made ready to search out Mr Wendover and his mysterious sister for himself.

Gareth stared blankly through the window at the curricle as it disappeared towards the stables. From the rear it looked to be a nobleman's carriage, but he had no idea who it belonged to or why it was at the George. Amelie had evidently gained a better view and she *had* recognised it. The thought came to him that this might be her previous employer, enraged by her dubious departure. He realised with a jolt that his initial suspicions had been completely lulled and now his mind could no longer consider the possibility that she was a deceiver. He dismissed the idea even as it came into his head. And common sense soon reasserted itself. If she were a dishonest maidservant, whatever she might have done and however furious her noble employer, the possibility of his seeking her out in a rundown country inn was extremely unlikely.

Annoyance at Amelie's abrupt departure mingled with feelings of self-reproach. He'd spoiled the warm companionship of the morning. One minute they'd been laughing, joking, funning with each other. And then everything had changed. He'd touched her and he shouldn't have. She was irresistible, but he should have resisted. God knew he'd had enough experience in escaping amorous situations, so why was this so different? He couldn't account for it. Indignation at the notion of sacrificing herself to family duty had rendered her beauty overwhelming, her eyes a molten brown and the sheen of her skin glowing fire. But it was more than physical beauty that had shattered his restraint. In that moment it seemed her very soul had been laid bare and spoken unmistakably to his. He gave himself a mental shake: such fanciful nonsense! Whatever the reason, he'd not been able to stop himself. Even now he could feel her mouth, soft but eager, opening delicately to his.

When he heard the bedroom door open he turned, a contrite expression on his face, but instead of Amelie he was confronted by Rufus Glyde, a man he'd not seen for seven long years. Both men stared at each other in amazement. Glyde was the first to find his voice.

'Surely,' he jeered, 'it cannot be Gareth Denville. Aren't you supposed to be resting on the Continent? Surely you haven't returned to claim the earldom? Even the blackest sheep might be expected to do the decent thing and stay away.'

Gareth stayed silent, his face impassive and his darkened eyes unreadable. For years unfounded suspicions had plagued his mind over Glyde's role in that ill-fated card game.

'Aren't you going to invite me to sit down, Mr Wendover?' Glyde tormented. 'I'm presuming it *is* Mr

Wendover? Why the false name, I wonder? A silly question no doubt. I imagine you would prefer to keep your identity hidden for all kinds of reasons. And staying in a place like this!' The smirk became more pronounced.

Gareth remained standing. His voice was cold and curt. 'State your business. Mine is none of yours,' he rapped out.

'Still hot-tempered, I see. Some things never change. Though you've aged—not quite as fresh faced as when I saw you last. Now, when was that? Ah, yes, the Great-Go. Quite a night, quite a sensation, I recall.'

'Cut to the chase, Glyde, what do you want?'

'Not you, for sure. Keeping company with the flotsam of society is not really my custom. But I am rather interested in the sister you appear to have acquired. If my memory serves me right—and, of course, I could be wrong, family genealogy was never my strong point—your father, another unfortunate I understand, had only one child and that child was you. So a sister?'

'It's none of your affair and I'll thank you to leave.'

'Now that's where we could disagree, I fear.'

'I've nothing further to say to you. Leave of your own free will or at the end of my boot, it's your choice.'

'Proud crowing from someone plainly unable to enforce their threat.' He gestured at Gareth's bandaged ankle. 'Tell me what I want to know and I'll leave as quickly as you could want. What about this sister?'

Gareth weighed up the odds of forcibly removing his antagonist from the room and decided it was probably not worth the pain he would inevitably suffer. He would give him the minimum of information and speed him on his way.

'She is merely an acquaintance who happens to be staying at the inn.'

'An acquaintance you call a sister. Come, Denville, that won't wash. Who is she?'

'She's a maidservant, no one you know and no one of any interest.'

'A maidservant? Pitching it rather low even for you, my dear Denville. A maidservant—and your doxy, I presume.'

Gareth's knuckles tightened until they were white. 'Get out!'

'Dear, dear, that temper again. Yes, I see, your doxy, and to pacify that dreadful harpy downstairs, you pass her off as your sister. You're right, of course, I have no interest in her. The woman I seek would not pass the time of day with you, and as for impersonating a maidservant and sharing this vile refuge, the idea is laughable.'

'Now you've had your laugh, you're at liberty to leave.'

'Indeed, and I shall do so very shortly. But first tell me how the cardsharping business prospers in Europe. Did you make a living?' Glyde glanced down at the elegant coat of superfine he was wearing and then at Gareth's outfit, daily looking more frayed.

'And I always thought such practised tricksters went on prosperously,' he murmured, 'but it would seem not.'

Ignoring the intense pain in his ankle, Gareth moved

with unexpected swiftness towards his enemy and clasped him violently round the throat.

'If ever you call me a cheat again, you will not live,' he ground out.

The door had remained open throughout their acrimonious exchange and with his hands still wrapped around Glyde's neck, Gareth thrust his adversary through the doorway and down the stairs.

At the moment Glyde had been dismounting from his carriage, Amelie had escaped through the back entrance of the inn. She ran wildly past the crumbling outbuildings and through the small wicket gate that led on to open pasture. Dismayed and frightened at the turn of events, she ran without thinking where she was going. Her mind was in chaos, refusing to accept that Sir Rufus had tracked her to this remote place. It was impossible. Nobody except Gareth Wendover knew her whereabouts and he was ignorant of her true identity.

Slowly through the confused toss and tumble of thoughts a chilling idea began to emerge. Was it possible that they were in alliance together, that Gareth knew who she was and had been Glyde's accomplice all this time? Was it coincidence that Rufus Glyde had appeared out of nowhere, just after she'd been abducted from the stagecoach? The fact that his carriage had mown Gareth down and thrown him into a ditch was probably an accident in their plan. Gareth had resolutely refused to tell her anything about himself. Was that in case she would unmask him too soon, before Glyde could catch up with them? And to think that she had so nearly put herself into his power, so nearly succumbed to his seductive charm.

By now breathless, she was forced to come to a stop. It was pointless running any farther across the fields. She had no idea where she was going and if she turned back again to regain the road, Glyde could overtake her in his curricle at any moment. A nearby clump of trees would provide shelter and from this vantage point she could observe the inn from a distance. She settled herself beneath a sturdy oak, her back against its grainy trunk. The gentle summer sun filtered through the leaves above and birdsong filled the air. It was hard to imagine there was anything wrong with the world. Gradually her breathing returned to normal and her disordered thoughts began to settle. It was madness to imagine that Gareth was in league with the man who was hunting her. How could he have arranged to be outside her house at the precise moment she'd climbed from the bedroom window? It was ridiculous. Even more ridiculous to think him an accomplice. She knew, as well as she knew herself, that he would loathe and despise a creature such as Glyde.

The time passed tantalisingly slowly. She told herself that her pursuer wouldn't be at the inn long. Even if he ran into Gareth, he would not know him and any description of Miss Wendover's appearance was unlikely to match that of the aristocratic woman Glyde sought. He would be eager to leave an inn as insalubrious as the George and make once more for the pleasures of

London. And once he'd driven away, she could take shelter for one more night. Early tomorrow morning she would get her lift to Wroxall and be on the stagecoach to Bath and safety.

She waited for what seemed an age, although in reality only half an hour had passed since she'd fled the inn so precipitately. In that time she'd neither glimpsed any activity nor heard a sound from the distant building. Maybe, after all, her hiding place was too far away to hear the noise of any departure? She debated what to do. At this rate she could be sitting under the oak tree until nightfall. Gathering her courage, she decided to chance a return. With some stealth she began slowly to approach the inn and, meeting nobody, crept through the back entrance to the passage that ran the length of the building to the open front door.

Almost immediately she became aware of Glyde's carriage being led back into the courtyard and turned to flee again. But at the same time raised voices sounded above and she was sure one of them was Gareth's. She strained to hear what was being said, but the voices were too indistinct. As she listened, there was a sudden noisy creak of bedroom floorboards overhead. In a trice she'd whisked herself into the shadows beneath the stairs. Just in time. Rufus Glyde clattered down the staircase, his face twisted in fury. He was so close that had she reached out her arm, she could have touched him. She remained frozen to the spot as he stormed past her and out into the sunlit yard, throwing himself onto the driving seat of the carriage and whipping up his horses in a frenzy.

She found she was shaking uncontrollably and her first thought was to seek the sanctuary of her bedchamber. But there were questions burning through her brain that needed answers. The angry scene she'd come upon in its dying moments made no sense. Her old suspicions began to return; she needed to know what connection existed between these two men.

Contempt was written large on Gareth's face. His ankle throbbed angrily, but it had been worth the pain to knock the sneering smile from the face of his foe. Glyde would be for ever associated with the scene of his disgrace and his heart rejoiced that he'd routed the man so completely. But if he were honest, it was the image of Glyde and Amelie together that had spurred him to extreme action. That image was seared on his mind's eye, even stronger for being intangible. He had no idea why Glyde had turned up at this remote inn or what connection he had to the girl, but speculation gnawed relentlessly at him. He doubted he would ever get the truth from her; he'd been a fool to believe that she was trustworthy.

He was still standing by the window, exactly where she'd left him. If she hadn't just heard that furious altercation, she might have imagined she'd been away for only a few minutes and that the intervening time was simply a bad dream. But Gareth's face told another story. She could see immediately that he was in a thunderous mood. He turned as he heard her footsteps, his eyes now blue flint and his mouth close-gripped. She started to speak, but was cut off abruptly.

'Why did you leave like that?' he flung at her. 'What is that man to you?'

She steadied her racing heart and replied in an even voice, 'He's nothing to me. I ran away because I feared being discovered.'

'Why should it matter that he saw you?'

'I told you, I feared being seen—by anyone.'

'Anyone? Do you take me for a fool? He came looking for a woman and I think that woman was you. You turned white when you saw his carriage in the yard. You fled. Can you really expect me to believe that it was because some stranger had suddenly arrived?'

'Believe what you wish, I don't know who he was seeking. I escaped from the inn because I didn't want to be found here. I'm an unmarried woman and have been living under the same roof as you for the last week.'

'You would have me accept that a girl who thinks nothing of throwing her lot in with a man she doesn't know is worried that others will see her with him?'

'I never threw my lot in with you. You forced me to accompany you.'

'It doesn't seem to have pained your sense of propriety too greatly.'

'You can mock all you wish. You may not have a reputation to defend, but I do. I have a living to earn and I can't afford to attract any gossip.'

She hoped that this was an inspired invention, but

instead Gareth immediately pounced on her words and shredded them to pieces.

'If you don't know this man, then how could it affect your reputation one way or another?'

'I didn't say I didn't know him,' she conceded.

'At last,' he muttered grimly, 'we're getting near the truth or as near as we're ever likely to with you.'

'What do you mean by that?' Her anger sliced through the airless room.

'Simply that you appear to have a rather slippery relationship with honesty.'

'If we are to call each other liars, then you hardly fare better. What about the lies you told my fellow passengers on the stagecoach? That was blatant.'

'And this isn't?'

'I was telling the truth when I said that I didn't want to be discovered. But I am acquainted with this man. He's an intimate of my young mistress's brother and visits the house regularly. Although I was only a servant there and beneath his notice, I was worried he might recognise me.'

Gareth was silent, seeming to turn this over in his mind. She was unsure he believed her and, to deflect him further, renewed her attack.

'I've told you how *I* know him, though I can't understand why it's any business of yours. Now perhaps you'll tell me how *you're* acquainted with him.'

He stared sightlessly through the window, once more in that overheated, overfurnished salon. The babble of rich men intent on their pleasure filled his ears, then the sudden silence, the incredulous stares, the shuffling of feet and finally the cool withdrawal of the well-bred from the social disaster in their midst.

Unrelenting, Amelie waited for his response, never taking her eyes from his face. Aware at last of her scrutiny, he raised his gaze to her, his expression bleak.

'My acquaintance with him is very slight.'

His discomfort was palpable and she decided to press home her advantage.

'You were quarrelling,' she insisted. 'You must know the man well enough to quarrel.'

'He angered me. He invaded my room without permission and then wouldn't leave.'

'And that was enough for you to throw him down the stairs?'

'A slight exaggeration? He's a particularly obnoxious man and I didn't care for his tone.'

'If all that annoyed you was his attitude, you seem to have argued for a long time. Why didn't you get rid of him earlier?'

'You may not have noticed,' he replied scathingly, 'but I've sustained an injury. You fled on the instant and I was left alone to deal with him. In the end I got tired of his importuning and decided to risk the ankle. It hurt like hell, but I'm glad I assisted him on his way.'

He seemed to have regained something of his poise and his face no longer bore the icy expression that she'd come to dread. She was almost encouraged to tell him her true situation—almost, but not quite. To do so might jeopardise her plans entirely. If Gareth were the man she believed him to be, he would be impelled to pursue Glyde when he knew the full extent of his infamy. That would cause a scandal she would never live down. And if he were not that man, if he were untrustworthy, then she could be in real peril, in danger of kidnap or blackmail once he knew her true identity.

'Does he know that you have a sister staying here?' she ventured tentatively.

'He knows,' came the short reply.

'You didn't tell him my name?'

'No,' he said in a distant voice.

Her face wore such an expression of relief that his distrust once again blossomed.

'Your fears are unfounded, my dear, your identity is safe.' His tone was caustic. 'I doubt that a man of Glyde's position would consider it interesting or worthwhile to spread scandal about a maidservant, even if he knew her name.'

Euphoric at her escape, Amelie hardly noticed his tone and unwisely pushed onwards.

'Thank you for not giving me away.' And when he didn't reply, she said again, 'Thank you.'

'Spare me the gratitude,' he grated.

There was a pause as he looked her fully in the face, wondering how he'd allowed himself to be taken in by a girl so adept at lying. He'd begun to believe his judgement of womankind faulty, but it seemed that she shared generously in the attributes of her sisters—she was no different from any of the women who'd passed briefly through his life.

'He thinks you're my doxy,' he said deliberately, then added with undisguised bitterness, 'And who could blame him? You behaved like one—scuttling for cover instead of facing him honestly.'

The words came out of nowhere and fell like hammer blows on her ears. Scarlet with mortification, she ran from the room. How could he throw such a vile insult at her? Even if she were the simple maidservant she purported to be, she would be justified in protecting her good name. Yet by his reckoning she'd committed an unforgivable offence in running away; she was no better than Haymarket ware.

Once in her bedroom, she grabbed the faithful cloak bag and hurriedly packed the few items she still possessed. Then she ran down the stairs and out into the backyard. Will was busy washing the cobbles.

'Will, come here,' she called urgently to him. 'Mr Wendover has taken a turn for the worst. He needs the medicine that the doctor prescribed in an emergency. I must get to Wroxhall immediately.'

Will rested from his labours, leaning on the broom with one hand and scratching his head with the other.

'Mr Wendover were fine this morning. Happen he'll come about again soon.'

'No, Will, he won't. He's been feeling poorly for hours, but didn't like to complain. Now his fever seems to have returned. We must get to Wroxall.'

'I'd like to help, Miss Wendover,' he said doubtfully, 'but I'll have to ask the missus. Mrs Skinner do like to know where I am. And she don't like it if the horse is taken out without her permission.'

'Mrs Skinner is out,' Amelie lied recklessly, 'and Mr Skinner, too. I saw them on their way to visit neighbours.'

Will shook his head slowly. The image of the Skinners visiting their neighbours was one he was having difficulty with.

'Please help me,' she pleaded urgently. 'You don't want Mr Wendover to become really ill again, do you?'

Will shook his head, but still looked unhappy.

'It could be a matter of life or death, Will. I wouldn't ask you otherwise.'

She felt guilty about deceiving him, but refused to think of his likely punishment for helping her. She had to get away. Unwillingly, Will put down his bucket and brush and went towards the trap, which stood backed into the corner of the rear yard. He carefully moved it into the centre and arranged the leather ties. The mare had then to be led from her stable and harnessed. For Amelie, desperate to leave the inn behind, every minute seemed an impossible age. One or the other of the Skinners could put in an appearance at any time and ruin her escape.

Will might be slow, but he was methodical. Finally the trap was ready and she jumped up on to the passenger seat.

'Please make haste,' she enjoined him as they turned out of the yard onto the highway.

Will, who had begun to enjoy his freedom from cobble washing and enter into the spirit of the adventure, whipped the placid bay into something approaching a trot. They were very soon out of sight of the inn and she sighed with relief. She never wanted to see Gareth Wendover again. His words flung at her so coldly and dismissively had finally cut whatever cord existed between them.

Chapter Six

She stood beneath the white portico of her grandmother's house. The rain had been falling in torrents ever since she'd alighted at the White Lion Inn and she was now soaked to the skin from the brief walk to Laura Place. The weeping skies seemed an echo of her present mood. After all the obstacles and alarms she had encountered since leaving London, the final leg of her journey to Bath had been deceptively simple. Once in Wroxall she'd given Will the slip, with only a few pangs of conscience. There had been less than an hour to pass before her coach had departed and she'd found it easy to hide herself away and board the stage without anyone recognising her. Now with her escape plan almost complete, she should be flushed with excitement. Instead, she felt a dawning fear. What if her grandmother were out of town? What if Brielle were so outraged by her granddaughter's conduct that she refused to receive her?

She stared at the ebony door with its brass lion head. In her disquiet it seemed to challenge her right to be there and she had to summon all her resolution to lift the knocker. The resulting clatter reverberated through the hall beyond. Tense minutes of silence followed. She was just lifting her hand to knock again when she heard footsteps coming towards the door and in a minute the butler's familiar person stood before her. Horrocks was looking at her strangely, seemingly trying to puzzle out just what or who had arrived on the front steps.

'You should go round to the back entrance,' he said reprovingly as he took in the bedraggled figure in front of him.

'Horrocks, it's me, Amelie,' she cried, pushing back the hood of her cloak to reveal her face fully.

'Miss Amelie?' Horrocks stared in disbelief. 'Whatever are you doing here? Her ladyship said nothing of your coming. And where is your escort? You surely cannot be alone.'

He peered up and down the empty street in a vain search. Then, recalled to his duties, he ushered her quickly into the house. She slipped gratefully past him into the warmth of the hall. The house looked little different from the last time she'd seen it as a child, perhaps a little smaller, a little less grand.

'Her ladyship is out this evening, Miss Amelie, but I can send a messenger to fetch her home immediately. She is only a few minutes away.'

'No, don't do that, Horrocks,' she said quickly. 'I'll wait until she gets back. I don't imagine that she keeps very late hours.'

The butler looked grateful. 'No, indeed. But you should get out of those wet clothes straight away. I'll send Miss Repton to you.'

She'd never heard of Miss Repton, evidently a new addition to the household whom she supposed must be her grandmother's dresser. Horrocks led the way upstairs to the small sitting room overlooking Laura Place. This was Brielle's favourite retreat, even though she had a far more elegant drawing room at the back of the house with views over a surprisingly large and immaculate garden.

Miss Repton turned out to be a disapproving middle-aged woman, manicured to within an inch of her life. She looked Amelie up and down with disbelief.

'You'll need dry clothes, miss.' She sniffed. 'Where is your valise?'

'My luggage was mislaid during my journey, Miss Repton. It will be coming on later.'

She hoped her lie would satisfy this haughty woman, but the dresser continued to gaze at her with barely concealed disdain.

'I'll try to find something of milady's to fit you, but it won't be easy.'

Amelie, unused to such disrespect from a servant, answered sharply, 'It really doesn't matter. If you will be so kind as to take my cloak, I will dry my dress by the fire.'

Miss Repton looked scandalised and even more so when the discarded cloak revealed Fanny's plain, and by now, severely dilapidated dress. Amelie looked her in the eyes, challenging her to make a comment. The woman remained mute and made for the door, carefully holding the sodden cloak at arm's length.

'I'll ask Horrocks to send up tea, miss,' she said tonelessly.

Relieved by the dresser's exit, she sank into a comfortable chair and closed her eyes. The fire burned brightly and warmed her chilled body. The peace of the room gradually soothed her and by the time Horrocks brought her tea and toast, she was in a fair way to thinking that all would be well once her grandmother returned. But as the minutes ticked by and there was no sign of Brielle, tormenting thoughts once more began to possess her. Her grandmother might have led an unconventional life, but she was a stickler for proper conduct. She would be greatly disturbed by her granddaughter's flight from home. Brielle must be won over, made to understand the nightmare that was in store for her if she were forced into marriage with Rufus Glyde. Perhaps that would not be too difficult. But how to explain where she'd been since leaving London, how to gloss over all that had happened this last week without provoking unwanted questions?

She suddenly felt very alone and a little scared. With a start she realised that all the time she'd been at the George, she'd never felt this vulnerable. Her mind drifted to Gareth and she wondered what he was doing.

Was he thinking of her, too? What nonsense, of course he wasn't. He would never have spoken so shockingly if he'd had an ounce of feeling for her. From the start he'd made it clear that she was simply entertainment for him; when she'd refused that role, he'd pursued her out of pique. Any fleeting moments of tenderness they'd shared were just that, fleeting. He was a loner, happy to use any woman who crossed his path, but just as happy to dismiss them from his mind if they angered him or ceased to be of interest.

The noise of the front door opening and closing drifted up the stairs. She heard voices below and her stomach churned. Suddenly, her grandmother was there and she was swept up in a warm, perfumed embrace.

'Amelie, dear child, what is this that Horrocks is telling me? Let me look at you, you poor little thing.' Brielle held her granddaughter away from her, taking in the drab dress now dried in creases, the sadly bedraggled chestnut curls and the anxious pinched face before her.

'You're in a sad way, my dear, but I cannot tell you how relieved I am that you're safe. I've been out of my mind with worry. This evening was the first invitation I've accepted since I knew that you'd left your home. And this is the evening that you arrive on my doorstep! But thank God for that.'

And once more Amelie found herself pulled into the jasmine-scented embrace she remembered so well from childhood. Whether her grandmother approved or not of what she'd done, it didn't matter. Brielle loved her and would care for her. She bit back the treacherous tears.

'I'm so sorry to have worried you needlessly, but I can explain,' she pleaded.

Brielle took her granddaughter's hands in hers and squeezed them lovingly. 'I'm sure you can, but first we must make you comfortable. I really don't understand why you're wearing that dreadful dress, but you should have changed it immediately. I can't think what my woman is about. Why didn't she find you a dressing robe at the least and order your bedchamber to be made up?'

'It doesn't matter. I was comfortable here and Horrocks brought me tea.'

'Tea! What are my servants thinking of? What you need is a proper meal and to get out of those clothes. The next thing we'll know is that you'll be running a fever.'

She rang the bell energetically and her butler appeared rather too quickly. Like the rest of the household, he had been greatly intrigued by Miss Silverdale's dramatic and, unexpected arrival and hovering by the sitting-room door, had been hopeful of learning more.

'Horrocks, ask the housekeeper to make up Miss Amelie's bedchamber immediately, and get Cook to put together a tray of something nourishing, and I don't mean just soup.'

'Yes, milady, immediately,' the butler murmured, suitably abashed by his mistress's sharp tone.

Brielle was still fiery, Amelie observed, even though

the years had begun to take their toll. Her grandmother, elegant in dove-grey Italian crepe, seemed smaller and frailer than when she'd last seen her.

'Horrocks is getting old,' Brielle said, excusing her butler's oversights. 'He doesn't think so clearly now.'

'He looked after me very well,' Amelie declared loyally, making ready to accompany the housekeeper upstairs.

She instantly recognised the room. Eau-de-nil hangings and bedcovers created a tranquil aura of pale green shadow: her mother's favourite colour. A portrait of Louise was displayed prominently above the dainty cherrywood writing desk. A deep tub was even now being filled with hot water by one of the housemaids. As soon as the servants had left, she quickly stripped off the despised dress and dropped it in a heap on the floor.

By the time her grandmother joined her once more, she was ensconced in one of the large easy chairs, wearing a robe of the finest chenille silk.

'This robe is far too beautiful for me to wear, Grandmama. Miss Repton must be in anguish.'

'Never mind about her. She has far too high an opinion of herself. Though she does have a way with my hair and makes her own complexion cream from crushed strawberries. Otherwise I would never keep the creature.'

Her grandmother put down the tray she was carrying. 'I've brought your food myself so we can be quiet together. Make sure you dine well. You look as though you've barely eaten all day.'

It was true. A sparse breakfast had not been followed by lunch. She'd been too busy hiding from Rufus Glyde to think of eating, and then Gareth's unexpected abuse had sent her flying from the inn to Wroxall and finally to Bath. She attacked the cold chicken with relish.

While she ate, Brielle kept her amused with anecdotes of Bath life. It was clear that she viewed English provincial society with some irony, but she had put down secure roots and now had many friends and acquaintances in the locality. The quintessential French woman had become almost English.

She let her granddaughter finish her meal in peace before saying, 'Now what's this nonsense I've been hearing?'

'Nonsense, Grandmama?' Amelie's stomach clenched. The inevitable moment had arrived.

'About a week ago I received a most unwelcome visitor. His name was Hyde or Glyde or some such. He told me some faradiddle about your being pledged to him in marriage.'

'He was lying,' Amelie said quietly. 'I never agreed to marry him.'

'Then why did he think you had?'

'Papa decided I should marry him. I decided I would not.'

'But why should your father wish you to marry a man you so clearly dislike?'

'Sir Rufus Glyde is a very rich man, I believe. Papa thought to help the family by marrying me to him.'

'The family, perhaps, but not you, it would seem. Your father is a selfish man and I won't hide from you that I do not hold him in a great deal of affection. But I've always thought his love for you showed him at his best. Why would he try to enforce such a marriage, knowing how you felt?'

She had no idea how much her grandmother knew of the Silverdales' financial difficulties and did not want to alarm her unnecessarily, so she said as nonchalantly as she could, 'The family have a few money problems.'

Brielle looked at her straitly. 'Your father has always lived high, that's certain, but surely the income from the estates he holds must be sufficient to cover even his expenditure.'

'There are other problems,' Amelie began awkwardly. 'Robert…' And her voice trailed off.

'Ah, Robert, an unfortunate boy by all accounts. Even in this backwater we've heard tales of his legendary gambling.' Brielle fixed her granddaughter with a sharp eye. 'Exactly how bad is the situation, Amelie? Tell me the truth.'

'Sir Rufus holds the mortgage on the house in Grosvenor Square and that is all we have left.'

Brielle let out an audible gasp. 'I knew your father and brother to be foolishly extravagant, but I had no idea that things had come to this pass.'

'Grandmama, I cannot marry Rufus Glyde. Please help me.'

'My darling, you shall not marry a man you hate. Your father will have to think again. And until he does, you will stay with me here in Bath.'

Amelie's brown eyes sparkled through a mist of tears as she launched herself at her grandmother and hugged her so tightly that the older woman was almost crushed.

'Hush, child, you've squeezed the breath out of me. You're a loving and beautiful young woman. You deserve better. We may even find you a Bath beau to take the place of this Glyde person.'

Amelie's smile faltered a little. 'I'm not looking for any other man. I don't wish to marry. Just let me stay here with you. I can be useful, I'm sure, even more as you get older.'

'What nonsense is this? To waste your youth and beauty on running errands for an old woman. Certainly not! Why are you so opposed to the idea of matrimony? It is every woman's destiny, after all.'

'I don't think it mine,' she retorted. 'In my experience men are either frivolous and foolish or they feel compelled to dominate me. I've no wish to be either the master or the mastered.'

'You have been unlucky in those you've met. But that's not to say that a strong man with the confidence to allow you independence does not exist, or that you won't encounter him.'

'Even if I were to meet such a paragon, how could I ever be sure that he would remain so?' Amelie ventured.

'Mama…' And she allowed the rest of her sentence to fade into the air.

Her grandmother gazed unseeingly into the fire, and it was a while before she spoke. 'You must not allow your mother's difficult life to determine your own choices,' she said at last. 'A woman's duty is to marry. But we'll say no more for now. I shall introduce you to Bath society while you're with me and who knows, the right person might just appear on the threshold.'

Brielle's thoughts were already ranging across the eligible males she knew and had begun to centre on one name that she thought might just alter Amelie's mind. But for now she was content to change the subject.

'You haven't told me yet how you escaped from Grosvenor Square.'

Amelie recounted the tale of the sheets and the stagecoach, carefully omitting the entrance of Gareth Wendover into her life. Brielle enjoyed the story immensely, even more so because it was a rebuke to a son-in-law she did not trust and a suitor she had disliked on sight.

'Grandmama, can we send for Fanny, please? I promised her I would do so as soon as I could.'

'I'm not at all sure about that, my love. Fanny aided you in what was a foolish and dangerous escapade. I've been enjoying your tale, but that's because you're safe here with me. When I think what might have befallen you! And Fanny would have borne a grave responsibility for it.'

'That's unfair,' her granddaughter cried hotly. 'Fanny tried to persuade me not to escape, but I made her help me. And no doubt she's suffered already for her loyalty. I cannot make her suffer doubly.'

Brielle blinked with surprise at this passionate outburst. 'You're far too hot at hand, my dear. I'm not surprised you've emerged from your first Season unwed. A fiery temper is not perhaps the best asset a young woman can possess.'

'Forgive me, ma'am, I didn't mean to be discourteous, but I owe Fanny so much.'

'Including a dress by the look of it,' her grandmother remarked drily, looking askance at the miserable heap of cloth lying abandoned in the corner. 'I was about to send a message to your father to assure him of your safety—I will ask him to despatch Fanny to you. We must hope that he hasn't already discovered her perfidy and sent her packing.'

Amelie smiled her pleasure and then gently stifled a yawn. She hoped Brielle would take the hint and leave her to sleep. So far she'd managed to evade all mention of her stay at the George. But as she'd foreseen, her grandmother was not so easily satisfied. The stagecoach had left the White Horse Inn in London over a week ago—so where had Amelie been in the interval?

'The stage had an accident,' she lied, 'and we had to find accommodation at a local inn. One of the passengers was hurt and I stayed to look after them. As soon as they were better, I finished the journey to Bath.' How glib that sounded and how very far from the truth!

'And were you the only two passengers at this inn?' Brielle questioned shrewdly.

'There were only a few other people on the stage. And they lived a short distance away and were able to finish their journey on horseback.' More lies, she thought guiltily.

'Who was this passenger you were so devoted to? Wasn't there anyone else who could have offered their services?'

'I felt obliged. They'd been very kind to me.'

'But who was this person?'

This was the question Amelie had been dreading. 'An elderly gentleman.' Age is relative, she told herself. 'You wouldn't know his name. He was actually on his way to Bristol, so he's not local.'

'A gentleman? You were looking after a gentleman? Surely that cannot be right.'

'I had to help. There was no one else who could devote the time to nursing him. The doctor called a few times and the landlord assisted when he could.'

Her grandmother was silent for a moment. 'Just how old was this gentleman?'

'I'm not very good at ages,' she prevaricated. 'A good deal older than me.'

'And who else was at the inn with you?'

'The landlord and his wife, and some of their serving staff. I shared a bedchamber with the kitchen maid.'

Brielle looked relieved at this information and decided not to probe any further for the moment. Amelie was looking tired and distressed. She sensed her granddaughter was not being entirely truthful and was determined in the next few days to get to the bottom of whatever mystery there was.

'You must sleep now. Tomorrow we'll begin to make up the deficiencies in your wardrobe. I understand from Horrocks that you arrived with only a cloak bag.'

'I'm afraid so. It will be wonderful to wear a dress other than Fanny's.'

'I should think so indeed,' Brielle lightly scolded her. 'After breakfast, we'll start our campaign. In the meantime I'll make sure that Repton looks out a dress from my younger years—not too old fashioned, I trust—and alters it to fit you.'

'Thank you. You're too kind—I don't know how I can ever repay you.'

'I'm sure I shall think of something,' Brielle replied, her mind firmly fixed on the man she intended to present once the girl was looking her best.

Amelie stayed awake longer than she expected. Her body was exhausted, but her mind continued to plague her. How was she to avoid telling her grandmother the true nature of her stay at the inn, for she knew that Brielle would not be content to leave the matter to rest? She smiled at the description she'd given of Gareth—he was neither elderly nor a gentleman!—but somehow she must maintain this fiction. Her smile died as suddenly as it had come—she must not think of him ever again. It had been foolish of her to allow an early attraction to melt her usual reserve and flourish unchecked. She'd grown far, far too close to him. She had never before felt such longing, such desire, and was left now bruised and baffled.

The insults he'd flung at her should have crushed such troublesome emotions. But apparently that wasn't so. As she drifted half in and half out of sleep, his powerful frame invaded the room. It was as though he were there with her. If she reached out, she could trace the outline of his smile with her finger. If she reached out, she could know the raw strength of his embrace. Shaken by her need for him, she buried her head in the pillow and tried to sleep.

Gareth was also finding it difficult to sleep. His anger still burned brightly, but he knew that he'd offended Amelie beyond pardon. His fury over her wild escape and his deep suspicions of her relationship with Glyde were justified, he was sure. But to call her a doxy had been inexcusable. She was no such thing, as he knew to his cost. He smiled mirthlessly as he considered the countless women of his acquaintance who perfectly satisfied that description. No, she was not a doxy, but she was just as cunning and manipulative as any other of her sex. He'd learned his lesson well; a woman was worth only the pleasure she gave. Amelie had given him pleasure, it was true, but not as he'd expected: it had been something altogether deeper, more exciting and more disturbing—a dangerous delight. It was as well that she'd left when she had. There was no place in his life for loyalty, tenderness, love, even if he could be sure of her. And he couldn't.

He would leave her in peace to find a new situation and be on his way. Within the next day or so his ankle would be strong enough to begin travelling, but where he knew not. He was close to Bristol; a journey to the port would take half a day at most and once there he could book a passage to France. It would not be difficult to resume his old life at the tables of the slightly less respectable gaming houses or take whatever menial work was offered. That way he would never touch a penny of the inheritance so long denied him.

But why shouldn't he enjoy his legacy? Would it not be sweet revenge to plunder the fortune his grandfather had so carefully conserved? Perhaps he would travel back to London after all, deal with Mr Spence and his formalities, and ensure a constant flow of funds to his pocket over the coming years as he wandered Europe. That would certainly spare him the discomfort of living off his wits. But what an existence! The one thing that had sustained him in seven long years of exile was the excitement and intrigue of a life on the edge. Take that away and what was left? A tedious round of places you didn't know, people you would never see again, plans that held no interest.

One way or another, though, he would leave England and this time willingly and for good. There was nobody to mourn his departure—except perhaps Lucas Avery. He'd been his one true friend. He knew him to be living in Bath, a short distance away, with a wife and children that Gareth had never met. He wondered if he could risk a meeting or whether Lucas might have changed his mind about his old friend in the years since that fateful evening. The unknown wife, too, might not easily welcome a convicted card cheat. But he would have liked to have bid him a final goodbye.

And Amelie, he suspected, was also in Bath. If he chose to make the journey, he might even see her there. If he chose! In his heart he knew that the decision had already been made. Of course he would make the journey, of course he would see her. Be truthful with yourself, he thought savagely. She was dangerous to him; a threat to his plans and to his peace of mind, but somehow he couldn't keep away. He might try to justify the trip to Bath in a dozen ways, but he was going there for one reason alone. He'd willed himself to forget this girl, but he could not: she was a constant refrain singing in his mind. London or France would both have to wait.

Amelie woke to the swish of heavy silk curtains being drawn and felt the warmth of the mid-morning sun streaming onto her bed. She hadn't heard the entrance of the maid on the deep pile carpet, but turning her head she saw that a cup of steaming chocolate sat waiting and a large jug of hot water was already on the washstand. A refashioned dress of her grandmother's was draped across the armchair, hardly the height of fashion, but acceptable enough for this one day. Miss Repton had been busy. She supposed she must thank her.

She lay back on the pillows and stretched luxuriously. Eventually she'd slept long and deep, cocooned in the comfort of the four-poster, a far cry from the straw mattress of recent days. At last she was at her grandmother's. She'd succeeded in what she'd set out to do and the world felt good. Or at least a part of it did. Gareth's figure once more crept unbidden into the corners of her mind. He would soon be preparing to leave the George and then where would he go? Whatever his decision, she scolded herself, it concerned her no longer.

This morning she was intent on pleasure for she knew it would be fleeting. She had no false expectations that Brielle would agree with her wish to remain single. For a woman of her grandmother's generation, indeed for a woman of her own, marriage had to be the goal of life and anyone who rejected it was either unwanted or eccentric. How much better to live alone, she thought, than be chained to a man with whom she shared nothing but a roof. That was likely to remain a dream. There was one thing of which she *was* sure: her heart would stay her own. It would not be a difficult vow to keep; until now she'd felt nothing for any man she'd ever met. Until now. But Gareth Wendover was clearly ineligible and destined to travel through life alone. A misguided passion for him would ensure the very unhappiness she was trying to escape.

The bedroom door opened and her grandmother came into the room fully dressed and looking businesslike. 'Good, you're awake. Are you well rested?'

Amelie smiled her assent.

'That's as well—we've a lot to do today. I'll see you in the breakfast room in thirty minutes.'

Brielle's brisk commands were diverting. Her

grandmother might be approaching old age, but she was as sprightly as ever and it was clear that she'd already been up some hours planning the day ahead. Amelie made haste to obey.

The carriage had been ordered to the door immediately after breakfast and very soon they were bowling along Bath's main thoroughfare. Brielle's destination was the small but elegant shop of a highly talented young modiste. She had heard on the grapevine that this new seamstress had the originality and skill of many a more expensive establishment. She had a very clear idea of what would suit her granddaughter, something in the French style, she thought, beautifully cut and simply adorned, to flatter the young woman's budding figure.

It seemed to Amelie that the next few hours were spent in a fantasy of fashion. There were outfits for every occasion: braided, embroidered, some adorned with knots of ribbon, others with spangled rosettes and silver fringes. Walking dresses, riding costumes, day *toilettes* and ball gowns floated past on a wave of elegance.

She tried hard to keep her feet on the ground, worrying about the mounting cost and how she could ever repay her grandmother even a fraction of the staggering bill for this dazzling wardrobe. Frantically she tried to catch sight of the price tags as the dresses were brought forwards for her inspection. An evening gown in sea-green tulle made her gasp as she gazed in wonder at her reflection in the mirror. She could hardly recognise the modish and graceful young woman looking back at her.

'How much did you say this gown was?' she asked the seamstress tentatively.

'That is one of our newest creations, *mademoiselle,* and made from the finest silk tulle. A very reasonable hundred guineas. It suits *mademoiselle* to perfection.'

Shocked by the price, Amelie began reluctantly to take off the charming creation when the modiste, catching a minatory look from Brielle, coughed apologetically and decided that she had made a mistake.

'Of course, for such a beautiful young lady we can come to an agreeable arrangement, I'm sure. You will wear the dress with a distinction that will bring honour to our small salon and build our reputation.'

After that Amelie gave up trying to keep count of the ever-increasing total. It was all way beyond anything she could ever have afforded from her allowance. The colours and fabrics flew past her eyes like a moving kaleidoscope. To the pile of dresses were added fur-trimmed pelisses, tiny pearl-stitched slippers, long white leather gloves and a Norwich silk shawl, all apparently necessities for a protracted stay in Bath. By the time they left the salon, the carriage was brimming with boxes and packages and had to be sent back to Laura Place while they made their way to Milsom Street to pay a call on Brielle's favourite milliner.

Amelie, who owned precisely two hats, was amazed by the information that she would need no fewer than six if she were to grace the Bath social scene successfully. One extraordinary confection followed another as Madame Charcot laid before them the finest of her wares. Amelie's London Season had been notable for its modesty. Lord Silverdale had neither the money nor the wish to expend large sums on his daughter's coming-out and expected her natural beauty to be sufficient to win a husband. An old acquaintance of his youth had acted as chaperone and since she also had a daughter to launch, she'd shown little interest in her new protégée or her clothes. Amelie had chosen almost single-handedly the restricted wardrobe her father had permitted for the three months of her London Season. Now Brielle, with her highly developed fashion sense, was intent on giving as much enjoyment as possible to her granddaughter.

Seated amidst a tower of hat boxes, waiting for the carriage to return, she revealed that she'd been busy first thing that morning putting together a guest list for a small evening party the following day.

'It will be more comfortable for you to meet a few people before going into society properly,' her grandmother explained.

Amelie made haste to reassure her, 'I won't be uncomfortable, Grandmama, not with you by my side.'

'That's as may be. I'm an old woman now. You need to meet younger people. It will be just a small, informal party. Nothing too overwhelming. But when we go the Pump Room or the Assembly Rooms, you'll already know a few faces.'

Amelie wasn't so sure. She'd expected to live quietly

in Bath, but it was evident from the morning's shopping that this was not what Brielle had in mind. She was grateful for her grandmother's unstinting kindness and she would try her best to conform. She had little desire to socialise, but that was something best left unsaid.

Like her granddaughter, Brielle decided on silence. It had been difficult to conjure up interesting guests at such short notice, but she'd felt it essential to introduce Amelie as swiftly as possible to many of those she would see in the coming weeks. She was intent on establishing the notion that her granddaughter's stay had been planned for a considerable time and that Amelie would be paying a protracted visit. That way she would limit any damage that rumour might do.

This morning while her granddaughter slept, she'd cast her mind swiftly over the people she might invite who would not be offended by the very short notice. Celine Charpentier, of course, a fellow *émigrée* and friend since the time they'd both left France for exile. Celine would support her in whatever plan she was hatching, Brielle knew. Then Major Radcliffe was a genial soul, always ready to add his bonhomie to any party. Unfortunately she would have to invite Miss Scarsdale. Letitia Scarsdale was a permanent fixture at all her parties, a difficult neighbour who had constantly to be placated.

But one particular guest would more than earn his place. Brielle had high hopes of him. Sir Peregrine Latham was well known in Bath, a handsome man and delightful companion. Perry Latham was no country bumpkin, either. He preferred a quieter pace of life, dividing his time between the Bath mansion and his Somerset estate, but he visited London regularly and was not devoid of town bronze. He was well into his thirties now and, gossip had it, the victim of a sad history. The story went that he had lost his fiancée when he was a very young man and had never recovered from the blow. Nevertheless, Brielle reckoned he might be persuaded to think again by the sight of her enchanting granddaughter.

The following day brought with it another whirl of activity. The hairdresser called early to trim Amelie's chestnut locks into submission. Her shining curls were artlessly twisted into a knot on the top of her head and then allowed to cascade down the sides of her face in loose ringlets. Before she had time to properly admire this transformation, it was the turn of the dressmaker. Hours the previous evening had been spent thumbing through the latest editions of *La Belle Assemblée* to decide on suitable styles. Now for several uncomfortable hours she was draped with muslin and stuck with pins. The dressmaker, she was told, would make her gowns for wearing at home when no one of any importance was expected. She began to wonder when she would ever have time to don even half of the wardrobe she'd so suddenly acquired.

Shortly before their guests arrived that evening, Brielle appeared with a pearl necklace and earrings that had belonged to Amelie's mother. They were the perfect accompaniment to the simple pink crêpe-de-Chine gown she'd chosen for her first party.

'Wear them for Louise,' her grandmother said with a catch in her voice, the closest she would ever come to expressing the pain she still felt.

Now that the evening was here, Amelie determined to take pleasure in it, if only for Brielle's sake. It was true that the guests assembled in the elegant drawing room were something of a motley crowd, but they were evidently all well-wishers. All except Lady Lampeter, who had two very plain daughters of Amelie's age and who was furious to discover that her acceptance of such a late invitation had been pointless. Not even the fondest of mamas could expect the Lampeter girls to compete with Amelie's beauty.

'Claudia Lampeter will come at short notice,' Brielle had confidently predicted to Celine. 'She has a mountain to climb with those girls of hers. One has spots and the other a sad figure. She will take them anywhere in the hope of finding a marriageable man.'

Knowing nothing of her grandmother's wiles, Amelie remained serene and unruffled as she made her way slowly around the mingling guests. Moving from one chattering group to another, she attracted admiring looks from around the room and Brielle was happy to see that in company her granddaughter was both modest and assured.

'She does you credit,' Celine remarked. 'A beautiful and unaffected girl.'

The Major took a long pinch of snuff and gave his considered opinion. 'With those looks and that charm she will take Bath by storm.'

As the evening proceeded, Amelie began to appreciate the gentle rhythm of Bath social life. The great society gatherings of her London Season had been a strain, but here she felt soothed. Even the man she imagined had been invited to partner her was unexceptional.

'And how do you like Bath, Miss Silverdale?' Perry Latham began as an opening gambit.

He had been stunned by the beauty of this young woman and was eager to see whether her intelligence matched her looks.

'So far, Sir Peregrine, I've seen only the inside of dress shops, but I'm sure I shall enjoy it immensely.'

'And Bath will enjoy you, too,' he rejoined gallantly. 'Can we hope to see you at the Pump Room shortly?'

'Indeed, yes. I understand my grandmother is planning our first visit tomorrow.'

'Excellent. I'll make sure I attend. I'm afraid you may well find the town a little dull. You will see many of the same faces there as are here tonight.'

'I shan't mind that. I find familiarity comforting.'

'I'm not sure you'll continue to think so after you've met the same set of people a dozen times.'

Privately, Amelie thought that was more than likely, looking around at the less-than-stimulating collection of people gathered there. She couldn't stop herself smiling at the thought of what Gareth would make of the company. 'An assortment of gargoyles,' she could hear him say. One of the older women, the scrawny Miss Scarsdale, bore an uncanny resemblance to Mrs Skinner.

'You smile.' Perry Latham had been watching her closely. 'You see, Miss Silverdale, you're already beginning to have doubts about Bath society.'

'No, Sir Peregrine. I was smiling at how very pleasant it is to be among friends.'

Diplomatic as well as intelligent and beautiful, he thought, already half-smitten with this entrancing princess who had appeared so suddenly in his world.

'Please call me Perry. I hope you will count me as one of those friends.'

The last guest departed well before eleven. She wasn't sorry that Bath inhabitants seemed to keep early hours. The party had been convivial and undemanding, but it had still cost an effort to play the role expected of her.

'I saw you talking to Perry Latham,' her grandmother remarked casually. 'He's a good-looking fellow, don't you think?'

'Very presentable.'

'A thorough gentleman, too.'

'Indeed, yes.'

'And not without town bronze,' Brielle pursued.

Amelie smiled warmly back at her. 'He's a veritable pattern card of all the virtues,' she replied laughingly, while her thoughts roved dangerously elsewhere.

Chapter Seven

The next morning dawned fair, a perfect day Brielle declared for her granddaughter's first visit to the Pump Room. Amelie felt little enthusiasm, but knew that her grandmother had been delighted by the success of yesterday's small party and was now eager to introduce her to wider Bath society.

Brielle did not take the famous waters, which she privately considered disgusting, but many of her friends drank a daily glass for a variety of complaints, imagined or otherwise. And she made sure that she attended the Pump Room regularly as a way of keeping in touch with what was going on in Bath. It was said that a morning spent there would vouchsafe the visitor all the current gossip of the town.

The room they entered was spacious with a wall of tall windows giving on to carefully tended lawns. A richly moulded azure ceiling was hung with ornate chandeliers glittering with light even on this bright morning. Small golden chairs were positioned around the edges of the room or marshalled by visitors into friendship or family circles. The salon emanated wealth and leisure, capturing the essence of Bath as a town of affluence and pleasure.

Almost immediately they spotted Celine Charpentier, who had just procured a glass of water from the pumper and was busy wending her way through knots of people deep in conversation. Brielle began to follow in her wake, zigzagging to avoid the couples who slowly paraded around the room, arm in arm, intent on seeing and being seen. Amelie was acutely conscious of the many pairs of eyes staring at her, some curious, some measuring and some frankly admiring. She gave thanks for the familiar faces already gathered at the far end of the room. As her grandmother had predicted, it was comforting to recognise acquaintances among a sea of unknowns. Perry Latham's sunny smile beamed across at her.

But before they could greet Brielle's friends, they were intercepted by a very thin, very richly clad figure. Amelie caught her breath—the man bowing profusely before her grandmother was none other than Rufus Glyde! He had returned not to London, but to Bath. He must have suspected that she would eventually find her way here.

'Lady St Clair,' he purred, 'my most humble apologies for intruding, but allow me to say how delighted

I am to see that your granddaughter has been safely restored to you.'

Brielle nodded briefly and went to move on, but Glyde was intent on detaining them.

'My lady, if I could beg you for a few minutes of your time… I wish to tender my heartfelt regrets for any misunderstanding that may have occurred when we last met.'

'I am not aware of any misunderstanding, *monsieur,*' Brielle said stiffly.

'I mean only that my motives for seeking your charming granddaughter were not clear and I fear I may have been misinterpreted.'

'Believe me, I understand perfectly your wish to pursue my granddaughter and since we are being frank, I will tell you now that your pursuit is unwelcome. Miss Silverdale stays with me for the foreseeable future. I am now responsible for her welfare.'

Amelie felt a glow of satisfaction. Surely that would get rid of him for good.

'Naturally I am more than pleased that Miss Silverdale has found sanctuary with a beloved relative. It is right and proper that she should do so.' Glyde's voice was smoothly persistent. 'My pursuit, as you term it, was a wish only to be of assistance to a young woman I had reason to believe was happy to become my wife.'

Unsure of precisely what Miles Silverdale had promised, Brielle was forced to concede the point.

Emboldened, he continued, 'Now that the position is clear to me, Miss Silverdale may rest assured that I will in no way incommode her in the future. Indeed, I would like to wish her very well whatever that future may be.'

Her grandmother had begun to look a little more gratified and answered neutrally, 'We thank you for your good wishes, sir, and for your reassurance.'

His thin lips arranged themselves into a tight smile, the sunken lines on either side of his mouth becoming more deeply etched. Amelie recoiled in distaste, but was forced to remain by her grandmother's side.

'In that case I hope that we may continue to enjoy a pleasant association. I had just begun a visit to friends here when I felt it necessary to interrupt my stay to search for Miss Silverdale. Now that the matter is happily concluded, I can look forward to enjoying the delights of Bath more thoroughly.'

'I hope the town will live up to your expectations,' Brielle murmured.

'If not, I have always the pleasures of my country estate, which lies nearby, but I can't imagine Bath will pall with two such charming ladies at the forefront of its society. I trust I am forgiven sufficiently to be included in your personal group of acquaintances.'

Brielle inclined her head slightly. 'Naturally, we are bound to encounter each other on occasions, Sir Rufus.'

'I look forward to meeting you and your granddaughter frequently. Bath is such a small society that I imagine that to be inevitable.'

Amelie had managed to put on a brave face during

this interchange, but her heart plummeted at these words. She was sure they carried an implicit threat and, glancing up at his thin, white face, she saw the wolfish eyes staring out at her from behind the social mask. Her grandmother, though, seemed to sense nothing amiss and, with another bow in Glyde's direction, moved towards her group of friends.

Glyde turned swiftly on his heel and left the Pump Room. Now that he was gone, she found her limbs were trembling and she had to fight to calm her breathing. His trite commonplaces had cloaked his true intent, she was sure. He had not given up his intention to marry her, whatever platitudes he mouthed to her grandmother. And Brielle appeared to have been completely taken in. With a sickening jolt Amelie realised that the sanctuary she'd sought and found with so much difficulty might now prove as dangerous as her London home. She could see Glyde's strategy clearly. He would make sure that he was constantly in her grandmother's company, presenting himself as a loyal and dependable friend. Gradually he would chip away at her grandmother's suspicion until Brielle began to wonder why her granddaughter had taken such a dislike to him. There would be nowhere else for her to run and little by little she would be coerced into an appalling marriage.

Her grandmother was already deep in conversation with the Major, and she saw with dismay that Perry Latham had begun to walk towards her. Unable to face him immediately, she fled towards the entrance hall, intending to stand in the cool, fresh air until she regained her composure. Looking straight ahead, she moved swiftly towards her goal, barely noticing the figure standing in the shadow of the large palm trees that graced either side of the doorway.

In an instant Gareth Wendover stood before her. She had a fleeting glimpse of his muscular figure, clothed now in a perfectly fitting coat of blue superfine, his shapely legs encased in skin-tight pantaloons of the palest fawn. Hardly had she absorbed his new image, when he advanced menacingly towards her and grabbed her by the wrist.

'You've evidently managed to acquire a very liberal employer since we met last,' he snarled. 'Such elegance, Amelie, such a taking coiffeure, but hardly fitting for a maidservant.' He thundered out the last word, his lip curling with disdain.

'Or a doxy, I imagine.' Her retort was swift and equally angry.

His face shadowed and he let go of her arm. He should apologise, but he was damned if he would. She had utterly deceived him. The girl he saw before him, so beautiful he could devour her on the spot, was thoroughly false. She had lied and lied again to him.

'May I enquire exactly who or what you are?' His tone was scathing.

She replied with as much dignity as she could, 'My name is Amelie Silverdale. My father is Lord Silverdale.'

'Well, well, a poor little rich girl. Wasn't being Miss

Silverdale exciting enough for you? Did you get some shabby thrill from dressing up as your maid?'

'There was no thrill. Disguising myself as a maid was the safest way to travel, or at least it would have been if I'd not been unlucky enough to meet you.'

'Not that unlucky, as I recall. You might still be dangling on the end of a rope if it were not for me. Or were you hoping your friend Glyde would happen by and execute a magnificent rescue? Was it a stunt to reel in a reluctant suitor?'

'How can you be so stupid! I was escaping from Rufus Glyde.'

'Another fantasy? I've just seen with my own eyes on what familiar terms you stand with the man.'

'Then your eyes tell you false. Sir Rufus has designs of his own. He wishes to ingratiate himself with my grandmother.'

'For what purpose?' he asked impatiently, pushing back the dark hair that had fallen across his brow.

'I don't see that it's any business of yours.'

'Really? You don't consider your constant lies give me any reason to demand the truth from you?'

She bowed her head slightly and said in a voice he could hardly hear, 'He wishes to marry me.'

'And…?'

'He hopes my grandmother will persuade me to agree.'

'How much persuasion will that take, I wonder?'

'I detest him,' she burst out. 'He's a vicious and

depraved man. He's followed me here when I thought I was safe and is plotting against me still.'

'He's certainly vicious,' Gareth said measuringly, 'but why are you running from him? You've only to tell your father that he's plaguing you and you'll be free of his demands.'

'I wish that were true, but my father has decided that Sir Rufus is the suitor he wishes me to accept.'

'The last time I looked we were living in the nineteenth century. Forced marriages no longer happen. You must have given your consent or at least appeared to do so.'

'I did not. I tell you I hate the man, but my father is adamant. I cannot speak of my family's difficulties, but Glyde wields considerable power over us.'

Gareth considered this for a moment, his athletic figure reclining lazily against a carved pillar.

'So you were the mistress who was being forced to marry for money? And your maid's defiant independence a mere charade, I imagine.'

Amelie flushed, but said nothing.

'And why go to so much trouble to deceive me? Why couldn't you have told me the truth and asked for help? Didn't you trust me?'

She swallowed uncomfortably. 'I was worried you might react unthinkingly. You might have chased after him and caused an even greater scandal than there was already.'

'Chased after him? With an injured ankle? You can do better than that.' His tone hardened. 'Wasn't it rather that you thought I might use the situation to my own benefit?'

She blushed. That was precisely what she had thought, imagining if only in fancy that he might be capable of blackmail or kidnap.

He saw the telltale flush and concluded bitterly, 'You didn't trust me. Only now that I've exposed your deception are you willing to be honest.'

'You shouldn't judge me harshly. You can't know what it feels like to be so besieged, without a friend in the world.'

He smiled crookedly. 'Can't I?'

'It's different for men—you make your own rules. A woman is always subject to others. Even a strong woman,' she added.

'You must have known I would stand your friend, yet you disappeared from the inn without a word.'

'I had to—you treated me abominably.'

'I regret my intemperance,' he muttered unwillingly. 'It was unfair, but Glyde provoked me and I knew you were lying.'

'It was more than unfair. It was a vile insult—I wanted never to see you again.'

'Nor I you.'

They stood facing each other, their figures tense, the air between them scorched by anger. Then quite suddenly his expression relaxed and he said lightly, 'But here I am.'

'And why exactly are you here? I thought you were

going to Bristol—or was it London? It seems to me, Mr Wendover, that you also have some explaining to do.'

'I have a particular friend in Bath. I wanted to say goodbye to him before I sail for France.'

She digested this news. 'You never mentioned this friend before. In fact, you were adamant you had no friends.'

'He slipped my mind.'

'Or maybe he's simply a figment of your imagination?'

'Like Amelie, the maidservant, you mean? No, he exists all right. His name is Lucas Avery and I'm staying in his house.'

'Even so, I'm not sure I believe you. Why suddenly do you wish to say goodbye? You weren't intending to do so. You'd no plans to come to Bath.'

'I've determined to quit England for good and since our little adventure brought me close by, it seemed right to say a final farewell.'

'And that's the truth?'

'Not quite.' She looked up into the blue eyes and their disturbing gaze. 'I needed to see you again. I needed to say a proper goodbye to you.'

The warmth of his glance produced a feeling of breathless discomfort. She felt a flutter of panic—she must remember her doubts, she told herself, remember his insults, stay angry. She mustn't allow herself to falter.

'You've seen me now and said goodbye,' she said

tightly. 'Let us end this chapter and wish each other good fortune.'

He did not reply, but took hold of her wrist again, this time with gentleness. Her heart turned a small somersault. Oblivious to the scandalised looks of people passing into the main room, he pulled her towards him and encircled her waist tightly. His mouth brushed her forehead and smoothed her hair. Crushed against his hard frame, she felt her body once more dissolve into the heat of his embrace. But it was over in a moment.

Breaking from her, Gareth took her hands and held them to his lips. 'We are deceivers both, Amelie. In another world we would belong together.'

Through a hot veil of desire, she became aware of the whispering voices around her and blushed deeply. Quickly, she disentangled her hands.

'I must go,' she managed in a constricted voice. 'My grandmother will be wondering where I am.'

And with that she turned and walked swiftly away.

Gareth made his way back to Lucas Avery's house, his mind a battleground of conflicting thoughts. He'd gone to the Pump Room that morning in the slender hope of finding Amelie in attendance on the new mistress she might have acquired. When he saw her across the room, he could hardly believe his eyes: not the beautiful but simple maidservant that he'd come to know, but an elegant and modish creature, moving effortlessly in the highest circles.

Transformed she might be, but she was still the same

girl who had stirred his senses so fervidly and anger over her deception fought with desire to possess her. Then Glyde had appeared and all his questions over their relationship were answered. It seemed that Amelie Silverdale was indeed a true daughter of Eve. She had lied and deceived as expertly as any of the harpies from his past. His anger had exploded into blind fury. And it was Glyde who crystallised a ferocious desire for revenge; he could have run the man through if he'd had a sword. And in the back, he thought grimly. Glyde's ingratiating smiles announced clearly that Amelie was destined for him, a man he held in the deepest contempt. He'd been sickened by what he saw and was about to leave when Glyde had hurried from the room, unnoticing of Gareth standing silently in the shadows. When Amelie had followed suit, he'd been unable to stop himself confronting her.

But now it seemed he might have read the picture wrongly. According to Amelie she was escaping Rufus Glyde, not embracing him. Did he believe her? If she was in truth being pursued by the scoundrel, why hadn't she confessed her troubles at the inn and enlisted his aid? In his heart he knew why not. She mistrusted him, mistrusted all men, and she was right to. He'd told her as many lies as she'd told him. If not lies, then omissions, and even now she was still ignorant of his true situation.

Lucas was at home when he knocked for admittance. From the moment he'd arrived in Bath, he'd been welcomed with open arms. His fear that Lord Avery would no longer be the friend he remembered had vanished with the first emotional clasp of their hands.

'Did you enjoy an invigorating morning with the old tabbies?' his friend greeted him gaily.

'Not exactly. I didn't make it into the Pump Room.'

'Was it that daunting?'

'It was singular, shall we say.'

And Gareth, who had briefly sketched for his friend the details of his stay at the George, told him of that morning's meeting with Amelie and the very different circumstances he'd found her in.

'But that's wonderful,' Lucas enthused.

'How is that?'

'A maidservant was an impossibility, but Lord Silverdale's daughter will make the perfect partner for the Earl of Denville.'

'Hold on a minute,' said Gareth, only half-laughing. 'You go too fast. For one thing I've no intention of playing the Earl of Denville and for another I'm not in the market to become leg-shackled.'

'Tell me, why *did* you come to Bath? I'm quite sure it wasn't just to meet your new godson!'

His friend maintained a discouraging silence, but Lucas persisted.

'We may not have seen each other for the past seven years, Gareth, but I know you as myself. In fact, I may know you even better.'

'I came to say a final goodbye, as you well know,'

Gareth was goaded to respond. 'And if Amelie Silverdale has crossed my path, that's pure chance.'

'Doing it much too brown!' his friend said crudely. 'You've just returned from the Pump Room—the Pump Room, for Heaven's sake! Why ever else would you visit such a place?'

'All right, I admit that I had it in mind to seek her out. I thought I'd make peace with her before I left. But that was before I realised I'd nothing to apologise for. She's as much a jade as any other woman I've known.'

Lucas looked thoughtful and it was a while before he replied. 'Do you know that when you speak of her, your eyes say something quite different?'

'Do they say that she's been thoroughly dishonest with me?'

'I can understand your anger at being deceived, but you're equally to blame. Have you confided your troubles to her?' He looked searchingly at his companion. 'No, I thought not. Neither of you has been entirely honest with the other.'

There was a long silence until Lucas once more broke it. 'Face it, my friend,' he said, his voice amused but sympathetic, 'she's got under your skin. Whether you like it or not, love is in the air.'

'I know nothing of love,' Gareth countered lightly. 'Now dalliance, that's where I'm an expert!'

During the following days Amelie was caught up in a whirl of social activity, a round of dance classes, supper parties and recitals which left little time to think about her recent meeting with Gareth. Only at night, when she could escape to the solitude of her room, was her mind free to roam over their brief, angry encounter. She'd been astonished to see him at the Pump Room and looking every inch a gentleman. Where had this sudden wealth come from and who was his supposed friend in Bath? She wasn't at all sure that either existed.

His fury at her deception had been real enough, but he was surely as guilty—she knew no more about him now than at their first meeting. Yet he seemed compelled to seek her out; she knew without being told that she was the real reason for his presence in Bath. If she'd needed confirmation, his scandalous embrace in that shockingly public place had been proof enough. But what had he meant by saying that in another world they should be together?

She had little time to puzzle over his words; every day her grandmother chaperoned her to what seemed a dozen different engagements and every day she was forced to appear unconcerned and happy. The week sped past, a constant bustle of movement, culminating in her first ball at the Upper Assembly Rooms. Its Master of Ceremonies had visited the ladies early in Amelie's stay. Mr King was a man who took his duties seriously and he had been concerned to introduce Miss Silverdale to any and every suitable young man he could find. The advent of a splendid evening of dancing promised him even greater scope. Amelie's lessons in the waltz, a daring new dance for Bath, were to be put to the test.

Her interest in attending the ball was mild, but the

minute she was ushered through the classical columns of the Assembly Room to its richly hung interior ablaze with light, she found herself responding to the colour and movement all around. Brightly clothed young women floated past on the arms of their black-suited escorts, while chaperones lined the walls of the ballroom, enjoying the opportunity for an agreeable exchange of news.

As she and Brielle entered the room, they were besieged. Within a very few minutes every slot on her dance card was filled; all the young men present, it seemed, wanted to dance with this beautiful new addition to Bath society. She couldn't help but give herself up to enjoyment. The sensation of being twirled around the highly polished floor in the arms of one admiring partner after another, and of knowing she was the toast of the evening, was gratifying. Perry Latham, revealing himself to be an excellent dancer, took to the floor with her twice, much to the delight of the Bath gossips.

It was certainly pleasurable to be the most sought-after girl in the room, but the froth and glamour of the night could not disguise the truth of her situation. This ball, like so many others, was part of an elaborate ritual that must lead eventually to the altar. It was a path she'd always been desperate not to tread, even as she'd realised her chances of escape were slim.

But recently it had become more imperative than ever that she stay true to herself. It was since meeting Gareth, of course. He was rude and overbearing, duplicitous, too, but he'd lit a flame within her that made it impossible to settle for the good enough. She'd believed herself to be cool, rational, even passionless. And yet within a few short weeks he'd destroyed that belief, but offered nothing in return. In the last moments of their meeting at the Pump Room, he'd shown her tenderness, but that altered nothing. He was getting ready to move on and his tenderness had simply been a prelude to his leaving.

Knowing nothing of what was passing in her granddaughter's mind, Brielle looked on complacently, secure in the knowledge that Amelie was the most beautiful girl in the room. Dressed in a gown of white sarsnet over a white satin petticoat with pearl fastenings and a circlet of pearls in her hair, she looked every inch a fairy-tale princess, Brielle thought with unaccustomed sentiment.

Halfway through the evening, when the gentlemen's starched shirt points had begun to wilt from the heat of the hundreds of wax candles burning in the wall-sconces, the orchestra took their break and everyone began to make their way towards the refreshments laid out in the adjoining room. Amelie had been dancing constantly and was grateful for the chance to sit down. As she went towards the door, Brielle following, Mr King caught up with them, clearly wishing to introduce an escort for the buffet which lay beyond. It was Rufus Glyde.

'Miss Silverdale, how very good to meet you again and in such pleasant surroundings. I hope you've enjoyed the dancing?'

The white mask of Glyde's face leaned towards her while his eyes ran lightly over her body. She felt herself squirming, but managed a brief curtsy without meeting his predatory gaze.

'Thank you, Sir Rufus, I have.'

'I wonder if you would be willing to add to *my* enjoyment by allowing me the pleasure of escorting you to tea?'

She looked desperately around for Brielle, who was now inconveniently deep in conversation with her neighbour. Following her glance, he said silkily, 'I have already asked your grandmother for permission and she is more than happy to entrust you to my care for half an hour.'

She was left with no other alternative than to agree. She felt the loathsome touch on her arm and stifled her repulsion, allowing Glyde to lead her through to the adjoining room. Here he found her a chair and went in search of food and drink. Escape was impossible.

In a very short while he was back and handing her a small gold-rimmed plate.

'I hope I've gauged your tastes correctly,' he murmured obsequiously, 'but tell me, please, if you would care for anything else.'

'This will do very well, thank you, Sir Rufus.'

'Please, Rufus. I feel we know each other sufficiently well to be on first-name terms. Do you not?'

'I would prefer our acquaintance to remain formal, Sir Rufus. I'm sure you will appreciate my reasons.'

'I'm not sure I do. I am a little disappointed that you

lack faith in me. Your father evidently holds another view or he would not have wished me to make you an offer of marriage.'

'My father has nothing to say in the matter. And I beg you to refrain from mentioning your proposal.'

'As to that, I would think your father has everything to say, notwithstanding your temporary stay in Bath. And I do trust that it is temporary.'

'I'm unsure of how long I shall be here, but certainly for some considerable time.'

'We shall have to see.' His voice held a sinister edge. 'In any contest of wills, Miss Silverdale, I think I might back your father.'

'Sir, I find the tone of your conversation not to my taste and I beg you to cease harassing me in this way.'

'I see that I must mend my tone. I have no wish to upset you unnecessarily. Please be assured that in future I will not burden you by making any further requests for your hand. I am not, after all, in the habit of requesting—as you will come to know.'

'If you will excuse me, I must find my grandmother.'

Unable to stifle her disgust any longer, she hastily gathered up her reticule and fled back into the ballroom. Brielle was nowhere to be seen, but she knew that even if her grandmother were to materialise before her that instant, she would not tell her of Glyde's menaces. What could she say? He was far too clever to issue direct threats. There was nothing you could pin down. Nevertheless she was aware that she had just been issued with a warning. Glyde was planning his revenge and it would be coming soon.

Scared that he might follow her, she kept moving through the long French windows which stood open, scarcely a breath of wind stirring the curtains, which had been pulled back to welcome the warm night air. She made her way rapidly out onto the terrace that ran the length of the building and descended a shallow flight of steps to one of the many paths that intersected the surrounding gardens, making sure that she could not be seen from the lighted room behind her. The night was still, as if holding its breath. The crunch of her slippers on the gravel was the only sound to disturb the warm enclosing peace.

The smell of lilac newly in flower floated towards her. Ahead the trees were motionless, a black mass silhouetted against the pale night sky. Her eyes gradually adapted to the darkness and now she could see shades of grey emerging from the gloom and close by, a pinprick of glowing red. For an instant her eyes focused directly on the light and with a start she realised she was looking at the tip of a cigar. She turned to flee back into the ballroom where the musicians had once more begun to play. A sardonic voice sounded softly in her ear.

'Tired of dancing so soon, Miss Silverdale?'

She spun round and saw Gareth Wendover's derisive smile. 'Surely as the belle of the ball, you cannot be leaving already?'

'I was merely taking the air. It's a beautiful evening.'

'Then perhaps we can take the air together,' he suggested in a voice that brooked no refusal.

They were now clearly visible from the ballroom and, not wishing to draw unwanted attention, she laid her hand lightly on the arm he proffered and retraced her steps along the pathway towards the knot of trees in the distance. The moon, which had been hovering behind clouds, swam free and the garden was suddenly bathed in silver. She saw her companion clearly for the first time. The white frilled shirt and black tailcoat and knee breeches deemed necessary for a formal occasion set off his tanned face and honed body to perfection. He looked magnificent. Her eyes felt bewitched, longing to linger on the seductive picture he presented, but she quickly averted her gaze. She had no wish to advertise the effect he was having on her.

'I see you've reacquainted yourself with your friend?'

'You've been spying on me,' she denounced hotly.

'Hardly.'

'Then why are you here?'

'I'm here because the Averys wished to attend the dance and I accompanied them.'

'I didn't see you dancing.'

'I prefer to watch. One notices all kinds of interesting things. Rufus Glyde, for example, your sworn enemy.'

'You don't believe that he is my enemy,' she said flatly.

'From where I was standing, it looked unlikely. That was a cosy little tête-à-tête—what did you enjoy most, tasting the sweetmeats or listening to sweet nothings?'

'I was forced into taking tea with him. They were threats he was uttering.'

'Forced? Threats?' Gareth looked quizzically at her.

'Hints, then, that I'd better do as he wishes and accept him as a suitor.'

'And do you intend to?'

'How can you ask me that?'

He gave a slight shrug of his shoulders. 'Your family is keen for you to make the match. Your life might be easier if you were to agree.'

'My life would be monstrous!'

Standing motionless in the cold, bright moonlight, her shoulders suddenly crumpled into defeat. She looked very young and very vulnerable and his heart was stirred.

'If you need help, you've only to ask,' he said, stopping beneath the broad leaves of a chestnut tree and turning to face her.

'Thank you, but I doubt you can aid me.'

'You could be wrong.' He reached out to trace the line of her cheek with one finger.

She took an involuntary step backwards; provokingly his brief touch had sent a shiver dancing up and down her spine.

'As you're leaving England very shortly, I'd be unwise to rely on your assistance,' she almost snapped.

His smile was lazy and assured. 'If you asked nicely, I might put my journey off.'

'Why would you do that? You believe me a trickster, a perfect deceiver.'

'You're certainly artful and scheming—like all your kind.'

'I bow to your limitless experience of women,' she said caustically.

'You should—it's been hard won and rewarding only for transitory pleasure.'

'If I'm no different from the countless women you scorn, why offer me help?'

'Maybe because you *are* perfect as well as a deceiver. And because you need help—it seems that the net is closing in.'

She shivered and he moved closer to her. Then, tipping up her chin, he gently kissed her on the lips. She knew that she should break away, ask him to escort her back to the ballroom. Already she had all the menace she could manage in her life without having to struggle against the temptation of this dangerous man. But the taste of his mouth was something she was desperate to know again and her lips opened unresistingly to receive his. He kissed her long and deep. She leaned back against the trunk of the tree, soft and pliant to his touch. He drew her towards him, the hard planes of his body pressing against her. His hands slowly and expertly caressed her bare skin until she was inundated by rolling waves of desire. The small pearl buttons of her dress were soon undone and the white flesh of her breasts exposed to his touch. His mouth found them and moulded them to his desire, his kisses becoming hotter and more urgent with every moment.

Somewhere an owl hooted and for an instant they were stilled, listening to the sounds of the night. Brusquely, he pulled away.

'You should go back and find your grandmother,' he said roughly.

Shocked, she began to put her dress to rights with shaking fingers. He watched her from a short distance, his expression impossible to read.

'You should be married, Amelie. And quickly. Surely there must be a suitor in the wings other than Rufus Glyde.'

She felt the anger exploding within her. How dare he use her like that and then suggest she marry another man? Was this just another version of the insult she'd already suffered from him? Did he indeed think of her as a doxy, permanently in a state of heat for any man who came her way?

She marched past him with her head high, but he caught her by the arm and pulled her back. 'I mean it, you know—if you're in trouble, send for me.'

She shook off his restraint and ran swiftly towards the ballroom. Thankfully, Brielle was seated near the window and alone.

'I'm afraid I cannot dance anymore, Grandmama, I have the most dreadful headache.'

Looking at her granddaughter's drawn face and hearing the agitation in her voice, Brielle hesitated only long enough to gather her belongings before summoning her carriage. Seated side by side in the town coach, her grandmother took her hands in a warm clasp and stroked them comfortingly. 'You're exhausted, my dear. We shall have a few quiet days and then you'll be more than ready to socialise again.'

If only she knew, Amelie thought, but she dared not mention the existence of Gareth or, even worse, her own impropriety. She needed to push the incident into the furthest recesses of her mind. She had behaved as unchastely as it was possible and with a man who cared nothing for her. It was obvious that he viewed her as an amusement, to be enjoyed when it suited. He'd made her frenzied with desire and then walked away. As she thought of their encounter, her face blazed scarlet with vexation and her whole body was suffused with shame. But she must not think of it, she must not!

'I admire your choice. A diamond of the first water!' Lucas grinned as Gareth entered the Avery family carriage. 'We caught a glimpse of her returning from your moonlight tryst.'

'She's a most beautiful girl,' his wife interjected. 'No wonder you're in love with her.'

Gareth glared at his friend. 'I won't ask who put that notion into your head, Katherine, but you have it wrong.'

She wrinkled her nose meditatively.

'I wonder,' she said gently.

'Admit it, you're in love, just as I said.' Lucas was

jubilant. 'And what could be better? I was worried when I thought you'd fallen for a girl who was completely ineligible, but now the situation is different.'

'No, it isn't,' was the terse reply as the coach trundled a slow passage over the darkened cobbled streets.

Once at the house, Lucas took his friend by the arm and ushered him into his den. No one ever entered this room except by invitation. He poured two glasses of brandy and handed one to Gareth.

'I may be stupid,' he began, 'so explain to me exactly why you're determined to walk away from this stunning girl?'

'Amelie *is* a beautiful young woman and I'm as red-blooded as the next man. But there it stays.'

'But why?'

'Women are a complication I can do without.'

'Women, maybe, but forget all the others who've flitted through your life—this girl is different.'

'I don't see that.'

'You said yourself that you can't get her out of your mind.'

'I have to and I will.'

Then, seeing his friend's perturbed expression, he said grimly, 'I'm not looking for a bride, Lucas. I'm not even looking for love. That would involve trust and I don't have trust to give.'

Lucas's eyes were troubled. 'Trust can grow—if you give it a chance.'

'I did—once. But we both know the end of that story.'

'It's a story from the past,' his friend argued, 'It doesn't mean you can't start again.'

'There is no starting again. I chose my path years ago and I can't now unchoose it.'

'It wasn't a choice, it was forced on you. I'm reluctant to speak ill of your family and of someone who isn't here to defend himself, but your grandfather treated you shabbily.'

Gareth gave a small, mirthless laugh and his friend continued, 'I can see you're a changed man, but don't let that accursed scandal ruin the rest of your life. You're innocent of any wrongdoing.'

'I know that and, thank God, so do you. But to the rest of the world I'm a guilty man and always will be. I can never ask anyone to marry me—even if I wanted to. It's as well that I don't,' he concluded roughly.

His companion sighed with frustration. 'If we could discover what really happened that night… Have you any idea who might have cheated? If it wasn't you, and it wasn't me, then it was one of the other three people around that table. General Tilney is an impossibility and Petersham is so wealthy that it would be laughable to suggest his cheating. But Glyde? He's a man steeped in all kinds of murk.'

'Of course I've thought about who cheated that night. I've thought about nothing else for seven long years. It could only be Glyde. But what would he have to gain?

The stakes weren't that high and in any case he's a rich man.'

'I'm not sure he's as well-breeched as he appears. There are tales that every so often he's forced to sell property and some of his horses. Then he has a lucky streak and all is well again. He replenishes his stables and says he merely fancied a change of cattle.'

'So where does that get us?'

'It means that Glyde might have had a motive after all—money. There's been a good deal of whispering lately about his keenness to play with very young men, those who have little experience, but are plump in the pocket.'

'I was certainly not one of those. Wet behind the ears, it's true. But I didn't have a fortune to lose. You know as well as I do how stringent my grandfather was. I received a very small allowance, hardly worth Glyde's effort if that was the plan.'

'It's true, I suppose, that he wouldn't have fleeced you of a great deal, but the man is spiteful and has a thoroughly malicious nature. He might just have wanted to destroy a young man with a golden future—good looks, charm, a title in waiting and a grandfather who loved and respected him.'

'It's not enough. It's never been enough. If there'd been a motive and concrete evidence of his wrongdoing, I'd have confronted him years ago, exiled and penniless though I was.'

'I think you may be underestimating our friend Glyde.

He would destroy anyone—for a wager, perhaps, or even for fun, his kind of fun.'

Gareth was sunk in deep thought and when he spoke his voice was harsh. 'And now he's hanging around Amelie Silverdale. I thought at first that she was playing games with me, pretending to dislike his overtures while angling to become the next Lady Glyde. But she appears to detest him. Despite that, he's determined to pursue her. First in London, then at the George and now here.'

'Then if you have a care for the girl—I won't call it love,' Lucas hastily interjected as he saw his friend's face, 'you must look out for her.'

'That won't be easy. She doesn't trust me and she's right not to.'

'Tell her the truth about yourself, then she will.'

'She's much more likely to turn away in disgust.'

'She needs to know the lengths to which Glyde will go, understand the peril she faces if she acts against him.'

Gareth stood up abruptly and began restlessly to pace the floor of the den. 'You're right,' he pronounced minutes later. 'France will have to wait. I need to warn her and defeating Glyde's plans will bring a certain savage pleasure.'

'Don't underestimate him, Gareth. He can be a dangerous man.'

'That I can believe, but *I* can be even more dangerous.'

Chapter Eight

It was the small hours before Amelie slept that night. Try as she might, she could not obliterate the stolen meeting with Gareth from her memory. Her mind replayed the scene constantly and every repetition made her feel worse. She knew that she'd behaved recklessly and immodestly. Yet what had she really been guilty of? Showing her feelings too obviously, allowing herself to trust? In return she'd been utterly humiliated. Witnessing her mother's distress all those years ago, she'd made a vow never to allow herself to get too close to any man. Now she'd broken that vow and was paying the price. Her only hope was that he would leave Bath instantly. She would never have to meet him again and see in his face the easy contempt he must feel.

A troubled sleep had left her tired and dispirited and it was with reluctance that she agreed to take a walk in the Sydney Gardens the next morning. Her grandmother had set time aside to wrestle with the household accounts and Fanny was deputed to accompany her mistress. Amelie had no wish to burden her maidservant with the emotional storm she was suffering, nor with her worries over Rufus Glyde. The girl had received a severe scolding for her part in her mistress's flight and the last thing Amelie wanted was to revive bad memories for her. It was best that Fanny thought her mistress perfectly happy.

The gardens were looking particularly inviting. An overnight shower had made the leaves gleam brightly and the flowers put on their most vivid colours. They strolled at a leisurely pace along meandering pathways that criss-crossed the well-kept lawns, making their way slowly around the grounds and back into Great Pulteney Street.

Fanny was eager to hear the details of last night's ball and her mistress was occupied trying to paint a reassuringly cheerful picture. Neither saw the clouds gather once more and the sky begin to darken until the rain started to pour in earnest. Snatching up their skirts, they ran for cover. A small wooden summer house at the end of the gardens offered what little shelter there was. They arrived there breathless and not a little wet.

'We should have brought our umbrellas, Miss Amelie, Bath weather is that changeable.'

The maid attempted to shake off the large drops of water that adorned her skirt and then turned to Amelie to help her do the same. But her mistress did not respond even when Fanny asked her with some puzzlement, 'Is everything all right, miss?'

Instead she stood, frozen and motionless, staring at the man who shared their shelter. Fate could not have been more unkind; Gareth Wendover was the last man in the world that she wanted to see. He bowed slightly to the two women, but remained silent. His blue eyes gazed into the distance without expression and a lock of wet hair shadowed his brow. The rain had moulded his coat of superfine to his form and the feelings she'd willed herself to suppress began to throb into life once more. Dumbly, she looked out at the teeming rain, unable to say a word.

At last, his voice broke the silence, the smooth tones seeming to travel from a vast distance.

'I trust I see you well this morning, Miss Silverdale.'

He'd turned towards her and his black brows were raised in enquiry.

Urgently, she gathered her wandering wits and somehow managed to reply in an even voice, 'I thank you, sir. I am well.'

'And fully recovered from the exertions of the last evening, I hope?'

She felt the anger seep through her; he was not content with mortifying her last night, but now must seek her out to taunt her with her shame.

'I'm not such a poor creature that dancing a few cotillions exhausts me, Mr Wendover,' she answered waspishly.

'Ah, *dancing*, naturally not,' he said with the slightest suggestion of a grin.

'You are unhandsome, sir.'

'How is that?'

'I may have been forced to take shelter here, but should not be forced to suffer your mocking.'

He looked genuinely surprised. 'That's far from my intention.'

'I find that difficult to believe, however. Since we first met you have treated me with contempt and last night you excelled yourself.'

Fanny, meanwhile, had gasped at the mention of Wendover. A distant memory had revived and she'd been gazing in astonishment, first at her mistress and then at the man who bore this disquieting name. Now, in an attempt to capture Amelie's attention, she shuffled her feet noisily on the bare wooden boards. Reminded of her maid's presence for the first time, Amelie made haste to send her away.

'Go back to the house, Fanny, and find our umbrellas.'

'But, miss, the rain has almost stopped.'

'Don't argue. The weather looks like to remain inclement and I don't wish to get any wetter than I am already.'

Fanny looked doubtful, but her mistress wore such a severe look, that she scurried away with hardly a backwards glance.

They watched the maid out of sight before Gareth

began to move towards her. She held up her hand abruptly, stopping him in his tracks.

'I don't know if you've happened here by accident or if you've followed me. It matters not,' she said bitterly. 'You've taunted me for the last time. I wish never to see you again, speak to you again, even hear of you again.'

A frown creased his brow. 'I've no idea why you should be so angry, but I'm sorry if I'm the cause.'

'No idea! When all you've ever done is play games with me. Save them for the women you meet and discard on your travels. I'm sure they'll be more appreciative. I'm not one of them.'

'As I know to my cost,' he murmured wryly. 'And I've never suggested you were.'

'No? Then how do you account for your despicable conduct last night?'

'I shouldn't have made love to you, I agree, but how is that despicable?'

'You were trifling with me.'

'Believe me, Amelie, I was far from trifling.' And he smiled in reminiscence.

She found herself remembering, recalling his smell, his touch, the feel of his body, and desperately sought to stoke her anger.

'You can't help yourself. You're so used to treating women as trophies that you think you can appropriate anyone.'

'It's true that plenty of women have passed through my life and I've let them go without regret.' His tone was sardonic. 'But they've hardly been trophies, merely ragged comfort along a stony path.'

'Very poetic, but it doesn't disguise the fact that you deliberately lured me into a compromising situation and then humiliated me.'

'You've a taste for the poetic, too, I see. I admit I should have resisted temptation, but you make that very difficult, you know.'

He smiled down at her in a way that made her body begin to crumple with desire. Alarmed by her own response, she sprang away from him, leaving as much distance between them as possible.

His expression turned wrathful. 'If you must cast blame, look to yourself. You're angry because last night you surrendered to your feelings. Be grateful that I saved you from betraying yourself further.'

'But of course, you're my knight errant, always rescuing me from disaster. I had forgot. How painful last night's episode must have been for you!'

'Inconvenient, shall we say. Such moments can benefit neither of us and you should have a care for your future.'

Her face wore a shocked expression, but he continued harshly, 'You don't want to hear it, but your best route out of the dangers that beset you is to find a good man to marry.'

'I shall never marry,' she said bleakly.

'Ah, the old refrain, but why ever not? There *are* decent men in the world, you know.'

'Few women find them or, if they do, manage to keep them. My mama did not,' she said in a subdued voice.

He looked at her for a long time and his expression softened slightly. 'Whatever your mother's experience you're not destined to repeat it.'

'Except that my own experience tells me otherwise. Did *you* play the decent man last night?'

'Do you really think that I wanted to lose control?' he grated. 'Of course I didn't. I've survived a brutal world by ensuring that I'm never at the mercy of my emotions.'

'Then why are you here, exposing yourself yet again to such peril?' she asked tartly. 'Or are you going to tell me that you accidentally just happened by?'

Even if his lovemaking had not been a deliberate ploy to humiliate her, it was at best an aberration, an inconvenience. And which was worse?

'No accident—I sought you out this morning. I saw you leave Laura Place and hoped to overtake you on your walk—it was fortunate that the rain brought us together.'

'*Fortunate* is not the word I would use. You deny spying on me, but spying is exactly what you're doing.'

'I sought you out,' he said deliberately, 'because I've something I must say. Don't fret, you'll be free of my presence very shortly.'

'I can't imagine why you're still in Bath,' she retorted childishly. 'How long does it take to bid your friend goodbye?'

He ignored her pointed rudeness and replied calmly, 'I've stayed because I have business to complete. When I go depends on you.'

'How very surprising—' the sharpness of her voice cut the air '—and there was I thinking you were a law unto yourself.'

'I need only a few minutes of your time, then you may be on your way. And I'll be on mine.'

His expression was impossible to read, but his tone was unusually serious.

'A few minutes then, Mr Wendover, although I cannot imagine that you've sought me out to exchange confidences. You seem to delight in posing as a figure of mystery.'

His face relaxed at this and he smiled. Once more the blue eyes were alight with warmth and, despite herself, she felt drawn into their orbit. He was standing very close to her again. She realised that just as his rain-soaked clothes had displayed his muscular form, hers were very revealing of her figure. The sheer sprig muslin she wore clung sensuously to her curves and he was looking his fill and clearly enjoying the sight.

'I'm glad you find it amusing,' she snapped, annoyed that her heart was once more in disorder.

'A figure of mystery sounds flatteringly enigmatic. My smile was simply for that.'

'And are you about to cease being a mystery? Do you intend to tell me your secrets?'

'Yes,' he said unexpectedly.

'Now?'

'Yes.'

'You're going to be honest with me at last?' she persisted.

'I'm going to be honest with you,' he replied solemnly. 'For your own sake, I need you to trust me. When you've heard what I have to say, you may choose to disown my acquaintance, but I still have to say it.'

The light had gone out of his eyes and his face was grave. She began to feel nervous. She'd always wanted to know his true history, but how troubling were the revelations he was about to make?

He remained standing close, their bodies almost touching, but not quite. He made no attempt to possess himself of her hands, no attempt to kiss her. She felt real fear now of what he was about to recount.

'Miss Silverdale, what on earth are you doing out in this dreadful weather?'

It was Perry Latham who had come bounding along the pathway with a large umbrella above his head. 'I met Fanny a while back and assured her that she could go home to dry and I would come to your rescue.'

'Thank you, Sir Peregrine,' she answered, flustered. 'That's most kind.'

'I am delighted to be of assistance. I am, in any case, a messenger from your grandmother.'

He caught sight of Gareth, standing still as a statue, and was somewhat disconcerted by the latter's scowling expression. 'Your servant, sir.' He bobbed his umbrella hastily as a token of respect.

'Yours, sir,' Gareth replied stiffly. Amelie hastily

made the introductions, but Gareth was in no mood for social niceties.

'If you'll excuse me, I have a number of affairs to settle. Now that you have an escort, Miss Silverdale, you have no further need of my company.'

'But…' began Amelie.

'It was good to make your acquaintance,' Perry called after the rapidly disappearing figure, as Gareth strode towards the gates across one of the Chinese-style bridges that dotted the gardens.

'A pleasant fellow,' said Perry Latham, 'I think.'

'What message did you have from my grandmother, Sir Peregrine?'

'Perry, please.' He smiled happily. 'She wanted me to tell you that a splendid excursion is arranged for tomorrow. A picnic to Severn Abbey. Always providing the weather changes for the better, of course.'

'A picnic tomorrow? How can this be? We were not to have any social engagements for a few days. It seems strange that Lady St Clair has arranged this without first consulting me.'

'She didn't arrange it. No, far from it. Everything taken out of her hands, everything done for her.'

'You've arranged it?'

'No, not me. I could have, of course. I thought about it, but I was pipped at the post. Some chap called Hyde or something like that.'

'Glyde?' Amelie faltered.

'Yes, that's the fellow. Good natured of him, don't

you think? He's gone to a lot of trouble apparently. Even booked musicians, I believe, and invited a big crowd.'

She had the presence of mind to pin on a smile of pleasure, but her heart was beating uncomfortably fast. This was to be the first strike in Glyde's renewed campaign. She had to go home and speak to her grandmother. Brielle must be made to understand Glyde's true purpose.

'Sir Peregrine—Perry, I was intending to visit the haberdashers after my walk, but I have just now realised that I've left behind the ribbon I wished to match. I'll have to return home after all.'

'Let me accompany you.'

'No, indeed, there's no need. The rain has stopped. Please don't let me keep you from your business. I will see you tomorrow, no doubt.'

And with that rapid dismissal, Perry Latham had nothing to do but bow politely and walk away in the opposite direction.

'Why are you so upset?' Brielle was clearly puzzled by her granddaughter's response to the invitation. 'It's simply a picnic, my dear. I shall be there and a good many other people that you know.'

'But so will Sir Rufus Glyde. The last thing I want is to be in that man's company. Why did you accept? Why didn't you ask me first when you know how I feel?'

'Dear child, strive for a little common sense. I accepted because to refuse would have been churlish. Sir Rufus has gone to considerable trouble organising this expedition—he made it clear to me that it was to compensate in some small way for the unpleasantness he unknowingly subjected you to. In those circumstances it was impossible to refuse.'

Amelie looked mulish. 'You could have said I was unwell and gone by yourself.'

'How could I have done that without appearing to lie? How many people have seen you today in the full bloom of health? You are refining too much on what has gone before. I do not believe that in the past Sir Rufus fully understood your feelings, but now that he does, he simply wishes to be a friend.'

'I love and respect you, Grandmama, but in this I believe you are judging wrongly.'

Brielle's expression was stern. 'You will allow me to know a little more about the world than you. I'll hear no more of this nonsense. The invitation is unexceptional, certainly nothing you need fear.'

'I do fear it. I loathe the man. I want nothing from him except his absence.'

'You are being unnecessarily alarmist, my dear. Whatever harm can come to you from going on a picnic?'

She had no answer and her grandmother continued smoothly, 'I'm sure that Sir Rufus means well. The trip to Severn Abbey is a kind thought on his part and will give you the chance of getting to know him better. It might even make you begin to change your mind.'

Horrified, she burst out, 'I will never change my mind

as long as I live. The idea of marriage to such a man is abhorrent.'

'And yet you seem not at all interested in marriage to anyone else, despite having been introduced to some of the most eligible bachelors living in Bath. Perry Latham is clearly entranced and one small sign of encouragement from you would produce an offer of marriage, I feel sure.'

'When I said I never wanted to marry, I spoke the truth.'

'I also spoke the truth, Amelie, when I said that you will have to marry, unless you are content to beg shelter as a poor relation for the rest of your life.'

She knew only too well that her grandmother was right. Not unsympathetic to her plight, Brielle tried gently to coax her towards accepting the inevitable.

'If you have no preferences, why not go along with your father's wishes for the time being? You may even come to think he has chosen wisely for you.'

'Never, never, never!'

'No histrionics, Amelie. You must begin to think sensibly. I accept that Rufus Glyde may not be the partner for you, but you cannot dismiss marriage entirely. Take heed of the fact that once you are wed, you will no longer be under your father's control. It will be your husband's duty to protect you from any interference from your family. If you choose a man like Perry, mature, independent and wealthy in his own right, he will have the power to do that. He will make you a good husband.'

'I don't want a good husband,' Amelie found herself saying while Brielle looked aghast.

In the silence that followed, her mind chased a maelstrom of thoughts, but always returned to a small insistent voice that would not be banished. What she wanted, she was learning, was a man who would possess her utterly, body and soul.

In the reaches of the night, she knew that man and he looked uncommonly like Gareth Wendover. But he was the last person who would feature as an eligible husband; marriage would never be for him. He desired her, that was obvious, and he would take her with a passion she could only begin to imagine. A streak of fire suffused her body as she thought of their lovemaking. But what then? She plummeted to earth. He would love her certainly, but just as certainly he would leave. He would cut loose with barely a backward glance.

Once again she lay awake for hours, a thousand different thoughts circling her agitated mind, Gareth always at their centre. His last words had disturbed her—what was it that he'd wanted to tell her with such urgency? She'd seen him angry, bitter, laughing and loving, but never before so serious as the moment when Perry Latham had interrupted their conversation. He'd deliberately sought her out that morning, but what was he about to confide and why now? Did it flow from that shared moment of passion in the moonlit garden? Did his feelings go more deeply than she suspected? Even if they did, he would not acknowledge them. He'd made it plain that emotion was a weakness he couldn't afford;

the moment's pleasure was his only interest. And yet… She longed to be able to seek him out on the morrow and know the answers. But convention decreed that a single woman must be sought rather than do the seeking. In any case the day was not even hers—it would be filled by an excursion she longed to forgo.

The heavy overnight rain had cleared by dawn and by ten o'clock the next morning the sky had mellowed to a clear blue, streaked with wisps of white cloud. It seemed there was to be no reprieve from the weather. She'd decided on the plainest of dresses, but her grandmother dismissed this plan immediately and insisted she put on one of the most fetching of the modiste's creations, a soft green lustring and matching cape. Miss Repton was sent to dress her hair. Her grandmother's maid had unbent slightly over time, Amelie's natural beauty providing her with the best opportunity she had ever enjoyed to display her professional skills. Her protégée acknowledged her efforts with courtesy, but with little interest. This was a day to be got through as quickly as possible.

From the outset it was clear that Sir Rufus had spared no effort or expense on the planning of his excursion. A cavalcade of carriages set off for Severn Abbey towards noon, the last two filled with servants, blankets, sunshades and hampers containing every conceivable kind of food and drink. The countryside was bathed in mellow sunshine and stretched before them fresh and green. As they swished through narrow lanes, the delicate scent of wild flowers wafted into the carriage from high banks on either side.

Amelie saw and felt none of it. This outing was simply a part of Glyde's plan to bend her to his will and she recognised miserably that her grandmother could no longer be counted as her ally in the battle against him. Sir Peregrine, dapper in dove-grey pantaloons and claret waistcoat, shared their carriage and ably maintained a flow of chatter. He tried and failed on several occasions to draw her into the conversation.

'Do you know the countryside around here, Miss Silverdale?'

'I regret that I don't. When I visited Bath as a child I never went beyond the town.'

'There are a great many places of interest, you know.'

'I'm sure, Sir Peregrine.'

'The Abbey we're visiting today, for instance? Do you know anything of its past?'

'No, I'm afraid not.'

He decided against regaling her with his potted history of Severn Abbey and said instead, 'You might be particularly interested in the legend that surrounds the building,' plunging into a somewhat confused account that interweaved a mad monk, a black crow and a murdered spouse who was forever dressed in white. She listened with an expression of interest on her face, but his words simply circled the air before disappearing without trace.

* * *

Once they had arrived at the Abbey, the carriages disgorged their occupants and the whole party began a walk around the ruins. Perry Latham, as an acknowledged expert on the Abbey's history, entertained a small crowd with anecdotes of its past. The most popular proved to be that of the ghost, although the story had grown even more confused in the retelling. Until called to order by their formidable mama, the Misses Lampeter giggled in nervous excitement at his description of the lady in white who floated through the ruins at full moon. Rufus Glyde pointedly ignored the storytelling, deciding instead to play the role of perfect host. He darted here and there, at one moment mingling with his guests and at the next snapping out commands to his servants. At his order the musical trio positioned a little way off struck up a cheerful air.

'This seems a little excessive for a simple picnic,' Amelie remarked to her grandmother.

'Don't be ungrateful,' Brielle chided. 'If the event is a little extravagant, I'm quite sure it is for your benefit alone.'

'I imagine it's rather to satisfy our host's love of ostentation.'

'You are unfair, Amelie, and unrealistic. It's clear to me that Sir Rufus cares for you a great deal and doubtless still wishes to marry you despite your stubbornness. You're not interested in Perry—I saw how you treated him in the carriage. If you won't take him, then you should seriously consider the very advantageous offer that's been made to you by your father's choice of suitor.'

Before she could respond, they were interrupted by Glyde himself, who appeared without warning at their side. Summoning up his most amiable smile, he turned to face Amelie.

'I hope you're enjoying our impromptu little affair, Miss Silverdale, and that all is to your satisfaction. Sir Peregrine's stories, I feel, have given the event an added *frisson.* Or perhaps, unlike the Misses Lampeter, you don't enjoy tales of ghostly visitations?'

'I've more interest in the present than the past, Sir Rufus.'

'How very sensible,' he murmured slyly, 'although one must never forget the future, either.'

'That is something I'm not like to forget, sir.'

'Exactly so. When one is young, the future is an exciting blank, is it not, just waiting to be filled.'

'And I shall fill it as I wish,' she retorted defiantly.

Glyde remained unruffled. 'He will be a lucky man who helps you.'

'I said nothing of any man. My future is mine alone.'

Brielle looked sharply at her granddaughter and decided to mediate. 'Sir Rufus is surely right to suggest that the most satisfying future is a shared one.'

'That's a matter of opinion,' Amelie replied, and looked pointedly away.

The excursion had started badly and continued so, even when the picnic lunch was served in the shade of the chapel ruins. As well as folding tables and chairs scattered across the close-cropped green, blankets had been spread for those who preferred the informality of eating close to nature. Servants circulated busily among the guests, offering platters spilling over with the finest food, followed by tray after tray of cool champagne in crystal glasses. Glyde hovered around their table, constantly offering Amelie a variety of delicacies, to which her reply was just as constant, 'Thank you, but, no.'

'In this heat I eat very little.'

'I really am not hungry.'

And as for champagne, 'I rarely drink wine and never during the daytime.'

Brielle became more and more incensed with her wayward granddaughter. Here was Sir Rufus making a concerted effort to give the girl an enjoyable day and Amelie appeared intent on treating him with an indifference bordering on rudeness. Over the past week Brielle had come to think that Glyde's proposal should not be dismissed out of hand. He appeared to be a man deep in the throes of love, but he'd shown a restraint and courtesy that she'd not expected of him. It was true that he was considerably older than Amelie, but that was no bad thing in Brielle's view. He was wealthy, a necessity now that the Silverdales' fortune was in such a parlous state. It was a little worrying to be sure that he'd acquired the mortgage over the house in Grosvenor Square, but Brielle thought that her granddaughter had perhaps misunderstood the nature of the transaction and that it had not been used as a threat, but as a way of helping a family with whom Glyde evidently wished to ally himself.

It was with relief that Amelie saw the servants begin to pile blankets and hampers back into the carriages and thought thankfully of the return to Bath. But the end of her misery was not yet in sight.

'Lady St Clair, I wonder if I might be permitted to drive your granddaughter?' Glyde had detached himself from the crowd of picnickers and was now bowing graciously to Brielle. 'I will undertake to deliver her safely at Laura Place.'

Brielle willingly gave her assent despite the pleading look on Amelie's face. It would be a chance for them to talk together without interruption. Perhaps they could sort through their differences, and if not, nothing had been lost.

'Grandmama, why don't you accompany Sir Rufus? I'm sure Perry will have room for me in his carriage,' Amelie appealed, hoping that Brielle would be content if she accompanied the second of her potential suitors.

'Perry has already offered me a seat, my dear—' her grandmother neatly cut the ground from beneath her feet '—and since Sir Rufus has been good enough to organise this wonderful excursion with you in mind, it would be fitting that you accompany him.'

This was the nearest Brielle had come to a public rebuke all day and it was one that Amelie could not ignore. Her face burning, she climbed into Glyde's carriage without another word. For the first few miles they drove in silence. She had no intention of playing the gracious guest and Rufus Glyde was biding his time. They were halfway back to Bath before he broke the ominous quiet.

'I'm so glad you felt able to accompany me, Miss Silverdale. I fear our acquaintance began badly and I have had no real chance to remedy this. You have given me now the opportunity to plead my true feelings for you.'

She remained mute and looked away at the blur of trees as they sped headlong through the country lanes. She was his quarry, hunted and cornered. She could escape ensnarement only by jumping from the curricle and that would mean injury for life, or worse.

Wholly undeterred by her silence, he began again, 'I would like to use this moment to tell you how much I hope you will consent to be my wife.'

'Did you not say, Sir Rufus, just one week ago, that you would not be renewing your proposal?'

'That is true, dear lady, but I think I was perhaps a little premature. I find that my feelings for you are stronger than ever and I am looking forward to making you Lady Glyde.'

'I thank you for your kind offer, sir, but I regret I must once more decline. I'm unable to return your affections.' She delivered her words as calmly as she was able.

'I hope in time you may be brought to change your mind.'

'I shall never change my mind.'

'Never is a very long time. You may think differently once you know me.'

'I know all I need to know, I assure you, and I will never wish to be your wife. I have no desire to hurt your feelings, but please accept this as my final word.'

'You don't hurt my feelings, Miss Silverdale. Very little does. But I've decided that you are the woman I shall wed. Your opposition merely adds spice to the quest.'

'If you persist in your delusion, there's nothing more I can say.'

'There is one word and that is yes.'

'I will never say yes.'

'I think you will. I have some powerful forces on my side. You see, I know you took at least a week to reach your grandmother's house from London and I ask myself just where you were during that time. Others might start to wonder, too, if they knew of your long absence from the protection of your relatives. I might even suggest to the inveterate gossips among us that you were up to no good. A possible love tryst? A scandal at all events. How would the *ton* react to that, I wonder? I imagine it might prove the end of all your hopes to shine in society, certainly all your hopes of a prestigious marriage.'

'I have no wish to shine in society. Nor have I any wish to make a marriage, prestigious or otherwise. Your threats leave me unmoved.'

They were now entering the outskirts of Bath and Amelie, her hands tightly clasped to prevent them shaking, could only hope that she would get to Laura Place with her head still held high. Her tormentor wore a marked sneer on his face and continued to drive at a spanking pace through the town's streets, seemingly undisturbed by her response.

They had begun to move into the more populated part of the town, when she gave an abrupt start. A familiar figure, his back turned, was walking purposefully along the pavement. It was Gareth. During the long day's ordeal she'd thought of him constantly—yearned for him, she admitted shamefacedly. And suddenly here he was, longing transformed into reality. Her start had not gone unnoticed by Glyde. He looked long and hard at the figure striding along the road, scarcely able to believe his eyes.

'And how do you know that fine gentleman?' he asked sharply.

'I doubt that is any concern of yours. But I believe I met him a few days ago at the Pump Room with my grandmother.' She was aware that this sounded less than convincing.

'Drinking the waters? Evidently, a new come-out for him.'

'Whatever do you mean?'

'I interest you at last! Strange, when the subject is a man you only *believe* you met.'

'He is of no interest to me—I simply did not understand you.'

'Then allow me to explain. The man we have just passed is a low scoundrel. A sharp, to be precise.'

'A sharp?'

'As a young lady of impeccable background, I doubt you will know the term. A sharp is a cheat who lives by his skill at manipulating the cards or dice. In effect, a thief.'

Her face paled, but she said in a voice that hardly wavered, 'I don't believe that he is any such thing.'

'Why? Is your knowledge of the gentleman so much greater than mine?'

'On what grounds do you accuse him of such base behaviour?'

'I saw him cheat with my own eyes. Pretty good grounds, wouldn't you agree, my dear?'

She sat rigid, in a state of shock. Glyde turned to her, a malicious smile on his face. 'The man is really not suitable company for any woman of quality.'

When she said nothing, he continued to taunt her. 'You seem a trifle upset at my revelation. Could it be that the gentleman is a little more to you than the casual acquaintance you claim?' And then slyly, delivering his crushing blow. 'So, we may have an answer to where you were for that missing week. With *that* man? And you refuse *me*!'

'I told you,' she said desperately, 'I hardly know him. And I doubt that you know him much better.'

She was far from feeling the certainty she expressed, haunted as she was by the remembrance of the quarrel she'd witnessed between the two men at the George.

'I hate to contradict a lady, but today I will make an exception. I know a good deal of him. He has recently returned from the Continent where I believe he has been pursuing his vocation with mixed success. He appears to have enjoyed better luck here. You are the first bird to be plucked, my dear, if not at cards.'

'How dare you! Kindly set me down. I'll not stay a minute longer in your company. I shall walk the rest of the way.'

'As you wish. But you are naive if you think you can flout society's rules and go unpunished. That is a grave error. If I know the truth, how long before others do, too? You will learn your mistake soon enough. Your biggest mistake by far is to tangle with me.'

Chapter Nine

She ran blindly towards her grandmother's house. Passers-by turned to stare at the young woman hastening past them, bonnet untied and hair flying free. Once in the house she rushed up the stairs to her bedroom and locked the door. She needed time and solitude to take in what she'd just heard. The threats by Glyde had hardly registered. She'd always known that he was a vicious man who would stop at nothing to gain what he wanted. But what he'd said about Gareth had turned her world upside down. It couldn't be true, it couldn't be true, echoed over and over again in her mind. Rufus Glyde would not hesitate to denigrate any man he thought might be a rival, but the confidence with which he'd delivered his damning judgement on Gareth had had its effect.

With all her heart she wanted to repudiate his words, but the fact that they accorded all too easily with what she already knew gave them a dreadful ring of truth. So many details fitted: Gareth's estrangement from his grandfather, his shabby clothes when she'd first met him and his air of having known better times, his wish to leave England and return to the Continent. The silence about his background would be readily explained if he were the disgraced man that Glyde had intimated. It would explain, too, the way he'd constantly deflected her questions and his anger when she'd continued to probe. And explain all too evidently why he'd looked so grave when she'd encountered him yesterday in the Sydney Gardens. He had something to tell her, he'd said, the truth about himself at last. Was that what he was about to confess when Perry Latham had interrupted them so inopportunely?

Perhaps after all not so inopportunely. If he didn't say the words, then maybe they wouldn't be true. She had no wish to hear such things from his lips, from the lips of the man she'd come to love. There it was...and she could no longer deny it. She'd fought so hard to preserve her heart, but in vain; she'd lost it to a man who cared for nothing and nobody, whose tenderness was a fleeting caress and who, it now transpired, was an outcast from society. She lay down on the silk bedspread and closed her eyes. She was too deeply upset to cry, but her head thudded painfully. Her mind darted here and there, going over and over all the conversations she'd had with Gareth, trying to find a chink of light, trying to find a different interpretation. The dreadful realisation dawned that there was no other.

How long she had lain there she had no idea but a discreet knock on the door brought her off the bed instantly. It was Fanny.

'Milady wants to speak to you, Miss Amelie,' she said softly.

'Tell her I'm indisposed, I have a headache.'

'I think you should see her now, miss, then I'll brew you something for the pain.'

'My grandmother will understand if you say I'm not well.'

'I don't think she will, Miss Amelie. She's in a rage and ringing a peal over everyone who dares come near. Best to go down.'

Why was Brielle in such a temper? She'd obeyed her grandmother's wishes and suffered a hateful journey for her pains. What, then, could be wrong? Lady St Clair's inexplicable mood seemed the final straw for a day so wretched that she wished for ever to blot it from her memory. Reluctantly, she combed her hair, smoothed out her dress and made her way to the library.

'There you are at last,' Brielle greeted her impatiently. 'That woman of yours takes her time.'

Amelie bridled. 'Fanny came as quickly as she could. I was lying down, Grandmama. I have a monstrously bad headache.'

'Another one? This seems to be getting rather a habit with you. Though after what I've heard today, it hardly surprises me.'

She stared at her grandmother uncomprehendingly.

'Yes, you may stare. I have never been more mortified.

To think I should hear of my granddaughter's appalling conduct from a man who, as yet, has no connection to the family!'

'I don't understand,' she murmured in a dazed voice, but her bewilderment did nothing to appease her grandmother's fury.

'I have just suffered one of the most uncomfortable interviews of my life. Sir Rufus Glyde made a point of calling on me after he'd set you down. He felt it his distasteful duty to relay the most shocking news. He wished to warn me of a thoroughly unsuitable friendship you have contracted with a man—Wendover was the name—a man who is an out-and-out villain.'

Amelie caught her breath. So this was Glyde's new plan. He intended to use her own grandmother to intimidate her and enforce his threats.

'I had to sit there,' Brielle continued bitterly, 'while he was kind enough to inform me that my granddaughter is acquainted with a man who is a proven thief, a man who has been shunned by his own family and is not accepted in decent society. This is a man apparently that you know well. Let's not be mealy-mouthed, a man you've stayed with alone in a solitary country inn. Sir Rufus was nothing but courteous, but can you imagine my feelings when he told me this? He expressed concern for your safety. He knows this man well and said he would be most anxious if it were his own sister involved. His feelings do him credit, which is more than I can say for yours, Amelie. You have let me down greatly—in fact, you have let the whole family down, by your scandalous behaviour.'

Her grandmother's harsh words struck a deep chill in her heart. There was no defence she could make without revealing her feelings for Gareth. And that could do nothing but make the situation a hundred times worse, if that were possible.

'I acquit you of any deliberate wrongdoing,' her grandmother was saying, 'but your naivety and lack of prudence are likely to make you the talk of this town and beyond. If that happens, you will be lucky ever to live it down.'

Questions nagged in Amelie's mind and forced her to speak, though she knew it would infuriate her grandmother further.

'How could Rufus Glyde know I'd spent time at the inn with this man? And what right has he to accuse him of such wrongdoing?'

'He *is* a wrongdoer. Sir Rufus would not voice such a serious charge if it were not true. And as for him knowing of your indecent stay with this man, he has been most discreet, never hinted that he imagines there is any more than a casual acquaintance between you. He didn't have to say more—I worked that out for myself. The patient you looked after so devotedly? An older man whom no one else could care for? How could you have deceived me so badly? Haven't I deserved better?'

Amelie turned a stormy countenance towards her grandmother.

'You are unfair, ma'am. You know that I would never

hurt you. Please believe that I've done nothing wrong. I was at the inn by accident, that is the truth, and I only withheld the full story from you because I didn't want you to worry unnecessarily, not because I wanted to deceive.'

'It's certainly necessary for me to worry now. How are we to avoid this becoming common knowledge?'

'I left the inn as soon as I could and no one knows I was there, except you.'

'And Sir Rufus, if only by supposition. However, he appears to be an honourable man and I'm sure will not spread rumours. In the circumstances he is hardly likely to. We must trust that the scandal will not leak out.'

Her grandmother looked at her sharply. 'You're extremely fortunate that, after this dreadful misdemeanour, a man like Sir Rufus is still willing to marry you.'

She turned sheet-white as her grandmother's words sank in. Of course Glyde was willing to marry her. He would get his desire and she would no longer be able to say a word against it. She had lost any moral advantage. Brielle was right: her family would consider it very lucky that anyone wished now to marry her, least of all a notable member of the *ton*.

Looking at her granddaughter's woebegone face, Brielle's heart softened. Amelie was so like her mother. She remembered seeing too often that same expression on Louise's face when things between her and Miles Silverdale had begun to go awry. She took her granddaughter's hands in hers.

'You've made a bad mistake, but you can recover from this. I have every faith in your good sense. Whatever may have happened in the past, you must immediately cut any links you have to this unsuitable man.'

Amelie said nothing and her grandmother tried to rouse her with a brisk smile. 'Put this behind you, my dear, you're still very young and you have your whole future in front of you. You should give thought to what that future is to be. Sir Rufus is not the only man who admires you. It's possible…' she pursed her lips thoughtfully '…that an early wedding will prove the best way out of this predicament.'

She felt too distressed to ask her grandmother what she meant and excused herself as soon as she could. Crushed by the shower of troubles that had descended, she could hardly drag herself up the stairs. The faithful Fanny was waiting in her bedroom with camomile tea and a handkerchief soaked in lavender water. At her insistence, her mistress lay down on the bed and almost immediately fell into an exhausted sleep.

It was daybreak before she stirred. As her mind swam out of slumber, a tide of wretchedness swept through her and drowned her in its misery. But she knew that she had to rise and dress and pretend all was well.

At breakfast her grandmother looked approvingly across the table as she sat pale-faced but composed. Whatever ailed the girl, Brielle thought, she had spirit and would recover.

'I thought we might make a short visit to the Pump

Room this morning,' her grandmother suggested over tea and toast.

'If it's possible, I would prefer to spend the day quietly, Grandmama.' The thought of the crowded room and the noisy chatter filled her with something near despair.

'Very well—' Brielle smiled agreement '—but you must not withdraw from society for too long. That way rumours start.'

She knew her grandmother spoke the truth. She would have to appear in public again very soon and could only hope that when she did, she would be able to wear an indifferent face. After breakfast she picked up one of the marble-backed novels recently arrived from the Circulating Library, thinking to divert herself, but it turned out that she had no interest in fantasy worlds. All the time her mind was tussling with the dreadful news that she'd learned and she could give thought to nothing else. Whatever occupation she chose was the same. It was a wearisome business and she was glad when at last the long day dragged to its close.

Two equally long days later Brielle rose unusually early and made her preparations. By the time Amelie came down to breakfast, she found her day already arranged and to her grandmother's liking.

'Perry Latham is calling this morning. We haven't seen him since the picnic and I thought it a friendly gesture to discover how he goes on.'

Amelie smiled absently and took a sip of tea. Whether

he called or not was unimportant. Her grandmother, though, continued to pursue the subject.

'I know he has business at Duffields and I thought you might wish to accompany him and choose some new reading for yourself.'

She didn't bother to disagree. Her grandmother obviously wanted her to take a walk with Sir Peregrine and, since she felt guilty at upsetting Brielle so badly, she was more than willing to go. She was even persuaded to wear the bronze-and-green walking dress that became her so well and to allow Miss Repton to dress her hair. She was determined to make it up to her grandmother in whatever way she could, short of consorting with Rufus Glyde.

When she returned to the drawing room, Sir Peregrine was already there, discussing with her grandmother the weather prospects for the next few days.

'Lady Blandford holds her open-air ridotto the day after tomorrow, but the omens are not good. It's said that the Blandfords have spent huge sums on the party. No doubt an attempt to launch the youngest girl in some style—a nice enough girl, but rather too plain to take, I fear.'

'It will need more than a ridotto to launch Georgiana Blandford successfully,' her grandmother was saying caustically as she entered the room.

'Miss Silverdale—' Perry Latham leapt to his feet '—allow me,' and he drew out a chair for her, smiling deferentially as she took the seat. 'Lady St Clair tells me that you have been slightly unwell. I hope you are now fully recovered.'

'I am well, Sir Peregrine, but thank you for your concern,' she answered tranquilly.

'You've been missed, let me tell you. You have been constantly looked for. Your army of admirers will be delighted to see you return to our midst.'

'You were talking of a ridotto, I believe,' she said to deflect the conversation away from herself. 'That sounds exotic.'

'Not so exotic, I fear, if we do indeed suffer the thunderstorms that are threatened. But I don't wish to put you off—I hope you will come.'

Her grandmother looked meaningfully at her. 'We have received our invitations.'

'Of course we shall come,' Amelie said quickly 'but perhaps take our umbrellas.'

Brielle relaxed and Sir Peregrine smiled with pleasure. 'We shouldn't need them this morning in any event. I hope you will feel able to accompany me to Duffields Library, Miss Silverdale?'

'That would be most enjoyable—it's time I explored the shop,' she lied glibly. 'I understand that you've already selected your volumes.'

'I'm most excited about them. I've ordered them especially from London—they are serious histories of this part of the country and one in particular is lavishly illustrated. If you are interested, I would be most happy to loan the books.'

'That is kind of you.'

'Perhaps you had better start for the library or they will be closed for luncheon,' Brielle reminded him. He looked a little concerned and rose quickly from his chair before he remembered his manners.

'When it is convenient with Miss Silverdale, of course.'

'I'm ready to leave now. I'll fetch my bonnet and gloves.'

Walking through the Sydney Gardens brought back some uncomfortable memories. Had it only been a few days ago that she'd met Gareth here and he'd said those fateful words about needing her to trust him, about wanting to tell her something that might change her feelings towards him? In the event, he had not told her anything—someone else had, and what she'd discovered had shaken the foundations of her world.

They threaded their way through the park and Sir Peregrine continued gallantly to make conversation. She felt sorry for him, trying so hard to entertain a companion whose thoughts were far away. When she looked up, she saw that he'd led them to the small summerhouse in which she and Fanny had taken shelter, the place she'd had her last meeting with Gareth.

Her instinct was to flee from the spot, but instead she asked with only a slight tremor, 'Sir Peregrine, why are we here? I thought we were making haste to Duffields.'

'You must forgive my little deception, Miss Silverdale. We will, of course, go to the library but I was hoping to have a few words with you in private and I thought this would be a perfect setting. I know how much you like it.'

She wondered fleetingly how he could have got things so wrong, but it was his desire for a private interview that gave her greatest pause. Before she had time to question, he had begun on what was obviously a well-honed speech.

'Miss Silverdale…Amelie, I would like you to know how much I honour and respect you. These last few weeks your company has given me so much pleasure. It is not too much to say that you have transformed my life. Meeting you has given me a second chance of happiness.'

She looked alarmed and held up her hand as if to stop him, but he was now well and truly embarked on his address and he was going to finish come what may.

'I said I respected you, Miss Silverdale, but my feelings run far deeper than this. I truly love you, Amelie, and I ask you to do me the honour of becoming my wife.'

She was stunned into silence and he went on quickly, 'In case you think that your grandmother would not approve of my having spoken, I have confided my feelings to her, and she has given me permission to address you.'

So this was the reason for Brielle's cryptic comment that an early marriage would be the most satisfactory outcome: she'd decided that it was time for Perry to declare himself. He was looking at her beseechingly.

She felt sorry for him and angry with her grandmother for her interference.

'Sir Peregrine,' she managed, 'I am greatly honoured that you wish to marry me. I esteem your good opinion very highly. You are a true and dear friend, but I fear that is all. I regret that I cannot accept your kind offer.'

He looked crestfallen. 'Perhaps I have been too precipitate,' he suggested. 'You may want time to think it over and I am more than happy to wait.'

'No, Sir Peregrine, it's only fair to tell you that I'm quite sure of my decision. I need no further time. I esteem you as a friend, but I'm not in search of a husband.'

'I see. I was led to believe that perhaps you would not be averse to marriage.'

'Then I regret that you've been misled.' She saw his face fall further. 'I hope that we can still continue to be friends. I wouldn't wish this uncomfortable situation to make that impossible.'

She held out her gloved hand to him and he took it rather limply.

'Of course, Miss Silverdale, I shall always be your friend,' he murmured chivalrously, looking abjectly into the distance.

'Shall we continue to Duffields,' she suggested gently, 'or would you prefer to abandon our visit?'

'No, no, naturally we will continue.'

'I'm sure you're eagerly awaited. The shop must be

looking forward to showing you the volumes they've managed to obtain.'

For the first time in the interview his face relaxed a little. 'By Jove, yes,' he exclaimed. 'I'd almost forgotten them.'

She took his arm and they once more moved off, this time towards the delicate wrought-iron gates that led them out of the gardens. His step had a slight spring in it now and by dint of talking to him about the publications he'd ordered and getting him to describe them in every particular, they managed to arrive at the library with Sir Peregrine in unusually good spirits for a man whose marriage proposal had just been rejected. In her desire to comfort him, she had for the moment forgotten her own plight.

Once in the shop he made haste to the counter and was soon lost in the new treasure awaiting him. She left him to his reading and began to wander around the shelves, listlessly picking up and putting down books without any real interest or intention of borrowing them. She drifted towards the back of the library where the shelves were even higher and the tomes even more dusty. A large volume bound in dark brown calf took her eye. The gold lettering seemed to leap out of the battered cover as though the title were intent on seeking attention. She lifted the book from the shelf better to decipher the words on its spine and found herself looking through the empty space at a face she knew well. In a second, Gareth Wendover had walked quickly around the end of the bookcase and was at her side.

'I've visited every shop in Bath these last few days, trying to find you,' he began abruptly. 'Where have you been hiding?'

'I've been indisposed.' The bald statement hid an avalanche of pain.

'And are you fully recovered?'

It was unlikely she thought that she would ever recover, but she answered in a toneless voice, 'Thank you, Mr Wendover, I am well.'

'I wanted to find you,' he repeated urgently. 'I never finished what I had to say.'

'There really is no need.'

'I think there is. Let me speak. I'll be brief.'

'There's no need, I tell you,' she said with anguish. 'I already know what you're about to say.'

'How can that be?'

'Others have told me.'

'Others? What others?'

She didn't answer.

His brow furrowed. 'Glyde? Was it Glyde?'

She nodded silently, a miserable expression on her face. The furrow deepened. 'How did he know I was in Bath?'

'He saw you as we were driving back into town a few days ago and was kind enough to apprise me of your history.'

'What exactly did he say?'

'Do you really want to hear?'

'Yes, I imagine his account differs markedly from mine,' he said curtly.

'He said you were a card thief—a card sharp, I think he called it—who preyed on naive people and made your living by taking their money. He said that you worked on the Continent usually, but hadn't been successful lately, so you've returned to England to try your luck here.' Her voice was dead and her eyes opaque. She could hardly bear to hear what she was saying.

He reached out and took her hands. They felt ice cold through her light gloves. 'Let me tell you the truth,' he urged.

'Truth? You once told me that my relationship with the truth was slippery. Yours, I think, does not exist. Spare me any more lies!'

With a sharp jerk she snatched back her hands just as Perry Latham came into view. He had been lost in the dream of his new acquisitions, but suddenly remembered that he was escorting a lady and one he had just asked to marry. He came bustling up to them, raising his hat to Gareth whom he vaguely remembered.

'Your servant, sir. Miss Silverdale, I am so sorry I abandoned you. Call it the excitement of an enthusiast. I can't wait to show you the books that have arrived. They are truly magnificent. I know you will be as entranced as I am.' He fairly danced with pleasure.

'Books!' Gareth growled.

'On the history of this area. Priceless volumes. Don't tell me that you are an amateur historian, too?'

Gareth's face was a mixture of astonishment and rage. He wheeled around to face Amelie. 'I can't talk to you here. Come with me.'

And without a further word he grabbed her arm and pulled her through the shop, leaving Sir Peregrine to gape helplessly after them. Once outside, he hailed a passing hansom and bundled them both inside. It was all too reminiscent of a previous journey she'd taken with him.

'How dare you kidnap me in this way!' she protested.

'I need to be alone with you.' With that he pulled down the blinds on the cab windows and commanded the jarvey to drive on.

'Where to, mister?'

'Anywhere, drive in circles if you wish, just leave us to be private,' he said abruptly.

'I geddit.' The jarvey gave a low whistle.

Incensed, Amelie made to open the cab door, but before she could jump to freedom, they'd jolted forwards and were bowling along the cobbles at some speed. He steadied her with one hand and turned to face her.

'You must listen to me, Amelie. Whatever Glyde told you has to be a distorted version of what happened. Give me the chance to tell you my story.'

'It would seem I have no option,' she returned, and stared rigidly ahead.

She'd spent fruitless hours trying to hate him, remembering every slight she'd suffered, every insult, every mockery. She'd told herself again and again that for all his charm he was as untrustworthy as any man and worse, guilty of a low crime for which he'd been justly punished. Pure chance had brought him into her life and now the dice had rolled once more and chance was setting her free. But try as she might, she could not forget him, let alone hate him. He was always there, always with her wherever she went, catching at her heart at each and every unexpected moment.

Undaunted by her silence, he began to relate the events of that long-ago evening. She listened to him, at first smarting and angry at being kept against her will, but then with growing concern as a very different account emerged from the shadows. Imperceptibly, her heart began to lighten; she wanted so badly to believe him.

'Why would Glyde have marked the cards?' she asked guardedly. 'What was in it for him?'

He shook his head. 'I've no idea. He must have known that I had little money and Lucas not much more. Petersham is a very wealthy man, of course, and as for the General, I imagine he's reasonably well-breeched. But to risk a thing like that makes no sense.'

'And to accuse you? That makes no sense either.' Maybe, she mused, it didn't have to make sense. Glyde was simply a vicious man.

As if to echo her thoughts, Gareth said, 'Lucas insists he did it out of malice, that he resented me for having what he didn't—a loving family and a promising future.'

'And do you agree?'

He shook his head again. 'I can't think a man like Glyde would care a jot about family and as for a golden future, his own was secure enough. It was an excessive thing to do out of spite. He didn't even know me well.'

'If it was spite, he was successful.' She reached out for his hand and gripped it very hard.

Gareth's expression was bleak. 'My grandfather disowned me on the spot and we remained unreconciled. Whatever Glyde's motives, he ensured that I lost everything.'

Her lovely face was alight with warm solicitude. 'And you've never tried to clear your name?' she prompted.

'A small matter of how,' he said grimly, 'without money, friends or influence. Glyde, on the other hand, was rich and well respected, if not greatly liked. I had not a shred of evidence against him.'

'Is that still the case?'

'Evidence? No, none.'

'But you have friends—Lord Avery for instance. And you appear now to be in better circumstances.'

He looked at her sharply, but then relaxed. She could have no inkling of his changed position.

'Let's say that I've come to a point in my life where it's immaterial to me whether society believes my story or not.'

'So why tell me?' she asked gently.

'I need *you* to believe, to trust me sufficiently that you'll heed my warning. Glyde will not easily give up his pursuit. He's a ruthless man and so steeped in vanity that he'll go to any lengths to achieve his goal.'

Amelie snuggled closer, a happy curve to her lips. Her heart was singing. Gareth had faced scorn, faced shame, in order to warn her and keep her safe—he must truly love her!

'I will be doubly on my guard,' she said at last, 'but I've always known that beneath his mask Sir Rufus was a vile creature.'

'It seems that others do not—unfortunately those who should protect and care for you.'

'I'm lucky, then, that they don't include you. If indeed you do care for me,' she ventured, catching her breath a little and blushing at her boldness.

He did not answer immediately and when he did it was to say obliquely, 'You could wreak havoc on my life, Amelie, and I on yours. But I'll not let that happen.'

His reply left her hot with embarrassment at having once more exposed herself so baldly. How stupid she was! Of course he didn't care for her, at least not enough. She was more to him perhaps than the women who'd previously skimmed the surface of his life, but she was not the anchor that would bring him home for ever. Well, she had her pride; she would take his warning and expect nothing else. He need not fear she would hang on his shoulder.

Silence descended. He sat unseeing and grim faced, a lock of hair shadowing his set expression. She sensed he was waiting for her to speak, but she felt too mortified to utter a word, and the silence between them gradually built in intensity. So intense it could shatter the carriage walls, she thought. But then he was turning to her, slowly, almost unwillingly, a storm-tossed question on his lips. 'You do believe me?'

The urgency in his voice made her look up and she found her eyes caught and held by his gaze. The unexpected longing that she saw there shocked her.

Stunned by the well of emotion she'd glimpsed, she tried for a light reply. 'Would you prefer I believe Rufus Glyde?'

But lightness was not what he was seeking. He pulled her roughly towards him. 'Don't ever say that name again in my hearing!'

Held tightly against his chest, she felt the magical warmth of his body begin to weave its spell once more; her doubts were stifled, her hurts submerged. Shyly she put up her face to his, aching for his touch. It was not long in coming. In a moment more she was in his arms and he was smothering her face with kisses, his breath warming her skin. Then his mouth was on hers, hard and demanding.

Even as she opened her lips to him, he knew that he should stop. He'd told her what he'd needed to say and she'd believed him. That was all that mattered. There could never be anything more between them. He did not belong in her world, nor she in his; they were always destined to journey apart.

Her mouth was soft and inviting beneath his and he could not bring himself to break away. His lips sought hers more and more urgently. He needed to taste her, all of her. He slid the loose sleeves of her dress down, exposing her shoulders to his kiss, his mouth working its way towards the soft swell of her breasts. His lips lit a fire in her. She was breathing quickly and he had an unbearable urge to make her his if only for this time. He must fight it, but she was matching him kiss for kiss; she was stroking his body until it was burning out of his control. He laid her down on the seat and she moaned with pleasure as he began to move against her. He would allow himself this one moment; he would take the memory with him and cherish it.

Suddenly the carriage came to a juddering halt and their entwined bodies were forcibly parted. There was loud shouting coming from close by. Dazed, they scrambled to their feet and Gareth carefully inched the blind upwards. A scene of carnage greeted him.

'There's been some kind of accident,' he said, still breathing hard. 'There's a large crowd milling about and people shouting at each other.'

She swiftly put her dress to rights and joined him at the small pane of exposed glass. They were at a crossroads and an overturned cart blocked the road opposite. Scattered sacks of potatoes bore witness to a collision and loud accusations of blame rent the air. She was alarmed at the number of people standing so close to the cab. At any time someone might notice them at the window or might even choose to open the door. She could not afford to be recognised.

'I must go,' she gasped. 'If someone sees me and tells my grandmother…'

'Your grandmother knows of me?'

'Glyde has told her and she's warned me that I must never see you again. If I disobey, she'll send me back to my father.'

'Then you must go. We should say our goodbyes now, Amelie.'

Still drifting on a hazy cloud of love, she was shaken from her dream by this splinter of ice.

'But why, why must we say goodbye?'

'I'll be gone from Bath very soon and we're unlikely to meet again,' he replied tautly.

'But—'

'Don't make it more difficult,' he ground out. 'This has to be. You know my story now—convince your grandmother of its truth and she'll send Glyde packing. Then you can look forward to a peaceful future. I have no part in that.'

His face was an expressionless blank and she felt like hitting him very hard. How could he be so obtuse? Whatever he was, whatever life he led, she was now a part of it. Glyde's shocking intelligence had forced her to confront her deepest and truest emotions. Even when she'd thought Gareth a cheat and a liar, she'd loved him, longed for him.

An idea flashed into her head. It was daring and dangerous, but it was what she wanted most in the world.

'Come to me tomorrow,' she said and her voice was clear and joyful. 'Meet me behind the Abbey after the lunchtime service. I'll be on my own—Grandmama attends the Catholic Church early in the morning.'

He shook his head. 'We cannot continue to meet, Amelie.'

'Come to me,' she pleaded again urgently.

He knew he must remain adamant. He must say

goodbye for ever, right here, right now. He looked at her glowing loveliness and felt a wild confusion of tenderness and desire wash over him.

'I should not. We should not.'

'Come!' she beseeched.

At last he said, 'I'll be there,' and his voice was thick with emotion.

He held her fingers to his lips for an instant and then she was slipping swiftly out of the carriage door, facing away from the mayhem. They had stopped near Pulteney Bridge, a walk of only a few minutes to Laura Place, and she hurriedly began to make for home. Before Perry had a chance to speak to her grandmother, she needed to concoct an explanation for her sudden disappearance. Stopping for a moment, she glanced back at the crossroads where an angry crowd of people were still spilling across the road.

'Such a shame you had your carriage ride curtailed,' a cold, reedy voice sounded behind her.

She wheeled around. Rufus Glyde blocked the pavement, a contemptuous sneer on his face. But where had he come from? He must have taken to tracking her through the town! She shivered inwardly at the thought of this base creature dogging her footsteps.

'I cannot think why you should choose to travel in such a disreputable conveyance,' he continued, gesturing in disgust at the distant hansom. 'And with the blinds closed!'

'I don't understand you, Sir Rufus.' She felt her stomach clench.

'Do you not? I believe I spoke in English. You alighted just now from a hansom cab, eccentric behaviour in itself, but with the blinds down? My dear!'

She flushed involuntarily, but her gaze did not waver even as he taunted, 'You are surely not bored already with the delights of Bath? Or was the view inside your carriage particularly enthralling?'

'Your remarks are offensive, sir. Allow me to pass, if you please.'

'Not so fast. I have, after all, a vested interest in your conduct.'

'On the contrary, my conduct has nothing whatsoever to do with you.'

'There we must disagree, yet again.' He sighed softly, but his face was alight with malice. 'I consider myself your affianced husband, you know, barring the formal announcement, and as such I have every right to concern myself with your activities.'

'You will never, ever be my husband,' she rejoined wearily. 'Please accept my decision and let me alone.'

'You are very wrong, my dear. I shall be your husband and soon.'

She shook her head with impatience and he said sourly, 'Let us have no more of this nonsense. You will do as I require. If you think to make a fool of me, you had better think again.'

'Only you can make a fool of yourself, sir. Now let me pass.'

'You will show me respect whether you like it or not. I have only to tell your grandmother that you are still consorting with a known criminal, and she will shower me with blessings if I still agree to marry you.'

'You may tell her what you wish. I have no fear of you or your threats.'

'I think you will find you will be very afraid. I shall do more than tell your grandmother of this incident. I will make sure that I publish your loose conduct far and wide. Your disgrace will soon be circulating way beyond Bath—it will make you the talk of London society.'

'I have little interest in what society says of me. Publish all you wish,' she threw at him belligerently.

'You may find that your interest quickens however, my dear Miss Silverdale, when your grandmother ejects you from her house and the rest of your family shuns you in disgust. Where will you go? Who will you find shelter with? Not a pretty future, is it?'

'I think I can endure it,' she said lightly and slipped past his outstretched hand to continue her journey home.

Glyde looked after her and snarled. He could not understand why she despised his threats. What could be lending her the strength to flout him? But that could not continue. If he was unable to intimidate her by menace or blackmail, he would do so by force.

Unaware of the cauldron of anger that she'd stoked, she walked away with a smile on her face. Glyde was a repugnant creature and it had cost her dear to maintain her equanimity in the face of his threats. But throughout the ordeal she'd held tight to the magnificent idea that had come to her as she left Gareth. A hansom cab ride had changed everything. It had begun with her believing that she'd given her heart away to a man incapable of caring deeply, but ended with a revelation: that profound flash of feeling that she'd surprised. She'd known then that she was loved and that was sufficient.

She believed Gareth innocent of any wrongdoing and willed the world to believe it, too. Yet it was clear that he no longer cared for society's judgement. His mind was made up and she would not seek to persuade him differently. He was determined to leave England and she was equally determined to leave with him. She would be ruined in the eyes of the world, but no more so than if Glyde made good his threats.

From childhood she'd set her face against marrying, her mother's fate hovering always before her. But she'd known that in reality she would be forced eventually to conform; the best she could hope was to be tied to a dull, well-meaning suitor such as Sir Peregrine. Yet her whole being cried out to live life large, to live for passion. How splendid, then, to follow her destiny with the man she desired and to do so on equal terms. She would go with Gareth to the Continent and share the rigours of his life, travel where he travelled, sleep where he slept. She had no illusions. His way of life was transient and insecure and their future together might prove the same. Poverty imposed its own tunes and desire could become blunted. But whatever dangers she faced, she would be fully alive at last. Tomorrow when they met, she would tell him her plans.

Chapter Ten

She awoke to a joyous morning—in just one day her life had been transformed. Though her head had acknowledged the likely truth of Glyde's accusations, her heart had always told a different tale. Now head and heart were one. Tomorrow she and Gareth would be together, friends, companions, lovers, for as long as he wanted her; she'd discovered the freedom she'd been seeking ever since her escape from Grosvenor Square.

Brielle did not appear at the breakfast table that Sunday morning. She was still suffering from a chill contracted a few days previously and sent a message to say that she would keep to her bed for most of the day. She would take tea with Amelie after her granddaughter had returned from church. Amelie was relieved. There was no possibility now of an accidental meeting with her grandmother while she was hurrying to the tryst she'd arranged.

Fanny was to accompany her to the Abbey and would have to be told of the appointment with Gareth, but she was sure that she could persuade her loyal maid to keep silent. It would be unfair to involve her any further. Whatever plans she and Gareth made that morning would be known only to the two of them. 'The two of them'—the phrase had a magnificent ring to it. He would be bound to oppose her wish to go with him to France and would paint in vivid colours the evils of permanent exclusion from polite society. But in the end he would capitulate. She would persuade him that a life lived with him was all she desired—and she knew just how to persuade him. He wouldn't hold out for long.

Her stomach churned with excitement and she ate little of the lavish breakfast that Horrocks served. Impatient to be gone, she slipped out of the front door as soon as the clock struck twelve and was soon walking briskly to the Abbey with Fanny in tow. She would wait until after the service before she revealed the meeting she'd planned. It was pointless to worry her maid before it was necessary. The weather had changed dramatically today and the sun now hid itself behind dark scudding clouds, but she was in no way downcast by the lowering skies. She bubbled with an inner joy.

As they approached the pathway leading to the Abbey's impressive front entrance, she paused for a moment at the lych gate. A few paces away a carriage was drawn up at the side of the road. It had a strange, solitary air about it. No one was in sight and horses and carriage seemed to have been abandoned. It struck her as odd. Normally residents walked to the Abbey for Sunday services or, if they were driven, their carriage was ordered to return for them at the appointed hour. She remarked on the waiting coach to her companion.

'It must belong to old Mrs Warrinder,' Fanny suggested. 'She hates to be kept waiting and never allows her carriage to return home.'

Amelie nodded and promptly lost interest, walking quickly along the paved way and in through the Abbey's main door. The church was full, as it was on most Sundays. Visitors and residents alike enjoyed the sensation of attending a service in such ancient precincts. The opportunity to show off one's finery and the chance to glimpse new arrivals in town was an added pleasure. She glanced briefly around the congregation and at first recognised no one. But when she looked again, she saw Perry Latham sitting in the shadow beneath the pulpit and carefully avoided him, making her way to a pew at the back of the church. He'd not visited Laura Place since she'd left him at Duffields and she had still to offer him an explanation for her abrupt departure. But this morning she couldn't afford to be delayed by conversation with anyone. Once the service had finished, she would have to make good her escape before he could catch up with her.

The well-remembered hymns and prayers proceeded at a leisurely pace. She heard hardly a word, making the responses automatically with her mind elsewhere. Surreptitiously, she looked at her pocket watch. In just over half an hour she would be seeing the man she loved, and for the first time they would be meeting as equals, all deception past. Then the rector was giving the final blessing and the congregation knelt for a last prayer. As soon as she felt she could, she got to her feet and made swiftly for the door. Fanny had to scramble up unceremoniously and move at a trot in order to keep up with her mistress. They both shook hands briefly with the rector, who was waiting at the door to greet his parishioners, but they did not dally. A quick smile and a nod and they were through the church porch.

'Why such a rush, Miss Amelie? You mustn't worry about milady, you know. I'm sure she'll be better soon.'

'I'm sure she will, too. Forgive me for hurrying you so, Fanny. It's not my grandmother I'm thinking of. I have an appointment to get to and I don't want to be late.'

'An appointment? Where? Who with, miss?'

'An appointment with Mr Wendover.'

Fanny drew her breath in and said with decision, 'I don't think you should go, miss. That man is trouble if ever I saw it.'

'Nonsense. This is a business arrangement only. I shan't keep you long. I need to see Mr Wendover for just a few minutes and then we'll be on our way home. You may walk round the churchyard while we talk.'

'Would your grandmother like you to be meeting him?' Fanny asked feebly. She had a lively apprehension of what Brielle's reaction would be and who would most likely be held responsible for Amelie's rashness.

'My grandmother need never know. If you don't wish to be involved, I'll understand. I'm going to meet Mr Wendover—you can come with me or not, as you please.'

'Miss Amelie, you know I would follow you anywhere, it's just...'

Suddenly her words died in the air. Two burly men had leapt from the coach they'd noticed earlier, and blocked their path. The women looked startled, but before either could make any move to escape, the men had scooped Amelie up and thrown her through the open door of the carriage. Fanny dashed after her, trying to hold on to her arm, but one of the men turned back and cuffed the maid soundly around the head. She fell to the ground, momentarily senseless. In a second, the horses had been whipped up and the coach was disappearing along the street.

'Fanny? It is Fanny, isn't it?' A kind voice sounded in the maid's ear. 'Are you all right? You look terrible.'

It was Sir Peregrine Latham. He bent solicitously over the girl and tried unsuccessfully to drag her to her feet.

'My mistress,' Fanny whispered urgently, 'Miss Amelie...'

'What about Miss Amelie?' Perry demanded. 'Where is she? I was trying to catch her up to have a word, but you both left the Abbey so quickly that I lost sight of you.'

The maid sat up groggily. She was shaking now,

hardly able to speak. 'My mistress,' she moaned, 'those men have kidnapped her.'

'What men? Are you sure, Fanny? You're probably suffering from concussion—you must have hurt your head when you fell.'

She looked blankly up at Perry, who was still bending anxiously over her. 'They hit me around the head and then I fell.'

'Hit you around the head? In Bath, in broad daylight and on a Sunday? Surely not!'

She nodded in a bewildered fashion while Sir Peregrine struggled to understand what had happened. 'Who are these men? Who could be guilty of such barbarism?'

At this a jumble of disjointed words gushed forth from the tearful Fanny. 'I don't know, I don't know. They were waiting… My mistress and I were passing a carriage and they sprang out and grabbed her and I tried to hold on to her, but the one with the crooked teeth turned round and hit me round the head and I wasn't able to hang on any more, and now they've taken her.'

She collapsed back on the pavement, sobbing violently. Sir Peregrine began to feel extremely agitated. He was not sure whether this poor maidservant was deluded or telling him some monstrous truth. And he had no idea how to cope with a woman deluged in tears. He was very worried that she would succumb to hysterics any moment now. It was obviously time to be decisive.

'We must return to Laura Place, Fanny, and tell Lady St Clair what has happened.'

'But my mistress…' Fanny moaned.

'Yes, yes,' Perry said soothingly. 'Her ladyship will know what to do, I'm sure.' His voice carried a certainty that he was far from feeling.

It was a matter of moments before they arrived back at Brielle's house. With encouragement from Sir Peregrine, Fanny haltingly told her tale. Brielle looked first astonished and then infuriated.

'What nonsense is this that you're telling me, girl?'

The maid looked crestfallen and ready to burst into tears again. Perry Latham thought it prudent to intervene.

'My lady, the girl is speaking the truth when she says she was attacked. I found her lying on the pavement, clearly having been injured in the head.'

'And why should that mean she has been attacked? She could have tripped. This girl has a history of not telling the truth. I have never found her to be wholly dependable.' She bent a basilisk stare on the unfortunate maidservant.

'But, Lady St Clair, your granddaughter is missing,' Perry pleaded. 'She has vanished into thin air.'

The stare became more pronounced, 'And where, Fanny, is my granddaughter precisely?'

'I don't know, milady,' she sniffled. 'Miss Amelie was took. I couldn't stop them.'

'Are you expecting me to believe that my granddaughter was abducted in broad daylight?'

'Yes, ma'am,' Fanny asserted, her voice trembling a little.

'As she came out of church?'

'Yes, ma'am.'

'Ridiculous,' Brielle pronounced. 'And who do you suggest is responsible for this outrage?' Her dawning fear was making her more imperious than ever.

'I think I recognised one of the men,' Fanny managed. 'He had crooked teeth.'

'Yes…' Brielle prompted crossly.

'He was at the picnic Miss Amelie went to.'

'What picnic?'

'The one at Severn Abbey. The one organised by Sir Rufus Glyde, ma'am. He was one of Sir Rufus's men, I'm sure.'

'Are you suggesting, you stupid girl, that Sir Rufus Glyde, a respected peer of the realm, has abducted my granddaughter? How dare you! If it were not so laughable, it would be a shocking accusation.'

Fanny hung her head. 'Miss Amelie was very afraid of him,' she muttered defiantly. 'She was scared he would force her to marry him.'

Sir Peregrine had listened to this interchange in growing bewilderment. The idea that Amelie might be forced to marry a man she feared, and that this man had been responsible for her disappearance, seemed to him something out of one of the local legends he so eagerly devoured rather than anything approaching real life.

'Sir Peregrine, will you put a stop to this nonsense once and for all. Please call at Sir Rufus Glyde's lodgings and ascertain his whereabouts. I'm sure we will find that he is as ignorant as we are of Amelie's plight. In the meantime I will send Horrocks and the footman to make other enquiries. I'm sure there must be a rational explanation for my granddaughter's disappearance and—' she favoured the maid with a contemptuous glare '—for this girl's sudden malady.' Inwardly, though, she had begun to feel very uneasy.

Sir Peregrine was not long in returning. His face was grave as he entered the room.

'I regret to tell you, Lady St Clair, that Sir Rufus left his lodgings this morning. Apparently, he quitted his rooms quite suddenly. The landlord was given no notice of his departure and…' Perry coughed delicately '…I understand there is a considerable amount of rent owing.'

'I cannot believe that of a gentleman such as Sir Rufus.' Brielle looked ashen. 'I'm sure if we can discover where he's gone, he will be able to tell us something of Amelie or at least reassure us that he has had no part in her disappearance.'

'As to that, the landlord naturally has no idea where Sir Rufus might be.'

'And you?' Brielle looked painfully at her young friend.

'I regret, my lady, that my acquaintance with him is of the slightest.'

A soft tap sounded at the door. The butler had returned from his mission and came quickly to the point.

Neither he nor Thomas had been able to find any trace of the young mistress. The rector remembered a girl who matched her description leaving the Abbey at the end of the service, but after that the trail had gone cold.

When Horrocks had bowed himself out, Brielle rose with unaccustomed difficulty from her chair and began slowly to pace the room.

'Who on earth can we turn to in this predicament? Who is likely to know where Sir Rufus would go? Who can we trust?'

There was no answer from her small audience. Suddenly she turned on Fanny.

'Sir Peregrine said that you were lying on the pavement beyond the Abbey. You must therefore have been walking away from the church. Why was your mistress heading in the opposite direction to her home?'

The maid swallowed hard, but did not reply.

'Come, girl, the truth, if you care anything for her.'

Fanny's voice was barely a whisper. 'She said that she had a business meeting, milady.'

'What do you mean, a business meeting? What has business to do with Amelie? Who was this person she was meeting and why?'

Fanny saw no escape from the question. 'I don't know why she was meeting him, milady,' she stuttered. 'Miss Amelie didn't tell me, but it was a man called Gareth Wendover.'

The name galvanised Brielle and she rushed over to the girl, and shook her violently.

'You allowed your mistress to meet that man? A man she was expressly forbidden to see?'

Sir Peregrine intervened in his quiet voice. 'I don't think we can blame Fanny, my lady. I know she would only have gone with her mistress to protect her.'

Fanny nodded gratefully while Sir Peregrine continued thoughtfully, 'I'm sure she knows as little as I do about this man. I have met him on a few occasions. A somewhat fierce person, I thought, but nevertheless decidedly a gentleman.'

He turned to the maid. 'Where was this meeting to take place, Fanny?' he asked her gently.

'Behind the Abbey, Sir Peregrine, I believe. I was to walk around the churchyard. Miss Amelie said she would only be a few minutes.'

'Then we must go there and find this man immediately. He may know more than we,' Brielle declared, invigorated now that she could take some action. 'Sir Peregrine, would you be so good as to assist in this?'

With an inward sigh, Perry Latham agreed and once more hurried from the house. It was beginning to be a somewhat energetic day.

Gareth arrived early at their meeting place, knowing he shouldn't have agreed to the stolen encounter. He had needed to tell Amelie the truth of his past, needed to be sure that she understood the full evil that was Glyde. But once she'd heard his story, he'd vowed that he would bid her a final goodbye. Why had he been unable to keep that vow?

Ever since he'd met her, he'd been acting irrationally. How could a slip of a girl do that to him? He'd never felt love for a woman, but that had been no hardship. Exiled from home and country, he'd been swift to put on the armour of indifference. An unsettled existence roaming Europe demanded nothing emotionally. But then Amelie had erupted into his life. He'd felt an immediate attraction, seeing her pirouetting uncertainly above him on that ridiculous rope, the chestnut locks framing her beautiful heart-shaped face. He'd been drunk, but not so drunk that he hadn't realised the pearl he'd stumbled on.

Since then he'd fought a constant battle with himself. Over and over again he'd argued the stupidity of a serious involvement with any woman, least of all with this green girl, and by dint of concentrating on her deceptions, her lies, he'd thought he'd managed to keep her from invading his heart. But it seemed that the heart wasn't interested in this tired ploy; it had its own ways to follow.

Sitting close in that musty cab, watching her beautiful face alight with happiness, and feeling her soft hair against his cheek, he'd been overwhelmed not only with desire, but something more, something deeper. He'd been unable to resist the urge to hold her, to caress and be caressed, to give himself to her body and soul. To take with him that one moment of love—yes, love. He'd been crazy; it should not have happened.

And here he was foolishly meeting her again, but this time there must be no repeat of yesterday's lovemaking. He could never offer her the marriage she deserved; even as the rightful earl, the taint of scandal would follow him wherever he walked and he could not bear to expose her to the venom of a spiteful society. She would say she cared nothing for her peers' judgement, but in time she would come to. They were destined always to travel different paths. His bags lay half-packed at Lucas's house: that was his future. Hers was the sensible marriage and no doubt Sir Peregrine Latham was being groomed at this moment for the role of husband. As for Rufus Glyde, he would cease to be a threat once Amelie's engagement to another was announced.

He made himself as inconspicuous as possible while he waited for the end of the service. The patch of grass where he loitered was shaded by overhanging trees from the churchyard and he was able to watch people coming and going without himself being seen. For some time there was little activity, but then the Abbey bells rang out and churchgoers began to saunter past in twos and threes. He felt a rising impatience to see her. He tried to remind himself that they had only a few hours left to them, but all he could think of was forbidden delights: to touch her, smell her, taste her again.

Time moved on and still Amelie did not come. He began to wonder if she were unwell or perhaps had been forcibly stopped from keeping the appointment. Perhaps her grandmother had discovered their intended meeting and kept her at home. The minutes ticked by. Surely, though, she would have sent an emissary to tell him if she'd been prevented from coming. That maid of hers, Fanny, was a devoted servant. She would have found a way of slipping out of the house and letting him know what had happened.

He stopped his pacing for a moment. She might have decided not to come. She might have thought better of it. In the fervour of their encounter yesterday she'd appeared to believe his account of that night at Watier's. But recalling their conversation word for word, he realised that she'd never actually committed herself. She'd pushed his direct question to one side. What if she'd had second thoughts once she was back in the quiet of her own room? Perhaps she was uncertain that this was finally the truth. After all, he'd consistently lied to her or at least avoided being honest. She might imagine that this story was yet another deception. She would think that the heat of the moment had deceived her and, now in the coldness of a new day, she would doubt. And doubting, she would not come.

Or perhaps this had always been her plan. The monstrous thought struck him off balance, apprehension turning to anger. She'd never had any intention of meeting him today; she'd meant him to wait fruitlessly. She'd enjoyed the physical pleasure he offered, but she didn't trust him. She didn't love him. He was the deceiver and always would be. This was her final riposte: she'd decided that she would be the one to practise the last deception.

That was the explanation, he was sure now. Why had he ever imagined otherwise? Amelie Silverdale was no different from any other woman he'd ever met. They'd shared a fleeting passion and that was all. He turned to go, disgusted with himself that even for a short time he'd thought he could know love. As he walked towards the corner of the street, a now familiar figure came into view. Of course, Peregrine Latham, her chosen go-between, he thought bitterly.

Perry Latham raised his hat and looked uncertainly at the glowering man in front of him.

'Mr Wendover, do excuse me for accosting you in this way,' he began with a worried look on his face, 'but would you be so good as to accompany me to the house of Lady St Clair?'

'Why on earth should I?' Gareth asked belligerently.

'Her ladyship is most anxious to speak with you,' Perry said in his most placating manner.

'But I'm not anxious to speak to her ladyship. I've nothing to say to her,' Gareth growled. Not only was he to be made a fool of by his false love, but he was to receive a raking-down from her grandmother.

Perry tried again. 'Lady St Clair is most worried about her granddaughter and feels that you may be able to help. I hope you will reconsider your decision.'

'Worried—why is she worried?' Gareth was seized with sudden foreboding.

Sir Peregrine answered repressively, 'That is something I cannot discuss in the street. If you will be so good as to accompany me, we can speak of the matter in private.'

'Has something happened to Amelie?'

'If you would come with me, Mr Wendover?'

'What's happened to Amelie?' Gareth rasped out, grabbing the other man by the coat lapels and nearly lifting him off his feet.

'I beg you, sir,' Perry gasped, 'let me go. All will be explained.'

Gareth reluctantly released his hold. All thoughts of Amelie's supposed treachery fled from his mind. She was in trouble and he must get to her.

Brielle looked long at the man who was ushered into her drawing room. He was lean and tanned and his dark hair fell carelessly over eyes that were as blue as a summer sky. At the moment they were blazing with a mixture of anger and alarm. As a woman Brielle could appreciate why her granddaughter had proved so wayward, but as a grandmother she recognised danger when she saw it. This man had no time for social niceties, she could tell—he was a soldier of fortune, a vagabond.

She wore her most haughty expression, but Gareth met her with an equal disdain. Neither cared for the other, but both were united in their desperate concern for Amelie.

'What do you know of Rufus Glyde?' she began.

'He's a villain,' Gareth replied shortly.

'You are entitled to your opinion,' Brielle conceded, even now finding it difficult to accept that she had been so badly mistaken in the man. 'But I meant—what do you know of his habits? Where might he go if he left Bath suddenly?'

'What is this about?' Gareth asked bluntly. 'I'm here

because something has happened to Amelie, not to discuss a blackguard such as Glyde. What trouble is she in? I need to know.'

Once more it was Perry Latham who intervened at a difficult moment.

'We very much fear that Miss Silverdale has been abducted, and possibly by this man Glyde.'

'What!' Gareth's voice exploded in their ears. 'And you're sitting here doing nothing!'

Sir Peregrine glanced at Brielle, but she remained bolt upright in her chair, her lips firmly compressed. 'Her ladyship hoped that you might know where this man could have taken her,' he explained tentatively.

Gareth regained something of his calm. Now was not the time for outrage. He needed to be in control of himself, to think rationally and to think fast.

'Glyde has a country estate some thirty miles from Bath,' he said curtly. 'That would seem a likely destination. Do you know what he was driving?'

'Fanny described a coach and pair.'

'Hardly designed for a lengthy journey, so I doubt he has decided to go out of the county.'

Brielle turned to Gareth and her voice shook very slightly. 'Do you have any idea of why he should do such a dreadful thing?'

'His threats against Amelie haven't worked,' he said roughly. 'Your granddaughter is a spirited woman. That would be intolerable to a man like Glyde. My guess would be that his abduction is a way of punishing her and making sure he wins in any contest of wills.'

Brielle wrung her hands and suddenly looked a very old lady; he felt a slight stirring of compassion.

'I will find her,' he promised and his voice held absolute conviction. 'I'll travel on horseback—that way I can ride cross-country and get there quicker. Time will be of the essence,' he ended grimly.

Brielle nodded, her face a study of wretchedness, understanding his meaning only too well. She came forwards and shook his hand.

'Mr Wendover, if you can rescue this dear child I will be for ever in your debt.'

'I have no need of gratitude, my lady. I do this as much for me as for you.'

He walked swiftly to the door and was gone. Sir Peregrine, who had been hovering by the window, felt it an opportune moment to escape. He preferred his dramas to be safely confined within the covers of a book.

Left alone, Brielle sank into her chair, exhausted and sick with fear. She had believed Gareth Wendover when he'd pledged himself to find Amelie. Despite what she knew of his reputation, she had instinctively trusted him. But he did not know the local country well and he was just one man. It was clear that Glyde had hired a team of thugs to do his bidding. What if Gareth never found her or, having found her, was overpowered, which seemed more than likely? She could not bear to contemplate what might happen to her beloved girl. And she, Brielle, would be responsible. She had promoted the pretensions of a man who had turned out to be a scoundrel. How could she have fallen into such gross error? She had always felt pride in her judgement, but now she would never trust herself again. And Amelie, all the time in this very house, fearful and alone, not daring to tell her grandmother of the threats against her. The tears began to trickle down Brielle's cheeks and she put her head in her hands and sobbed.

She was not allowed to indulge her grief for long. A diplomatic tap on the door by Horrocks heralded another visitor, and one who could not have been less welcome.

'Lord Miles Silverdale, milady,' the butler announced.

'How good to see you, Brielle.' Lord Silverdale's hearty voice sundered what little peace was left. He seemed to fill her dainty drawing room with his presence and she was forced to her feet, offering him a feeble smile as he came towards her.

'Miles, what a surprise! Whatever brings you to Bath?' she asked somewhat inanely.

He looked nonplussed for a moment. 'Amelie, of course. My daughter? I need to see her. She is here, I take it?'

Brielle made a brave attempt to mask her discomfort. 'I hope to see her soon,' she extemporised.

'When exactly?' he sounded agitated. 'I've urgent business with her. I've been travelling since dawn to get here.'

For the first time Brielle regarded her son-in-law closely and saw that he was looking tired and travel-stained.

'I'm so sorry, Miles, you must be fatigued,' she prevaricated. 'Where are my brains wandering? I must order refreshments to be brought and have a room made up immediately.'

'Yes, yes,' he said testily, 'but Amelie—when will she be back?'

'Why is it so urgent to see her?' Brielle parried.

It was his turn now to look uncomfortable. He shifted uneasily on his feet and fixed his gaze on the far wall. 'You might as well know, Brielle, I've been a damned fool. The man I was intent on her marrying has turned out to be a complete blackguard.'

'Sir Rufus Glyde?'

'Yes, Rufus Glyde. The man is a very devil. He has deliberately set out to ruin this family!'

He began pacing jerkily up and down the room, evidently labouring under a great upswell of emotion. Hoping to calm the situation, Brielle gestured to him to sit down beside her.

'He started with Robert, you know,' he blurted out, then trying to compose his voice, 'gradually drew him into gambling well beyond his means—truth to tell, the boy needed little encouragement—but until he met Glyde the sums he wagered were within reason. Since then he has become more and more reckless. I've had to sell just about every piece of property we've ever owned to cover the boy's debts. The last straw was the mortgage on Grosvenor Square.'

Brielle said nothing, but took his hand. He looked tired and defeated. 'I believed in Glyde,' he continued.

'I thought that if he married Amelie, the family would be saved. And she would have a secure future.'

'And now?'

'Robert came to me late last night. For once he wasn't drunk and he hadn't been gambling. He told me a dreadful tale. A young friend of his had blown his brains out. Just twenty-two. Such a tragic waste. He owed money to Glyde and Glyde was threatening to foreclose on his parents' property.'

Brielle could not speak. This was the monster who had taken Amelie. She hoped desperately that the story was false or at least exaggerated.

'Could there have been any mistake?'

'No mistake, I'm afraid. Robert said that as soon as the suicide became known, half a dozen other young men came forwards with similar stories. They'd gambled with Glyde, lost heavily and been encouraged to pledge more and more until they were ruined. Glyde would make sure they paid up—his threats were taken seriously.'

'And nobody realised what was happening?'

'Not until now. The young men—boys, really—were reluctant to publish their troubles.'

'How dreadful,' Brielle said faintly.

'Dreadful indeed. It was the shock of losing his friend that gave Robert the courage to tell me last night just how badly things have gone with him. It is worse even than I knew. There's nothing I can do about the money or the estate—the Silverdales are ruined. But I can prevent another of my children becoming Glyde's victim.'

Miles opened his arms as if to plead for absolution. 'I've been so stupid. I knew that Glyde had followed Amelie to Bath and I hoped she would get to know him better here and be more willing to contemplate marriage to him. That's why I left her with you.'

'It didn't make her any more willing. She hated Glyde and has continued to hate him despite every effort he's made to attract her.'

'Thank God for that.'

'Don't be too thankful,' Brielle said with difficulty. 'I fear that Sir Rufus Glyde has lived up to his reputation.'

'What do you mean?'

'I hardly know how to tell you. Glyde has abducted Amelie.'

'Abducted!' Miles Silverdale's voice reverberated around the room, making the crystal decanters on the sideboard tremble.

'If you please, Miles, we must be as calm as we can.'

'Calm! How can I stay calm when you tell me my own daughter has been abducted and by this villain? When did this dreadful thing happen?'

'This morning. Amelie attended the lunchtime service at the Abbey and Glyde's men swooped on her as she walked away from the church.'

'And what has been done to get her back? Have Bow

Street been alerted?' His face had turned a bright red as he once more began furiously to pace the carpet.

'You really must seek to compose yourself, Miles, or you will become ill. I am trying to find Glyde privately. Calling in the Runners would lead to a scandal that neither of us would want.'

'But how are you trying to find them?' Miles Silverdale was almost pulling at his usually sleek silver hair. 'Can you trust the servants you've sent?'

'I haven't sent servants. A man called Gareth Wendover has gone. He knows where Glyde's country estate is situated. He is a friend of Amelie's.' She passed over this quickly, hoping he would not enquire too deeply.

'I've never heard of him. What do you know of this man?'

'Little except that Amelie trusts him and he is intent on finding Glyde and bringing her safely home.'

'And meanwhile we are to sit here and wait like clunches.'

'What else do you suggest we do?' his mother-in-law asked, an irascible edge to her voice. Her nerves were overwrought and the constant effort of appearing self-possessed was beginning to take its toll.

Miles pulled himself together. 'You're right of course. It wouldn't be sensible to career around the countryside looking for this wretch. We can only pray that this Wendover fellow runs him to ground. If he rescues my girl, he will have deserved the highest reward—though God knows I have nothing left to give him.'

Brielle thought otherwise, but decided to keep her counsel.

Chapter Eleven

It seemed as though she were emerging from a pitch-black tunnel. The echo of far-off sounds filled her ears, but she could see nothing. A suffocating darkness enclosed her. Her breath came in short, sharp gasps.

Now the tunnel was expanding and the darkness was not so opaque. There seemed to be a slight chink of light in the distance. She opened her eyes a fraction and pain arrowed through her head. In response, her eyelids quickly shut and she drifted back into a black haze.

When she tried to look again, she was sure that she could see sunlight. Her head was heavy and throbbing and seemed detached from the rest of her limbs. Minutes ticked by and gradually her body began to come back to life. She stretched out her hands and realised that she was lying on a bed. A shaft of light lay brightly across the faded counterpane. Cautiously she turned her head and saw the sun streaming through dusty, mullioned windows. She turned her head in the other direction and this time the shape of a door swam into her vision. She felt wretchedly sick.

There was a bitter taste filling her mouth, which she couldn't understand. Her throat felt raw. She puzzled over this for some time and gradually her mind began to recall incidents, voices, actions. She'd been in a coach, she remembered, and her arm was hurting badly. She tried desperately to focus her wandering mind, to piece together the fragments of memory. She'd been in a coach, against her will—yes, that was it, someone had thrown her into the coach and she'd hurt her arm. A large, rough hand was covering her mouth. She'd struggled, she'd bitten that hand and freed herself. But not for long. Her head was being jerked back. What then? A hot, evil-tasting liquid was forced between her lips—she'd been drugged! Two men there'd been, nasty and brutish. She'd recognised one of them from somewhere. And Fanny had cried out. Fanny, where was Fanny?

And where was she? Gingerly she tried to raise herself into a sitting position, but instantly fell back onto the bed. The walls were moving in disturbing circles. After a while she tried again and saw that she was in a large room, wainscoted with dark oak panelling. Heavy Jacobean furniture filled the chamber, sombre and intricately carved. The bed she lay on was massive, the bedstead as black as jet. Leaded windows filled the entire side of a wall, diamond-shaped panes giving on to tall trees that swayed in the wind. Their branches scratched against the glass. She was in an old house and in the countryside, but whose house and where remained a mystery.

She lay back on the pillow and tried to concentrate her mind, but it wasn't easy. Waves of nausea constantly engulfed her. She'd been with Fanny, she remembered, they'd been walking along the pavement, just past the Abbey. They'd been to Sunday service and were going to…meet Gareth, she finished in a rush. She'd been going to meet Gareth when two men had jumped down from the coach she'd seen earlier, scooped her up and thrown her into the carriage and driven off at high speed. She'd struggled, but it was hopeless. She'd been forced to swallow the drugged liquid and she'd known no more. Until now.

She sat up groggily, then very slowly swung her feet to the ground. So far, so good. She tried to stand, holding on to the bed for support, but was forced to sit down again as the floor spiralled up to meet her. Allowing herself a short rest, she once again tried to stand. She had to get out of this house, wherever it was. She had to get back to Bath and find Gareth.

He would think she'd failed their appointment, that she was no truer than any other women he'd met. He would not wait long before deciding that he was wasting his time. His eyes had spoken a depth of feeling that had taken her breath away. But she knew him well enough to realise that if he thought himself rejected, he would cloak his emotions in ice. He would cut his losses there and then and start immediately on his journey. She had to get to him before he left Bath.

Dragging herself up to a standing position, she shuffled very slowly to the door. She tugged at the handle, a huge, plaited-iron circle, but the door did not budge. Slowly she inched her way in the other direction towards the windows. Looking through the dusty panes, she saw that she'd been right: she was in the country. Rolling hills were the backdrop for what appeared to be a neglected park. The grass almost reached the window sill and ragged bushes ranged far into the distance. The room had an air of neglect and the grounds of the house were no better.

If she could just open one of the windows, she might be able to climb over the sill. She fumbled with the latch, but it was stiff with rust and appeared to be jammed. As she struggled with it, the door of the room opened. She turned quickly, too quickly. Head spinning, she clung to the window seat to prevent herself from falling. She looked at the man framed in the doorway. She had always known who it would be, of course. Rufus Glyde. It could be no other.

'I'm delighted to see you on your feet, my dear. You have a strong constitution, which is most gratifying.' In the gloom of the doorway, his thin mouth was like a knife slash across the white face.

She tried to speak with authority, but her mouth was dry and her voice came out in a hoarse whisper. 'You are a villain, sir, to serve me thus.'

'A villain? Quite possibly, although I have been called worse.'

'You have drugged me, kidnapped me and now I am imprisoned.'

'Yes, all those things. But it will get better, I promise.' His thin face broke into a mirthless smile.

'Let me go immediately!' she demanded in as strong a voice as she could manage.

'I don't think so, not immediately. What would be the point of all the hard work in bringing you here? There is some business outstanding between us and we must first attend to that.'

'What possible purpose can you have in locking me up here?'

'I warned you, did I not, that you would bend to my will?' His cold voice slid icily through her consciousness. 'My purpose is to ensure that you do just that. Really quite simple.'

'And what is your will, pray?'

'I think you know very well, Miss Silverdale. By the way, do tell me when you think I may call you Amelie. Miss Silverdale is a trifle formal, I feel, for what lies ahead of us.'

'If you're referring to marriage, you must surely know that I will never agree.'

'Indeed I do.' He sighed with tedium. 'However, I regret that I must disappoint you a little. I find I am no longer desirous of marrying, or at least not just yet, so perhaps we should not be too previous.'

'Then why am I here?'

'So that we can become more closely acquainted. What else? And what better place to get to know each other intimately? No one lives within ten miles of this house and there is no staff to speak of. Only your two gallant companions of the coach and they, of course, do my bidding like the faithful dogs they are. We shall be completely alone. Won't that be pleasant? Just the two of us, getting to know each other.' His voice jeered, and a wave of revulsion broke over her.

He looked at her face, which had grown even paler as he spoke. 'But you must not despair, Miss Silverdale. Not entirely. I may still discuss marriage at a later date. We shall just have to see how you please me.'

She said nothing and he continued, his voice now harsh and peremptory, 'And you *will* please me, you know. You are completely at my disposal.'

She sank back on to the window seat. Her body was weak, but her mind was racing. Let him but go and she would try the window once more. Ten miles was a long way, but if she could once reach the road, she might garner help from a passing traveller.

He seemed to know exactly what she was thinking. 'I do hope you won't try to escape.' His voice was languid but its arctic menace was clear. 'It would be so tiresome. As you've already discovered, the windows are bolted and the door securely fastened. You will remain locked in this room and whenever you leave it, for whatever purpose, you will be accompanied. I shall leave you now. You will find hot water by the dressing table and fresh apparel in the wardrobe. I wish you to wear the dress I have selected for you.'

Despite her weakness, Amelie felt her temper

rising. 'My own clothes are sufficient, I thank you,' she exclaimed.

'Perhaps I did not make myself clear. You will do as I command. Your own clothes are no longer fit to be seen.' And he gestured with distaste at her dusty skirt and torn bodice.

'And who is responsible for that?' she demanded angrily. 'The men you employ are thugs.'

'Regrettably so, but very efficient, would you not say? I'm sure you will find the clothes I have provided more than ample recompense. You will put them on and wait to be fetched for dinner.'

Her heart lurched. Might this provide her with an opportunity for escape? The relentless voice told her otherwise.

'So far you have been treated with restraint, but if you should attempt to escape or resist in any way, you will be bound closely. Do I make myself clear?'

She made no sign that she had heard his words as he went out of the door, locking it noisily behind him. Once he had gone, she sat for a long time looking into nothingness. She would not weep. Somehow she must find a way to escape this evil man. She dared not think of the threats he had made. Instead, she must concentrate on getting away, but her spirits faltered as she looked at the locked door and the bolted windows. The sun had disappeared over the horizon and a cold darkness had stealthily encroached on the room, finding a cheerless echo in her heart.

* * *

Once he'd left Brielle's house, Gareth moved rapidly. He went first to the livery stables and ordered them to saddle their fastest mare as quickly as possible. His urgent tone sent the usually sleepy ostlers scurrying to do his behest. From the livery stables he hurriedly retraced his steps along the main thoroughfare towards the Averys' house. The family was visiting friends and he was relieved to find only the servants at home. No time would be lost trying to explain the situation. He dashed off a brief note to his friend and left it with the footman to give Lucas immediately when he returned. Then up to the bedroom two stairs at a time and a rapid change into riding breeches and topboots, headlong down the staircase once more and quickly back to the stables.

The head lad was fastening the last buckles on the harness as Gareth walked through the gate. Minerva stood waiting, her legs twitching with anticipation and her head jerking up and down as if to shake off the bridle and be gone. He was in the saddle and away within minutes.

The location of Guestling Manor, Glyde's country estate, was already known to him. Just last night Lucas had related the latest *on dit* from town, now going the rounds of Bath. It was said that Sir Rufus Glyde's affairs were not flourishing and he would very soon be putting his country estate up for sale. It was generally held that he'd be lucky to find a purchaser. The mansion was old and dilapidated and its surrounding park untamed.

It would require a mountain of money to make any improvement and was, in any case, not large enough for the needs of a gentleman and his family. It was large enough to conceal a prisoner though, Gareth thought grimly.

He was soon out of the environs of Bath, making for the country roads beyond. Almost immediately Minerva fell into an easy stride that seemed to devour the miles effortlessly. But Gareth did not relax for they had far to travel and the time was short. The image of Amelie, bewildered and frightened and in Glyde's power, tormented him and he was tempted to spur the horse forwards in a headlong gallop. But he knew he had to save her strength for the cross-country riding, which would soon be upon them. He felt the mare trembling with excitement, eager to speed like the wind, but reined her in and forced her to maintain a slower pace. The hedgerows were ablaze with pale gold honeysuckle and the scarlet of poppies newly opened, but he saw none of it.

Amelie was the picture that filled his mind. He knew she would fight with every breath in her body, but how could she successfully defend herself, a vulnerable girl held prisoner in a hostile place? He could only guess what Glyde intended towards her and none of it was good. Back there in Brielle's genteel salon, that scoundrel's name had sent his mind blazing, hot enough to set the room on fire. He'd been overwhelmed with the need to choke the life out of a man who sowed wickedness wherever he went. Such bloodthirsty ferocity was new to him. As a young man, wandering Europe friendless and penniless, he would have given his soul to wreak revenge on the man he suspected had authored his downfall. But he'd lacked the power to do so; all his energy and ingenuity had been employed in simply keeping alive.

His situation today was very different and he might have avenged his injuries any time since he returned to England. Yet he hadn't done so. He hadn't wanted to soil his sword on such a contemptible creature, but in truth he no longer cared enough. He believed Glyde responsible for sending him into exile, but it was exile from a society he despised; responsible for severing the ties to his family, but his grandfather had proved cold and unforgiving. Was avenging such wrongs worth more scandal and possible death? He'd considered not. But now it was no longer just about him; it was about a girl who'd lodged herself deep within his heart. His face hardened into an expressionless mask as he considered the revenge he would exact.

And he would exact revenge. He'd insisted to Lucas that he knew nothing of love, unwilling to acknowledge the powerful feelings Amelie had stirred in him from the very beginning. It had been easier to concentrate on her shortcomings. He'd taken refuge in anger at her deception. He'd pretended that they shared only a physical passion, which would burn itself out as quickly as it had ignited. But in the end he'd failed to subdue the emotions shaking him to the core. If he'd ever doubted that he knew the meaning of love, it had been put to flight the instant he'd realised she was in such desperate peril.

He would rescue her or die in the attempt. He would bring her safely back to Bath and to those who should have the greatest care of her. She would, must, find happiness in a match deemed suitable by her family; for all his title and wealth, that could never be him. It was ironic that after all the years of uncaring liaisons with women of the *demi-monde*, he should have finally fallen in love with a virtuous daughter of *ton* society.

He'd had a taste of that society as he'd stood in the doorway of Watier's salon. He would not be ignored—his inheritance would make sure of that—but he would attract the worst kind of attention. For himself, it mattered not a fig, but for Amelie... Confronted by the whispers, the nudges, the nuanced glances, she would die a thousand deaths. She would trust him to defend her and he would be unable. He loved her too much to put her through that. No, she was destined to be another man's bride and when he found her it would be to say a last farewell.

His mind thus occupied, he rode onwards, hardly conscious of time passing. The going was easy at this stage, the country lane soft underfoot. For the first hour, he made excellent time but just outside the village of Marksbury he received a check. Precious minutes were wasted at the toll where the keeper had absented himself. Gareth was forced to bribe a small boy to go and find him. After what seemed a lifetime, the guardian of the tollgate returned, very much the worse for drink, and was only persuaded to allow Gareth through by another hefty bribe. It was fortunate that only that morning he'd withdrawn a large sum of money in anticipation of his journey to France.

The experience of Marksbury decided him to avoid the toll roads and begin to travel cross-country where possible. The young boy had described a short cut through Witham Woods, which lay ahead and to one side, its eastern border running parallel to the toll road. The sky had gradually been clearing and the afternoon become hot, but the woods were blissfully cool. Strong branches reached skywards, interlocking overhead to form a shadowy vault, hardly pierced by the sun. The mare showed her appreciation of this welcome change of temperature by a willingness to pick up speed once more, but again Gareth reined her in. The forest floor was uneven; dead branches were strewn here and there and tree roots erupted haphazardly through the soil. The path, pleasant though it was, meant potential danger. Whatever happened he had to keep the horse in good shape.

From Witham Woods he took the path that skirted the southern end of a lake. Once past this large expanse of water, the countryside opened up and he could at last allow the horse an unrestrained gallop. Pounding over the soft turf, he was able to make up the minutes forfeited earlier at the tollgate. And even when the open country was left behind, he continued to make good time, speeding through leafy lanes and along rough tracks. Candlelight began to appear in the few lonely cottages he passed, but still he travelled on, never slackening his pace.

The last rays of the sun had created shaded folds in the patchwork of surrounding hills. It was a beautiful evening, breezy but warm, and the pink tinged clouds that streaked across the wide sky promised another fine day on the morrow. But he was too anxious to care much for nature. A dilapidated signpost warned him that the manor house was still some five miles distant. He had to get there before nightfall. A moon gently climbing into the sky offered little help, its light diffused and pallid behind the scudding clouds. The thought of Amelie in Glyde's power as night came close was unbearable. Once more he spurred Minerva onwards, whispering in her ear to make one last effort. She whinnied softly in response, and though her breath was beginning to come short and fast, she redoubled her pace. They were back now in open country and leaning low over her neck, he urged her to a last gallop. The miles once again flashed by. The mare was almost spent when the rusting iron gates of Guestling Manor at last came into view. They were locked and barred, but an overgrown screen of dark ilex surrounded the property. Gareth sidled the horse along the hedge and very soon found a small gap. He pushed the horse swiftly through and prayed he was not too late.

Reluctantly, Amelie took the gown from the wardrobe. It was an elaborately embroidered silk gauze and the diaphanous folds billowed over her arms. A very expensive dress, she thought, its amber sheen lustrous and its beadwork intricate. But when she slipped it over her head and viewed herself in the tarnished mirror, she hated what she saw. The sheer material and the low-cut neckline made her feel horribly exposed and she looked in vain for a handkerchief to cover her breasts as they surged above the plunging bodice. Eventually she tugged a faded cloth from the small table, which stood nearby, and fastened it around her shoulders. It made her feel considerably braver. The shoes she was forced to wear were as flimsy as the dress, and would surely make any chance of escape impossible. She saw with satisfaction that her face was chalk-white and made even paler by the deep gold of the gown. Her hair was left tumbled and unkempt. She aimed to be the least attractive of dinner companions.

She had only just finished dressing when the ancient lock once more ground into action and one of her erstwhile captors stood on the threshold.

'Come with me,' he ordered abruptly and seized her by the arm, dragging her out of the room and along a maze of flagged passages. Small, cell-like doors dotted the stone walls, but appeared to lead nowhere. There was no other sign of human life. They seemed to walk for ever, the man striding ahead and dragging her roughly behind him. It took all of her strength to remain on her feet. She had completely lost her bearings by the time he arrived at a door that was more imposing and less dilapidated than the rest.

The man's knock was discreet, a surprise given his

general brutishness. But she imagined that Glyde was an unpleasant master to serve and his hired hand would want to be as inconspicuous as possible.

'Come!' The thin tone rose clear in the air and she shivered. She could never hear Glyde's voice without feeling an upsurge of disgust.

She was pushed unceremoniously into the room and the door locked behind her. The furnishings here were slightly more comfortable, but the room still bore all the signs of prolonged neglect. The brocade curtains, once a deep sapphire, now hung greyly at spotted windows, their fraying material incubating layers of dust. The *chaise-longue* beside the window had lost most of its gold embellishment and the two wing chairs that guarded either side of the fireplace had sunken seats and stained coverlets. Someone had attempted to polish the large rectangular table that dominated the middle of the room. Its surface reflected the light of a wrought-iron chandelier hanging above, also newly cleaned, it seemed. The table was set for two.

Glyde was lolling at his ease in one of the massive carved chairs drawn up to the table, but as she stood wavering in the doorway, he rose in a leisurely fashion and moved towards her. With a twitch of his hand he tore the material from around her shoulders and cast it on the floor.

'Allow me to see just what my very considerable efforts have purchased,' he sneered.

For what seemed minutes on end, he stared lustfully at her, his sulphurous eyes undressing her inch by inch.

She could do nothing but stand and endure his gaze. Then reluctantly he stepped back, waving a negligent hand at her as he returned to his seat.

'Come to the table, Miss Silverdale. You must be hungry after the exertions of the day.'

She'd never felt less like eating, but she feared that he would return to her side if she did not obey. She could not bear him anywhere near. She moved slowly towards the end of the table and sat down. Glyde had evidently been drinking while he waited. His face was already slightly mottled and drops of red wine stained the frilled white shirt that he wore beneath a suit of rich ruby velvet. He saw the direction of her glance.

'Don't worry, my dear. I've merely been filling in time until you got here. No more wine this evening—at least not for me. *I* need no Dutch courage.' He smirked unpleasantly. 'But allow me to pour *you* some. You will undoubtedly find it beneficial. Such an excellent relaxant.'

'I thank you, no.'

'You will drink some wine. It is my wish.'

He said it with a finality that brooked no argument. Before she had time to realise what was happening, he was at her shoulder and filling her glass to the brim.

'Now drink,' he ordered.

She did as she was told, but tried to sip as small an amount as possible. Satisfied that he was being obeyed, he resumed his chair and reached for the tattered bell pull. Its noisy clang echoed through the passageways beyond. Almost immediately, the man who had brought her to the room appeared in the doorway. He carried large bowls of soup and was followed by a companion bearing the remaining entrées, the man with the crooked teeth.

'This is most pleasant,' Glyde murmured expansively as he sipped from the bowl in front of him. 'The moment has been so very long in coming. But triumph is even sweeter when it is hard won.'

She didn't answer, but played with her spoon, pretending to consume the soup while in reality watchful and alert, hoping for a chance to escape. She'd noted that this time the door behind her had not been locked. It was possible that Glyde's two henchmen were lurking just beyond, but she reasoned they would have to return to the distant kitchen after each course to collect the next serving. For a few minutes at least the door would be unguarded. If only she'd not been forced to wear these stupid shoes! Perhaps she could slip them off under the table without being noticed. She hoped Glyde might forget his vow and begin drinking again. She needed him torpid and lacking in vigilance.

When the next course arrived, though, it was brought by just one man. Where was his companion? She could not be sure and if she made a dash for the door and he was on the other side, she would have lost any chance of escape. Her fate would almost certainly be another drugging, only this time when she awoke she would find herself securely bound.

Serving followed serving and there was never more

than one man in the room at any time. She felt bitterly disappointed.

Glyde read her mind with uncanny ease. 'Escape is impossible. You might as well sit back, my dear, and enjoy the evening. For my part I can assure you of many hours of future pleasure.' He leered hungrily across the table, but almost immediately recovered himself and continued smoothly, 'The food, for instance, is in a class of its own. Naturally not cooked by the clods who have served it, but produced by the very finest chef that my money can buy.'

She wondered, but only for a moment, whether the chef was still on the premises and, if so, whether she would be able to appeal to him for help.

'Of course he isn't here now,' Glyde said, reading her mind once more. 'As I told you, there is just Amer and Figgis—yes, they do have names—and myself. A cosy little foursome, don't you think? Though naturally Amer and Figgis will be absenting themselves very shortly.'

She tried to eat slowly and delay each round of food as it came to the table. He saw through the ploy immediately.

'I have all the time in the world, Miss Silverdale. Do please savour your food. I like that in a woman. It suggests appetite.'

She continued to eat at the same pace, trying to maintain an air of indifference. His face, scored by the gash of his thin mouth, broke into the familiar icy smile.

'The longer the meal, the greater the anticipation and the more satisfying the finale. Do you not agree?'

All too soon the fruit was removed and coffee served. She was allowed to decline the liqueur, which Glyde tossed off in one gulp. He nodded sharply at his two henchmen, who were clearing the last vestiges of the meal, and they disappeared promptly. The occasional noises emanating from the passage gradually ceased.

Glyde strolled to the door and turned the heavy rusting key. He returned to his chair and leaned back with a cruel smile on his face. She cast around for ways of deflecting him, anything that would win her freedom.

'Sir Rufus,' she ventured, 'my grandmother is a wealthy woman. She would come to an accommodation with you—you have only to say the word.'

His face wore an expression of incredulity. 'You foolish chit, I do not desire money. Money is mine whenever I wish,' he boasted. 'What I require is a far rarer prize, as you well know. Spare me the play-acting. After all, you are hardly an innocent.'

'You have been misinformed. I am a virtuous woman.'

He scanned her cynically. 'As you wish, my dear. Your recent conduct would suggest otherwise. The man in question is fortunate to be many miles away, else I would have ordered his disposal. Chastity is not a requirement of mine—virginal pleasures in my experience are much overrated—but when I make a woman mine, that is how she will stay.'

He gestured to her. 'Come here to me, Amelie.'

She made no move.

'Now,' he barked, 'unless you wish me to come and drag you here.'

She got up and walked with as much dignity as she could summon to stand in front of him. He pulled her down roughly onto his lap, his eyes devouring her greedily.

'You are very beautiful, Amelie, and you are now mine—mine as and when I desire. You will stay with me here until I have finished with you. If you entertain me well, I may consider renewing my proposal of marriage.'

One hand fitted itself around her waist while the other stroked her hair. She was overcome with nausea and fervently hoped that she might be sick over him.

'However, if you do not please me, you will be sent back to your family,' he continued impassively. 'They may do as they wish with you though their options will be severely limited. Damaged goods are so difficult to sell. And the family home will be no more. I will be forced to foreclose on the mortgage. Dear, dear, let us hope that it will not come to that.'

She remained immobile, dazed by his depravity, while he held her tightly against his chest. Her body was rigid, withdrawn into itself in a desperate attempt to avoid contamination. He began stroking the inside of her arm and crooning to himself. It was too much. She leapt to her feet and ran across the room to the window.

'Of course,' he jeered, 'I must not forget how young you are. Naturally you want to make it a little more exciting. I'm only too willing to oblige.'

And he was there beside her, grabbing her round the waist again, only this time managing to encircle her whole body with his arms and pulling her tight against him. His shirt smelt of wine and his breath on her bare skin was noxious. She tried to escape his grasp, but this only caused him to tighten it still further.

His right arm imprisoned her, holding her so that her face was buried in his chest and she could hardly breathe. With the other hand he began caressing the soft cream of her shoulders. She cried out in disgust, but this seemed only to excite him further. He pulled at her dress, trying to untie the ribbons single-handed. Taking advantage of his preoccupation, she managed to tear herself away. But not for long. He came after her immediately.

This time she had fled to the corner of the room nearest the door in a vain attempt to effect an escape. But there was no help from that quarter—the door was impenetrable. She was fighting for breath and knew she would not be able to hold off her abductor for much longer. A vision of Gareth, sparkling blue eyes and mocking smile, sprang improbably to her mind. She clung to it as though it would somehow save her. But how could that be? It was a figment, a phantom only. By now he would be well on his way to France, unknowing and perhaps uncaring of her fate.

Glyde was advancing on her once more, incensed now by her recalcitrance, and tore at her dress, exposing her breasts to view. For a moment he stood back, examining her with a salacious intensity as she cowered partly naked against the wall. Then he threw himself at her, hoisting her skirt upwards while he fumbled urgently with his breeches. She knew that he would have no compunction. He would rape her, here in this dreadful room. She closed her eyes, trying to abstract her mind from the frightful deed that was to be perpetrated on her.

A loud crash sounded from across the room. Then suddenly all was changed. There was a whirl of movement, a muttered curse from Glyde, and she was left alone, her hands trembling and scrabbling to cover her nakedness. An intruder had smashed his way through one of the leaded windows and stood brandishing two swords. One he retained in his right hand while the other he threw to Glyde, who caught it awkwardly. The man waited for his adversary to regain his balance. Glyde, deliberately ignoring the courtesy of touching swords, lunged without warning at the stranger, attempting to catch him off guard as the man's eyes adjusted to the lighted room. In response the intruder cut the chandelier cord and brought it tumbling down on to the table, the small crystals tinkling eerily as they shattered. The only light was that of the moon, now floating free of its cloudy coverlet, and streaming through the open casement. The two men faced each other.

Chapter Twelve

Glittering moonlight flooded through the window pane, lighting the centre of the room like a stage complete with its actors. The two figures circled each other cautiously for some minutes, their swords disengaged. Then Glyde, impatient to free himself of this unwanted visitor, delivered a lightning strike. In return he was parried gracefully. He lunged again and was once more deftly countered. Over and over again he pressed forwards, often seeming to be on the point of breaking through the other man's guard, but miraculously his opponent always regained his position, meeting Glyde's blade with steel.

In one of the pools of darkness that filled the corners of the room Amelie stood, hardly daring to breathe. She had snatched a cloth from a side table and wrapped it around herself to conceal her torn dress. Her lips were parted and her eyes wide. She had recognised Gareth instantly, a phantom miraculously made flesh. He had found her! How he'd done so, she had no inkling. It was enough that he had found her. He was here and fighting for her life, and for his: a darting force, lithe and nimble, biding his time, waiting to make a kill. She saw his eyes aglow with the primitive joy of revenge.

The fight went on, their blades clashing harshly in the silence of the room. Glyde continued to attack fiercely, but his opponent was able to parry the blows with ease. Gradually the younger man began to gain ground, his thrusting sword pushing Glyde back farther and farther. It seemed he would pin his adversary to the wall. Then, in a sudden violent movement, Glyde gathered all his strength into the riposte and with his whole body weight lunged straight at his opponent's chest. Gareth stepped back as quickly as he could, but the blade caught him on the arm and ripped the sleeve of his shirt. A trickle of blood seeped through the white cambric and began to drip on to the floor.

Amelie's eyes closed in horror, but when she looked again she saw that Gareth had managed to steady himself. Tight-lipped and with a deep furrow scarring his brow, he had recovered his ground. He began to fight more defensively, hoping that an opportunity would occur that would enable him to snake below his enemy's guard. Sensing his advantage, Glyde continued to assail his opponent savagely, strike after strike. At any moment Amelie expected to hear the dull thud of her lover's body falling to the floor. A dozen times he might have been run through, but he always managed to block the attack, disengage his blade and return to the fray. He was tiring, though. The loss of blood was taking its toll and he was no longer as nimble on his feet nor was his swordplay as sharp as it had been. Every fresh charge from Glyde tired him further. His face had turned ashen and his breathing was laboured.

Glyde's face wore a devilish expression. Once more he drove forwards ferociously, intent on making an end of it. But with an almost superhuman effort, Gareth blocked the blow and with a supple flick of his wrist twisted his sword in a rapid half-circle and slid smoothly under his opponent's guard. Glyde's sword hand wavered and he staggered back. With a mighty slash, Gareth struck the weapon from his hand and directed the point of his own blade to the other man's throat.

'Villain, I have you.' He was breathing raggedly, but his voice rippled with triumph.

In a moment he had staunched his bleeding with a tightly bound strip from his shirt sleeve. The fallen man, his face whiter than ever, snarled defiance. With the point of his sword Gareth pricked the skin of his enemy's neck and brought a pinhead of blood to the surface.

'If you wish to live, you will do as you are told.' He looked down commandingly on the prostrate figure.

'And what might that be?' Glyde spat out, infuriated by the ignominy of his position.

'You will grovel to Miss Silverdale for the torment you've inflicted and then tell her exactly what happened on the night you say I cheated at cards.'

Glyde, his head awkwardly angled away from the

sword point, looked contemptuous. 'I will not grovel. Naturally as a *gentleman*, I apologise to Miss Silverdale for any misunderstanding.'

Gareth's expression remained one of iron control, but his sword hand gripped the weapon ever more tightly.

'You are a cur and I would whip you if *I* were not a gentleman!'

Unperturbed by Gareth's disdain, the fallen man sneered. 'A somewhat besmirched gentleman, however. You will never free yourself of that particular stain, I fancy.'

The sword quivered and the gash on Glyde's neck grew redder. 'You mistake—you are about to free me from the lies I've lived with for so long.'

'How very dramatic. But hardly likely.' Glyde's smirk became more pronounced even as the wound in his neck began to bleed freely.

Gareth ignored him and continued in a voice that was icily indifferent. 'You will recount the circumstances of that evening and you will do it truly. If not, I can assure you that you will feel more than the tip of my sword.'

His implacability seemed to affect his enemy more than any show of anger. The man glared at him, his face sullen and set.

'I must first ask you to remove your weapon from my throat. It is hardly conducive to talking.'

Gareth reluctantly withdrew the point of his sword a little, but still held its position fast.

'You have it. Now talk.'

'What am I to say? It was an evening like any other.

I was engaged to dine with Petersham and we wandered into the Great-Go to make up a table with the General and whoever else was in the mind for a little light gambling.'

'Hardly light, as I recall.'

'Not for a Johnny Raw, that's true. It was unfortunate for me that you and your friend Avery, such an innocent, should happen to arrive at that moment. I would have preferred a plumper bird for the plucking.'

'That was your purpose for the evening?'

'I had some debts that were becoming a little pressing.'

'And you decided to pay them by cheating those you played with.'

'Not entirely, but the cards fell badly for me that night. I really had no choice.'

'So you marked the cards?'

'A very little, just sufficiently for me to recognise the ones I needed.'

'And when it was discovered?'

'I was amazed. Tilney spotted it. His eyesight must be a good deal sharper than his brain. Nobody else at the table had a clue. Petersham is so indolent that he hardly looks at the cards. And so disgustingly rich, that the result of a game matters nothing to him.'

'When General Tilney alerted the table to the cheating, you didn't own up.'

'Are you mad?' Glyde's voice was waspish with irritation. 'Of course I did not "own up." One would think I was some cadet on probation.'

'But you had no compunction in implicating me.' Gareth's hand quivered on his sword, but, controlling his fury, he kept the point just short of Glyde's throat. He was finding that after all such gross treachery roused an incendiary rage.

'None whatsoever. Striplings who think they are old enough to play with the grown-ups get all they deserve.'

'You must have known that I had little money of my own.'

'That's what made it so perfect. I saw in a moment that you were the one who would shoulder the blame. The General was out of the question, Petersham's too rich and as for Lucas Avery, everyone knew that his trustees were liberal to the point of insanity and would pay his debts instantly. But it was also common knowledge that your esteemed grandfather kept you on a tight allowance. So who more likely to cheat than you?'

'And that was your sole reason to tarnish the name of a man you hardly knew?'

'There was an additional pleasure, I must admit. I had a score to settle with your grandfather. You settled it nicely.'

'And now? Are you still settling debts in the same way?'

'Naturally one must live and, contrary to society's opinion, I am not a wealthy man. Fortunately, there's an inexhaustible supply of callow youth. The money I've won off that fool Robert Silverdale has kept me afloat for many a month.'

Amelie's eyes had been wide with dismay, but now she looked stricken. It was bad enough that her brother had gambled so stupidly, but to know that his downfall had been deliberately plotted by this depraved man was horrifying. She could not stop herself crying out, 'You are the worst of men.'

'Indeed, and it is a great pleasure to know that I exceed in this,' he gloated.

'And Miss Silverdale, was she to be part of the debt?' Gareth asked savagely, thrusting the sword once more against Glyde's throat.

'We are all fools for something, are we not? She has been my one failure. I should have known she would be more trouble than she was worth. But as soon as I saw her, I meant to have her. The mortgage on the Grosvenor Square mansion was a master stroke. I had thought to make her my wife and then sell the house to provide some much-needed funds. But damaged goods…'

His vanquisher's weapon cut into Glyde's flesh. 'You will pay for every moment of suffering you've caused her.'

'How touching,' the injured man croaked, his voice faint with pain.

Gareth ignored him and for the first time looked directly at the frightened girl standing transfixed in the corner of the room. He gave her an encouraging smile.

'Unlock the door, Amelie, and ring the bell for those ruffians to come.'

'Are you sure we should? They may overpower

us,' she said uncertainly, emerging from the shadowy darkness.

'Have no fear. They're as cowardly as their paymaster. I need a light and paper and ink. This black-hearted monster is about to make a full written confession, a little keepsake from our encounter this evening.'

The prostrate man recovered sufficient strength to snarl angrily, 'I'll not be signing anything. My men will finish you in a second.'

But when Amer and Figgis appeared over the threshold and saw Glyde's situation, they seemed in no hurry to come to his aid. Gareth snapped out his orders, warning them to follow his commands or he would execute summary justice on both them and their master.

They scurried from the room and he looked down at his antagonist.

'Somehow I can't see them staying for too long. My guess would be that they'll be gone from the house as soon as they can make their escape.'

In a few minutes the men returned, bringing the items he'd demanded. He moved towards the door to take the lighted candlestick and momentarily released his sword grip. In that instant Glyde staggered to his feet, his hand crept into his pocket and he withdrew a small duelling pistol. Standing behind him, Amelie saw in an instant what he meant to do and shouted a warning.

Gareth spun round as his adversary lifted the gun to eye level and made ready to fire. He waited for what seemed an endless moment, knowing there was no way he could escape, but then Glyde's body was crumpling to the floor, the gun harmlessly firing into the ceiling. Amelie, her breathing coming fast, stood clutching a branch of the broken chandelier.

Gareth smiled with relief. 'You certainly know how to fell a man,' he murmured wryly.

'Have I killed him?'

He felt for a pulse. 'Fortunately not. We don't want him dead yet.'

Amer and Figgis turned tail at this new course of events and made off towards the nether regions of the building. Gareth, meanwhile, had bound Glyde's legs with curtain ties and was busy throwing a jug of water from the table over his face. He came round, groaning and looking decidedly green.

Gareth dragged him roughly across the floor and into a chair, propping him up against the solid oak table. He dipped the quill in the ink and placed it in Glyde's hand.

'Now write to my dictation.'

For long minutes, the pen scratched across the paper, the writer looking ever more sickly. Inwardly, Amelie fretted that he would faint or worse before he could finish, but she remained silent while Gareth's inexorable voice spelt out the long confession. When the last word had been written, and Glyde's signature appended, he carefully rolled the document and stored it safely in his shirt front.

'That is the price for my not killing you,' he said, binding his adversary's hands behind him. 'The price of my silence, however, is a little more exacting. You will leave England within the next five days. And leave for good. You will never show your face in society again.'

Glyde started angrily, but his legs were still bound and he was unable to move.

'You would do well to heed my words,' Gareth warned. He patted his chest. 'I have here the means to expose you to your peers for what you are.'

'And if I choose exposure?'

'Somehow I don't think you will. A life wandering the world isn't the most fulfilling, as I can testify, but better far than being blacklisted by your fellows. Think, too, of all those opportunities to exercise your talents. Johnny Raws are everywhere!'

He opened the door and ushered Amelie through. Glyde was already struggling with the ties that bound him as Gareth turned to leave.

'Remember,' he warned, 'five days and you will have left these shores.'

His voice was implacable and with a last hard look at his enemy, he followed Amelie into the passageway and walked her slowly through the hall and out of the front door.

Once outside she turned to him and said wonderingly, 'You came.'

'How could you doubt that I would?'

She smiled slowly in response and held her hands out to him, but he took them only briefly. For a moment she wondered at his reticence, but a more important matter needed an answer.

'Why did you let him go?' she asked, perplexed.

'What else could I do? If I called in the Runners, your abduction and my pursuit would be the talk of the town for months. There's already been more than enough scandal and I don't want any more to taint your life. This way, Glyde has his liberty, but only to spend it miserably—and you're free of him for good.'

'But if he disappears, you may not properly clear your name. People may continue to think ill of you.'

'I have his signed confession, but, in any case, I've no interest in what people think. You know the truth and that's sufficient for me.'

He smiled gently down at her and she looked once more for the warm embrace she'd been expecting ever since they left Glyde to his fate. Instead he tossed her up into the saddle of the waiting Minerva, and said, 'I'm afraid that this time you *will* have to share a horse with me!'

The mare, still tired from her earlier exertions, ambled placidly along the same lanes that she had flown down just a few hours ago. Although night had fallen and the surrounding countryside was in inky darkness, a shaft of moonlight revealed clearly the thread of packed earth that was the pathway leading back to the main Bath road.

Amelie leant back into her rescuer's arms, weary but overwhelmingly happy. Above, the clear night sky was silvered with a cascade of stars and only a breath of wind sighed through the trees as they passed on their way.

It was she who broke the calm. 'How did you know where to find me?'

'I didn't. I knew it was Glyde who'd abducted you, thanks to Fanny, but I had no means of knowing for certain which direction he'd taken. It was a hunch. I'd been told that his country estate lay nearby and I guessed that he would instinctively go to ground there once he'd got his prey.'

She shuddered. 'You talk of him as though he were a wild animal.'

'What else is he, beneath the paint and the polish?' he asked grimly.

'How clever of Fanny to recognise Glyde's men.'

'She got precious little thanks for it.' Gareth smiled reminiscently. 'Your grandmother has the devil of a temper. Do you know that?'

Amelie didn't reply.

'Like grandmother, like granddaughter, I guess.'

'Why do you say that? Is that what you thought when I failed to arrive at the Abbey? That I was angry for some reason and wanted to punish you?'

'I thought you might have regretted making the appointment.'

'But we made a promise to meet. You didn't trust me to come.'

'Of course I did,' he blustered.

'No, you didn't. You didn't trust me!' She paused. 'But then I haven't trusted you, either.'

There was a long silence between them until she said

quietly, 'Neither of us is blameless, Gareth, we've both been guilty of deceit.'

His lips brushed lightly against her soft curls. 'We've done a lot of silly things,' he murmured, 'but they're in the past. Now we can both face our futures honestly.'

She hardly noticed the odd expression as she once more nestled against his strong frame, Minerva slowly and surely carrying them towards Bath. They had been passing along a stretch of the road where the trees overhung, pressing tightly together and almost barricading the moonlight from view. Then quite abruptly the trees fell away from either side and they found themselves in clear country, with the lake before them, the moon shimmering across its surface like a lustrous ribbon. Carefully, the mare began to pick her way around the shoreline. The warm night air wrapped them in its velvet touch. All was tranquil.

But dozing in Gareth's encircling arms, Amelie suddenly became aware of a warmth dripping on to her hand. She raised her fingers slowly in the moonlight and gasped when she saw them blood-red.

'Gareth, your arm!'

In the semi-conscious state into which he'd sunk, he hardly heard her.

'Gareth, wake up. You're bleeding and badly. We must stop. We must bind up your arm immediately.'

She tugged urgently on the reins and the horse came to a halt. Slipping from the saddle, she pulled him down, trying to support his weight as he slid to the ground.

His face in the moonlight was chalk-white, but he was alert now and tried to reassure her.

'I'm pretty sure it's just a surface wound.'

'Surface wound or not, you seem to be doing a good job of bleeding to death.'

'One of your faults, Amelie, is that you're prone to exaggeration.'

'One of your faults, Gareth, is that you're prone to stubbornness.'

And with that she pulled down her silk petticoat and ripped off a large strip of soft white material. She led the way down to the lakeside and gently took off his shirt. The wound looked livid. She only hoped it hadn't already become infected. She bathed the angry weal with care and swiftly bound it up again, this time more tightly and thoroughly than Gareth had managed in the heat of conflict. With some difficulty he shrugged on the remains of his shirt.

The horse had followed them down to the lake and was now thirstily drinking the water. After a few moments they took hold of her bridle and led her back to the trees where she began placidly to crop the grass.

'She should have a rest,' Amelie said, 'and so should you. Here…' and she quickly pushed a mound of leaves together to form a bed '…lie down for a while and try to sleep.'

He protested, but only feebly. He knew that if he were to return her safely to her family, he needed to be in stronger case. A short rest could only do them both good. In a moment he was asleep while she watched over him. At length when he showed no sign of waking, she curled up beside him and slept herself, her head on his chest, the glinting curls fanned out across his body.

It was one of those curls tickling his chin, as the breeze ruffled her hair, that finally woke him. He ran his fingers through the soft tresses and kissed her gently awake. Her eyes opened and for a moment fear engulfed her as she recalled the locked and darkened room of her imprisonment. But the rustle of the leaves and the breeze on her warm cheeks steadied her racing heart.

Gareth was looking down at her tenderly. 'I have no idea how long we've been sleeping, dear child, but your grandmother must be going out of her mind with worry. It's time we were gone.'

He looked over at Minerva. 'The mare is well and truly rested. She should carry us swiftly back to town.'

Amelie stretched lazily. Her ordeal was over and the man she loved was by her side. 'I've never thanked you properly for rescuing me.'

'Thanked me? What nonsense is this?'

'You risked your life.'

'But think of the prize,' he said lightly.

'You came for me because I'm yours and always will be.' Her voice grew husky and her eyes glistened with unshed tears.

'You'll always be the one girl I've truly loved, Amelie,' he said carefully.

She felt a shiver of apprehension and sat up swiftly. 'Why does that sound like a farewell?'

'Because, my dear, it is. As soon as we reach Bath and you're reunited with your grandmother, I must be on my way. Lucas will be wondering what on earth has happened. I've my valise half-packed and ready to go.'

'You can't still mean to leave England,' she burst out.

'I must, Amelie.'

'I don't understand you,' she cried passionately. 'Why must you go? You have a confession from Glyde. Everything is changed.'

'Nothing is changed, my love. I'm still the same man with the same history—and it's not an edifying one. I'm not a proper suitor for you.'

'But you've proved Glyde a villain, you can clear your name.'

'No matter how much I may wave his confession, scandal is like to follow me wherever I go. You deserve better.'

'This is nonsense.' The alarm in her voice hurt, but he must keep to his vow for her sake.

'It's the way the world wags,' he said as calmly as he could. 'And your grandmother will know that better than anyone. She will advise you.'

'You mean in the same way she advised me about Glyde.' Amelie's tone was acid.

'She's learned a painful lesson, I think you'll find. She'll be anxious to discover a man who is good and kind and not at all like Glyde. And not like me, either—

someone whose skeletons from a misspent life will not always be threatening to reappear.'

'I don't care how many skeletons are hidden deep in your past, Gareth,' she said in a taut voice. 'They may all make an appearance if they will. I want no other man, and I intend to have no other.'

'Fighting talk,' he said, with a sad attempt at a joke.

'And why not?' she demanded. 'You've just fought for my life, but now you seem intent on denying it to me. So, yes, it is fighting talk.'

In the silver light that threaded the landscape her face was ardent with feeling and her eyes, no longer velvet soft, sparkled with indignation.

'Why am I not to be allowed to choose my own destiny?' she went on. 'Why should everyone feel they have the right to make my decisions for me? First my father, then my grandmother and now, unbelievably, you!'

In her vexation she'd moved a little away and sat facing him, her back ramrod straight and the chestnut tendrils of her hair blowing in the breeze. The torn dress had been hastily patched together, but now the cloth she'd wrapped around herself slipped from her shoulders, revealing an expanse of luminous skin, gleaming pearl-like in the moonlight. Gareth had to force himself from feasting on this radiant vision, for both his heart and his body were urging him to forget his steadfast resolve to walk away and never return.

He cast around in his mind for an argument that

would convince them both, but she was in no mood to listen.

'*I* have made my own decision,' she was saying proudly, 'and I'll allow no one to gainsay it, not even you, Gareth. When I asked you to meet me at the Abbey it was to tell you that I wanted to go away with you, that I wanted to live with you for as long as you desired me.'

Astonishment ranged across his face. Did she love him so much that she was willing to relinquish all vestige of virtue, in order to be with him?

'And I still want to,' she announced defiantly.

'But...' A vagrant part of him began to leap hungrily to life. He found his resistance crumbling, the power of her love destroying his last defence.

'No buts, I'm sick of buts,' she commanded. 'Sick of other people trying to arrange my life. You followed me to my prison and from now on I intend to follow you—wherever you go!'

'What a spitfire!' He was gathering his scattered wits. 'I see you do have your grandmother's temper.'

'I may pull caps with you from time to time,' she admitted, 'but only when you deserve it. Will you still be able to love me?'

In response he pulled her roughly into his arms, the misconceived vow consigned at a stroke to oblivion. 'Now it's your turn to hear *my* decision, my fiery one,' he whispered into her ear. 'You *will* go with me wherever I go, but with a wedding ring on your finger.'

His expression shadowed for a moment. 'If we stay in

England, it won't be easy—there'll be gossip, innuendo, even direct snubs. You'll have to learn to bear it all with an indifferent face. Do you think you can? Brave the world with me?'

'I can and I will, but I'll need kisses, endless kisses.' She sighed slyly. 'You've been particularly mean with them of late.'

He pulled her down onto their bed of leaves and searched her face lovingly.

'You're sure of this, my darling?'

'I couldn't be more sure,' she breathed and stroked the hard planes of his face as he bent over her.

His eyes were the deepest blue, dark and mysterious, and his gaze penetrated to her very heart. He gave her a long, lingering kiss and the heat of his mouth made her hungry for him. She closed her eyes, drinking in his musky scent and melting, melting into his body like warm honey as he hardened against her. Her fingers buried themselves in his dark hair and pulled him closer as his kisses became ever more urgent, covering her face, her arms, her neck, with a fierceness that left her breathless. Then, more gently, he pushed aside the tattered remnants of her bodice. Cupping the soft swell of her breasts, he brought them to his eager lips. A deep, aching pleasure shot through her body.

'I see your arm is a good deal better,' she managed to murmur.

'Don't be pert, miss, or...'

'Or?'

'Or this', and with one deft movement he rolled her

beneath him, fitting his form to hers. Slowly and thoroughly his hands began to move over her body, undressing her as he went, his mouth following where his hands led. The warm night air caressed her bare skin as it took fire beneath the heat of his lips. Gradually she began to move as he did, responding to his forceful rhythm until every fibre sang with hot pleasure. Her body ablaze, the world around her vanished into nothingness—the soft grass, the hushed lake, the clear night sky. Her world was contained only in this moment and she gave herself up to it.

Neither Brielle nor Miles Silverdale could bring themselves to eat. They sat at either end of the mahogany table, maintaining the pretence of dining while their faces, mirrored in the sheen of the wood, reflected back at them an overwhelming anxiety.

Horrocks carefully served the modest meal: soup and entrées followed by salmon, then a braised ham and a haunch of venison, and finally an assortment of pastries, jellies and creams. They sat in silence as the butler expertly brought and removed courses. But every dish was returned to the kitchen barely touched.

The dismal meal at an end, they removed to the drawing room and settled themselves in seats flanking the fireside. It was early June, but Horrocks had thought it wise to kindle a small blaze and provide a little cheer. Both had given up trying to make polite conversation and instead gazed intently into the flames, sunk in their own thoughts. Forbidding images danced in front of them, pictures of Amelie terrified and alone, at the mercy of a villain they had both championed. Older heads had not been wiser and it was their lovely girl who was paying the price.

At around ten o'clock Horrocks brought in the tea tray. They sat still silent and cradling their two cups, their eyes now forever drawn to the hands of the clock slowly turning. An hour later the door bell pealed. Miles, slumped in the brown leather chesterfield, jumped from his seat in one movement. Brielle held up her hand for silence and strained her ears. Two voices sounded from below, but she was certain one of them was Horrocks. Could it be that Gareth Wendover had returned empty-handed? She sat perched on the edge of her chair while Miles paced up and down, unable to rest.

Horrocks opened the drawing-room door and in a voice muted by disappointment announced, 'Lord Lucas Avery.' The servants, too, were keeping their own vigil below stairs.

Brielle pulled herself together sufficiently to make the necessary introductions. Their visitor looked uncomfortable, but also extremely worried.

'Please accept my apologies for this intrusion at so late an hour. Only very real anxiety for my friend's welfare could prompt me to impose on you in this way.'

'Your friend?' Brielle queried.

Lucas turned to her and in his overwrought state, the words poured out unchecked. 'I had a note from Gareth… He's staying with me, and I couldn't really make head or tail of it. Something about his having to leave Bath at short notice, but that he'd be back to collect his baggage. He was due to leave for France tomorrow.'

He paused for breath and then continued more slowly but with some awkwardness, 'He mentioned in the note that Miss Silverdale was in danger. Naturally, I've no wish to intrude on a private family matter, but he hasn't returned, and it's now many hours since he left.'

'Don't apologise, Lord Avery. As you see, we are in similar case, waiting helplessly for news.' Brielle sank down in her chair. She looked very tired and very old. 'You're most welcome to sit and wait with us.'

'But where has he gone, ma'am?'

'To find Rufus Glyde. It appears that the man we trusted—' and she included Lord Silverdale in her gesture '—is an out-and-out villain.'

'That I have always suspicioned, but your granddaughter?'

'Abducted,' she said abruptly, but her voice faltered. The young man looked horrified.

'This is the most shocking news. What can I say? But don't despair, Lady St Clair. Gareth is a resourceful man and a tough one. He's had many years shifting for himself in difficult circumstances. If anyone can help her, it will be him. Depend on it, he will bring her safely home.'

'So I hoped when I agreed to his going, but that was many hours ago. Will he even find Glyde?'

'I'm sure he will. Glyde will not travel far with an

unwilling woman in tow. His country estate is not too distant from Bath and Gareth knows its general direction.'

She refused to be comforted. 'Glyde is not alone. Amelie's maid has told us that two ruffians in his employ swooped on her mistress. Your friend is just one man. How will he fare against the brutality of such low creatures?'

'*And* Sir Rufus is a notable swordsman,' put in Lord Silverdale, still pacing the room and in despair for his daughter's safety.

'Gareth is a first-class fencer. He will be more than a match for Glyde,' Lucas said staunchly, but his heart felt leaden. He had a very good idea of the odds his friend would face. If only he'd waited. But Gareth would have refused his help, he knew. Lucas had a wife and children and the mission was dangerous, if not suicidal.

Frustrated, he suggested riding out towards Glyde's estate. 'I could try to discover news of them. At least I would be doing something useful.'

Brielle shook her head. 'I appreciate your offer, Lord Avery, but I doubt that you would learn much. You might, however, give rise to speculation. One of the reasons that persuaded me to let your friend go alone was the need to keep this whole shocking business from becoming an open scandal.'

Lord Silverdale interjected with a sombre shake of his head, 'We shall know soon enough what has happened to them, I fear.'

His words effectively silenced the trio and they sat

mutely, each encased in private thought. The hours wore on. Horrocks appeared regularly to make up the fire and offer unwanted refreshments. As the minutes ticked by, Gareth's mission looked increasingly hopeless and by the time the small hours arrived what little spirit had earlier been present had vanished entirely.

The breaking dawn, chill and grey, found the three of them dozing fitfully by the embers, unwilling to give up their watch, but knowing in their hearts that whatever news came, it could only be bad. Then a bell pealed below. A sudden noise, a flurry of voices, footsteps springing up the marble staircase, and the door flew open.

Gareth and Amelie stood framed in the doorway, tired and travel weary but with hands held fast and faces lit with gladness. Brielle started forwards and flung her arms around her granddaughter, tears streaming down her face.

'It's all right, Grandmama. I'm all right,' Amelie calmed her.

She smoothed Brielle's hair and kissed her on both cheeks and then, putting her grandmother gently aside, moved towards her father where he stood alone and forlorn. His emotions choked him and for a moment he could only cling to his daughter, silently hugging her to his chest.

'Papa, why are you here?'

'My darling, thank God you're safe. Thank God,' his voice choked again. 'Will you ever forgive me?'

'There's nothing to forgive.'

'Indeed there is. I was the one intent on forcing you into marriage with that villain. You must believe me, Amelie, I had no idea what manner of man he was. I have only just discovered the evil he has practised against our family and I came immediately to warn you. But by then he had done his worst.'

'Not quite his worst, Papa', and she turned with a radiant face to her lover. 'I have my rescuer to thank for that. Grandmama, I believe you already know Gareth, but, Papa, let me introduce you. This is Gareth Wendover.'

The name made Lucas Avery's brows twitch, but Gareth signed to him to hold his peace.

'I don't think we've met before,' Miles was saying, 'but you have my most grateful thanks for what you've done this night. How can I ever repay you?'

'I wish to marry your daughter, Lord Silverdale. To have your consent will be ample repayment.'

Miles Silverdale looked taken aback. 'That will need some discussion, young man,' he began to bluster.

'Her father means that he'll be only too pleased that she is to marry a man of such courage and principle,' Brielle interrupted, giving Miles one of her basilisk stares.

'Is that what you wish, Amelie?' he asked his daughter mildly.

'More than anything, Papa.'

'But I had such hopes for you, my dear. Mr Wendover is obviously an honourable man who deserves the highest consideration. I would not wish you to think that I'm unappreciative of what I owe him. However, marriage is another matter and I'm sure he would agree himself that you could look a lot higher for a husband.'

Once more Brielle interrupted her son-in-law. 'Miles, we have already made the most dreadful mess of Amelie's life between us. Do you not think that she knows her own mind best?'

'I do,' said Amelie firmly. 'I'm going to marry Gareth and I hope you'll be happy for me. But I shall marry him even if you're not. He is the only man I will ever want and I intend to share the rest of my life with him.'

She looked mischievously around at the gathering. 'I shall make an excellent vagabond, I'm sure!'

'There will be no need for that,' her father rejoined hastily. 'Mr Wendover may not be the husband I had in mind, but he is a man of integrity and if he is your choice, I am happy to give my blessing. But not,' he added, 'to a life of vagabondage. I'm sure that between us—' and he glanced across at Brielle '—we can start this young man in a respectable profession and provide a home for you both.'

Brielle nodded her head vigorously. 'Naturally, Mr Wendover, it will be quite unnecessary for you to resume your former life.' Gareth smiled at the thought of the inward shudder she must be suppressing.

The presence of Lucas Avery had all but been forgotten, but now he was staring at them open-mouthed as though he could hardly believe what he was hearing. Then he began to laugh, amusement bubbling up in him, mixed with relief at his friend's safe return, until it exploded in a riot of noise that rang around the room. His companions turned to him in surprise. Gradually his mirth subsided and he whisked out a handkerchief to dab the tears from his eyes.

'I'm so sorry. Forgive my merriment. But to hear you talk about setting Gareth up in a profession…!'

He had all their attention, their eyes fixed on him in enquiry. Between laughs he managed to splutter, 'I think you'll find Gareth already has a profession. Meet the new Earl of Denville.'

Lord Silverdale and Brielle looked at first astounded, then their faces flooded with relief.

'But why are you travelling in this fashion?' Miles asked him in amazement.

The whole sorry story of Glyde's villainy had to be told and the signed confession passed around. Lord Silverdale read it and reread it, shaking his head, and muttering inaudibly from time to time. Then he looked up from the sheaf of papers and spoke with determination.

'Glyde is already widely discredited and I will make sure that everyone of my acquaintance, and their acquaintance, too, is aware of this confession. *You* may have promised him silence, but I have not. If I have any influence, the tale of his infamy will soon be known to every member of the *ton*.'

Reaching out to his future son-on-law, he clutched Gareth's hand. 'It's clear that you've suffered even greater harm from this devil. No one could be more worthy of my beautiful daughter.'

'Your beautiful daughter has something to say,' Amelie interrupted bitingly. She had kept silent until this moment, her lips firmly sealed, but now she turned a furious face to Gareth.

'Were you by chance ever going to tell me who you really were?'

Conscious of the seething indignation flooding her granddaughter's lovely face, Brielle made a decision. 'It is more than time that we all had some rest,' she said briskly and moved towards the doorway with surprising speed. In an instant she had shepherded her companions out of the room.

The door had barely closed behind them before Amelie repeated her question, her tone even more imperious.

'Well, were you ever going to tell me who you were? Or perhaps it just slipped your mind that you'd inherited a title?'

'Strangely enough, it did. Or at least has done these past few weeks.'

His blue eyes sparkled with an errant sweetness. She longed to reach out and feel him close again, but steeled herself against his charm.

'How could it slip your mind? It isn't possible. You vowed there would be no more secrets between us, yet the biggest secret has remained untold. How can I ever truly believe you?'

'Amelie, my darling, you must believe me when I say that I'd pushed the Earl of Denville out of my mind. You met me as Gareth Wendover and I've loved you as he.

The Earl of Denville is as foreign to me as to you. We must both get to know him.'

For a long minute she did not speak, her eyes scanning his face intently, searching and searching again, and knew he spoke the truth. Her anger drained away. This *was* the final deception, she thought, and the first brick in the bridge of trust they would build together.

He was by her side and looking directly into her eyes, wrapping her in stardust. She felt a wild, dancing joy surge headlong through her. His arms were back where they belonged, his lips close.

'I love you, Amelie Silverdale,' he whispered.

'I love you too, Gareth Wendover,' she replied.

* * * * *

THE RETURN OF LORD CONISTONE

LUCY ASHFORD

Lucy Ashford, an English Studies lecturer, has always loved literature and history, and from childhood one of her favourite occupations has been to immerse herself in historical romances. She studied English with history at Nottingham University, and the Regency is her favourite period.

Lucy has written several historical novels, but this is only her second for Mills & Boon. She lives with her husband in an old stone cottage in the Peak District, near to beautiful Chatsworth House and Haddon Hall, all of which give her a taste of the magic of life in a bygone age. Her garden enjoys spectacular views over the Derbyshire hills, where she loves to roam and let her imagination go to work on her latest story.

You can contact Lucy via her website—www.lucyashford.com.

For my alpha male, AJR—
who not only helped with the research,
but also provided endless cups of tea

Prologue

May 1810—Portugal

His four men huddled round a meagre fire and played cards for *escudos*. But Lucas Conistone stood apart, his hooded grey eyes scanning the peaks like a hawk's as the fiery sun set over the mountains, the iron wind tugging at his tousled black hair and his travel-worn clothes.

Here, he'd been told. Here was the meeting place. If it was a trap, he was ready. His hand went to the pistol in his pocket and softly caressed the cold metal.

And then he turned round quickly, and his men also were on their feet, because someone was hurrying along the rocky path to this isolated mountain pass, a silhouette against the blood-red sun.

Lucas gestured to his men to sit again as he recognised the small, sinewy figure coming straight for him. '*Como vai*, Miguel?' he said softly in fluent Portuguese. 'I hear you have news.'

The man called Miguel grasped his hand, his dark head barely up to Lucas's powerful shoulder, and said in the accent of the Portuguese mountain people, 'News, yes, *meu amigo*. The body of the Englishman has been found at last.'

After nearly a year and a half of searching. 'Where?'

'He must have been swept downstream by the flood waters of the River Vouga. His body was trapped under rocks, and rotted in the water as the months went by—a suitable end, *nao*? And—this was found on him.' Miguel handed Lucas a small package; something saved, miraculously, from the water by the oilskin in which it was tightly wrapped.

Swiftly Lucas tore the package open.

A compact, leather-bound journal. And the first entry was dated—September 1808.

No. He wanted to shout his protest across the mountains. No. Where was the old one, the previous one?

He flicked through it—two, three pages only, of hurried notes. The rest was blank. A blow indeed.

Wild Jack, I have followed you to hell and back for this.

Curtly he held out silver coins to the man Miguel. 'Where is the body now?'

'We buried what was left of it, *Inglês*. For the spies of Napoleon Bonaparte are on the trail.' He looked up at Lucas slyly. 'And they offer our people rewards also.'

Lucas clenched his teeth. 'And what exactly have your people told them, Miguel?'

The man gave a crooked smile. 'Why, we babbled of treasure. The old, old legend of gold buried somewhere in the steep hills high above Coimbra. Isn't that, after all, what the English traveller you call Wild Jack died for?'

Let the French believe that, thought Lucas swiftly. *Let the Portuguese, like Miguel, believe it.* He was scanning the diary's sparse contents: ramblings of a sea voyage from

England, of a swift ascent into the mountains. The writings of a man knowing he was being pursued, and that the end was near…

Already he was turning to his waiting men. 'Get your things together. We're heading homewards.' They moved instantly to roll up their thin blankets and tie them to their packs.

But the man Miguel pointed suddenly at the blood that stained Lucas's shirt, all too visible where his long coat had fallen open. 'You have been wounded, *Inglês*. Stay with us in the mountains for one night at least! We have food we can share.' Miguel's black eyes gleamed mischievously. 'And our girls—pretty girls, eh?—will be only too happy to make a man as handsome as you forget the perils of war!'

'*Obrigado*, *meu amigo*, but it's nothing.' Grimly Lucas pulled at his coat to hide the bloodstain.

'An ambush?'

'Of sorts. We had a run in with some French outriders on our way up here.'

'Did they live to tell the tale?'

Lucas was already turning to go, but he swung round one last time. 'What do you think?'

Miguel grinned. 'They did not. You'll be back soon with the key to the treasure, *Inglês*?'

'I hope so,' Lucas breathed. 'For if others get it first, we are lost indeed.'

So Lucas Conistone and his companions set off down the barren slope, each of them as lithe and hard-muscled as any of the Portuguese who herded goats on the sparse spring grass of these high mountains. Lucas's men were intent on their route, sometimes cursing softly under their breath at the difficulty of the terrain.

But their leader was thinking of another time. Another place.

Of the Hampshire countryside in early autumn. Of the English sun, warming a flower-scented garden whose acres of lawns swept down to the cliff's edge, where the azure sea gleamed far below. Of a time when he'd thought he'd found love, and a purpose to his life.

But then the vision was gone, the dream over. And he was back in this foreign land, clambering down a treacherous path in the knife-sharp night air, with an almost impossible task facing him.

He was remembering, too, the last words spoken by a man about to die. *Look after her for me, will you, Lucas? Tell her I did it for Wycherley. For all of them... For God's sake, look after Verena.*

Chapter One

Early July 1810—Wycherley, Hampshire

'They are ruined, you know,' whispered the malicious female voice, 'quite ruined! But, my dears, what can you expect, with four daughters and a father who was hardly ever here?'

Verena Sheldon froze, hidden from the three gossiping old busybodies by an ornate lacquered screen to which she was tying a label. *'Three guineas,'* the label read. *'Or nearest offer.'*

Like everything else in Wycherley's great hall, it was for sale. Like everything else—herself and her family included, it seemed—it was up for inspection, assessment and—condemnation.

During all this hot July day, neighbours, dealers from Chichester, and local businessmen with their wives and families had rolled up Wycherley's long drive in carriages or on horseback. Some had also brought servants with open drays ready to cart their purchases away. Every hour Verena had seen the precious memories of her past and all her hopes for the future slipping away.

She put her hands to her burning cheeks as the vicious whispering went on.

'Such a *foolish* woman, that Lady Frances,' continued the rancid female voice. 'And the way she's brought up all those daughters of hers, with *such* airs and graces! Why, my dears—' a cackling sound followed '—to *think* that only a short while ago her ladyship was boasting that her eldest was being courted by the Earl of Stancliffe's heir! One would laugh, if it weren't all so pitiable! *Oh…*'

She trailed off as Verena Sheldon marched out from her place of unintended concealment, her amber-coloured eyes flashing fire.

'Good afternoon, ladies!' She squarely faced the Chichester tabbies. 'Do you know, I somehow expected you would be here! Mrs Marsham, how did your daughter's London Season go? Plenty of suitors—well, of *course*—and she's engaged to…? Oh, I see, no one suitable yet, well, never mind… Do, pray, enjoy the rest of your spying—I'm sorry, *buying*!'

The gossiping trio went off rather hastily, muttering. But everyone else continued to prowl round the hall, poking and prodding at the furniture, paintings and ornaments that had all been an integral part of Wycherley, her beloved home.

Verena found to her dismay that a great lump had risen in her throat. The vultures were everywhere. She even saw, through the crowds, one bold, shabbily dressed fellow with spiky black hair pulling out the drawers of an old walnut cabinet and bending to peer into the empty recesses. Really! Indignation welling again, she started pushing through the crowds towards him, but was distracted anew by the sight of a couple of porters going by with a delicate inlaid table. 'No!' she blurted out. 'My father's chess table—'

Her brother-in-law David Parker, who owned a farm that adjoined the coast road to Framlington, was quickly at her side. He'd been helping all day, and now she clutched at his arm. 'David, we cannot let that go!'

'We have to sell as much as possible before the bailiffs move in, I'm afraid, Verena. And it has been sold for the asking price,' David said gravely.

The man who was buying the table—a dealer—broke in. 'Which is more than you'll get for this pair of Chinese vases just here!' He was picking one up, to weigh it casually in his hand. 'No more Chinese than I am, I'd say!' He turned to David. 'I'll give you a guinea for the pair on top of the three guineas for the table, and that's being generous.'

David hesitated, glanced at Verena, then nodded. The dealer hurried off to gather more booty.

Verena bit her lip. *I won't cry. When I heard about Lucas, I vowed that I would never, ever cry again.*

Once the contents were sold, the house would have to go too. Mr Mayhew, the family's attorney, had told her that. Kind Mr Mayhew was here now, collecting payments at a desk by the door and issuing receipts. Earlier he'd taken Verena aside and said, 'You do realise, don't you, Miss Sheldon, that there is actually a potential buyer for the whole estate?'

'The Earl. Yes.' Her voice, miraculously, was steady. 'And I had rather it went to anyone else!'

Mr Mayhew had glanced at her over his spectacles and sighed. 'Very well. Very well… But take my advice, my dear Miss Sheldon, and don't make this harder than it needs to be. No need for you to attend the dispersal sale; your brother-in-law Mr Parker and I will manage the business perfectly well, I do assure you.'

But Verena believed that *someone* had to represent their family! Her one sensible sister, Pippa, married to David, was at home looking after their twin baby boys. Verena's other sisters, Deb and Isobel, were up in their bedrooms, and both of them, like their mother Lady Frances, were loudly lamenting the collapse of their family fortunes—about as useful as leaking buckets, the three of them.

Lady Frances had tackled Verena before the sale began. 'Verena, there will be *gentlemen* here this afternoon! Some of them with prospects!' She'd glanced waspishly at Verena's day gown of brown cambric, its only adornment the tiny mother-of-pearl buttons running firmly up the bodice to her throat. 'Now, I know that your looks bear no comparison to Deb's or darling Izzy's—but if you do insist on being present, you might make *some* effort with your appearance! After all, your godfather is none other than the Earl of Stancliffe!'

'And much good that has done us!' Verena had snapped, her patience worn to a thread.

Lady Frances had retreated upstairs with her smelling salts.

Verena made a point of not changing her drab gown, and of only carelessly pinning up her chestnut-coloured hair before facing the seemingly endless onslaught of strangers cascading through the house.

And she had thought she would be able to bear it. But suddenly the plaintive tune of 'My Soldier Love' drifted across the crowded hall, and the emotions she'd tried so very hard to suppress came sweeping back in a wave of blinding memory.

That was her music box.

She'd put it in the sale herself, but…

She remembered Lucas, riding along the track towards her that golden autumn nearly two years ago; his body toughened by war, but his expression softening in glad surprise when he saw her.

Herself, twenty years old, stumbling towards him, her heart racing, yet full of joy, blurting out, 'Lucas. You're safe. I was so afraid…'

He'd laughed as he sprang down from his big grey mare. 'I'm untouchable,' he'd said. 'The bullets just fly past me.'

She would not cry for him ever again. But that little silver music box was his last gift to her.

She started to plunge through the crowds to where a corn merchant and his wife were greedily pawing over its delicate casing.

Then she stopped; remembering what David had said. *We have to sell as much as possible, before the bailiffs move in…*

Best to let it go, along with her memories. She turned round slowly and walked out through the open French doors into the west-facing gardens, where the sun was sending rays of gold across the sea below the cliff tops, and the scent of roses wafted towards her on the warm evening breeze.

With its mellow brickwork clad in ivy and climbing roses, Wycherley Hall was one of the most picturesque dwellings between the South Downs and the Hampshire coast, and had belonged to the Sheldons for generations. But now, her family would have to leave, and go—where? What would they do? How would they live? There was no answer except the sad cries of the gulls high above.

Last winter there had been troops posted all along this part of the coast, because of rumours that the Emperor Napoleon was sending an invasion fleet across the Channel. Now the troops were gone. But just sometimes lately, when she was alone, she felt as if she was being watched, though she told herself it was nothing but the rustling of birds, or small animals in the nearby woods. She was growing fanciful in her despair.

The dark clouds were piling up to the south, and though the sun was going down, the air seemed hotter, more sultry than ever. Verena turned, heavy-hearted, to go back into the house.

Lucas had once told her that it was the happiest house he had ever known. 'I'll carry my memory of you and Wycherley wherever I go, Verena,' he'd said to her quietly. 'Whatever you hear, please trust in me.'

And she had. More fool her.

'Verena!' A man's voice broke abruptly into her reverie. 'What on earth's going on here? All those people—taking your furniture, your things…'

She swung round to see the scarlet-jacketed Captain Martin Bryant, twenty-six-year-old war hero, marching towards her from the stable courtyard where he'd just sprung off his horse. She drew a deep breath. 'I'm afraid we are quite done up, as they say, Captain Bryant. This is just the start.'

Martin, with his pleasantly boyish features and brown curls, looked horrified. 'But—you won't have to leave the *house*?'

She nodded, feeling a sudden constriction in her throat.

'My dear Miss Sheldon!' His light blue eyes were ardent. 'May I call you Verena? I am, first and foremost, a man devoted to my military duties—duties that have too often taken me away from here!' He was stammering a little; his face had turned slightly pink. 'Otherwise, I would have asked you before.'

Oh, Lord. What was he talking about? Verena's heart was beginning to thump. 'Captain Bryant, I really should be getting back inside…'

He grasped her hand and clung to it almost desperately. 'Verena. I want to ask you—I must beg of you the honour—the precious gift—of your sweet and lovely hand in marriage!'

She snatched her hand away and stood, frozen with shock.

Once, almost two years ago, she had walked with Lucas through these gardens, as the shadows lengthened, and the harvest moon encrusted the old house with fairytale shards of silver. Once Lucas had cupped her face in his strong but tender hands and breathed, 'Some day I'll be home again, Verena. Home for good. Will you wait for me?'

There was no need even for him to ask, because she'd not been able to imagine life without him. Hadn't *wanted* life without him. 'For ever,' she'd breathed, with the ardent belief of a twenty-year-old. 'For ever, Lucas.'

'Captain Bryant,' she said steadily, though the ache at the back of her throat threatened to choke her, 'I'm sorry, but I cannot marry you. It wouldn't be fair to you, you see, because I do not love you!'

His expression was imploring. 'But perhaps you can grow to love me, in time!'

Again, she hesitated. Everyone would tell her that life as Captain Bryant's wife would surely be preferable to employment as a governess, trapped in a dreary half-world between family and servants. Indeed, that was a prospect that filled her with dread.

'I'm not rich,' Captain Bryant was going on, 'but believe me, I will do *anything*, my dear Verena, to provide you with the life you deserve! Your family also!' he added hastily.

That, at last, made Verena smile just a little, and eased the pain that was squeezing her wretched heart. '*All* my family?' she teased gently. 'You don't know what you're saying, Captain Bryant. We are really quite a frightening prospect, I do assure you!'

'I don't care!' he declared defiantly. 'I don't care!'

He lunged towards her. She desperately sprang away from his outstretched arms—and felt the shoulder of the gown her mother so despised being firmly hooked by the sturdy thorn of the clambering pink rose shrub that grew by the back wall. She pulled herself away violently; the serviceable fabric held, but she felt, then heard, some of the tiny mother-of-pearl buttons that fastened her bodice at the front snap off with an alarming ping, their threads weakened by age. *Oh, no…*

She flung her hands across her breasts, but too late; Martin was staring, transfixed.

Verena, as even her mother reluctantly acknowledged, was slender but full-bosomed. And her gaping and shabby gown could no longer conceal that underneath it she wore something that could not be more different—an exquisite cream-silk chemise, scalloped and embroidered at the edges, low enough to reveal the full curve of her breasts. It was her one piece of finery. The one relic of the beautiful garments she had started to acquire when her future was full of hope.

In utter mortification she tried to tug her gown back across her bosom, making use of the few buttons that remained. But that dratted rose briar had left a thorn in her sleeve, and it pricked her every time she moved. 'Ouch! *Botheration!*' she gasped. Her long chestnut hair was starting to fall from its pins.

Martin Bryant, still wide-eyed, jumped to the rescue. 'Here! Let me help you!'

'No!' She almost smacked him away, like a troublesome fly. But he persevered, drawing close to tackle the offending thorn; and things took a turn for the worse, because her efforts to escape from Martin meant that the bodice of her gown slipped apart again, and now she heard the sound of male voices and hoofbeats drawing exceedingly close; and just as she was frantically struggling to push Martin off, two horsemen rode into the yard.

And stopped.

Martin swung round angrily to face them. Verena, hot and dishevelled, had flung her arms across her silk-draped bosom. Already the first of the riders, dark-haired and clad in a long grey riding coat and polished boots, was dismounting with a lazy sort of grace to stand, wide-shouldered and imposing, at the head of his big roan mare.

She froze. She tried to speak, but the words would not come out.

The tall newcomer turned to his companion, who was also dismounting, and said languidly, 'Hold the horses, Alec, will you?' The fading beams of the setting sun drifted over his aristocratic face and figure, highlighting the slightly overlong thick black hair; the cold dark eyes with those deceptively hooded lids, the sharply defined, almost over-handsome features.

Oh, no. Please God, no.

What must he think? And why should she care any more?

She cared because this was Viscount Conistone, grandson and heir to her family's enemy, the Earl of Stancliffe. This was Lucas. The man to whom she had, almost two years ago, given her heart, only to have it smashed into a thousand pieces.

Chapter Two

Lucas Conistone's first impulse had been to knock the foolish fellow he'd seen mauling Verena Sheldon to hell and back; his next, to crush her full and passionate lips beneath his own. Dear God, Alec was right. He was an utter fool to have come here. That gown. The glimpse he'd got, of those sweet, full breasts… And his memory had not played him false; her heart-shaped face was still as exquisite as ever. Yes, her chestnut-coloured hair had slipped from its pins in some disarray; but only to fall in utterly tantalising curls round her neck and throat. Her smooth, creamy skin was still flawless, and her almond-shaped eyes were just as he remembered, amber in some lights, gold in others…

The army fellow was about to say something, but Verena Sheldon spoke first. 'My lord!' She tilted her chin in unspoken defiance. 'Some warning of your arrival would not have gone amiss. You were not—expected!'

Not invited. Not *wanted*, anywhere near Wycherley, she might as well have declared. Her arms were still folded tightly across her breasts as her eyes burned darkly up at him. *She had lost weight. There were shadows beneath those beautiful eyes, as if she had been grieving...* What the deuce had been going on here just now?

'Alec and I were just passing,' Lucas said expressionlessly, 'on our way to Stancliffe Manor.' He was pulling off his riding gloves and thrusting them into his deep pockets. 'As my grandfather's still in Bath, I promised him I'd visit the house to see that all was well. But then we saw the carriages. And decided to—investigate.'

'Oh, you mean the *sale*!' Her amber-gold eyes were wide and innocent. She even endeavoured to smile. 'Yes, it really is *so* entertaining! We thought we'd have a clear out—one gets bored, Lord Conistone, with the same old pieces of furniture—'

Gammon. Lucas cut in, 'I heard from your attorney that you're selling Wycherley, Verena.'

He saw the colour draining from her face. She whispered, 'You have no right to discuss our family's affairs with anyone! No right at all, do you hear?'

A warning glance from his very good friend Captain Stewart, resplendent in the blue of the Light Dragoons, flashed Lucas's way. *I told you, Lucas, that this was a bad idea...*

The young army fellow nearby stepped forward like an angry turkeycock. 'You heard what Verena—Miss Sheldon—said, Lord Conistone! I think you would be doing her an enormous favour if you and your friend left immediately!'

Lucas let his gaze rake his bright uniform. Then he blinked. 'I'm sorry? Have I had the pleasure?'

'I am Captain Bryant, of the 11th Regiment of Foot!'

'My congratulations,' drawled Lucas. 'No doubt your duties call. Off you run, now, Captain, there's a good fellow.'

Some spluttering ensued, and a further reddening of

those already pink cheeks. 'Don't you give orders to me, you—you—'

'Let's call it a polite suggestion, shall we?' said Lucas softly. 'After all, we're not on the army parade ground now, are we?'

'So you actually *remember* the parade ground, do you?' retorted Martin Bryant bitterly. 'My God, you got out of the army just about as quickly as you could, didn't you, Conistone? Before the bullets flew too close?'

'Martin!' cried Verena.

Alec Stewart, at Lucas's side, had taken a step forwards, muttering, 'Too far, that, Lucas. Pray, let *me* sort the blackguard!'

But Lucas stopped him with a calm, restraining hand, and said directly to Martin, 'Perhaps I left the army because I became weary of idiots like *you*.'

Martin lunged. Verena let out a low cry. Alec Stewart was swearing. But Lucas had already moved swiftly to one side, and his right fist flew. Martin staggered, then pulled himself up dazedly, wiping at the blood on his lip. 'Damn you, Conistone!'

Lucas towered over him, powerful shoulders still braced, his eyes hard as iron. He said curtly, 'That was just a warning, Bryant. Stop being a damned idiot. You'd best go and clean yourself up, before someone—and I assure you it won't be *me*—receives a more serious injury.'

Still Martin hesitated. 'Captain Bryant,' Verena pleaded. 'Do as he says. *Please*.'

'I'm not leaving you alone with—'

'Lord Conistone and his friend are going,' interrupted Verena quietly, wretchedly. '*Now*.'

Alec said tersely to Lucas, 'I'll get someone to see to our horses. Then—I think you'll now agree—we'd best be on our way.'

Martin Bryant had already hurried off, holding a handkerchief to his bleeding lip after shooting a look of hatred at Lucas. Alec turned to Verena, saying, 'Do you still have your man Turley, Miss Sheldon? The horses need water and I must adjust my mare's curb chain. Then we can ride on.'

She was fighting back the bitter mortification. What could she do? What could she *say*, that would not make things a thousand times worse than they were already?

Nothing, except speed their exit.

'I will find Turley for you, Captain Stewart!' she said. 'We wouldn't want you—*detained* for any longer than necessary!'

Alec hesitated. 'Very well. I'll take the horses to the stables, if I may?'

She nodded and turned for the house.

But she was too late. As Alec disappeared, a strong hand stretched out, almost casually, to grip her. 'Wait,' Lucas commanded.

This was—*intolerable*. Her whole body trembled with rage. With shock. With the longing—the *treacherous* longing—to be in his arms again, to feel his body pressed against hers, his warm lips caressing her skin…

Harlot. Fortune-hunting harlot, that letter had said. She spoke in a tight voice, staring into the distance. 'Will you please let go of me, my lord?'

'Oh, Verena,' Lucas said tiredly. He had turned her to face him. She would not, she *would not* meet his eyes! But his long coat had fallen open, so she could see all too clearly how his cream shirt moulded itself to his powerful shoulders and chest, against which he had once cradled her so close that she could hear his heart beating…

'Turley,' she said blindly, 'I must fetch Turley.'

'Alec will sort all that.' Lucas Conistone's voice was

harder now. 'Deuce take it, Verena, if you're in difficulties of some kind, why didn't you ask me for assistance? Why didn't you write?'

'Oh, pray forgive me, my lord!' Her eyes flashed up to his now. 'But, absurd as it seems, I did not once think, "Dear me, we are in trouble, I must ask Viscount Conistone for help!"'

He had always been stunningly handsome. But now there was something different, a dangerous cold light in those inscrutable grey eyes. Only perhaps it had always been there, and she'd been too much of a lovesick fool to see it.

He said in a quiet voice, 'I suppose I cannot blame you if you have come to hate me.'

She swallowed hard, suddenly aware that the air out here was oppressive with heat. As the shadows deepened, she heard a rumble of ominous thunder. And his eyes were already as dark as night. 'Hate you?' she replied, summoning false brightness. 'No such powerful emotion, my lord; you see, the thought of you simply never crossed my mind! Though, may I say, I do not *warm* to your idea of arriving here, unannounced, to gloat over our misfortune.'

'Verena. Stop it. *Stop it*,' he grated out, so savagely that she flinched. Then he raked his hand through his dark hair and said, almost tonelessly, 'I'm sorry if I ever gave you cause to think that I might find your plight—amusing.'

His hands. His long, beautifully shaped fingers. The way he used to caress her... 'No apology needed, my lord!' Somehow she managed to keep a smile fixed to her lips. 'You see, you never gave me any cause to think of you at all!'

She turned resolutely back to the house; but again he caught her, swinging her round to face him. 'Verena.' His voice was almost a growl. 'Wait. Please, I beg you. You *must* speak with me.'

She stood, unable to ignore the pressure of those warm fingers on her shoulders—a pressure that cruelly awakened feelings she'd thought long since dead. 'What is there to say?' she whispered. The thunder rolled nearer. A heavy drop of rain splashed on the ground by her feet.

'Verena,' he murmured, his fingers tracing tiny circles on her bare skin just above her collarbone—oh, no, she could feel her pulse racing at his merest touch. 'You haven't really forgotten me, Verena. You *can't* have…'

She jerked herself away from his treacherous hand and crossed her arms over her bosom. Dear God. Less than two years ago this man had walked out of her life, leaving her utterly bereft, and a target for the sneers of the whole county. Now he was here again. Why? She said with passionate defiance, 'I have succeeded in forgetting you completely, my lord! And as for your sympathy—I can live without it, I do assure you!'

'I was hoping to offer more practical help,' Lucas Conistone said flatly. He looked up at the dark clouds, and a flash of lightning suddenly illuminated the hard line of his jaw. 'Perhaps we could go inside and talk?'

'Inside? The *house*?' She looked as though he'd suggested they torch the place. 'But—my mother is in there! Deb is in there!'

'Deb?' Lucas repeated the name almost blankly. Then he remembered that Deb was one of her three younger sisters, the foolish blonde one, the one he had least time for. He frowned. 'Of what account, pray, is she?'

And Verena's face, where before it had been anguished, was frozen into first shock, then shuttered coldness. 'Oh, Lucas,' she whispered. 'Enough of this. I never expected to see you again. I never *wanted* to see you again. Please. Just go.'

So that was it, thought Lucas bleakly. She hated him.

Just as well, he reminded himself. Yet she was so beautiful, with her hair tumbling now to her shoulders. And as for that damned gown, what buttons were left were barely managing to contain her luscious breasts; dear God, his blood surged with wanting her… Grimly he fought down his arousal. 'Verena,' he said. 'Verena, at least tell me why you are on the brink of losing your home.'

She stared. 'Are you really going to pretend you don't know? But of course, our activities are of no account in the kind of circles you move in…' She gave a brittle laugh, but could not disguise the pain in her eyes. 'It's really quite simple, my lord. All our creditors have withdrawn their loans. And as the house is mortgaged, we must sell—everything.'

'Everything?' he echoed harshly. 'Have you put *everything* up for sale?'

She gave a little shrug, then her fingers flew instinctively to secure her gown. 'All that my family can survive without, yes. Furniture, paintings—the dealers have been through the house room by room.'

He drew a sharp breath. *Here goes.* 'You might have other items of value, without realising it,' he said quickly. 'Have you thought of that?'

She looked shaken. 'Such as?'

'Such as your father's personal possessions. Some people would pay good money for things you consider almost worthless. His papers, for example.'

'His *papers*?'

He'd taken her by surprise, he could see. Her bewildered eyes—amber-gold eyes, dark-lashed, beautiful—met his again in shock.

'Yes,' he went on swiftly. 'All his records of his travels abroad. Letters. Maps, perhaps. And—he kept some kind of diary, didn't he?'

'Yes, oh, yes,' she whispered, 'he was always writing, about *everything*. But who would pay for such trifles?'

'I can think of several people. In London, for example, there are Portuguese exiles from the war, rich men who would dearly love any descriptive mementoes of their homeland.' *You liar, Conistone*, he rebuked himself bitterly. *You deceiver.*

She jerked her head up, her eyes over-bright. 'Then I'm sorry, my lord, to have to inform you that, firstly, I would never dream of parting with my father's private letters to me. And, secondly, he always kept his diary with him.'

That was true, thought Lucas grimly. His *latest* diary. But… 'What about his older diaries? Weren't there any he'd completed, and left here?'

'No! And if he did, I would never, *ever* sell them!' Her voice trembled, then recovered. 'Excuse me, my lord, but I find your pretended—*interest* in our plight nothing short of humiliating!'

She tossed back her head in defiance, just as she used to; the gesture afforded him yet another glimpse of those creamy-smooth breasts. His anger boiled. Damn it, had that fellow Bryant really been *kissing* her? The thought of it tipped him over the edge; desire lurched at his groin as she struggled to cover herself. That was the kind of trick used by whores in London.

And she was daring to play high and mighty with *him*?

'Humiliating?' he grated. 'You speak of—*humiliation*, when, good God, the moment I arrived, you were outrageously flirting with that witless army boor?'

Her eyes flew up to clash with his. 'I was not flirting! And do not speak of him like that!'

'I'll speak of him exactly as I like! What is that man doing here? Why isn't he with his regiment?'

'You may as well ask the same of your friend Captain Stewart!' Verena cried. 'For his—*reputation* leaves a deal to be desired!' It was true; she knew it was a long-standing joke that Alec Stewart, a year or so younger than Lucas, spent a good deal more effort on hunting heiresses than he did on hunting the French. 'Besides,' she went on furiously, 'Captain Bryant is *not* a boor, he is our friend! He was injured at Talavera, and his wound is not yet completely healed. So he makes himself *useful*. He helps the Revenue men watch this part of the coast for smugglers and—French spies!'

She saw him almost sneer. 'French spies? Things *have* been busy at Wycherley.'

'Meaning?' she snapped.

'I also heard that four weeks ago there was a burglary here.'

She went very still. 'How do you—?'

'Gossip travels.'

She seemed to sag. 'Yes,' she whispered. 'I, of all people, should know that…' Her voice faltered, then recovered again. 'Indeed, there *was* evidence of an intruder. But—' again, that toss of the head '—nothing at all was taken, my lord! And even if it had been, what business is it of yours? Besides, Captain Bryant himself has offered us his protection.'

'Protection!' Now his scorn was rampant. 'That spineless fellow couldn't fight off a damned flea.'

Her eyes whipped up to his, flashing with defiance. The rain was starting to fall all around them in the courtyard, the thunder rumbling; she had to raise her voice to be heard.

'You are wrong, quite wrong! Captain Bryant is not spineless! And—and he has asked me to marry him!'

He found himself horrified. Furious. 'My God. You will not do so?'

'Why not?' she declared bitterly. 'Does anyone have a prior claim?'

Damn it, me. I do. He wanted to crush her in his arms, and feel those sweet, full breasts against his chest. Wanted to drown his aching arousal in the slender lushness of her body. He wanted…

Look after her for me, will you, Lucas?

The words that haunted him, every minute, every day. His mouth set grimly. Easier to let her continue to hate him. Though—utterly abominable for him.

But Bryant—her *suitor*? 'Very well,' he said in an iron-hard voice. 'Very well. I can see, Miss Sheldon, that your troubles are overwhelming. I can see the lure of any port in a storm.'

Her eyes blazed. She tilted her chin. 'Lord Conistone. I would be obliged if you would leave our home this instant. *Now.*'

'Oh, I'm going,' he said. 'But before I leave, I thought you might want this back.' He reached into the inside deep pocket of his coat. And pulled out—the little silver music box.

She gazed at him in utter disbelief.

'I saw someone leaving with it.' He shrugged. 'I gave him twice what he'd paid in the sale. Sell it again if you wish. But this time—' and his lip curled '—ask more for it. You shouldn't find it difficult. You're on the way to becoming a mercenary creature, Miss Sheldon.'

And Verena felt that her heart was breaking anew as she took the box in hands that were as numb as her heart.

Her despairing eyes flew up to his. Dear God. He was still—*Lucas*. But he despised her.

Perhaps he always had. And now, she'd as good as told him she might accept Martin as a suitor… 'Lucas!'

'Yes?'

'I—I never believed you were a coward, Lucas,' she whispered. 'Never that!'

The falling rain intensified every feature of his starkly masculine face. 'Ah. Playing hot and cold with me now, are you, Miss Sheldon?' he said softly. Suddenly he cupped her chin with one strong hand. 'Hoping, perhaps, that if your gallant Captain realises he has a rival, he might rush you to the altar?'

She gasped with fresh pain. 'That is *despicable*—'

Before she could say more, Lucas had pulled her close. She felt the light caress of his hands on her back; then he touched her scalloped silk chemise, her half-exposed breasts, running one tantalising thumb over her tightening nipple so she arched yearningly, helplessly towards him.

'I can see for myself,' Lucas Conistone grated, 'that as well as selling your house's contents to the highest bidder, you're also selling yourself. A pity that the best offer you can get is from an utter nonentity like Martin Bryant.'

For a moment she was too frozen even to move. Too numb even to *hate* him as she should. Then she pushed him away and ran inside, still clutching the little music box, as her life fell to pieces around her.

Lucas stood very still as he watched her disappear into the house. Desire, frustration and black despair surged through every muscle of his powerful body.

Parting after that sweet autumn almost two years ago was for the best, he told himself bitterly as he walked slowly in the direction of the stables. *It was the only thing to do. You knew that.*

And yet he hadn't expected to still want her so badly. Hadn't expected her to be so damned beautiful. And he hadn't expected her to look up at him with those wide, beautiful eyes, as if he were the devil himself.

Who could blame her? He'd lied to her. Deceived her.

His visit to Wycherley had not been a matter of chance, far from it. Five days ago in London he'd seen the notice in the newspapers of the Sheldon family's dispersal sale. And then he'd heard of the attempted burglary.

His good friend Captain Alec Stewart, in London also, had tried to warn him. 'For God's sake, man. She's no fool. Why all this "passing by" pretence? Can't you trust her with the truth?'

'The truth?' Lucas answered sharply. 'How much of it—how little of it will she be able to bear? And why should I expect her to believe a word I say?'

Well, he'd lied to her and achieved—nothing.

Lucas Conistone was aware of the occasional whispers that he had left the army because he had no stomach for war. But most people gave no thought to his resignation. The fact that, since his father's early death ten years ago, he was heir to his grandfather's earldom, with all the responsibilities that entailed, meant that many people had thought him irresponsible to have joined the army in the first place.

Verena clearly thought otherwise. He just hadn't expected her to actually *despise* him.

Now Alec was approaching from the stableyard, with the reins of both their horses in his hand. 'Everything's sorted, Lucas—horses watered, curb chain fixed—but other than that,' commented Alec drily, 'I'm saying nothing. Nothing at all.'

Lucas took the reins from him. 'I know,' he said tersely. 'You told me. I'm not welcome here, and I should have realised it. I'll go on to wait for Bentinck, at the place and time we arranged, and you—will you set off back to Portugal?'

Alec, already mounting his horse, nodded. 'Portsmouth

first, then Lisbon—I should be back there in ten days. Any messages?'

'Yes. Let them know in Portugal, Alec, that I still believe what I'm looking for could be here.'

'At Wycherley?' Alec's face creased in doubt.

'At Wycherley,' Lucas emphasised.

And it was true—he did.

The diary. A year and a half ago, Lucas had followed Wild Jack across the mountains in hopes of getting that diary. Thought he'd seen Jack clutching it, as he faced death.

But now the body had been found, the diary with it—*and it was the wrong one.* Which meant that what Lucas really wanted must be here, somewhere, at Wycherley…

And he cursed the fate that had brought him here.

'The girl will have nothing to do with you,' Alec warned as he started gathering up his reins.

'There are other ways.'

Alec's pleasant eyes narrowed just a little. He said quietly, 'In that case, I'm glad, for her sake, that she's over you.'

Lucas watched him ride off towards the Chichester road before mounting his own horse. Alec was right. But for her to throw herself away on *Bryant…*

Something inside him twisted like a knife as he remembered the Verena he'd known. She'd been young and beautiful, and full of hope and, yes, love, for him. And he'd thought, *this is the one…*

But now, she hated him. And, by God, it was as well.

Chapter Three

Swiftly Verena, up in her bedchamber, pulled on an old cotton shift instead of the silk chemise, and then over it a shabby print gown, which did an excellent job of disguising her full breasts and narrow waist. Not even Lucas could accuse her of playing the whore in this.

She pulled it up viciously high at the neck, then, turning to her looking-glass, began to tug a comb through her rippling chestnut curls, which were damp from the rain. She stopped and gazed at herself. Her eyes were still bright with emotion, her skin still tingled from Lucas's insultingly casual caress.

Meu amor. My love. That was what he had once breathed to her. One of his many damnable lies.

She pulled on a shawl and hurried to knock on the door of a nearby room. No answer—but she thought she heard the sound of sobbing. 'Deb. Deb? It's me—Verena.' She pushed the door open, and saw her sister sitting on the edge of the bed, her head bowed. When Deb looked up, her blue eyes were brimming with tears.

Verena quickly shut the door. 'Oh, Deb!' she cried, and rushed to embrace her, but Deb shrank away.

'Why didn't you tell me he was coming?' she whispered. 'I will not, I will not face him!'

Dear God. Had her sister observed that insult of a caress? 'Did you—did you see him out there?'

'No, but Izzy told me! She saw him and his friend Captain Stewart riding up the drive, and was full of it…'

Be grateful for small mercies. Verena drew a deep breath and sat down beside her. It had been the final blow—almost laughable, really, were it not so cruel—to find out that less than one year ago Lucas had tried his luck with Deb also. What fair game her family must have seemed.

'Deb, listen to me,' she urged. 'Lord Conistone is leaving. He only called here because he was on his way to Stancliffe Manor.'

'You mean—' Deb shivered '—he said nothing about me?'

'Nothing at all.' Verena sighed. 'Look, he will have gone already… Deb, you must forget him. You must be strong.' *And so must I.*

'Oh, Verena.' Deborah flung herself into her arms, in a fresh storm of weeping.

And Verena did her best—an almost impossible task—to soothe her, then left her sister at last, returning to her own room to endure fresh heartbreak herself as she remembered how nearly two years ago she herself was fool enough to fall in love with Lucas, Lord Conistone.

In the early August of 1808, all of Hampshire was deluged by heavy rainfall, and the harvests were ruined. Verena's father had gone away again on his travels—from which, in fact, he was never to return—and Verena, young as she was, found that their tenants and villagers were coming to *her* for help, since their mother, Lady Frances, could do nothing but bewail their troubles.

Verena had been supposed to be preparing for her come-out the following Season. The dressmaker had even completed part of her new wardrobe, of which the silk chemise was a sad relic. But instead of looking forward to parties and balls, she had found herself having to discuss their woeful finances with Mr Mayhew, her father's attorney.

With Mr Mayhew's help that summer she had dug deeper into the dwindling family coffers to save the home farm—save the estate, in fact; during discussions with the estate's tenant farmers, she struggled to comprehend all the talk of crop rotation, winter fodder and seasonal plantings.

She still dreamed of going to London, with its theatres and fashionable parties. When her father returned, she told herself, everything would be as it should be once more! The last week of August seemed to echo her optimism, with days suddenly full of sunshine. Though Verena, riding back on an old pony from a meeting with some of the tenant farmers to discuss, of all things, the virtues of planting turnips as a fodder crop, knew that her return to Wycherley would be greeted by her mother with near hysterics.

'Verena! You have been riding about the countryside like—a farmer's wife! Oh, if any of our neighbours should see you!'

It was hot, it was beautiful outdoors, and the larks were singing above the meadows. And so, in a sudden impulse of rebellion, Verena had jumped off her pony near a haystack and let it amble towards some grass. Then, after pulling a crisp red apple and two books from her saddle bag, she sat with her back against the sweet-smelling hay.

With her spectacles perched at the end of her nose, she started on *Miss Bonamy's Young Lady's Guide to Etiquette*, a parting gift from a former extremely dull governess that her mother was always urging her to read. She tackled the first few pages. *A young lady never rides out without a chaperon. A young lady always dresses demurely and protects her complexion from the sun.*

'Oh, fiddle!' Verena had cried, and flung Miss Bonamy's tome at the hayrick, turning instead, with almost equal lack of enthusiasm, to the treatise on agriculture that David, her brother-in-law, had lent her.

It was actually not as boring as she'd expected. She read through it, frowning at first, then with growing interest, until—

'Oh!'

He was riding towards her along the track, and the sound of his horse's hooves had made her start.

Lucas, Viscount Conistone. Of course, as she grew up she'd seen him from afar. Dreamed about him from afar, like her sisters, like most of the girls in the entire county, no doubt. She'd even met him occasionally, because her father had been a friend of his grandfather, the old Earl, and the Earl was her godfather. She dropped the treatise on turnips and dragged herself to her feet, snatching off her spectacles, pushing back her tumbled hair; then she just said, with utter gladness, 'You're safe! I was so afraid!'

He'd dismounted, and stood lightly holding his big horse's reins, smiling down at her. He would be—yes, twenty-four years old, four years older than she was. He was hatless, and his thick black hair, a shade too long for fashion, framed a striking, aristocratic face that was tanned now by the sun. He wore just a loose cream shirt—no coat, in this heat—riding breeches and dusty leather boots.

'Very much alive,' he agreed heartily. 'Did you hear news to the contrary, Miss Sheldon?'

She coloured. 'They said you'd gone overseas, with the army. And I heard there were some terrible battles…'

That was when he told her he was untouchable, and the bullets just flew past him. She wasn't going to tell him that every time she read the news sheets, or overheard talk of the war, she thought of him.

'I did not know you were coming home,' she said simply.

He'd smiled down at her again. Since she'd last seen him—it was at a gathering of local families at Stancliffe Manor several years ago—he'd changed, become wider-shouldered, leaner, yet more powerful. His face, always handsome, was more angular, his features more defined. And there was something—some shadow—in his dark grey eyes that she was sure had not been there before. *A soldier now.* He would have lost friends in battles, she thought. He would have killed men.

Lucas said lightly, 'Even my grandfather didn't know I was returning till I turned up on his doorstep yesterday. I was intending to call on you all at Wycherley, but I'm glad to find you on your own.'

It means nothing, he means nothing, don't be foolish… She suddenly remembered, and her heart sank. She said, 'You must have heard from your grandfather about—the matter with my father. I wouldn't have been surprised if you'd decided *not* to call on us, my lord.'

His eyes were still gentle. 'They had an argument, I'm afraid, as old friends will.'

'It was more than an argument, I fear!' she answered.

'And your father's away again? On his travels?'

'Indeed, yes.'

'And you—' his eyes were scanning her, assessing her in a way that made her blush '—you, Verena, should be in London, surely, enjoying yourself, surrounded by flocks of admirers!'

At that moment, with Lucas smiling down at her, she

would not have been anywhere else for the world. 'Oh, there's time enough for all that,' she said airily.

'Time enough, indeed. Though this…' he picked up the book that lay where she had dropped it '…is hardly everyday reading for a young lady.' He flicked through it, eyebrows tilting. 'The cultivation of—turnips?'

She blushed hotly. He must think her a country clod, for no London lady of fashion would ever glance at such a thing!

'It belongs to—someone else, and, yes, of course you are right, I wouldn't dream of reading about—farming! *Turnips!*' She laughed. 'Ridiculous!'

He put his head on one side, not smiling back, and said seriously, 'I have heard that since your father last went away, you've had to take on responsibility for the estate yourself, Verena.'

She bit her lip, then, 'What nonsense people do talk!' she declared. 'Why, soon Mama and Deb and I will be going to London, and we will have such fun—going to the theatre, attending parties…' She casually picked up her copy of the *Miss Bonamy's* book and fanned her warm cheeks with it, so he should see it and consider her a lady.

He cut in, 'I heard there was a bad harvest. And that you're short of labourers to plant the winter crops.'

She was mortified. 'It's true that the summer rains did great damage. But by next spring all will be right again at Wycherley!' *I wish, I wish he hadn't seen me like this, in my old print dress that must be flecked with dust and straw. He will be used to the company of such beautiful women, and I must look like a farm girl…*

He said suddenly, 'I'm interested in the new ways of farming too. Everyone should be.'

'Sh-should they?'

'Indeed. Unfortunately, this war will go on and on, and

it's vital that every acre of English land should be made as productive as possible. But Turnip Townshend's ideas are a little outdated now, you know! Have you come across Blake's new harrow yet, I wonder? My grandfather's agent has ordered one, for drilling seed in rows, rather than scattering. You could borrow it for Wycherley, I'm sure. Would you show me round your estate's farms some time, Verena, and I'll see how I can help?'

She was stunned. So he *didn't* despise her after all, even though she was reduced to learning about turnips. He was actually offering to help her!

She realised the sun was beating down on her unruly hair, her cheeks; oh, Lord, her freckles would be coming back! She exclaimed, 'The Earl, your grandfather, does not approve of my family at all, you know!'

He shrugged. 'Then I shall tell him it's a matter of neighbourliness and of mutual benefit. The Stancliffe estate can perhaps help Wycherley for now, but some day, in different circumstances, you might be able to help *us*!'

She could barely restrain an incredulous laugh. Stancliffe was a vast and rich ancestral home; its estate always ran at a profit, and it had a water-powered corn mill that minted money, David Parker said. Wycherley was paltry in comparison.

He touched her hand. A gesture of friendship, no more, but his long, lean fingers burned her; she felt that silken touch through every nerve ending.

'Are you in a hurry *now*?' he asked her suddenly.

'No, not at all,' she lied. Really, there was a great deal to be done: the household accounts to be sorted, Cook's monthly order for the stores to be cut back as much as possible, Turley's laments about the leak in the roof of the north wing to be placated...

'Then let's ride together,' said Lucas, Viscount Conistone,

'now, around Wycherley's farms. I know the harvest has been a bad one, but there's time yet to remedy things.'

Her eyes were wide with wonder and surprise. 'But—you're home *on leave*. You must have so many things you'd rather be doing, my lord!'

'As a matter of fact,' he said rather quietly, 'I haven't.'

Her heart leapt; her soul sang. Quietly, wonderingly, she packed her things into her saddle bag. And as he helped her on to her pony, her thoughts were in utter turmoil. For she'd fallen head over heels in love, and her world was suddenly a different, a marvellous place.

And so, during those weeks of late August and September when the sun shone as if in apology for the dreadful early summer, Lord Lucas Conistone called for her almost daily and they would ride around the Wycherley and Stancliffe estates together, with either Turley or one of her sisters accompanying them as chaperon, talking about crops and harvesting.

Verena's complexion became golden in the sun and her mother chided her to wear a wide-brimmed sunbonnet. But Lucas laughed at her headgear and told her that he disliked ladies with pallor; he told her also that her eyes were like amber in the sunlight. 'You must have inherited your grandmother's colouring,' he said.

She didn't even realise that he knew about her father's Portuguese mother. 'Her name was Lucia. And yes, I am told that I look like her,' she said shyly.

'Then she must have been beautiful.'

She was not used to being complimented on her looks. Her mother had always bemoaned the fact that she was not blonde and blue-eyed, like Deb and Izzy. Her heart thudded. 'You are making fun of me. I'm sure I would never gain approval at Almack's!'

'No, because the others there would die of jealousy,' he answered lightly. And he added, even more softly, *'Minha querida.'*

The Portuguese endearment—*my dear one*—went through her like an arrow. A light aside. A frivolous compliment, nothing more, she told herself swiftly.

She also had to damp down her mother's excited speculation. 'Lord Conistone has no intentions towards me whatsoever, Mama, I assure you! We are friends, nothing more.'

But it seemed truly marvellous to be Lucas's friend as they rode together that September, talking about the agricultural improvements that were needed to feed a country at war. Though Lucas never talked about the war itself.

Of course, she always knew that soon he would have to go back. She knew that the harvest festival, in the fourth week of September, would be his last night at home; he was due to rejoin his regiment the next day, he had told her. But it was easy to believe, that warm, moonlit night, that the cruel war was a whole world away.

His friend Captain Alec Stewart, whose reputation as a high liver was just starting to gather pace, was there, too, and of course there was great excitement amongst the local girls when Alec and Lucas stayed on after the supper for the dancing. Yet Lucas danced with Verena nearly all evening. When she suggested that he should ask some of the others, he answered lightly, 'How can I *not* dance with someone who is a student of Turnip Townshend? How could anyone else be my amber-eyed harvest maiden?' Somehow he danced her away from the others, into the shadows offered by the outbuildings, and there, while the music still played, he kissed her.

She'd glimpsed his dark smile seconds before he lowered his head and brushed his lips against her own. His strong arms cradled her close and soft yearning had flooded her.

Nothing less than a tremor shook her body as his warm, firm mouth caressed hers, and she felt his tongue lightly trace the parting of her lips, then flicker against her moist inner mouth.

Her hands were trapped, pressed flat against the hard wall of his chest. She could feel the heat of his skin through the fine lawn of his white shirt. Feel the ridges of sculpted male muscle under her fingertips. His hips and thighs were moulded to hers, so close she couldn't help but be aware of his desire, hard and powerful, where he held her tight. *For her. He wanted her...*

Verena recognised her own answering desire at the pit of her stomach. Hazy, heated images filled her mind. The whispers she'd heard, about what women and men did together; her sister Pippa's sighs of rapture as she hinted at nights in her new husband's arms…

It was Lucas who drew away. But he still held her hands. And whispered, '*Verena.* Remember this night, because I will.'

The sounds of music and merrymaking drifted through to her as if from a great distance. For a moment all she could do was gaze up at him. Every inch of her skin where he had touched her was aching with acute awareness, as she saw something so dark, so rawly male in his expression that it almost frightened her.

Then they were interrupted. A crowd of his friends were coming to see where he was. 'Best get back to the others,' Lucas said lightly. And it was over.

That kiss was nothing to him, she told herself. It was just an evening of joyous celebration, when everyone was dancing and drinking a little more than they should.

It was just a kiss. But later, as she prepared for bed, she looked at herself in the mirror; for the first time in her life she wished that she was a tantalising society beauty, from a wealthy family, because then, then, he might love her in return.

Love. She'd thought that being courted—being *loved*—would be sweet and pleasant—and easily resisted.

But no. What she felt for Lucas was a dark, a dangerous, a living thing. Her whole being throbbed with need. She longed to be in his arms, to feel his lips on hers, and more, for he'd awakened her body, and her heart.

Lucas called at Wycherley briefly before he left the next day. He was in uniform, and obviously in great haste, but he gave her the little music box. As she opened it, and the tender tune filled her heart, he took her hand and said, his eyes searching hers, 'I'll be away for a little while, Verena. Can I ask you something?'

She had been tormented by the knowledge that soon he would be sailing away to Portugal, to war with the French, to terrible danger. 'Of course,' she breathed. 'Anything.'

'Will you keep your trust in me, whatever you hear? Will you remember we are friends?'

Friends. Her heart plummeted, but she managed to say lightly, 'Good friends indeed. And we owe you so much, Lucas! Next time you are home, you will see the Wycherley farms *transformed*!'

He nodded almost curtly. 'As long as you yourself do not change, Verena. As long as *you* stay the same.' Then he took her hand and pressed his lips to it. She wanted to fling herself into his arms and cling to him and never let him go.

As he'd walked towards his waiting horse, he had turned to her once last time, as if he was about to say something else. But then he mounted up, gave a half-salute, and was gone.

She thought—*everybody* thought—that he'd gone back

to the battlefields of the Peninsula. But news came a few weeks later that he'd resigned from the army and was instead living the high life in London with the Prince's set. After that came whispers, too, of secret *affaires* with beautiful society women—and each piece of news about Lord Lucas Conistone stabbed Verena to the heart.

Still during that winter of anguish, there'd been no word from their father. And hard on the heels of the rumours about Lucas had come an ominous visit from Mr Mayhew, their father's attorney. Verena's mother had felt a migraine coming on, so it was Verena who had to listen to Mr Mayhew's grave explanation that the loan on which Wycherley depended was being withdrawn, due, Mr Mayhew feared, to personal pressure on their bank from the Earl of Stancliffe, Lucas's grandfather.

Verena had first thought, *This must be a mistake. The Earl is my godfather. Despite his disagreement with my father, he cannot intend to harm us so!* She wrote to the Earl that same day, explaining their predicament; and that was when she'd received the devastating answer:

The Earl of Stancliffe does not respond to begging letters. Especially when they are sent by a fortune-hunting harlot—yes, my grandson Lucas told me of your pitiful attempts to entrap him...

Verena had locked herself in her room on receiving that note, shaking with shock. She read it again and again, remembering every conversation, every look of Lucas's, trying to make sense of it and failing.

She'd told Lucas that when he returned to Wycherley, he'd find it transformed; it was unrecognisable indeed, within months of his departure, for, by the January of 1809, the Sheldons, and the Wycherley estate, were starting to face the road to ruin.

Soon afterwards, the Earl made a ludicrously low offer for the entire estate, which Verena refused outright. *Something* would happen, she thought desperately. Her dear father would return, filling the house with his beloved presence, making everything all right…

Her father had been abroad for months, and still nothing whatsoever had been heard of him, though Verena took the gig or rode every fortnight to the shipping office in Portsmouth ten miles away to ask if there was any news.

And early in February 1809, during bitter winter weather, the news finally arrived. Sir Jack Sheldon would never be coming home again.

Chapter Four

Jack Sheldon was dead. And there was no body to bury, either. They were told he'd been exploring the snow-covered peaks on Portugal's Spanish border when he fell into a raging mountain river and was swept away downstream, never to be found. Verena had been grief-stricken and, more than that, desperately afraid. She honestly did not see how they could go on.

The Earl of Stancliffe was in Bath when the news arrived, taking the waters for his health; they heard nothing from him, and after his insults Verena did not expect to. Then Lucas wrote to her, to send his condolences. She was horrified by his duplicity. She didn't understand how he could pretend to care. She'd secretly fallen in love with a gallant hero, who'd asked her to trust him, when all the time he'd been planning to leave the army, and must also have betrayed her infatuation with him to his grandfather.

Of course she burned Lucas's letter and did not reply. He wrote again. This time she did not even read it before destroying it.

Verena had her father's letters for consolation. He was

a compulsive writer, and as she leafed through them, with their vivid descriptions of the wild hills of his mother's country where he'd felt so at home, she could almost hear Jack Sheldon's loud voice, almost see his dancing dark eyes, which had glittered exultantly as he confided to her, on the night just before he left for the last time, that summer two years ago, that he had discovered a great secret, something that would make them all rich.

Oh, Papa. She hadn't believed him. But how she missed him: his stories, and his zest, and his unquenchable optimism—and how secretly fearful she was as she faced life without him, under a mountain of burgeoning debt.

Lady Frances Sheldon was still determined to marry off her daughters, and wanted to take Verena and Deb to London as soon as the minimum period of mourning was over. Verena told her mother that they simply could not afford the expense of a London Season; Pippa, usually Verena's staunch ally, was by then expecting her twins, so Verena took on the full brunt of her mother's anger.

'I would hate to think you are jealous of Deb's prettiness, my dear,' said Lady Frances.

'Jealousy, piffle! I am not going to London, Mama!' declared Verena. 'And you should not either!'

But Lady Frances had insisted on taking Deb to London that autumn, for an extended stay with a rather foolish friend of hers, Lady Willoughby. Verena remained at Wycherley, trying to hold the estate together and to fend off their mounting debts. She was startled one afternoon to see a hired chaise rattling into the courtyard; when she'd hurried to see who it was, Deb and Lady Frances were climbing out.

'Deb! Mama!' Verena had cried. 'I had not expected you back so soon!'

Lady Frances, hurrying towards the house, waved her

hand dismissively. 'The disappointments, Verena! Lady Willoughby is *no true friend*, and I've decided that I've had enough of her! Pray have tea sent up to my room while I recover from the journey!'

Deb, her pretty face clouded with ill humour, was about to follow, but Verena had barred her way. 'Deb. What on earth's happened?'

Deb had burst into tears.

Oh, Lord, Verena had thought, ordering the staring Turley to unload the luggage. 'Deb. Come inside. Tell me everything.'

But Verena had rather wished she'd been spared at least some of the details when Deb told her in the parlour, between fits of tears and outbursts of anger, how she'd met Viscount Conistone at one of Lady Willoughby's parties and that he had made severely improper advances.

Verena had been stunned. 'No!'

Deb had started crying again. 'Oh, yes! I thought I would be *safe* with Lucas! After all, last September *you* used to ride around the countryside with him, didn't you, Verena? Often with only one of us for company, and no one said a thing! He—he took me into a side room, and gave me wine to drink—and then he attempted to *kiss* me, and murmured that we must meet, later! Oh, I would die if anyone else knew of my shame!'

Until then, there had always been the faint hope in Verena's beleaguered heart that the stories she heard about Lucas were somehow false, and that the Earl's comment that Lucas had called her a silly fortune-hunter was a wicked concoction.

But—*this*? For a start, what was Lucas doing at one of Lady Willoughby's entertainments? He was part of the Carlton House set—he would never normally attend such a shabby affair! And—what did it matter? Any last hope had died within her. She'd felt cold, alone and afraid.

'Deb. Deb, listen to me. Maybe Lord Conistone had been drinking—'

'Oh, you *would* say that! You are jealous; I might have known!'

Verena bit her lip and tried again. 'I'm only trying to say that you must pretend it never happened. Lucas—Lord Conistone—will say nothing either, if he has any sense of honour. Does Mama know anything of this?'

'Mama? No, of course not! She insisted that we leave London because she fell out with Lady Willoughby over some petty business of who should pay for the theatre or some such thing. And some unpleasant people were starting to say that I should not be appearing at parties and routs, since I was not properly out… But, Verena, listen. You don't think—' Deb had lifted her pretty, petulant face enquiringly '—that Lucas might perhaps really care for me? That if I'd stayed in London, he might have continued his attentions in a more proper fashion?'

'I don't,' Verena had said flatly. 'No gentleman of Lord Conistone's standing initiates a serious courtship in such a way.'

Deb had burst into tears again. 'I hate you, Verena! You are jealous, and spiteful, because I am so much prettier than you!'

'Deb, please—'

But her sister, still sobbing, had flounced out of the room, slamming the door behind her.

Verena had still refused to believe that Lucas had resigned from the army out of fear. But she was forced to believe everything else she heard about him, because the stories spread throughout the following winter and into the spring of Lucas's high living amongst the Prince's set, of the gambling and the parties that lasted for days and nights on end in London, Brighton and even the Channel Isles—for, like many of his aristocratic companions, he had his own sea-going yacht.

Captain Alec Stewart, his services in the Light Dragoons clearly minimal, was often his companion in these outbursts of revelry. Their female conquests were legendary; that spring, the rumour had spread that Lucas was about to announce his betrothal to one of the diamonds of the Season, Lady Jasmine Rowley.

True or not, Lucas had betrayed Wycherley. And had shattered her stupid heart.

Now, suddenly, on the day their fast-disintegrating fortunes were put on public display, Lucas was back in her life again. And she wouldn't accept any of his offers of help, for she could not believe a word he said.

Yet the trouble was that not a night had gone by, since that magical autumn, without her thinking of him. Missing him. Wanting him so badly that it was as if her life was broken without him.

It was nine o'clock and the ordeal of the dispersal sale was almost over. The chaises and carts had departed along the Chichester road, piled high with items that had been in Wycherley Hall for centuries. Verena, feeling tired and alone, set off down the stairs. At least Lord Conistone and Captain Stewart would have gone by now.

But the day was not over yet. As she entered the great hall, that this morning had been piled with furniture and ornaments and was now almost bare, she saw Turley, looking hot and distressed.

'Turley, what on earth's the matter?' *Not Lucas again, causing trouble, please...*

Turley rushed towards her. 'There's bad doings down at

Ragg's Cove, Miss Verena! The militia, they're roundin' up some local men who've bin fishing!'

'The militia? Fishing? Why on earth—?'

'They're saying our men are in league with French spies, Miss Verena! And they're plannin' on taking them off to Chichester gaol!'

'This is ridiculous! French spies? I will deal with this!'

Now Turley's kind old face was truly tight with alarm. 'You mustn't go down there, miss! You know as well as I there's been strange things goin' on around here lately! Oh, I wish I'd never told you…'

'This is Wycherley business,' she replied crisply, 'and you did quite right to tell me, Turley. Believe me, I'll be back before anyone's even missed me. No need to make matters worse with a general hue and cry!'

Ignoring Turley's protests, she went to put on her cloak, glad that at least it had stopped raining, and the thunderstorm was past. It would take her very little time to hurry through the gardens and down the steep track that she knew so well to Ragg's Cove. French spies? Martin Bryant was always muttering about them, but no one else took the notion in the least bit seriously. She would vouch for the local men and get rid of the interfering militia. And then this dreadful day would be—almost—at an end.

Waving Turley aside, she found a lantern and headed out into the darkness, towards the cliff path.

And did not see, in the black shadows beyond her lantern's glow, the figures moving behind the trees, following her

Chapter Five

Lucas Conistone was waiting on horseback by the deserted lodge where the Wycherley drive met the toll road to Chichester. The lights of Wycherley Hall twinkled a quarter of a mile away, through the darkness.

His horse was growing restless, and so was he. He constantly scanned the long driveway back to Wycherley Hall, until he saw that someone was coming at last, trotting up the drive from the house on a stocky bay cob.

'My God, Bentinck,' said Lucas, urging his horse forwards to meet him, 'you took your damned time!'

Bentinck, who had once been a prize fighter, ran his hand through his spiky black hair and grunted. He had been Lucas's aide and valet for many years; now he looked mildly aggrieved at Lucas's comment.

'Done just as you asked, milord, all right and proper! I took a good look round all the books and desks and so forth that were up for sale—did pretty well until I almost got caught!'

Lucas's face tightened. 'Who by?'

'The young lady of the house. The pretty one, with

chestnut hair and proud eyes, and, ahem, luscious figure… She saw me opening drawers and havin' a good poke around and started coming over to take me to task, but I was too quick for her! A tasty armful, I'd reckon, in spite of them drab clothes—'

Lucas broke in, 'Did you find anything?'

'Nothing to our immediate purpose, milord. But I did find something of interest, you might say. I got into the study and took a good long look at the window that we'd heard on our way here was the one that was used to get in to burgle the place…' He paused weightily.

'And?'

'Some villain did indeed 'ave a go at that window, milord, to make it look like it had been forced. But he was doin' it from the inside. Get my meaning?'

'From the inside. Thank you, Bentinck,' breathed Lord Lucas Conistone softly. 'Thank you very much.'

'One thing more, milord.' Bentinck frowned. 'As I was leavin' just now, all quiet-like, to find my nag, I heard a bit of an argument between the girl—the beauty—and a servant. Seems as if there's trouble down at the beach, Ragg's Cove they call it, between the militia and some fishermen. And the girl's gone hurrying down there to investigate.'

'Not—on her own?' Lucas's voice was harsh. Incredulous.

'Sounds like it, milord. Weren't nothing I could—'

'I know Ragg's Cove.' Lucas looked grim. 'There's a path down to it from where the Wycherley gardens end at the top of the cliffs…' He was making rapid decisions. 'We'll both ride quietly back towards the house, then you must keep yourself and the horses hidden. If I'm not back in half an hour—come after me.'

'But—'

'That's an order. Understand?'

Bentinck sighed. 'Understood, milord.' And followed.

As Verena hurried down the last few yards to the shingle beach, a hoarse cry of welcome rose from the half-dozen or so figures who cowered from the militia men's pointed muskets. 'Miss Verena! It's Miss Verena!'

Drawing nearer, she recognised them: old Tom Sawrey, Billy Dixon, Ned Goodhew, and two others. Wycherley tenants, they farmed smallholdings and fished to supplement their income.

She also knew the officer in charge of the militia. 'Colonel Harrap! Yes, it's me, Verena Sheldon! I have no idea what you and your soldiers think you're doing! French spies indeed!'

Colonel Harrap puffed himself out like a peacock. 'I'm afraid you aren't acquainted with the full facts, Miss Sheldon! Are you aware, for instance, that these scoundrels—' he pointed at the Wycherley men '—made a signal—a fire, up on the cliff—to lure the enemy into land? And as a servant of his Majesty, it's my duty to arrest them!'

Her heart lurched sickly. *A fire.* She looked sharply at the villagers again.

Fish weren't the only haul they landed at night. Occasionally she and her family had received good French brandy, and sometimes even a bale of silk. Tonight—yes, tonight it was all too possible that they'd lit a fire to guide in a boat—to help not French spies, but French smugglers.

Then Billy Dixon stepped forwards, desperate. 'We didn't light that fire, Miss Verena, honest! We'd just been out fishin' and we saw the flames while we were out at sea!'

'A likely story!' snorted Colonel Harrap.

'It's true! We rowed back in to see what it could be,

but just after we pulled our boat in, that—that officer and his men came running down from the top of the headland and told us we was all under arrest! See, there's our boat, look!'

He pointed to the big rowing boat heaved up on to the shingle, to the folded nets and baskets of glistening fish. Verena was just starting to breathe again.

But Colonel Harrap hadn't finished. 'Their word against mine, Miss Sheldon! And the lighting of a signal to the enemy amounts to treason, as I'm sure you know! This will go before the magistrates, I promise you!'

Verena gave him her best frosty glare. 'I think the magistrates, Colonel Harrap, will require more evidence than you've just given me!' she declared stoutly. *Oh, Billy. You'd best be telling me the truth about this, or else...*

'We'll see! If I should find proof that some French villains have indeed landed, there'll be the devil to pay!' blustered Colonel Harrap. And, after muttering 'You've not heard the last of this!' he led his men surlily back to the steep path that led up to the headland.

Verena drew her hand across her eyes, feeling a little faint. 'Billy, Tom,' she said, 'I really hope you've been honest with me.'

The Wycherley men had quickly surrounded her, their faces shining with relief. 'Oh, yes, Miss Verena!' said Billy. 'But—' and he glanced at the others '—there's somethin' else you ought to know. Something we wasn't going to tell old Harrap and his bunch of brass buttons!'

Verena's heart sank anew. 'Tell me, Billy.'

'Well,' said Billy, 'we were out at sea, like I said, when we saw that fire lit. We saw nothing else. But when we landed, young Dickon—he's Tom's lad, he's only thirteen—he'd been watching for us, to help us in with the catch, and he saw a boat come in, saw them land, three of them, and he said they were mighty quiet about everything, but he's got sharp ears, and he said they talked real strange!'

Verena's heart thumped. *French.* Oh, no. Maybe the villagers should have told Colonel Harrap this from the start. If he found out now, Harrap would jump on the chance to accuse them all of conspiracy. *If I should find proof that some French villains have indeed landed, there'll be the devil to pay!*

'Then tell Dickon to keep quiet about it,' Verena said swiftly. 'You must *all* keep quiet about it! As long as you are innocent…'

'We are, Miss Verena, we are!' said Billy. 'Should we go with you, back up to the house?'

'No, Billy.' She knew they'd be anxious to get their catch in safely. 'No, I'm all right. I'll make my own way up in a little while.'

Thanking her again, they slung their baskets of fish over their shoulders and went trudging up the steep path.

She stood there, gazing out to the moonlit sea, the only sound the gentle rasp of waves on shingle. And her heart was heavy.

They'd escaped trouble for now, whether or not their story about the mysterious French boat was true. They thought life would go on as ever. Those villagers had worked on Wycherley land and fished from Ragg's Cove for generations. And, yes, had landed smuggled goods from time to time as well…

But soon the Wycherley estate would have a new owner, and if the Earl bought it he would be a harsh and grasping landlord who would give bullies like Colonel Harrap a free hand. The old and easy ways of her father would vanish into distant memory. What could she do? Nothing.

She picked up her lantern and started to climb slowly back uphill. It was raining again; by the time she reached the top of the path, her bonnet and cloak were sodden. She could just see the lights of Wycherley Hall, dimly shining through the mist and rain.

The Earl. *Lucas.* She suddenly stopped and pressed her palm to her forehead. *Why* had Lucas come here today of all days? Had he come to gloat? To satisfy himself that he could still reduce her to a quivering, needy mess, by just being near her?

And—her face burned anew—she had let him think she might accept Martin Bryant's proposal! Oh, what a foolish, stupid lie! Well, soon he would be going back to his London parties, to join his friends of the Prince's set, with his loose-living companion Alec Stewart. She would never see Lucas again, and nothing could give her greater pleasure than his complete *absence* from her life!

That was a lie, too. The terrible ache in her heart told her so.

The danger erupted so suddenly. One moment she was quite alone. The next, three heavily cloaked men were crashing through the thicket beside the path towards her, with pistols gleaming in the lantern light. Something like a blanket was thrown over her face, so she could not see, could not breathe. The lantern was snatched from her. Hands were grabbing at her roughly, hurting her.

She remembered in those brief, terrifying moments the sensation of so often being followed, remembered the break-in at Wycherley Hall. Fight as she might, they were pulling her, hustling her towards the trees. Smugglers? But why attack *her*? And she thought she heard them muttering, *'C'est elle. C'est la fille.'* Her blood froze.

Then she heard a man's voice roaring, 'Verena!'

She heard the sound of a gun exploding within a few feet of her and realised the restraining hands were gone. Pulling the blanket from her face, gasping for air, she saw the three cloaked men running off, heads low, into the dark woods.

'Verena!' The same desperate male voice, close now.

Turning, she saw Lucas, his long coat and hair glistening with the rain, standing there with a gun in his hand. At first she did not understand. At first she thought he was the one who had fired.

Then she realised that Lucas was sinking very slowly to his knees, and where he clutched his left hand to his arm, bright blood was welling through his fingers.

Chapter Six

Lucas was kneeling on the ground. She ran to crouch beside him, her heart hammering.

'*Lucas*. Oh, we must get your coat off.' Her voice shook with emotion. 'We must tie something around your injury, I must get help!'

'They told me you'd gone down to the beach—alone!' he grated out. 'How could you have been so—so *foolish*?'

'Foolish?' she cried. She felt faint with fear. 'Some militia men were threatening our villagers—was it *foolish* to try to protect them?' She was striving, with trembling fingers, to ease his coat from his shoulder, but she could see the perspiration pouring from his forehead, indicating his pain. *He is your enemy*, she reminded herself, *your family's enemy…*

'Who were your attackers?' he rasped.

'I've no idea. Not smugglers, definitely not—' she was thinking of the danger Billy and his friends might be in '—so they must have been robbers, and it was my misfortune to be in their way.'

'I never thought they were smugglers,' Lucas said bluntly.

'Smugglers don't attack innocent girls. And they were not robbers either. Verena, they were trying to drag you away. Did you hear them speak?'

Swiftly she tore aside the fabric of his shirt and pressed her clean folded handkerchief to the wound, remembering Colonel Harrap's warning: *If I should find proof that some French villains have indeed landed, there'll be the devil to pay!*

'They sounded like Portsmouth men,' she lied. 'I heard a few words I wouldn't care to repeat, I'm afraid—' Then she realised that his blood was still welling through her handkerchief. *Oh, no.* 'Have you got anything else I can bind it with?' she asked rather faintly.

'There's my cravat.' He was already loosening it, with his left hand; his face was very pale, though the corner of his mouth lifted in a faint smile. 'I didn't realise your numerous skills extended to nursing.'

She reached for his loosened cravat. So much blood. She struggled to stay calm, to say matter of factly, 'Oh, my sisters were for ever getting into scrapes—literally—when they were small, and my mother tends to faint at the sight of a scratch, so it's almost a matter of necessity… Can you hold your arm up, Lucas, just a little? That's right. Then I can bind it—it will help to stop the bleeding.' Her voice was tight with strain.

Too close. He was too close. Difficult to concentrate on her bandaging, difficult not to notice the taut, tanned skin, the underlying muscle and sinew of his warm, powerful arm… *A young lady should never be nearer than two feet to a gentleman who is not a close relative…*

Miss Bonamy's Young Lady's Guide to Etiquette wasn't much use here.

She tied the knot with a snap. 'There,' she breathed.

'Now, if you will stay here and rest, I'll run to the house and fetch help.'

His good arm grabbed for her. '*No.* You must not be by yourself!' He rapped out the warning.

She shivered and retorted defiantly, because she was afraid, 'You cannot really think that—those men will be back?'

'Who knows? You're not going anywhere on your own! I can walk, if you'll let me lean on you a little! It's not far to Wycherley.'

Her eyes jerked up to his. 'You cannot stay at *Wycherley*!' With Deb. Herself. *A thousand times, no.*

'I see,' he said quietly. 'But I could, perhaps, make use of your family carriage to get to Stancliffe.'

She felt her stomach lurch sickeningly at the thought of Lucas, in pain, being transported along the rough road to Stancliffe Manor, two miles away.

Wasn't it what he deserved? He had made her fall in love with him, he had betrayed her…

But then she saw that he was swaying where he stood, and his face had gone very white. 'We'll go to Wycherley, of course, it's far nearer,' she muttered. She guessed from the little she knew about bullet wounds that he must be in acute pain, and losing blood fast. 'Put your arm around my shoulder, *quickly*. Can you really walk all the way there? Shouldn't I fetch some men from the house to help you?'

'I said—no!' He tightened his arm around her. The close contact of his lithe, muscular body set into motion all the long pushed-aside memories that still haunted her every waking moment. 'And anyway, who would you fetch? Captain Martin Bryant? He'd most likely cheer and put a second bullet through me, for making advances to the woman who's to be his wife—'

She gasped. *Oh, Lord, her lies.* 'Stop it,' she breathed, 'please stop it, Lucas...'

'Stop what?'

'Talking.'

'About Bryant?'

'About anything,' she whispered. 'Anything at all.'

He was quiet for a few moments as they stumbled along. Somewhere in the woods an owl hooted. She jumped and his arm tightened around her.

'I'm sorry,' she muttered.

'Sorry?' Somehow they had come to a stop. 'Maybe I'm the one who should apologise. My blood is ruining your gown and cloak.'

'Do you think I *care*? Please, keep going...'

His arm was heavy and warm on her shoulder. 'You've already had one gown ruined tonight. Do you usually get through them at such a rate?'

She caught her breath. *Those buttons.* That scandalous silk chemise... She wanted to laugh, she wanted to cry; she wanted to nestle into the warmth of him and cherish him and never, ever let him go...

'It's all part of the excitement of country living,' she said crisply. 'We run up such a bill at our dressmakers in Chichester, you really cannot imagine... Lucas. Please *hurry*, it's not far now...'

Trudging and slipping lopsidedly, they'd almost reached the lawns—only a few hundred yards to go.

'I'd like to buy you a new gown,' he muttered as the night-time fragrance of the rose gardens enveloped them. 'A new gown, in pink, or jade, or lilac, for my amber-eyed girl. You wore lilac at that harvest dance but your skin was scented with lavender... Oh, God.' He stopped suddenly. 'I've missed you, Verena.'

He was wandering. He must be. Her heart was thumping.

'Lucas,' she begged, 'you must stop talking. You must concentrate on getting back to the house. *Please...*'

But he didn't move. His grey eyes, suddenly molten with flecks of gold, burned down into her anxious face. Then he lifted his left hand and let his fingertips trail down her cheek. His touch was like a flame searing through her.

'I'd rather concentrate on something else,' he murmured, his fingertips still stroking her skin in that wicked caress. 'And this time, you will *not* push me away.' Then everything faded, as he pulled her close with his sound arm and captured her mouth in a kiss that jolted the breath from her body. A whimper of protest rose, then died in her throat.

For in spite of her fear and exhaustion, there was suddenly nothing else but Lucas. Nothing but the strength of his powerful body against hers; the taste of his warm, silken mouth as he brushed his lips over her lips and coaxed them apart; nothing but her own wildly instinctive response to the sensual thrust of his tongue and all that it promised...

It could not be happening, it *should* not be happening, but somehow she'd wound her own hands round his neck and arched her body into his. And with a groan he was drawing her nearer, his thighs pressed against hers, as he kissed her more deeply, his tongue twining with hers. Verena felt the need spiralling from deep within as she opened to him, revelled in his hard maleness, wanting more, *needing* more as he withdrew, only to feel his lips trailing down to her throat, to the swell of her bosom where her cloak had fallen apart...

She dragged herself away. '*No.* Are you out of your senses?'

'Not for what I just did,' he answered quietly. 'But I was mad to ever let you go.'

A sudden wave of despair all but overwhelmed her.

'Lucas.' She struggled to make her voice steady. 'Lucas, you did not let me go. There was nothing between us. Ever.'

'If you say so,' he answered in a low voice, his eyes opaque again. 'And, of course, you're betrothed.'

'Stop it!' she cried desperately.

'Why?' His arm was still tight around her waist.

'Because—because I'm not marrying Captain Bryant!'

He gazed down at her, his brows gathering. 'Not…?'

She swallowed hard. 'I'm not betrothed to Captain Bryant,' she muttered. 'I—apologise if I let you think it.'

His grey eyes were hooded, inscrutable. After a long moment he said quietly, 'And what did I do to provoke this—setting up of Bryant as a suitor?'

She sought the words, desperately. 'He *did* ask me to marry him! I only told you of it, because—because you were so hateful about him!'

Because you left me, Lucas.

Because you were not there when I needed you. When I trusted you with all my heart…

He said at last, letting his hand drop from her waist, 'It is, after all, none of my business, I know.'

She nodded, blinking hard. 'Indeed, my lord, it's not!' But inside she was shaking. He had kissed her. He had said, *I was mad to ever let you go.*

Silently they trudged on. It was as if Lucas Conistone had wiped the last two years from his mind, thought Verena blindly, and the wrongs he and his grandfather had done to her family.

Oh, Verena, she told herself bitterly, *he only came here today by utter chance. Just passing, on his way to the vast house he will one day inherit. Yet his presence is—lethal. You are going to have to be stronger than this.*

And she was not sure that she could, because once more

she was fighting her own stupid physical longing for a man she should have kicked out of her heart long ago.

'Verena! Verena!'

David Parker's voice. Help was coming. A search party with lanterns was hurrying in their direction across Wycherley's lawns, headed by David and Turley. As they came close, they explained they'd heard gunfire.

'Miss Sheldon was attacked by robbers and they fired at me when I went to help her,' she heard Lucas explain swiftly; Verena said nothing, simply glad to leave the care of the injured Lucas to David and Turley.

But there was someone else there. Someone who had materialised out of thin air as they reached the courtyard; a thickset man with roughly cut black hair, who looked faintly familiar, and who rapidly seemed to be taking charge of Lucas's well-being with a sharp command to all and sundry. 'Now, then. We'll be needin' a nice private room on the ground floor for his lordship, if you please! Some clean sheets and hot water. With a good log fire…' Already he was helping Lucas into the house.

Where had she seen him before?

Then David was next to her. He must have seen her staring at the man, because he took her aside to explain. 'He's Lord Conistone's valet, apparently. His name is Bentinck. Looks like we'll need his help.'

'Really?' she breathed bitterly. 'Really?' Because she had suddenly remembered. He was the man who had been at the sale this afternoon. Opening drawers, looking around in an odd and shifty manner…

Oh, no. This meant Lucas had been lying to her—yet again—when he had told her he was just passing on his way to Stancliffe, because Bentinck had been here at least two hours before his master arrived! Did he take her for a complete fool?

Oh, she was so right not to believe a word Lucas said! And as to a suitable room—*difficult*, because most of their spare furniture had gone.

She summoned Turley. 'There's a day bed in my father's study. Would you get that man—*Bentinck*—to help you carry it into the back parlour, please? And get a fire lit there. It will serve as a bedroom for Lord Conistone!'

'Certainly, Miss Verena.' Turley nodded dourly at the valet. 'Though I wouldn't trust *that* one further than I can throw him.'

Verena agreed heartily.

Lady Frances appeared to be in almost as much need of attention as Lucas; she was clearly close to fainting at the thought of the Earl's grandson being shot on Wycherley land. The fact that Verena had also been in grave danger appeared not to occur to her.

Verena somehow managed to persuade Lady Frances to retire for the night. 'You'll do no good here, Mama. I will cope. And Deb will bring you your headache powders,' said Verena firmly.

Which disposed for now of Deb, also, and the likelihood that she too would have hysterics once she realised that Lucas was actually staying under their roof.

But—he kissed me. He told me he was mad ever to let me go…

One thing was for sure. Getting himself shot was definitely not part of Lord Lucas Conistone's plan.

It was close to midnight when Turley informed her that Dr Pilkington had arrived from Framlington. Squaring her shoulders—*Lord Conistone must leave as soon as possible, I will tell the doctor so!*—she went downstairs to the back parlour, which Turley, obeying her orders, had converted into the patient's room.

Bentinck was there, building up the fire with his back to her—hateful man. And grey-haired Dr Pilkington, who'd been their family physician for as long as she could remember, was bending over—

Oh, no. Her hand flew to her mouth. Oh, no. She'd thought—what had she thought? That Lucas would be sitting up, laughing, talking? No. He lay prone on the day bed that had been covered with sheets. His eyes were closed—*such pain, he must have been in such pain, how did he walk all that way with me?*—and a sheen of perspiration covered his haggard features. His shirt had been removed entirely; Verena felt a shock run through her, her mind blurring wildly with an image of wide male shoulders and powerfully sculpted muscles. No hint here of the dissipated gentleman of leisure that society assumed him to be.

Dr Pilkington swung round and quickly ushered her out of the room. 'Miss Sheldon! You will want an account of his lordship's condition.'

She'd been going to say, *He really must be moved to Stancliffe Manor as soon as possible, Doctor. I'm sure you'll agree it's not at all appropriate that he should be here...*but all her prepared words evaporated. She cleared her throat. 'Will—will he be all right, Doctor?'

'Lord Conistone is sleeping,' answered Dr Pilkington, closing the door on the sick room. 'It's only a flesh wound, but there's always the risk that a fever might set in. I will see, of course, about getting him moved to Stancliffe Manor in your carriage, within the next hour or so; I was told by David Parker that you cannot possibly have him staying here, you clearly have a good deal already to see to, and besides, it would not be suitable—'

'No!' she said, too strongly.

He looked crestfallen. 'You mean that you cannot spare your carriage? In that case, I—'

'No! I mean he must stay here! At least—until he is somewhat recovered!'

Oh, Lord. What made her say it? Was she quite mad?

'My dear,' said Dr Pilkington, looking happier, 'that would certainly be for the best! It shouldn't be long; he's a strong young fellow, and the bullet passed cleanly through the flesh. We can, of course, hire a nurse from the town to tend him—'

'That will not be necessary, Doctor!' said Verena crisply. She had seen plenty of hired nurses when she and Pippa had visited the hospital for wounded officers in Chichester. They struck her as rough and unkind. 'I mean,' she went on quickly, 'that his valet, and our own servants, will be able to tend him quite adequately. That is, if it is not for long?'

'He should recover quickly; a couple of days and he'll be on his feet. He's clearly a survivor. This is nothing compared to another wound he's sustained in the not-too-distant past.'

'*Another* wound?'

'Yes, a nasty one, must just have missed his left lung; done by a French sabre, I'd say.'

Verena had been striving to be businesslike. But now she felt rather sick. 'How can you know?'

'Oh, I used to be an army surgeon, so I've seen similar injuries. They jab and twist—that's how the French foot soldiers are trained—up through the ribs, to strike for the heart. Lord Conistone was lucky to escape with his life.'

The army, of course. He must have been wounded in the army, before he resigned.

But…

'Well, now,' went on Dr Pilkington, 'I must go back in

and dress his arm for the night. One more thing—though I gather Lord Conistone wants no fuss, I'll have to make a report to the constables, but I fear those villains will be long gone by now. I will call on the patient again in the morning.'

Nodding, she turned to go up to her room, her mind churning with confusion. Those men who shot Lucas must have been French smugglers, straying from their usual part of the coast, and they'd planned, perhaps, on demanding a ransom for her. That *must* be the explanation. Billy and Tom and the others had been caught up unintentionally in the drama; for their sakes, Verena was more than happy for the whole frightening episode to be forgotten.

But why did *Lucas* want tonight's violent incident kept quiet? And earlier, when he'd confronted her outside the house, he had said he was leaving for Stancliffe; why, two hours later, was he still so close that he had been the first to come to her rescue?

People whispered that Lucas Conistone was a coward. But he had not been a coward when he rescued her. And then he had kissed her; and all her carefully built defences had tumbled as his embrace set fire to her yearning soul…

Oh, you fool, Verena.

That night she slept badly and woke long before dawn, her heart full of despair, wondering how she would endure his presence here.

Harlot. Fortune-hunting harlot.

Chapter Seven

'Is it true, Verena? That Lucas will have to stay here till he's better? And will they catch the ferocious band of smugglers who shot him?' Verena's youngest sister Izzy was first to join Verena at breakfast the next morning, bubbling with excitement.

So the rumours were already spreading. 'We're not absolutely sure who did it, Izzy,' Verena told her gravely. Cook's strong, sweet tea and the normal demands of the household had restored her to relative equanimity. 'But, yes, he will stay for a day or two, until he's well enough to move. And you must call him Lord Conistone.'

Seventeen-year-old Izzy's face fell, then brightened. 'But he's actually in our house! And he's so handsome, Verena. Wait till I tell my friends! I shall write to them all this minute…' She was already on her feet, breakfast forgotten.

Verena cut in. 'No gossip, please, Izzy. Remember, he is our guest!'

Izzy pouted and ran off. But Pippa, her red-headed, lively, *sensible* sister, had ridden over from the farm near

Framlington that morning with a basket of eggs and had appeared just in time to catch Verena's last words.

'Well,' Pippa declared, 'David says Lord Conistone most certainly won't want to stay for long in a place that's been stripped of half its furniture!' She settled herself at the table and started pouring tea. 'Why *did* he come here in the first place, Verena? I'm intrigued. Was it to gloat?'

'Over our misfortunes? Our *disasters*? I don't know, Pippa. I really don't know.' Verena was shaking her head, still fighting to dispel the dreams that had haunted her sleep. 'And do you know, yesterday Luc—Lord Conistone—actually had the effrontery to offer me money for our father's private papers? Or rather, he said he knew people who would pay for them! I don't understand why *anyone* would want them, do you?'

Pippa frowned. 'You mean our father's letters to us?'

'Oh, letters, maps, diaries, I think; you know how he always wrote about everything on his travels, in the minutest detail! But I told Lucas I would never, ever sell anything of Papa's!'

'Good for you. But now you're stuck with his lordship in the house. It really is appalling luck.' Pippa sipped her tea. 'Although dear Mama will be delighted to have Lord Conistone a captive, as it were, under her roof.'

Verena absorbed herself in buttering a piece of toast. 'They say he is as good as betrothed already, Pippa.'

Pippa snorted. 'That story about Lady Jasmine, you mean? London tattle. Anyway, you think that would deter Mama? Here is her dream: a real-life viscount on the sacrificial altar of marriage, so to speak…'

'Oh, Lord, *don't*, Pippa!' Verena feigned lightheartedness. 'Mama must be kept away from him at all costs. And,' she added more quietly, 'it's going to be hideously awkward for Deb.'

Pippa knew nothing about the Earl's terrible letter to Verena. But Pippa did know about Deb's encounter with Lucas at Lady Willoughby's ball.

'Deb? I see the problem.' Pippa frowned. Then her face brightened. 'My goodness, I might have *part* of the answer! Don't you remember? Mama and Deb and Izzy were supposed to be going to Chichester later today, to stay with Aunt Grace for a few days and visit the shops…'

'But then Mama vowed she could not travel into Chichester because of the shame of the dispersal sale!'

'Nevertheless,' said Pippa, eyes gleaming, 'we will tell Mama that even if *she* doesn't go, the girls absolutely must, this very afternoon! How will that do? I'll persuade her, never fear!'

Verena's spirits lifted. Aunt Grace, their father's widowed cousin, often played host to the Sheldon family. 'If you *could*, Pippa! But we must remind Mama and the girls that—'

'That we've no money for Deb and Izzy to spend on frivolities, I know!'

'We've no money to spend on *anything*, I fear.'

Pippa hurried to hug her sister. 'Oh, Verena. Anyone would think it's all your fault! You—you don't feel anything for Lucas still, do you?'

'Goodness me, not a thing,' lied Verena, forcing a smile. 'Unlike Deb, I can't deceive myself that the heir to an earldom could be interested in a Sheldon sister!'

'Oh, Deb's a fool.' Pippa was silent a moment. Then she said thoughtfully, 'You know, Verena, I always wondered about Lucas and you. So did David. We both used to notice the way he looked at you…'

'Marvelling at my absurdly rustic clothes, no doubt,' said Verena lightly.

'My dear, you are beautiful!' said Pippa abruptly. 'Just

don't let him give you any more trouble, do you hear?' She kissed Verena and went to tackle their mother.

Anyone would think it was all your fault, Pippa had chided. But that was the trouble—perhaps it was, for she, and she alone, had stirred up the old Earl's vindictiveness. Her head aching with conjecture, Verena was crossing the main hall when she suddenly saw that the door to her father's study was ajar. Frowning, she drew quietly nearer. Someone was going through the drawers of the writing cabinet.

Bentinck. Lucas's sinister-looking servant.

She rushed into the room. 'What is this? What on *earth* do you think you are doing in here?'

He didn't look in the least ashamed of being caught. He merely blinked and said, 'His lordship wants pencil and paper. I was just looking for some.'

'You should have asked me. Or one of the servants,' she said crisply. She found paper and pencil and thrust them at him. 'Although I appreciate you are needed by Lord Conistone, I would be grateful if you would not make yourself free with our house, Bentinck!'

'My thanks, ma'am,' was all he said. And he didn't even sound as though he meant it.

More than ever, Verena was determined to get Lucas—and his manservant—out of here at the first opportunity.

Dr Pilkington made his morning visit, and assured her that the patient was making good progress. Pippa kept her promise, and by two that afternoon Izzy and Deb were squeezed into the old family carriage for the five-mile journey to Chichester. Izzy was highly excited. What Deb thought was made clear to Verena.

'Thank you,' Deb said to her with an expressive shudder

as she leaned out of the carriage window. 'I really could not have borne staying in the same house as—that man. You will not listen to anything he might say about me, will you?'

The carriage rolled away; Verena and Lady Frances waved them goodbye. 'Oh,' said Lady Frances, 'this is a wonderful opportunity for my girls! The latest fashions will be in stock in Chichester, and they will need so many things if we are to visit London again in the autumn!'

Oh, no. 'Mama, we have no money! A stay in London is completely out of the question, and in Chichester they will have to window-shop only!'

'Who says we have no money?' said her mother, looking slightly pink. 'Didn't dear Lord Conistone tell you? I spoke to him just half an hour ago.'

Verena froze. 'You have no business—'

'But he is our guest after all, and so obliging; he has money with him, you know! He told his servant to give me ten guineas and said that our families are linked by neighbourly ties, so I am to think nothing of paying it back!'

Verena went white. *No.* This was *impossible*… 'Where is the money? Give it to me!'

'Oh, Deb has it. I told her to share it with Izzy, and to buy from only the best *modistes*—and to get themselves a ready-made gown each. For with Lord Conistone in the house, who knows? *One* of my daughters might find she does not have to go to London to look for a bridegroom!'

The carriage was disappearing into the distance. Verena watched it go, speechless with dismay.

Her mother gave one last fond wave, then turned with a sigh to go back into the house. But she had not yet finished with Verena. 'I do wish, my dear, that you, too, would make some attempt with your appearance while Lord Conistone is here! Such an opportunity, even for you!'

Ten guineas. Verena, burning with shame, resolved to dress like one determined on lifelong spinsterhood for the rest of Lord Conistone's enforced stay. *Whatever he is up to, with his insulting gifts and his spying manservant, he will not get round us in such a shabby way. He will not humiliate my family any further!*

She hurried up to her own room first, then marched to the kitchen where Cook, she knew, was preparing the thin gruel for Lucas that had been recommended by Dr Pilkington. 'Is it ready, Cook? I'll take it to his lordship!'

Cook's face dropped. 'Now that's not right, Miss Verena, and you know it. That servant of his, he said he'd take it.'

'Then I'll save him the bother!' If Lucas was well enough to make condescending gifts to her mother, he was well enough to explain his conduct. Verena picked up the tray and headed towards Lucas's room, practising her speech. *You must realise that we are badly in debt. And yet you come here and lavish money on Mama—for fripperies!*

Half-expecting to be barred by Bentinck, she knocked sharply, and, hearing nothing, eased the door open and carried in the tray with its bowl of steaming gruel.

Lucas was alone and asleep.

She put the tray down on the nearby table, rather carefully. He lay back on the pillows with the sheet pulled up to his waist. He wore a loosely buttoned shirt with the right sleeve cut away to make room for the bandaging on his upper arm.

Her heart thudding, she glanced again at his sleeping face; at his thick black hair, just a little too long for fashion; his lean, hard-boned features with the aristocratic nose and square jaw, lightly stubbled now. At the expressive, wickedly curving mouth that had kissed her and made such enticing, false promises. *The man is utterly dangerous.* Yet somehow he looked so vulnerable in sleep.

She felt a small, tight knot of yearning set up in her stomach that throbbed and grew.

Here was the man who had betrayed her callously. And yet last night he had somehow known that she'd been in danger, and he'd saved her at the risk of his own life—*why*?

Why had he come here at all?

He was stirring. He was trying to heave himself up, but his eyes were still half-closed, and perspiration gleamed on his high cheekbones. She should leave, *now*…

'No one must know,' he was muttering agitatedly. 'Do you understand that, Bentinck? No one—'

'My lord!' She hurried close. 'It's not Bentinck, but Verena!'

'Bentinck,' he went on hoarsely, as if she'd not spoken, 'soon it will be too late, the French are on the trail, damn them, they know it's here…'

Oh, no. He was feverish; she needed help. Already making for the door, she said, 'I will fetch your valet, my lord—'

'Verena.' Suddenly he was awake, and lifting himself again on his uninjured arm; those slate-grey eyes were clear and penetrating. 'Verena!'

Oh, my goodness. If he knew how she had gazed at him…

She turned round, swallowing on her dry throat, her heart thumping.

He was hauling himself up further. She saw him flinch at the fresh pain in his arm, before he said, 'I am exceedingly sorry to intrude on your family like this.'

He is not telling the truth. Remember it. Be strong. 'No, you're not sorry!' she broke in, almost wildly. 'I know now that you *planned* to come here, Lucas; you even sent your man Bentinck on ahead, to spy on us—and now you've given my mother a purseful of money! You treat us as if we were paupers, to be pitied and mocked—*why*?'

He said quietly, 'I didn't plan on getting shot. And your mother came to my room earlier and begged me to lend her the money.'

'Oh, no…' She stood stock still, sick with shame.

She remembered the day he'd let her ride side-saddle on his big grey mare. Verena had been both excited and terrified. 'Trust me,' he'd said softly, 'only trust me.' Afterwards he'd helped her dismount, catching her in his strong arms, and she'd found herself straining, exhilarated, towards him, wanting to be pressed against that warm and powerful body for not just a few moments, but for ever…

Now she said, her voice shaking with hurt, and the effort to suppress those and many other sweet, painful memories, 'Lord Conistone, while you are our guest, I would be more than grateful if you—and your servant—would interfere as little as possible in our lives. And as for my mother asking you for money—I apologise, and here is the money you gave her!' Defiantly she reached into her pocket and handed him her little purse with ten guineas in it—her entire savings.

He took it and cast it aside. She reached across to grasp for it and his sound arm suddenly snaked around her waist.

'I don't want that damned money,' he said. His hand was relentlessly pulling her closer, so that she had to sink to the bed beside him, her entire being fighting the longing to be held by him, cherished by him, kissed by him.

'Please,' she whispered. Her voice was agonised. 'Please let me go.'

'Stop struggling,' he said, 'or you'll hurt my injured arm.'

She gasped. 'How can you use your injury as a weapon, to humiliate me still further? *Let me go!*'

'What if I don't want to let you go?' he answered softly. His lips were close to her cheek, her ear. 'What if this is the only way to get you to tell me the truth? Look at me, Verena! Why didn't you answer my letters?'

Enveloped by the scent of warm male skin, she closed her eyes briefly. 'I destroyed your letters, Lucas! I *burnt* them!'

He released her. For a moment she thought he might actually push her away, he looked so angry. 'In God's name, *why*?'

She was backing away from him. 'You must know!' she cried. 'You must know that, thanks to you, your grandfather brought about the ruin of my family!'

For a moment he stared, incredulous. Then he rested his head back against the pillows and said in a dangerously mild voice, 'It appears I don't know a damned thing. You'd better tell me.'

Verena remembered, almost sickeningly, that night at the harvest feast when he'd kissed her. The passion in his eyes and voice as he'd begged her to wait for him.

Harlot. Fortune-hunting harlot.

No more, Verena. No more. To repeat those—*abominable* insults would achieve no purpose now.

She dragged breath into her lungs. 'Strange, I thought all of Hampshire knew. Thanks to the Earl, all our creditors, including the bank that holds our mortgage, withdrew their loans. Which is why we now have not a feather to fly with, as the gossips like to say. Why we must sell everything.'

Lucas looked stunned. 'My grandfather… Verena, you should have told me! I begged you to trust me!'

'*Trust* you?' Again she felt disbelief, confusion, swimming through her head. Harlot. Deb… Her throat tightened. 'Lucas, I should not be alone with you, like this—'

He was grim-faced. 'Rest assured I will say nothing of my stay here.'

Of course. She flinched. *He was ashamed, of being here at Wycherley...*

She swept towards the door, saying in a bright voice, 'Naturally. Imagine the shock, my lord, if your friends knew you were reduced to lodging at such a lowly place! If Lady Jasmine knew...'

'Lady Jasmine Rowley?' He looked angry and bewildered. 'What the devil has *she* to do with it?'

'They—they say you are about to become betrothed to her, Lucas!'

'Am I?' he said sharply. 'Then it's the first I damned well knew about it.'

She stared. 'But—everyone said...'

'Who said?' His face was tight with anger; he was breathing hard.

Pippa had warned her it was just London tattle. Her stomach lurched. Impulsive, stupid to come out with it... 'Does it matter?' she breathed.

'It does to me, if you're listening to damned lies!'

A rebuke she deserved. 'I'm sorry,' she said quietly. 'I had better leave. You have your ten guineas back, Lord Conistone, and I apologise again for my family.'

'Oh, rest assured,' he drawled, leaning tiredly back against the pillows, 'I can deal with your family! And by the way, it was twelve guineas I gave your mother, not ten.'

Her hands flew to her cheeks. 'Twelve! Believe me,' she said, blindly, 'I'm sorry, I will make sure you get it all back.'

'Don't be silly,' he retorted. 'Pretend you're charging me for board and lodging. It's nothing to me.'

'No doubt.' Already she was pulling from round her

neck a tiny gold locket. And she almost slammed it down on the table with the purse. 'This was from my father. I trust that will go towards covering our debt, my lord, until I can refund you the money in full!'

'Oh, for God's sake.' Lucas was tired now, tired and in pain. 'I'm not arguing any more, but I'm not taking it. Verena, listen to me before you march off in high dudgeon. Have you really no idea who your attackers were last night?'

She shook her head stubbornly. 'I told you, they sounded like Portsmouth men, but I would much rather forget it—'

'Portsmouth men. Yes, you *did* say that. But I wondered if you might have changed your mind, because I, personally, found it strange that they had French pistols.'

She stared. 'How could you—?'

'Thanks to your lantern, I glimpsed the weapon that was fired at me. It was French. I know quite a lot about guns. I was in the army once.'

He knew.

Just then she heard Bentinck's loud whistling of 'The British Grenadiers' coming nearer along the corridor, and the heavy tread of his feet, and she only had time to say, quite desperately, 'Please, Lucas, I know the Wycherley men would have nothing to do with anyone who would wish me harm! You said you wanted to help me and my family; if so, please, I beg you, say nothing of this.'

His face was grave. 'I won't, believe me,' he emphasized. 'In return, you must promise me that you won't go anywhere by yourself.'

'But—'

'If you need to leave the house, tell Bentinck to accompany you.'

'Bentinck?'

'I mean it,' he said in a low voice. The door was opening. 'I mean it, Verena.'

She bit her lip and left, exhausted by the welter of emotions that surged through her.

She could not trust him again, ever. And she must not let herself be alone with him again, either, because quite clearly she could not trust herself.

You practically threw yourself into his arms, Verena. You can't stop wanting to feel the sweet caress of his lips on your hands, your lips, your breasts...

You fool. You stupid fool.

Her mother was waiting for her at the end of the corridor. Looking—gleeful.

'Cook told me you were taking in Lord Conistone's soup!' Lady Frances pronounced in a conspiratorial whisper. 'But next time, Verena, wear something more *flattering*, for heaven's sake!' She tugged at Verena's demure neckline and reached to pat at her few stray curls. 'A little rouge, perhaps, also; you are too pale. It's a start, though. A start!'

Verena closed her eyes in despair.

Why had Lucas come here?

She had been resigned to her fate. To the sale of her beloved house. To finding herself some death-in-life post as a governess, or a lady's companion. And now...

Oh, Lucas. Oh, how unspeakably bereft she would be when he left.

Bentinck waited until the door had shut behind her, then muttered darkly, 'She really has no idea at all, milord?'

Lucas lay back wearily.

What in Hades had his grandfather been up to? And why did Verena blame *him* for it?

His arm was hurting like hell and the encounter had exhausted him. Not least because he'd found himself becoming spectacularly aroused as her luscious breasts heaved beneath the confines of that ridiculously outdated gown and her lovely eyes flashed fire at him…

Hell and damnation, didn't she realise how he ached for her? Probably not. She was an innocent. A virgin. He replied heavily, 'She has no idea about many things, including the fact that there are some remarkably dangerous people after her.' *Not least of them myself.* 'Did you get over to the steward at Stancliffe?'

'Old Rickmanby? Aye, and a miserable soul *he* is…but he told me the Earl should be back any day now.'

'Good.' It was time—more than time—for Lucas to tackle his grandfather.

Bentinck, who was busying himself with the fire, suddenly swung round on Lucas again. 'I know I'm harping on, milord, about those fellows who shot you—'

'You are indeed, Bentinck.'

'But Miss Verena, she's got a sharp brain, as well as bein' a prime piece, beggin' pardon—she must surely guess those men who attacked her were Johnny Frogs, so why isn't she saying anything?'

'She does know. But she's afraid that if she confirms her attackers were French, then the villagers will be charged with helping the enemy to land. And we'll say nothing either, Bentinck. Is that clear?'

'I suppose so, milord. But—who lit the fire to guide them in?'

'I wish I knew,' said Lucas, laying his head back against the pillows and closing his eyes.

Bentinck looked dubiously at the cooling dish of gruel. Then he burst out, 'We should get you to Stancliffe Manor. You're not amongst friends here.'

Lucas opened his eyes again, narrowly. A visit to Stancliffe Manor was most definitely required. But— 'While I'm here, Bentinck, I have the perfect opportunity to find what I need. And to discover who else is after it.'

'The maps and that diary, you mean? Pity you 'ad to take a bullet in the arm to get yourself in here!'

'It's not exactly what I planned, admittedly. But make use of every minute, will you, Bentinck, to search and listen?'

'She's on to me. Doesn't trust me a damned inch. A shame you couldn't tell her exactly why you left the army—'

Lucas cut in softly, 'If you whisper one word of it, Bentinck, I'll have your guts for fancy garters. I mean it.'

'Have you tried just askin' her, milord? For the diary and things?'

'I've asked. She's told me she has no idea where any diary might be. She *certainly* wouldn't let me see her father's private papers—I know that without asking. Questioning her again would seem distinctly suspicious; besides, I rather fear that the diary might give the game away.'

Bentinck made one last try. 'Would it not be easiest to be honest with her, milord? To kick the blarney and tell all, so to speak?'

'Two things: firstly, her ignorance is, at the moment, perhaps her greatest security. And, Bentinck,' Lucas went on softly, 'if I were—as you say—*honest* with her, she would pitch me out of this house and aim a pistol at me herself. Straight to the heart. For which I would not blame her, in the slightest.'

And that was the trouble, he thought, lying back with a stifled groan against the pillows. She really did have no idea, about anything. She had no idea that, weak though he was, her visit just now had been a torture of self-control for him.

A prime piece, Bentinck had called her. Yes, indeed, she was as utterly ravishing as he'd remembered, with her clouds of rippling chestnut hair and her amber eyes that gleamed like molten gold in the candlelight. And what made her even more entrancing was that, thanks to that ridiculous family of hers, she had absolutely no idea of her own beauty.

She was lovely, and vulnerable. And though clearly afraid of what life had cruelly thrown at her—not least his damned grandfather—she sought to mask her fears with cool efficiency. But beneath that coolness, he knew, raged tempestuous fires. That autumn she had been full of life, and hope, and love, and at the harvest feast he'd felt her tremble in his arms when he'd kissed her.

And the devil of it was, he knew she had not changed. Dear God, the thought of awakening her to the delights of full passion made his loins throb again, damn it. Last night on the clifftop path, as his mouth caressed hers, and he felt her tender breasts peak against the hard wall of his chest, he'd known she was the same Verena, the girl he had fallen in love with two years ago. *Before everything changed. Before the catastrophe that had altered everything irrevocably.*

He cursed himself softly. To indulge in any sort of hope that things could be as they were before was impossible. Tiredly he picked up the purse and the gold locket that she'd left on the bedside table and saw that the locket was, in fact, made not of gold, but of a cheap alloy.

Well, he wasn't going to be the one to tell her *that.*

When Bentinck came back in, he said sharply, 'Bentinck. You must follow her every time she leaves the house. Keep her in sight at all times, do you understand? And—get this message to Mayhew the attorney.' He handed Bentinck a folded sheet of paper. 'There's something I wish him to investigate.'

'Thought you hated legal fellows!'

'This one's better than most. And...' Lucas shifted himself on his pillows '...I've thought of a way to help the Sheldons.'

Bentinck grunted morosely. 'Hmph. Just don't expect them to be grateful, milord. That's all.'

Chapter Eight

'I heard that Lord Conistone was staying here, Verena! This is a terrible situation for you.'

It was ten in the morning. Another day and night had gone by since Lucas had been brought to the house; and Captain Martin Bryant had galloped round to call at Wycherley, his amiable face full of concern.

'Perhaps even more terrible for Lord Conistone,' said Verena. 'He was shot.'

She had not visited Lucas again; she mistrusted him deeply, herself even more. Dr Pilkington still called three times a day, and reported that Lucas needed to rest. But surely now he was well enough to travel to Stancliffe Manor?

And yet—and yet…

'Yes. I heard what happened!' exclaimed Martin. 'That you went down to Ragg's Cove and were physically attacked. My dear girl, did you see your assailants? Did they speak to you?'

Poor Martin. He was well meaning and well mannered, except when he was proposing marriage, and Verena, sighing inwardly, decided to keep things on a business-like footing by offering him tea in the parlour, while Cook bustled to and fro nearby.

'They made quite sure I didn't see their faces,' she replied, calmly pouring the tea. 'It was dark, of course. And as for their voices—no, they were remarkably silent. It was all over within minutes.'

He clenched his fists. 'Some of the Revenue men reported rumours that a boat full of Frenchmen landed somewhere along the coast that night! A sinister coincidence, surely, Conistone arriving here at the same time as the French are said to be around! Perhaps Conistone is not only a coward, but also a spy!'

Verena spluttered over her tea. 'Lord Conistone a spy? What nonsense you do talk, Martin! He *saved* me from my attackers!'

'Convenient, that he was there on your trail,' Martin muttered. 'I still say he might have been in collusion with them.'

'As I pointed out—he was *shot*, Captain Bryant!'

'And so you are burdened with him! Having to go up and down all day to see to him…'

'He is in the back parlour, so there's no need to go up and down at all. And his valet Bentinck sees to most of his needs, so it is no burden, I assure you!' *Unbelievable.* Martin's objections were actually forcing her to *defend* their unwelcome guest.

Martin didn't give up. 'It is a gross inconvenience for you and your mother, none the less. You take too much on yourself, Verena, you really do.' He stood up. 'You must not allow money and social position to sway you!'

She felt the colour warm her cheeks. 'You really are being rather insulting, Captain Bryant.'

'Then you must blame my feelings for you,' he urged in a low voice.

He was coming nearer, with an ominous intensity in his eyes. *Oh, no.* Verena jumped to her feet also, saying brightly, 'More tea, Captain Bryant? I will just ask Cook to bring us more hot water. And I am sure my mother would be delighted to join us.' She raised her voice. 'Cook! Cook, are you there?'

That did the trick. 'I must go now,' he said quickly, stepping away. 'But—remember I will be here whenever you want me, Verena!'

He departed, leaving Verena cross, upset and more disturbed than ever. As her own tea grew cold, she paced to and fro. Martin was warning her against Lucas. And perhaps he was right to do so. The trouble was that in Lucas Conistone's presence all reason left her, and her body and her brain became a mass of seething, forbidden emotions…

As soon as she could, she must get him out of the house, and out of her life, for her own peace of mind. Her own sanity.

Shortly afterwards, they had another visitor. Mr Mayhew arrived in his gig at eleven, to speak with Lord Conistone, he said.

Verena was astonished.

'His man Bentinck delivered the message,' Mr Mayhew said almost apologetically. 'I have done some work for his lordship in the past, you know.'

'No. I didn't know,' she said tartly. 'He is not thinking of making his will, I hope?'

Her attempt at levity was wasted. Mr Mayhew, not to be drawn, replied, 'Nothing so serious; though I was sorry to hear of the—fracas the other night, and about his unfortunate injury. I understand that you also were drawn into a situation of considerable danger, Miss Sheldon.'

'It was nothing,' she said quickly.

'I'm extremely glad to hear it. Your mother is well, I trust? Good.' Mr Mayhew bowed to her and turned to Turley, who was waiting to show him the way to Lucas's room.

'Mr Mayhew!' she called suddenly after his retreating back. 'About the other night—has Colonel Harrap been making trouble for the Wycherley men, do you know, with his foolish talk of French spies?'

Mr Mayhew hesitated. 'Nothing you need concern yourself about, my dear Miss Sheldon,' he said, then proceeded to follow Turley.

Why was he visiting Lucas? She frowned in perplexity. And suddenly remembered another of her worries.

Mr Mayhew had not yet mentioned the bill for his services on the day of the dispersal sale. In fact, he had not sent the Sheldons *any* bills for his advice for, oh, many months now.

She had intended to catch him before he left, but half an hour later she heard the sound of his gig rattling away down the drive. She bit her lip. *Botheration.*

Dr Pilkington was the next arrival; after visiting his patient, he came as usual to make his report. 'His lordship is recovering quickly, Miss Sheldon. But it's still just a little early for him to be moving to Stancliffe; he has lost a good deal of blood… I do hope that's not a problem?'

Verena hesitated. 'Of course not.' What else could she say?

But another night went by; and then, it most definitely *was* a problem, because that day at two, Izzy and Deb returned after their stay in Chichester, laden with hatboxes and parcels. Their mother rushed out to hug them and Pippa was there, too, to hear the news, as Lady Frances began to escort her chattering daughters inside. Then Izzy caught sight of Verena and ran over to her.

'Wait till you see the new gown I've ordered, Verena! I shall wear it in London, for my come-out, and I shall be the most beautiful of them all! Oh, I'm sorry—perhaps you're thinking we should have spent the money on that leaking roof instead, shouldn't we, and saved Wycherley?'

Verena felt instant remorse. Twelve guineas wouldn't save Wycherley. A thousand guineas wouldn't save Wycherley.

'Not at all, Izzy,' she said quickly. 'I'm glad you've had a lovely trip.'

'Oh, I have, I have! And now—I shall go and see Lucas! He is still here, isn't he? I shall tell him what a delightful time we had, and how he must attend my coming out!'

Verena jumped to block her way. 'Izzy, you'll do no such thing. It's not at all proper for you to be alone with Lord Conistone!'

Izzy was crestfallen, then brightened. 'Then I'll go to my room to unpack my new things!'

Deb had come over meanwhile, to fetch her hat from the carriage.

'Not proper for any of *us* to be alone with him,' Deb said silkily to Verena, 'but what about *you*? Trying your chances again with his lordship, are you? Is that why you bundled us all off to Chichester?'

Verena gasped. At that moment Pippa came up, just in time to hear the last barbed question. 'What did you say, Deborah?' Pippa exclaimed.

But Deb had already flounced off to her room with her parcels.

'Leave her, Pippa,' said Verena tiredly, 'it's of no matter.'

'It is,' said Pippa, putting her hands on her hips. 'Sooner or later I'm going to have a word with that sister of ours!'

And Pippa did. Half an hour later she came to Verena, who was sewing in the parlour, and her eyes were glittering. 'Listen. I've had a word with Deb. And there is something you absolutely must know. You realised, didn't you, how upset Deb was when Lucas turned up the other day without warning? She'd been hoping never to see him again!'

Verena sighed. 'That's understandable, after what happened at Lady Willoughby's party.'

'Perhaps it is, but not for the reasons you're thinking of! I was wondering—wasn't it rather *odd* of Lucas to turn up at the house of a girl he was supposed to have lured into a private room and attempted to kiss?'

'Yes,' said Verena honestly. 'But some men take such flirtations very lightly.'

'Maybe. As it happens, I've had my suspicions for some time, but only now have I— Well, let Deb tell you for herself.' Pippa raised her voice and called, 'Deborah!'

Deb was just outside the door, looking sullen. Pippa said silkily, 'Come in, sister mine. Tell Verena *exactly* what you told me.'

Verena got to her feet, her pulse inexplicably racing. Deb glanced at her and muttered, 'Oh, such a fuss. It wasn't true, my story about Lady Willoughby's party.'

Verena gasped.

Pippa snapped, 'Speak up, Deb!'

'All right, I made it up. About Lucas trying to—to kiss me.'

Verena took a step backwards. 'Oh, Deb—why?'

'I wanted him, that was why!' said Deb sullenly. 'What girl wouldn't? I knew it wouldn't be easy, because I come from an absolutely useless family with no money, but I knew

I was much prettier than the other girls who throw themselves at him! So—I asked him to bring me some wine; I said I would sit in the anteroom, where no one else was, because I was too hot in the ballroom. But—he just sent a footman to me, with a glass of lemonade!' Angry tears sparkled in her lovely blue eyes. 'I was so disappointed. I didn't see how he could turn me *down*…'

'Perhaps because he's equipped with common sense!' cried Pippa.

Deb clenched her fists. 'You're jealous, both of you, that's your trouble, because I'm so much prettier than either of you! You've ended up with just a farmer, Pippa. And Verena, the saintly Verena, you've ended up with nobody!'

Fiery Pippa's colour was high. 'That's enough, I think. Quite enough.'

Verena said softly, 'All right, Pippa. Let her go. The harm's been done.'

But Pippa turned to Verena when Deb had left. 'The little cat! She was jealous because it was you Lucas was interested in! You always deny it, but you and he were always together.'

'Please let it rest, Pippa.' Verena's voice was sharp.

But she was thinking, in anguish, *That night, after he was shot, he kissed me. He told me he cared for me—and I refused to listen. I couldn't believe in him, because of his grandfather's insults, and Deb's lies…*

Oh, Lucas. Did he really feel something for her after all?

It was too late. Far too late.

Pippa put her hand on her shoulder. 'I have to go now. But come round later, love, and stay for the night. David will call for you.' And Pippa with a nod, left; but then Verena realised that Turley, who'd driven her sisters back from Chichester, was in the room.

'Miss Sheldon. May I have a word?'

'Of course, Turley. What is it?'

He was looking grave. Her heart sank. 'Didn't want to tell her ladyship, or your sisters. But I heard, in Chichester, that the magistrates' court is sitting today. And the whole town was talking of it, because some of our men—Billy Dixon and the rest—were facin' a charge of treason, Miss Verena!'

She went white. '*Treason?* I should have known. I should have been told…'

Turley looked embarrassed. 'Fact is, Miss Verena, I thought you *did* know. You see, I heard Mr Mayhew and his lordship talking about it when I took them in tea yesterday…'

Talking about it. Behind her back… She bit her lip. 'Is there any news of the case yet, Turley?'

'No one here's heard anything yet, Miss Verena.'

But Turley could be wrong. There was *somebody* who might know. Somebody who seemed to know everything.

When Verena flew into his room, Lucas was dressed and sitting on the edge of the bed while Bentinck adjusted the sling in which his arm rested. Lucas got slowly to his feet, his eyes unreadable. 'Miss Sheldon. It's been a couple of days since you last made one of your—impromptu visits.'

'A word, if you please, Lord Conistone!'

'Is it a word,' he said gravely, 'that Bentinck is allowed to hear? Or would you prefer him to leave us?'

'No! I mean, yes!'

Lucas nodded to Bentinck, who plodded out, his face a picture, and closed the door.

Verena clasped her hands together. Alone with Lucas Conistone—*again*. How she piled the torment upon herself. Yet this was something that could not be stalled for mere etiquette. 'I have just heard this morning, my lord, that the Wycherley fishermen were up before the magistrates. And I've also been informed that you have discussed their case with Mr Mayhew! Those men are our tenants. Why was I not informed?'

He said quietly, 'Because Mr Mayhew had the matter in hand and I did not want you troubled.'

Her heart was thudding. 'Since when have Wycherley's villagers been your concern?'

'*You* are my concern, Verena,' he said.

She stumbled. That look in his eyes. Those dark, hidden, inexplicable depths. She was reminded, all too vividly, of the sweet sensation of his kiss. The heated tenderness of his hands, on her shoulders, her throat, her breasts. And she'd been wrong about Deb. But… *His grandfather. He utterly betrayed you to his grandfather.*

She breathed, 'This is—impossible. I should have *been* there.'

'They will be all right, believe me,' he repeated gravely.

The door opened. Her mother tiptoed in. 'My dear Lord Conistone—oh, Verena! You are here, my love! Lord Conistone, I was going to ask you if—to relieve the tedium of your convalescence—you might care to join us tonight for one of our musical soirées! Izzy and Deb are home again. They sing, you know, and Verena plays the piano quite wonderfully; but perhaps you are quite happy alone here with my dear Verena—such an *accomplished* girl! And—'

'Mama,' Verena broke in. 'Mama, will you go outside, please? I will join you in a minute.'

'Oh, if I have interrupted something—'

'You have,' declared Verena flatly. 'One minute, please.'

Lady Frances, simpering, left the room and closed the door very softly.

Lucas said to her, 'The villagers are safe. Bentinck went into Chichester earlier to get me the latest news. I think Mr Mayhew wanted to explain to you himself.'

'To explain *what*?' Her voice shook with tension.

'As you know, Colonel Harrap accused your villagers of signalling to the French, on the night in question. The magistrates said there was not enough proof, so the case was dismissed.'

'*Entirely?* They are quite free?'

He hesitated. 'There was a small matter of surety, as a guarantee of their good behaviour in the future.'

Oh, no. Surety. How could the estate ever afford it? 'H-how much?'

'There is no need whatsoever to concern yourself,' Lucas went on quickly. Too quickly. 'A friend, a well-wisher, has settled the matter.'

'Mr Mayhew! But he has already done so much for us, he has never charged us for *anything* since my father went away, I cannot allow this—'

Something in his face made her break off. Suddenly, with a sickening lurch of her stomach, she knew. 'Lucas. It was you, wasn't it?'

'I told Mr Mayhew that I wanted to help if the question of surety came up, yes.'

She stared at him, her heart thudding. 'And his bills? For his services to my family?'

He said nothing. She breathed, 'You have been paying those too. *Why?*'

He spread out his hands. 'I wrote to offer my help, Verena, when your father died. I suggested that paying your legal bills might be one way in which I could serve your family. You told me earlier that you got my letters, but didn't read any of them. Because you never replied, I assumed the arrangement was acceptable.'

She had burned his letters without even reading them.

And Mr Mayhew too had perhaps assumed that for the sake of her family she was happy to quietly accept Lucas Conistone's money…

Never. Never. Nothing would make up for either his grandfather's callous cruelty, or for Lucas's betrayal of her. Now she whispered, 'You must go. Please. I will speak myself to Mr Mayhew, of course, but this—your being here—is impossible…'

He gave a slight bow. Said quietly, 'Of course.'

As she was turning to leave, she saw suddenly that there was a plan laid out on the table, a plan of the Wycherley estate, and froze. 'What is this?'

'It's something Mayhew brought over,' he said, walking over to gesture at it with his uninjured arm. 'Verena, did your father ever say anything to you about a stream that ran through Wycherley's lands, close to the border with my grandfather's estate?'

She lifted her head to him almost in despair. 'No. *No.* Lucas, when will this interfering stop? When will you leave us alone?'

He folded the map away, his face sombre. 'I will make arrangements to depart first thing in the morning,' he said.

She lifted her chin. 'Very well. As it happens, I'm visiting my sister, Pippa, tonight—'

He broke in sharply. 'You're not going there alone?'

'David, her husband, is calling for me! So you may well have gone, my lord, before I return tomorrow!"

'Then it's—farewell,' he said softly.

She nodded and stumbled towards the door. Once outside, she stood there in the passageway, shaking.

What else was going on that she had not been told about?

He had to go. He had to leave Wycherley as soon as possible. Because with just one word, just one touch, he could hurt her with the kind of pain she hadn't even realised existed.

But then she would never see him again. A black abyss of total despair opened up before her. She stood there a moment, looking—as Turley, who passed by the end of the corridor, told Cook later—as if the life had gone out of her.

'Damn,' Turley, with awe, heard her breathe. 'Damn, damn, *damn*. I will *not* accept his charity, I will not accept *anything* from him, I will not have him in this house any longer!'

Chapter Nine

After Verena had gone, Lucas slept for an hour on his bed. He'd refused Dr Pilkington's laudanum, because it disturbed his dreams; but the dreams came anyway, and they were about Verena. He dreamed that he held her slender yet enticing body in his arms. Dreamed that he was kissing her, making love to her, clasping her silken hips to his and she was responding with passion, and breathless desire…

Then in his dream she broke away from him, saying to him with loathing in her voice, *'My father. Why are you telling these terrible lies about my father?'* And she was running, running away from him, and suddenly she had disappeared, and there instead was the figure of Jack Sheldon, climbing along the ice-capped ridge of that mountain in Spain, while Lucas called out, 'No! It doesn't have to be this way, Jack! Stop, for the love of God! All I want is your diary…'

And the last thing Lucas remembered of Wild Jack Sheldon was the look of sheer horror in his eyes as he clutched that oilskin package close and went tumbling, tumbling into the raging torrent of a river hundreds of feet below.

Look after Verena.

Lucas sat up, the perspiration beading on his forehead. Then he saw that the late afternoon sun was pouring through the window, and Bentinck was sitting there, morosely offering him a tumbler of brandy. 'You bin havin' them bad dreams again, milord?'

'Yes. *Yes.*' He wanted her. Jack's daughter. And it was—quite simply—impossible. 'What time is it, Bentinck?'

'Four in the afternoon. You must rest, milord. Everything you asked about is bein' attended to.'

'Even so, there is danger—*everywhere.*'

Bentinck allowed himself a crack of a smile. 'Wot, amongst all these women? Now I'll agree with you there, milord.'

Lucas responded with a faint grin, and lay wearily back against the pillows. His arm was hurting like the devil again. 'You're damned right. But you must tell me what you've discovered.'

'Now, I don't want you crocking yourself again, milord, gettin' up before you're ready and landin' yourself with a hellfire fever again!'

'I swear I most certainly *will* get up if you don't tell me your news,' replied Lucas evenly.

'Well, I told you about the magistrates' court.'

'You did.'

'And the Earl your grandfather's just got back from Bath.'

Lucas clenched his fists. 'Has he now?'

'And then, in between, I've bin lookin' round 'ere, room by room, just like you said. Especially up amongst those boxes of papers and stuff they'd cleared from the north wing when the roof leaked in spring. There was no sign that anyone else had bin searchin', like you feared. All covered with dust, them boxes; I'd have known if someone had been in. So we're still ahead of the game. And I found—*these*.' He handed Lucas some scruffy, folded sheets of paper.

Lucas scanned them swiftly. 'Good,' he breathed. 'In fact—excellent. But no diary?'

'No diary.'

Lucas was swinging his legs to the floor, easing his arm out of its sling. 'Then I'll manage—somehow—without it. Bentinck, tomorrow I'll have to leave here.'

Bentinck sighed. 'You're not off on your travels again, milord? With that crocked arm?'

'Yes, but I'm leaving you behind.'

'Oh, my God…'

'Yes. As well as continuing to look for that diary, you must watch constantly for any strangers around the place. And you must try to be aware at all times of where Verena—Miss Sheldon—is.'

'Bloomin' difficult,' muttered Bentinck. 'She don't like me one bit. And I just ain't built for creepin' around, fiddling locks and peeping through keyholes. Give me a proper battle any time, milord.'

'Me, too,' agreed Lucas with feeling. 'But one of the rules of warfare, Bentinck, is that we need to know—precisely—who our enemies are. Agreed?'

'Agreed, milord,' said Bentinck heavily. 'And I've done just as you asked—saddled up a horse for you and left it round the side of the house, where, if you go out now, no one will see you. Though how you can ride with that arm—'

Lucas interrupted. 'You say the coast's clear?'

'The servants have been given what's left of the afternoon off, as well as the evening. There's a wedding in the village.'

'Good.' He was already easing his arms into his coat. 'I'll follow you out, past the servants' quarters. I might be a little while. Verena is visiting her sister—the sensible one—and staying overnight, so you can have a few hours away from here. Ask some questions for me. Visit the Royal George in Framlington, if you wish.'

Bentinck squinted. 'The alehouse? You sure? Don't want that Miss Verena tearin' a strip off me hide for neglectin' you!'

Lucas laughed. 'Afraid of her, Bentinck?'

'She's got a strong will in her, that one! She'd fight like the devil himself for what she believes in, I'd say!' He eyed the locket Lucas had picked up suspiciously. 'What in tarnation have you got there, milord?'

'You could call it another of Wild Jack's false promises,' Lord Lucas Conistone said grimly. 'Now, go and check that my escape route's clear.'

'You are coming back tonight, milord, aren't you?'

'Indeed. One last night here, then I'm on my way.'

Bentinck moved off. Lucas looked quickly again at the papers Bentinck had brought him, which were all covered with Wild Jack's sketch maps of a hitherto-uncharted region. He read aloud the words written at the foot of one of them: *'Route of the River Tagus; its source and progress through the Portuguese mountains, 1808...'*

He put them in the deep inside pocket of his coat.

Perhaps, after all, these were as good as he was going to get. Perhaps he should be *satisfied* with these...

He glanced at a document Mr Mayhew had brought him: an old plan marking the boundary between the Stancliffe and Wycherley estates.

He pushed that also in his pocket. Then, after locking the door of his room, he quickly followed Bentinck through the silent house and out into the late afternoon sunshine, to mount the horse Bentinck had ready.

Lucas had forgotten what a huge, dusty old mausoleum of a place Stancliffe Manor was. But he remembered how he had felt when, aged sixteen, he was told that both his parents were dead of a fever and that some day all this would be his.

The heavy curtains in the north-facing bedchamber were drawn shut against the daylight. The Earl sat in an armchair by the fireplace, in dressing robe and cap. Despite the blazing logs, the room was cold and the candles few.

'You have been interfering, Lucas,' said the Earl in a quavering voice. 'You have meddled behind my back while I was away.' He pointed a gnarled, accusing finger at his only grandson. 'Remember, my boy, Stancliffe is not yours yet!'

And the Earl, who was seventy-five years old and almost a recluse except for his trips to Bath for his failing health, broke into a fit of coughing.

Lucas, whose arm throbbed like hell from the ride there, forced himself into patience. He said, 'Twenty years ago, Grandfather, you diverted a stream that used to run through the Wycherley estate in order to power the corn mill you built on Stancliffe land. Did you divert that stream legally? Did you ever ask Sir Jack Sheldon's permission?'

'Legally?' the Earl snorted. 'No one knew, no one cared. That stream flowed through uncultivated land, and Wild Jack didn't even damn well notice, he was away so often!'

Lucas pulled a document from his pocket. He said steadily, 'I have a plan here, showing its former route. You had no right to divert it. And now it's time for you to make compensation.'

'Pah!' The Earl's gnarled hand shook on the stick he gripped. 'Why all this concern for a bunch of country nobodies? Next you'll be bringing in this French revolutionary nonsense, telling me we have to give every damn thing away!'

'If you won't compensate the Sheldons, then I will,' said Lucas flatly, shoving the folded plan back in his pocket.

The Earl stared. 'You'll do it with your own money, then!'

'I will,' answered Lucas calmly. 'With my mother's money. Why do you wish the Sheldons such harm, sir? Why did you use your influence to persuade the bank to foreclose on Wycherley's mortgage?'

The Earl was wringing his hands. 'My revenge was just! It was because he *cheated* me!'

'Who? Jack Sheldon?'

'Who else? The damned rogue, he told me he'd found treasure in the Portuguese mountains! Gold from the Americas, brought back by explorers long ago and hidden—my God, are you after the secret, too?'

Lucas drew his hand tiredly across his forehead. *That rubbish again.* 'I'm not after gold, because there was none,' he said quietly.

The candles were burning low. Several had already gone out. The Earl banged his fist on the arm of his chair. 'I offered him money, yes, I did, to pay for his knowledge. He took it, but then he went back to Portugal two years ago to gather up all that treasure for himself!'

Lucas sighed. 'I repeat. There was no—'

But what was the use? Lucas looked around the dreary room and started again. 'You should live in more comfort, Grandfather. Open the house up. Let in light and air.'

'No! The damp air will kill me!' the old man wheezed. 'Besides, I have to watch, all the time!'

Lucas repeated softly, 'Watch?'

'Yes, indeed! In case Jack comes back, trying to steal!'

'Grandfather, Jack Sheldon is *dead*. Did you ever see a diary? Jack's journal of his travels?'

The Earl darted a fierce glance at him. 'I told you, I have nothing that belongs to that scoundrel. But he took my money!'

Lucas ran his hand tiredly through his dark hair. 'You told the banks to withdraw credit from the Wycherley estate—you all but ruined them—just for some petty revenge against a dead man?'

'Not only that, Lucas! I was thinking of *you*, my boy! You see, I'd heard the little hussy was after *you*!'

Lucas was suddenly rigid. 'You heard what?'

'Rickmanby told me!' The Earl was starting to whimper now. 'Two years ago, when you came home from the army, she was always pestering you, always tempting you, Jack's oldest! She was after your fortune!'

'Never,' said Lucas curtly. 'Never.'

But the Earl hadn't finished. 'You were a fool not to see it; you deserve a far better wife than that little harlot, and I told her so…'

Lucas was on his feet. 'You did *what*? You used that actual word? *Harlot*?'

'I called her that in my letter, yes!' The Earl looked sullen, almost defiant.

Lucas sat down again, his face bleak. 'I don't deserve *her*, that's for sure. My God, you've done her a great, great wrong, sir.' He passed his hand briefly across his eyes.

He knew his grandfather had treated her family vilely, but not *this*. Now he understood everything. Her refusal to accept his help, to even read his letters. *Harlot*. Oh, Verena. If his dreams had seemed desperate before, they were surely impossible now.

'Her father was a cheat!' The Earl rapped his stick on the floor for emphasis. 'I tell you, he promised me a share in the gold, then tried to tell me there was none!' A look of cunning suddenly crept over the Earl's face. 'You and Jack were close for a while, weren't you? I remember him teaching you those faradiddle languages, Spanish and Portuguese. But now you say that Jack is dead. So everyone assumes the secret of the gold is lost. Died with him, that's what they all think, that's what I told him when he came the other day…'

'*Who* came the other day?' Lucas spoke with renewed harshness.

The Earl started coughing. 'Oh, my memory—sometimes my memory tricks me, and I think I see Jack Sheldon again…'

Lucas stood up tiredly. 'Grandfather, you've done more harm than you can begin to imagine. I have to go away now, but believe me, I'll be back very soon. And you will do nothing else, absolutely nothing, to harm the Sheldons, do you understand?'

'Always leaving me,' muttered the Earl bitterly. 'Parties, London. Horses. Sailing off overseas… *Compensation?* To Jack Sheldon's profligate family? Ridiculous!'

'I'll be back soon,' Lucas repeated. He bowed, and left.

The Earl's rheumy eyes were like slits as he muttered to himself, 'The girl. The hussy. *She* was Jack's favourite. *She* was closest to him!' Suddenly he got up and hobbled to the window, pushing back the curtains so he could see Stancliffe's acres of wild garden, the lakes. The island pavilion, where he and Jack used to meet…

Two days ago he'd had another visitor, who'd pretended to be his friend. Who'd told him it was his duty to his country to reveal, if he knew it, where Jack's diary was.

They all wanted that diary, but it was his! For he, the Earl, had paid Jack Sheldon dearly for it. And its whereabouts was a secret he intended to keep.

Chapter Ten

By the time Lucas got back to Wycherley, the sun was setting. Quietly he stabled the horse and let himself in, preparing to spend just one more night here.

By the morning he would be gone.

Guessing Bentinck would still be at the Framlington alehouse, Lucas extinguished all the candles except one and, wearing just his breeches, sprawled on the bed and slept.

Suddenly he was wide awake. He thought he'd heard someone, or something, outside the west window. Glancing at his watch, he saw that it was past ten. He reached under the pillow for his pistol.

He blew out the candle and edged up to the wall by the window, angling his head to look out. In the garden all was dark.

There was the sound again. Someone was creeping through the bushes that grew close to the house.

Lucas padded barefoot across the room to pick up the long iron poker from the grate, dangled his pale handkerchief from its tip, then swiftly raised it up against the window pane. A bullet came crashing through the glass. He dived aside, landing on the floor, jarring his injured arm. Glass splinters scattered around him. He lay cursing softly. *My arm. Hell and damnation, my arm...*

He heaved himself up and grabbed for his pistol again. Through the broken window, he glimpsed someone running away into the darkness. He took aim and fired.

Too late.

And in falling he had broken open his wound. Blood was seeping through the bandage.

Swiftly he searched for and found the spent bullet that had smashed into the bookcase opposite the window. He pushed the books around to cover the damage and slipped the bullet into his pocket. He carefully broke away more of the window pane, dropping the glass outside, then re-lit the candle and a few others round the room—*whoever did this was a coward, and would doubtless have run as far as his legs could carry him.* Then he went over to the washstand where there was a roll of fresh bandaging, and began the laborious task of re-dressing his wound single-handed.

Give me a proper battle, any time.

But then he'd known, hadn't he, what he was letting himself in for?

Verena was upstairs in her bedroom. David had indeed called earlier, but only to tell her that her visit must be postponed, as one of the children had a mild fever.

She'd expressed her concern, and sent Pippa her love; but the empty hours stretched ahead. Desperate to distract herself, she turned again to the London newspaper David had brought; to the latest news of the war. *Our Portuguese correspondent reports that Lord Wellington's army has vacated the fortress of Almeida and is planning a two-*

hundred-mile march to Lisbon, which is held at present just by a small British force.

She could picture it all, because she'd seen her father's maps, heard his travel stories. To get from Almeida on the Spanish frontier to Lisbon meant, she knew, climbing across mountainous terrain before the coastal plain was reached. Lucas had told her once that whoever held Lisbon, with its vital port, would control all of Portugal…

She put the newspaper down slowly. *Lucas*. Everything always came back to Lucas. He had been paying Mr Mayhew's bills. He had known more about the court case than *she* did. Unforgivable! Tomorrow, she would ensure that he kept his word and left forthwith! *And then she would never see him again.*

She stared blindly out of the window into the darkness. Even losing Wycherley seemed nothing, compared to losing Lucas…

The house seemed eerily quiet. Her mother and sisters had gone early to bed. Cook and Turley had asked permission to go to the celebration of a wedding in the village and were not back yet. Their other servants did not live in.

When she heard the sound of breaking glass and—*Lord, was that a gun shot?*—she was on her feet in an instant, her heart pounding. The noise came, surely, from Lucas's room downstairs. Clutching her shawl about her, she almost flew down the stairs and rapped sharply on the door.

'Lucas? *Lucas?*'

No answer. She hurried in—and froze.

He was standing with his back to her by the table on which the water jug stood and the rolls of bandages. Nearer to her, the floor was strewn with splinters of glass. She realised the curtain to the west window was pulled back, revealing a jagged hole in the centre of one of the panes. She let out a low cry.

Lucas whirled around to face her. And what had registered only faintly at first in her mind became all too clear. *Verena, you fool, charging in without waiting.*

He was clad only in hip-hugging buckskin breeches. His calves, strong and shapely, were unclad, as were his feet. She was presented with the full sight of that manly golden torso rippling with muscle, the broad chest and shoulders tapering down in smooth sculpted ridges to the perfection of his slim waist and loins.

Her throat was dry. No man had the right to look so beautiful.

In the unfortunate event of a young lady finding herself alone in a room with a man, she must avert her eyes, say nothing and leave immediately…

Miss Bonamy should try looking at Lucas Conistone, half-undressed, and see if *she* could avert her eyes.

Verena swallowed and said, as steadily as she could, 'What has happened, my lord?' and then she realised. He had been trying his best to hold a wad of bandaging to it, but his wounded arm was bleeding again. 'Oh, *Lucas.*' She hurried instinctively towards him, all embarrassment forgotten. 'Let me see to that, before you bleed to death. But *how…*?' She glanced in distress at the broken window again.

He said through gritted teeth, 'It's nothing. Just the gale outside. A piece of a branch came flying through.'

There was a breeze from the sea, but she wouldn't have called it a gale. Doubt assailed her. She stiffened. 'Really? Then where is it, this branch?'

'I tossed it outside again,' he swiftly replied. 'You weren't meant to be here, you were meant to be at your sister's.'

'The visit had to be cancelled,' she muttered. 'Just as well—I cannot leave you for one hour, it seems. Please sit on the bed, my lord, and I will bandage your wound again.

Where is Bentinck? I must send him for Dr Pilkington in Framlington—'

'No.'

His voice was so harsh that she looked at him wonderingly. 'No?'

'There is no need, Verena,' he said more gently. He sat down at last, on the edge of the bed.

Then she saw it. The ugly scar snaking along his left ribs, a raised and angry seam, still not fully healed; the result, Dr Pilkington had said, of a vicious thrust from a French sabre... *'Lucas.'* She was staring at it, horrified.

'An old wound,' he said quickly. 'It's nothing.'

'It's *not* old! I'm not a fool, Lucas!'

He sighed. 'You're determined to out all my secrets, aren't you? Very well—I fought a duel a few months ago.'

A duel? With a man wielding a French sabre?

She thought not.

None of her business. None of her business... But her hands were shaking.

'I'd better patch you up again,' she said as steadily as she could.

'Yes, but, Verena, look, the bleeding's all but stopped.' He had turned so she could no longer see that scar, but instead she saw the blood that still trickled steadily down his right arm.

'It hasn't stopped and I must bind it.' She did so quickly and efficiently, finding a pad of clean linen and getting to work. She pretended to herself that it was just like seeing to one of her younger sisters' scratches when they used to romp in the garden; pretended that the warm skin overlaying taut sinews against which her fingertips brushed was having no effect on her whatsoever...

A downright lie. She had never realised a man's body

could be so exquisite. The strong, golden musculature of his chest and shoulders made her pulse race sweetly. Her head was swimming at his nearness. At the male scent of him. 'There,' she said, with a passable effort at brisk efficiency. 'Now, I will fetch you some tea, or brandy, and something to eat. Cook left a tray for you in the kitchen, for your supper, but I saw it has not been touched.'

'No!' he insisted again.

She lifted her shoulders in near-despair. 'Lucas, you need to restore your strength! Wherever has Bentinck got to? He might persuade you into some sense!'

Lucas said shortly, 'I sent Bentinck to the village earlier.'

'To the village…'

'Yes. To the alehouse.'

'Then we are alone?'

'We are alone.' He added, disarmingly softly, 'Is that so terrible?'

She tried to draw away, pushing back her tousled chestnut hair from her cheeks. 'What's happened to this room is terrible!' she declared, trying to hide her confusion by feigning housewifely concern. 'My goodness, I really must tidy up the broken glass, and see about getting the broken window boarded up before I go—'

'There are shutters,' he gently reminded her. 'Will not they suffice? And Bentinck will sweep up the glass when he finally returns. There's no reason for you to do the work of a servant.'

'Nevertheless, I—'

He caught hold of her shoulder. 'I meant it. You should value yourself more, Verena.'

She froze at his touch. Her eyes were wide and heartsore. 'Value myself more?' she whispered. 'When you do not even value me enough to tell me the truth? Ever since you arrived on the day of that hateful sale, things have *happened* here, Lucas, bad things! Those men above Ragg's Cove, who shot you. Now, this!'

'Sit down, Verena,' he commanded quietly.

She did so, almost numbly, on one of the chairs beside the bed. He poured her some wine, kept by his bedside, and pushed the glass towards her. 'Drink,' he said. 'It will help.'

Her fingers trembling, she took a tiny sip.

He dragged another chair across and sat astride it, his eyes never leaving her face. 'Do you know,' he went on softly, 'when I saw you two years ago I thought you were something out of a dream.' Her pulse began to race. 'It was that wonderful autumn,' he went on. 'You were sitting in the shade of the haystack, Verena, in your sprigged muslin gown and sunbonnet, with your spectacles perched delightfully on the end of your nose. You'd flung aside your book on etiquette and were reading about farming. Turnips.'

Her heart thumped. She gulped down too much wine. She said tightly, 'I suppose you found me—and all of us—amusing!'

'Amusing?' He refilled her glass; his face was serious. 'I was home, from the war. And you were my island of sanity, Verena. You were at the heart of my dream of another life.' His hooded eyes darkened. He whispered, 'I need that dream now.'

For a moment she was unable to speak. He went on, 'They were happy days, that autumn, weren't they? You know, I'd made such plans for myself, Verena. But then I found my world turned upside down. Because I'd fallen in love with you.'

She could hardly breathe. She was sure he must hear her heart breaking all over again, for she could. His grandfather's hideous message still seared her mind.

She drank more wine. She said, striving to keep her voice steady, 'Lucas, there is no point in going back over all this...'

'There is,' he said. 'There is *every* point. Now I have some idea, at last, of the damage my grandfather has done. Not only did he try to ruin your family financially; but he has insulted you quite vilely.'

'How do you—'

'I've been to see him. This afternoon. I know everything, Verena. And I want you to know that I've said nothing at all to him, either two years ago or at any time since, of how I felt about you; of my plans, for the two of us...'

Her heart was thudding wildly. 'Oh, *Lucas*.'

He caught her hand. 'I loved you,' he broke in. 'But you stopped caring for me. Tell me, for God's sake, *why* you despise me so much. Why you were so ready to believe slanders about me, even though I begged you to trust me before I went away. Is it because you think I'm a coward?'

'No! Never!' Her voice broke. 'I've told you—how could I possibly think you a coward, when you were actually *shot* for saving me from those vile men who attacked me?'

'Having observed for myself how intrepid you are,' he said drily, 'I believe you could probably have taken them on yourself.' And he smiled. But suddenly he looked deathly tired. She wanted to take him in her arms, and soothe that pale, handsome face, that strong jawline now shadowed by stubble, with soft, cherishing kisses. He'd talked of his love for her. He said he *hadn't* betrayed her to the Earl. Too late. Far too late. All in the past. And oh, Lord, she'd had too much to drink...

She said, her heart and mind in turmoil, 'Lucas, listen to me, please! I *cannot* let you pay Mr Mayhew's bills, or the surety! We must talk of this again, tomorrow, perhaps, or with Mr Mayhew present—'

'No,' he said. '*No.* We might not get this chance to talk again, for some time!'

Her eyes clouded. 'You have had opportunities before, Lucas. Long before, if you had wished to take them.'

'I wrote to you. You never replied. You told me yourself that you burned my letters.'

Her hand flew to her throat. *True.*

'Then,' he went on steadily, 'I heard your sister Deborah would be at Lady Willoughby's party in London—though what your mother was doing taking her unmarried daughter to such a shabby affair I could not understand—so I went, and asked your sister to tell you that I needed an answer to my letters, for all sorts of reasons. Obviously my plea did nothing to change your mind.'

She gazed at him, transfixed. 'My—my sister did not pass on that message.' She felt sick to her stomach. *Oh, Lucas.* No point in telling him about Deb's lies and multiplying the mischief already done.

Lucas raked his hand tiredly through his hair. 'Deuce take it,' he said tersely, 'between us we have been ill served by our families! I'm sorry. You loved your father very much, I know. Verena—is it true he promised you that some day he would make you all rich?'

She swallowed, hard. 'He did, yes. He—he spoke of some secret that is gone now for ever…' Her low voice resonated with heartbreak. 'We lost my dear father. We lost everything.'

Lucas was silent for a moment and the candles flickered fitfully. 'Do you know how he died?'

'It was an accident, in the mountains. A terrible accident.'

Lucas bowed his head so she could not see his eyes. Then he lifted his face again and said, 'Verena. What if I can help you? What if I can help Wycherley?'

She lifted her head with a jerk. *Guard yourself, Verena.* 'We will not accept charity! We will not be any further in your debt!'

His jaw was set in determination. 'I'm not *offering* charity! What if there's a sum of money that's legally *owed* to you, Verena? Do you place your damned pride higher than your concern for the estate, its workers, your own family?'

Her distress showed in her amber-gold eyes. 'How can you even ask? I care more than anything! Not just for us, but—if the Earl buys Wycherley, our villagers will suffer. I *know* the Earl will be a harsh landlord.'

'If you just trust me,' he said, 'I will see that justice is done.'

She stood for a moment in stunned silence, her face a vivid picture. At last she breathed, 'Each way I turn, you are there ahead of me. It is as if you are pulling strings over which I have no control. Oh, Lucas, I cannot take the *risk* of trusting you!'

He said—nothing. She clenched her hands at her sides, and went on, rather desperately, 'This must be tiring you. I will leave you to rest.'

He sighed. 'Come here,' he said quietly.

Lucas knew this was the moment. *'Come here,'* he murmured again.

And slowly, as if mesmerised, she obeyed.

Chapter Eleven

His grandfather. Her foolish mother and sisters. They'd all worked their mischief on this beautiful woman. Lucas Conistone steeled himself. Now he, with full knowledge of what he was doing, was about to take the greatest of all risks with her future happiness.

'Verena.' With his free hand he again took her by the shoulder. Turned her to face an oval looking-glass hanging on the wall. 'Look at yourself, Verena.'

He, too, gazed in silence at her huge dark-lashed amber eyes set in that perfect heart-shaped face. Saw the gleaming chestnut hair, rippling loosely past her shoulders; saw those full, curving lips that looked as if they remembered his last kiss, and longed for another.

This was the moment. Enemies were closing in. He had to make her his, before it was too late.

Before she found out—everything.

And, God forgive him, innocent that she was, wronged as she was, she was making it so damned easy.

He lifted her rich heavy hair that was faintly scented with lavender and kissed the nape of her neck. Before she could say anything, he began to gently ease her shabby old gown from her shoulders. Her creamy smooth skin glowed in the candlelight. His long fingers pushed her bodice lower.

The silk chemise. No corset, but—she was wearing that silk chemise.

'Lucas…' she breathed. 'Lucas, *no*…'

He let his warm hand rest on the sweet swell of one breast. Felt his loins tightening. He said, 'Once I thought you loved me.'

She bit her lip and tried to pull away. 'Ridiculous! Why should I imagine that there could be anything more than friendship—'

He clasped her closer. *'Friendship?'* he broke in. 'What about—desire? Look into that mirror. If nothing else, I want you to see how beautiful you are. You have been cast into the shade by your selfish family for far too long. What man in his right mind would *not* desire you?' He swung her round to face him.

'Lucas,' she whispered, 'this is impossible…'

The silk chemise had slipped, to reveal one cherry-tipped breast. He put his left arm round her and drew her close.

He was standing over her, towering over her. He put his finger to her cheek and drew it lightly down her skin. Scorched by his touch, Verena instinctively backed away, only to feel his arm curl more firmly around her and tug her towards him so she all but fell against his naked chest. 'Lucas—' Strong fingers caught hold of her chin, tilting it as his mouth closed over hers in a kiss that stopped the breath in her throat.

And Verena was lost. To his tenderness. To his silken voice. The sensation of her acutely sensitive bosom chafing gently against his rippling, hard-muscled chest, his silken warm skin, was so delicious as to make her almost swoon.

The wine, she told herself. But it wasn't the wine. It was Lucas.

'You are beautiful, Miss Sheldon,' he murmured in her ear.

And it was then that his kiss began. A kiss that reached in and tugged at her heart and deeper. A kiss so exquisite she thought she would die of joy, except that she wanted more; her breasts ached for more and at the juncture of her thighs was liquid longing.

She leaned into the welcome of his warm enfolding body, weak with desire. Now he was prising her lips apart, his tongue assertively tracing the soft inner flesh of her mouth, then probing, teasing, enticing.

Little flames began their dance of desire at the pit of her abdomen. His hand slid up to cup the nape of her neck as he deepened his kiss and she felt herself responding.

Lucas. Her eyes fluttered shut. She felt her nipples pucker and tingle as his firm tongue began an insistent, rhythmic probing in her mouth that awakened still further the tormenting desire at all the sensitive parts of her body. Her own hands were sliding round his shoulders with a will of their own, pressing flat against the firm, muscled flesh of his back that was so silken, so warm. She let his tongue in deeper, shyly caressed it with her own, becoming so lost in this wondrous feeling that embroiled all her senses that she forgot everything as she clasped him tighter and felt—oh, Lord, she felt the hard, pulsing arousal at his loins…

'*Hell.*' It was he who pulled away from her, gasping. 'My arm…'

'I'm sorry, Lucas. So sorry!'

'Don't be.' He was still caressing the nape of her neck where her chestnut curls tumbled free. Circling the spot rhythmically with the pad of his thumb, in a meaningful pattern that made her go hot and cold. 'No harm done.'

But much harm had been done. *A harlot. No better than a fortune-hunting harlot.* The Earl's savage words lashed her anew, for that was what everyone would think… She jerked away. Stood clumsily, straightening her hair and pulling up her gown, unable to meet his eyes. She could still taste him. Still feel that strong, warm body, lithe and hard against her own, compelling her, so clearly desiring her…

No more than she desired him.

As if he guessed her innermost thoughts, he rapped out, 'My grandfather is a fool and a liar. Forget his wicked insults. Stay with me.'

She whispered, 'But this is madness. Someone might come in.'

He went to bolt the door. 'Stay.'

It was nothing less than a command. And resistance was useless, for by the time he returned to take her in his arms again, her body had already surrendered.

His long, fine fingers stroked her velvety throat, then tilted her chin as he lowered his lips to hers. Gently he savoured her; it was not enough. The touch of his silken skin, the strong smooth muscles beneath, the male scent of him, the feel of his tongue stroking hers rhythmically, all were intoxicating. Heady as rich wine, causing the blood to pound heavily through her veins, making her languorous, dizzy with desire.

With the utmost care, he eased her gown down to her waist. *That silky undergarment: sensuous, gorgeous…* He felt lust rearing, fought it down; he needed, above all, not to frighten her. He slipped off one delicate shoulder strap with care, with devotion. The peak of her breast stood out, coral-red, from its flushed areola; he caressed the nub with his thumb pad, then bent to take it in his mouth. She cried out as tremors ricocheted through her and clung to his shoulders for support, arching her back in an intense spasm of primitive desire. He lifted his head, watching her face, his eyes dark and unfathomable. *'Meu amor,'* he whispered.

He guided her to the bed and eased her down against the pillows. She was clad now only in her flimsy chemise and stockings. Verena clung to him, heavy with need, wanting him to lie with her, wanting to feel his muscled body hard against her nakedness, wanting him to fill her aching emptiness. But he kissed her mouth instead, until she was liquid with hunger, and then she felt his hand pushing up her gown, touching the delicate skin of her thigh above her white stocking.

His lips moved to her breast, drawing in the exquisitely sensitive peak again. *'Lucas—'* She was writhing against him. Begging him. Wanton.

A gasp of pleasure escaped from her lips and her thighs fell apart as his fingers found her very core of need and caressed her insistently there.

No, she told herself. *This is wrong. The Earl was right to think you a whore.*

But the room was swimming around her in spiralling circles of pleasure as the candles cast sensual golden shadows across the beauteous male curves and planes of this man's exquisite torso as he hovered purposefully beside her, over her. She was beyond control. Utterly in his power. And she wanted to be nowhere else.

She dug her fingers into the lean muscle encased by his breeches, her whole body pulsing to the rhythm of his fingers, crying out his name over and over as he caressed her to her extremity. *Lucas.* Her entire being, her very soul, melted with incandescent pleasure.

Lucas Conistone knew that he'd made her—almost—his. His plan was underway. *You are a bastard*, he told himself. *A cold, cynical bastard.*

It would be so easy to make love to her. He knew she was beautiful and brave, but he had not realised she would be so incredibly sensual. His own arousal throbbed devilishly within the constraints of his clothing. *You must control yourself. You could easily take her.* But—not yet.

Forcing himself to subdue the pounding at his loins, he held her until she was quite still. He smothered her sighs of ecstasy with his deep, sensual kisses. She clung to his wide shoulders as if she were drowning, and he was her only safety in the whole wide world. *If she knew…*

Suddenly she pulled herself away. 'Lucas,' she cried desperately. 'Lucas, what must you think of me?'

He planted a trail of kisses from her throat to her lips. 'I think you are perfect,' he murmured, easing his muscled thighs against hers, praying she wouldn't realise how hard he still was for her.

She coloured. She *did* realise. She started, in anguish, to pull herself up, to gather her things, to leave.

She must never be alone with him again. To have let this happen was madness. Lucas could not be serious in his love-making, he could not. Her family was poverty-stricken; the Earl his grandfather had detested the Sheldons ever since he had that last, terrible row with her father, before Jack went away for ever. The Earl still had the power to spread ruin.

Lucas tried to stop her. 'Verena. What are you doing?'

She tugged at her dishevelled hair. 'This is a mistake, Lucas. I must go…'

'No. Stay a moment.' He stood up quickly, enfolding her in his arms again and pressing his lips to her forehead.

'Please do not stop me!'

'I thought,' he told her softly, 'that I heard someone out in the hall. A servant, perhaps. Or one of your inquisitive sisters. You don't want anyone to see you coming out of my room looking as you do, do you?'

She twisted to glance at herself in the mirror and saw her flushed cheeks, her disordered hair, her reddened lips. She looked anguished. 'People will say your grandfather was right to call me a—harlot, Lucas!'

'I know that he is wrong,' he said. He pressed a finger against her lips. 'And, believe me, I have dealt with him.'

Her eyes flew up to his, wide with alarm. 'You have—*how*?'

'You look exhausted,' he said. 'Tomorrow, we will talk properly. About your family and Wycherley, and you, Verena.'

'Yes. Tomorrow.' She let out a little sigh. 'Oh, Lucas, I'm so tired, so very, very tired…'

He drew her close. Guiding her with his free arm, he led her to the bed and sat gently beside her. Her eyelids were heavy. To sleep safe in his strong arms was all Verena wanted. To forget all her cares.

She snuggled into the crook of his arm again. So tired…

This was bliss. To be here, safe, with him. 'I will stay for just one minute,' she whispered. 'Then I will go. Poor Miss Bonamy, I always was her worst scholar…'

'What?' He thought she was rambling.

'Miss Bonamy.' She almost chuckled. 'She wrote *Young Lady's Guide to Etiquette*.'

He smiled. 'The book you threw into the haystack.'

'Exactly,' she said rather faintly. 'Tomorrow, Lucas, as you say, we will talk.' And she curled up against the pillows, her eyes fluttering shut.

'We will indeed,' he said steadily. His hand was on hers as he gazed down at her. 'Verena, my brave, sweet, amber-eyed girl, I want to marry you.'

The wine had fogged her senses, but for an instant her eyes shot open. 'Ridiculous man,' she murmured.

'But, Verena—'

She nestled closer to him, with a little smile. Soon her breathing steadied. She lay asleep, her hand still curled with trust in his.

After a while Lucas eased himself away from her and got up very carefully to unbolt the door.

Then he went back to pull the sheet to her shoulders. His heart was full. He felt as if he had something infinitely precious in his care. She was passionate, beautiful and brave—and he had the power to shatter her life into tiny pieces.

The door opened softly and Bentinck padded in, only to pull up in horror when he saw Verena's sleeping figure.

'Oh, my saints,' he hissed. 'You said she was away… Have you taken leave of your wits, milord?'

Lucas answered in a low voice, 'No. Clear away that broken glass, will you? As quietly as possible. There's some outside as well.'

'But wot the devil's happened? I've only been to the alehouse, like you said, and—'

'Someone fired at me, from the garden.'

'Don't you want me to—?'

'No point now in pursuit. Please do as I say.'

Bentinck pursed his lips, scratched his head, then went for a broom. When his task was completed, he left the room in a way that expressed utter bewilderment and total despair.

The candle went out. The fire went out. Lucas settled his tall frame in the armchair and slept fitfully, prey to uneasy dreams. Like Jack Sheldon, he was falling down, down to damnation. He heard Wild Jack's voice, calling out, *'Tell her I did it for Wycherley. For all of them…'*

He woke, perspiring.

Now was the time to conclude. To give up on the diary, to deliver what he had found and to walk away.

He cursed softly under his breath. It would have been so easy, if it weren't for the damnable fact that two years ago he'd fallen in love with Verena Sheldon. And try as he might, he could not kill that love.

Marriage was the only way now to protect her. For soon, somehow, the truth would come out about Wild Jack Sheldon.

Soon he would have to tell her, before anyone else did. But how in God's name was he going to break the news to her that her beloved father was—a traitor?

Chapter Twelve

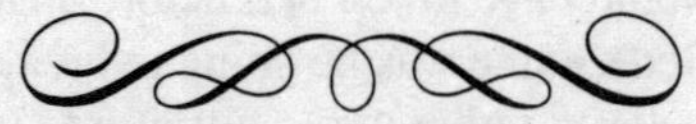

Verena woke in the cold grey light of dawn. In Lucas's room. In Lucas's bed.

He was standing by the window with his back to her, clad in shirt and breeches and riding boots. He was opening the shutters, letting the daylight pour in.

She pulled herself up, blenching as she remembered. *Last night she'd allowed this man to caress her into bliss, then had fallen asleep in his arms...*

Her cheeks burned. Just as her body still burned, to be in his arms again. She remembered his strong hands, so skilfully stroking her into surrender as she clutched at him and begged for...ecstasy. *Dear Lord, Verena.* She started struggling into the clothes that lay on the chair beside her, her fingers shaking.

He turned round. Began to come towards her slowly, with a light smile on his face. 'Good morning, Verena. Did you sleep well?'

He looked stunning. His loose shirt was tucked into those close-fitting buckskin breeches that enhanced rather than concealed his superb physique. His lean, strong-jawed face, framed by that mane of black hair, was all taut planes and shadows in the morning light.

She wanted to touch him. Wanted to kiss him, hold him…

'Lucas. Lucas, I must go, before anyone finds me here!' *Oh, God. He must think me such a fool.* In a state of near panic, she was fumbling with her buttons.

'Why worry?' His finger traced a line up to the fullness of her lower lip. 'Last night, Verena, I asked you to marry me.'

She froze. 'You—you did?'

'Don't you remember?'

Yes. Yes, but he could not mean it, he could not. She said in a low, hurried voice, 'Lord Conistone, last night we made a mistake, and I am as much to blame as you…'

'A mistake?' He caught her close, his grey eyes smouldering. So close that his thigh was pressed against her hip, a reminder of masculine potency that set all her hidden longings pulsing down *there*. 'If it was a mistake, I'm happy to make it again, and again. Do you want me,' he went on ruthlessly, 'to prove to you just how much I desire you, Verena?'

She pushed at his shoulders. 'I do not want you to feel forced into something you can only regret later!'

He stepped back. This time his voice held a cutting edge. 'No one forces me into a damned thing. As I told you last night—I want you to be my wife.'

She was slowly shaking her head.

'Your mother, at least, will be delighted,' he went on drily. 'The rest of them can go hang if they don't like the prospect.'

She lifted her face to his. His smile lingered, but his grey eyes were unreadable now.

'What about your grandfather, Lucas?' she whispered.

'He's tried to ruin us. And you know what he thinks of *me*…'

His expression grew harsher. 'Leave my grandfather to me. Verena, I need to have your answer before I leave today.'

Today. 'But you must not ride yet!' she cried.

'I thought I had my marching orders.'

She blushed. 'Your arm…'

'Is almost mended. I'm quite fit again.' He grinned suddenly. 'Didn't I prove that to you last night?

The colour flooded her face anew. 'Lucas.' She drew herself up. 'Lucas, you must give me time. You must give *yourself* time, to think this through. And—I must apologise, because my behaviour last night was quite unforgivable!'

'Really, Miss Sheldon?' he murmured, a wicked gleam in his eye. 'What particular aspect of it? Would you remind me? I found it rather delightful.'

She bit her lip. 'You will find that you regret your proposal. Due to ill luck, we have been thrown together—'

'Ill luck? Then I could wish for more of the same.' He went, quite casually, to pull his coat on. Then he turned back to face her. 'No necessity for panic, Verena. You need say nothing at all about what has passed between us until I return. And while I'm away, I'll leave Bentinck here.'

Her face clouded. *Oh, no.* 'Why?'

'I just feel you might have enemies.'

'Those men on the path…' Her fingers flew to her throat. 'Lucas! You knew they were Frenchmen, didn't you? And I did not tell you before—but I was afraid they were after *me*. Do you think that's possible? And—why?'

She saw a shadow cross his face; but his voice was still gently reassuring. 'It's something I'm hoping to resolve very soon; it might be nothing. But in the meantime, Bentinck stays here. I'm taking no risks with your safety, *querida*.

Or your future… Verena, do you remember that last night I told you I wanted to help Wycherley?'

She whirled to face him, her amber eyes burning in defiance. 'And I told you I would never accept charity!'

'This is not charity. It's justice. Twenty years ago the Earl diverted a stream from Wycherley lands to power a new corn mill on his estate.'

'You asked me about this stream yesterday…'

'Yes, indeed. And now I'm sure that my grandfather never got your father's permission to divert it, and he owes your family compensation, Verena.'

She blinked. 'But the Earl hates us! He will never give us anything!'

'He has no option. He's been profiting, basically, from a resource that he stole from you.'

'I had no idea…'

'How could you have known? There'll be a generous settlement, because what my grandfather did could be construed in a court as unlawful, and he will not want trouble. The money you get could be several thousand guineas.'

Her eyes widened. *Enough to pay their debts. Enough, at last, to enable them to live within the income of the estate, and more…*

She pressed her fingertips to her temples. 'So—our villagers will be safe, and Wycherley will remain ours?'

'Exactly. I'm only sorry I didn't uncover this earlier. It would have saved you the harrowing business of losing so many of your family's possessions at the dispersal sale.'

She clasped her hands together. 'Forgive me, but this will take a moment to absorb. I—I will have to speak to Mr Mayhew about all this…'

'He already knows.'

'You have certainly been busy.' Her voice was tight.

'To make up for lost time. And I'll get him to hurry

matters along, just in case my grandfather should prove awkward. Or in case anything were to happen to me.'

Verena jumped. He said the last words so lightly that she wasn't sure she heard them. *That dreadful scar...* 'What do you mean, if anything happens to you?'

Lucas pulled a wry face, then grinned. 'Oh, you know. Anything could put me out of action. Taking a tumble from my horse and breaking my leg. A dose of the migraine after staying up too late drinking and gaming at Watier's. There's all manner of things a wastrel like me can get up to.' He was buttoning up his coat awkwardly, his injured arm still hampering him. 'I might be away for a week or so, I can't be sure.'

She nodded, biting her lip. *Compensation.* Wycherley could be restored. Deb and Izzy could have their come-outs. Oh, wretched Deb, for not giving her Lucas's message and telling her falsehoods instead!

But marriage! No, he could not mean it. This was a dream, an illusion. *Best to put her own truly disgraceful behaviour last night from her mind and hope that Lucas would do the same.* Yet...

She heaved a deep breath. 'There's an annual fair up on the Common, in September. Now it can also be a cause of celebration,' she told him almost shyly, 'for Wycherley is safe at last.' She could still hardly believe it. 'Will you be back in time for it?'

'I'll be back before then, be sure of it,' he said quietly. He held her and kissed her lightly on the cheek; though she had not needed that kiss to set her whole body yearning for him. Even his lightest touch did that to her. 'And when I return, I want you to say, "Lucas, I will marry you". Apart from that I want nothing—nothing at all about you—to change.'

She tried to smile, even though her heart was thudding so rapidly she felt faint. 'You mean, you want me to remain a country nobody, with patched dresses?'

'I want you to be—Verena. I want to roam around the country lanes with you, talking about turnips and clover.'

'And what would the Prince and his set think of you then?' she teased. Her voice suddenly altered. 'What would they think of *me*, Lucas?'

'They will be charmed,' he'd told her. 'They will fall utterly in love with you, as I did. Now, off you go. I can hear my tormentor on his way.'

'Your—?'

He pointed towards the door; she could faintly hear the off-key whistling of 'The British Grenadiers'. 'Bentinck.' He grinned. 'He's like an old mother hen.'

She gazed up at him earnestly. 'Lucas. I will wait for you,' she whispered. 'And please—take care.' Then she hurried away, leaving behind the faint scents of silk and lavender, and of soft, gleaming hair.

'This, milord, is the rummest thing I ever heard,' grumbled Bentinck. 'First you get yourself shot at through the window, and have Miss Sheldon in here all night—and now you tell me you're good as hitched! Beg pardon, but have your wits gone astray? Did that bullet catch you a thump on the 'ead, by any chance?'

'Not quite—hitched.' Lucas was looking for his gloves. 'She's not accepted me yet.'

Bentinck grunted. 'And what lady in her right senses would turn you down, pray? Not said yes *yet*, perhaps. She's just playin' games, like women do.'

Lucas winced as his valet untenderly straightened the collar of his coat. 'Don't you approve of my choice, Bentinck?'

'Drastic measures, milord! Not but what she's a pretty piece and all that, but to be leg-shackled! 'Tis more than the call of duty, surely?'

Lucas said quietly, 'Talking of duty, I must leave today.'

'For London?'

'Just a little further. Will you have my horse ready for me as soon as possible? Thanks to you, I've enough to be going on with. Oh, and you're staying.'

'So you said yesterday, milord.' Bentinck looked acutely glum.

'I want you to watch her,' went on Lucas, 'wherever she goes.'

'You don't think that whoever's popping pistols at you—?'

'I don't think they'll actually harm her, no. But she realizes herself now that she needs protection. She knows those Frenchmen were after her—what she doesn't know is why. It's your job both to guard her and also to make sure that she never finds out why. Oh, and I want you to carry on looking for more maps, private letters and especially for Jack's diary.'

'I did get in her bedroom, milord, but didn't find anything.'

Lucas nodded grimly. *Setting your servant to ransack a woman's bedroom. I hope you're proud of yourself.*

'You still think that she might have it, that diary?'

'I still think it's here, yes. Somewhere.'

'Hmph. Well, it strikes me that if Miss Verena gets just one little hint as to what you're about and why, she'll hate you for ever, milord. And you plannin' to make her your wife! A pretty pickle you got yourself into now, and no mistake!'

Lucas, his face bleak, did not contradict him.

* * *

Verena went to her room, praying she would not meet a soul until she could wash and change. Would they be able to see? Would they *know*, just by looking at her face, at her eyes?

She had spent the night in his bed. Allowed him such intimacy… She felt ashamed. She felt full of bewildering joy. She put her palms to her face in a vain attempt to cool her heated skin.

Why does he have to go? What is there in his life that is so urgent? Will he once more ask me to marry him when he returns, or will he realise he's made a grave error and laugh about me, with his London friends?

Those Frenchmen—he knew about them all the time. And now Lucas had gone; she'd watched him from her window riding away towards the Chichester road; watched him till he was out of sight. Where was he going? Why wouldn't he tell her more?

He had asked her to trust him. And this time, she would—for he had ensured that Wycherley was safe.

Soon, the usual clamour of the household took up her attention, and it was some time before she could get up to her room again and think of Lucas.

He and her father would perhaps have become great friends. Her heart lifting at the thought, she went to where she kept his letters locked away in a secret compartment of the dressing table. On that table stood the silver music box, which looked as if it was a little nearer the window than before…

Nonsense. She was imagining things.

She started, smiling, to look at the letters. Her father had written to her more than he did to anyone else, corresponding regularly while on his travels in Spain and Portugal before the war began. *You would love it all, Verena! Some day I will bring you here, to see the cities, and the plains, and the high mountains!*

The letters from his last journey of all were different. Written in the Portuguese dialect of his mother's family, they were troubled, darker, for the shadow of war was engulfing the Peninsula. She thought again of the British army about to set off over the mountains towards Lisbon; her father would have known that terrain so well…

His last letters grew shorter, the notes folded many times. Damaged, torn even, during their uncertain journey to her. Several of them were inscribed with his rough-sketched maps, together with footnotes about distances and heights. One of the maps, drawn in more detail than usual, was labelled *Busaco.*

This was the final communication she'd received from him. And the last words were: *The e-r of Sta-iffe. Do not trust him. He is our enemy.*

She'd looked at those words, some of them half-obliterated, many times.

But now, her heart suddenly seemed to stop beating. She walked across her room, to hold the letter closer to the window. Her fingers started to shake.

She'd always assumed—*believed*—that her father was writing about the Earl of Stancliffe, with whom he'd argued so bitterly.

But now, she realised she could make out the letters more clearly in the bright morning light. And they spelled out not the *earl of*, but the *heir of Stancliffe.*

Lucas. Oh, dear God.

Verena stumbled blindly for a chair, and in doing so she sent the music box crashing to the ground. It fell open and the poignant melody of 'My Soldier Love' filled the room.

She snatched it up and slammed the lid shut, her mind reeling in the stunning silence. *You fool, Verena. You utter fool.*

'You have failed again. You were mad to even try such a thing, Englishman. Yes, it appears our enemy has decided to pass this incident also off as an accident. But truly now he will be even more on the alert.'

In the grey morning light a confrontation was taking place less than half a mile away, down on the shingle beach at Ragg's Cove, between three men who spoke in harsh, fractured English and Captain Martin Bryant.

'You have blundered too!' Martin fought back, attempting defiance. 'You tried to kidnap the girl, although you swore to me that she would not be touched!'

For some moments the only sound was that of the rolling waves dragging at the shingle. Then Bryant saw the gleam of the pistol in the first man's hand and he stepped backwards, sweat breaking out on his forehead.

'*Vraiment*, she will not be harmed,' murmured the man with the pistol, 'if you get us the information we need. We want to see her father's papers. His maps. Especially, we must have the diary that he kept of his travels in Portugal two years ago.'

Bryant muttered, 'I'm not sure that she knows anything. I'm not sure that what you want even *exists*. I visited the old Earl, who's half-mad and just rants that Sheldon swindled him; and at Wycherley I've been through Sheldon's study quite thoroughly.'

'You told us. That you'd got inside the house with a key you'd purloined, and made it look like a burglary. Clever. And yet you found—nothing. Be careful, my friend. It was you, after all, who promised us these items in return for your freedom, a year ago.' The three men were moving in closer.

Martin Bryant faced them with squared shoulders. 'At least my shot last night means that Conistone is laid up again, useless!'

'Ah. Your bullet caught him then, *mon ami*?'

Martin flushed. 'Not exactly. But I heard that valet of his telling a servant this morning that Conistone stumbled last night and re-opened his wound—an accident no doubt caused by the shock of my bullet flying so close!'

'In that case,' said the first Frenchman silkily, 'why has he just gone riding off along the road, to the devil knows where?'

'What?' Martin Bryant's face was quite white. 'I swear I don't know! I honestly thought he was bedridden…'

'We have let him go—for now. He has powerful friends. But you must try to do better, Captain Bryant. There is so little time left. Do you understand?' The Frenchman moved closer to Martin, his pistol raised threateningly now. 'To where does he go? And on what business? What has Lord Conistone found that you could not?'

Chapter Thirteen

Three weeks later—Jersey, Channel Isles

A magnificent private party was being hosted by the Comtesse de Brouet in her mansion overlooking the sea at St Helier. Amongst her glittering guests were other French royalists who had similarly taken refuge here, as well as an assortment of handsome British army officers and several English travellers on business they preferred to keep to themselves. Jersey was British territory, but only a few miles from France; in this time of war, nobody asked too many questions.

Candlelight shone in the beautifully furnished salons, and a string orchestra filled the evening air with sweet melodies. The widowed Comtesse de Brouet was only in her thirties and had several suitors, but she had her eye on a tall, dark-haired Englishman who went by the name of Mr Patterson.

He was engaged in the wine trade, she'd been told, and had been in St Helier for a week now. Waiting for someone, he said.

Disappointingly, instead of joining the dancing, the rather delicious-looking Mr Patterson was at present outside on the terrace, leaning against the balustrade, watching the moonlight on the sea. It was August, and the night air was pleasantly warm, but even so, such a waste…

The Comtesse went sweeping out to him in her gown of draped white satin embroidered with gold thread, and declared, 'My dear Monsieur Patterson, do not brood alone, pray!' She tapped her feathered fan flirtatiously against his broad shoulder. 'Are none of our St Helier beauties to your liking?'

Lucas Conistone, for it was he, answered as required, with a bow and in equally fluent French, 'Since you have declared your intention to remain single, I fear not, Comtesse!'

'Dancing is not the same as marriage, *monsieur*,' she said, coyly smiling up at the handsome, powerfully built Englishman. 'Will you promise to partner me in the cotillion before supper?'

'I would be honoured.' But when she nodded, satisfied, and returned inside, Lucas turned back to gaze at the harbour below. The summer seas just lately had been rough, but today had been calmer, and Lucas had tonight seen several British navy vessels drop anchor in the bay. *Tonight. Come on, man. Make it tonight.*

'Mr Patterson?'

Lucas spun round to see a waiter addressing him.

'There's an officer in here, sir, looking for you…'

Lucas hurried inside. There, eye-catching even in this crowded salon, was a familiar figure clad in the dashing blue jacket and white breeches of the Light Dragoons, who came straight over to him.

'Got your message, Lucas, almost the minute I got into harbour,' grinned Alec Stewart. He looked around appreciatively. 'You've chosen a mighty fine place for our rendezvous this time.'

Lucas was already leading the way to the balcony again. 'Apart from the occupational hazard of man-hungry French comtesses, yes. Come out here. We'll be more private.'

Alec seized two glasses and the almost-full bottle from the waiter's tray, and jauntily followed his friend out to the table and two chairs set in the shadows beyond the doorway. 'Man-hungry French comtesses,' he breathed. 'My God, after over a week on board ship, that sounds good…'

'Tell me the news before you let yourself fall prey to one.'

Intelligence reports when he reached London from Hampshire had informed Lucas Conistone that Alec Stewart was making his way to England from Lisbon on board a ship that was due to call in at St Helier for supplies, so Lucas had set sail here himself and waited.

For Alec was not a wastrel, as was popularly supposed, but a vital messenger for Lord Wellington himself. Now Alec poured them both wine and his expression became graver. 'Lord Wellington's started his march towards Lisbon from the Spanish border, Lucas. But the bad news is that the French, I'm afraid, are after him, in almost double the numbers.'

For Lucas, the sounds of music and laughter seemed suddenly to recede, and he was picturing, in all its brutal vividness, Wellington's army on the march. The thousands of footsore soldiers with their heavy packs; the gun-carriages; the vital ammunition and supplies borne on mules and lumbering bullock carts, which were the only transport fit for what rough Portuguese roads existed. And the huge French army in pursuit…

'A gamble,' Lucas said softly. 'A brave but almighty gamble.'

'Exactly. Lord Wellington gave me a message for you. He urgently needs more maps—detailed maps—of the wild and difficult terrain he's about to cross. He's sent out his own scouts, of course, but you and I are both aware of one man who knew that territory like no other.'

'Wild Jack Sheldon,' nodded Lucas. 'Alec, I've found—*these*.' He pushed across the maps Bentinck had found at Wycherley.

Alec scanned the maps eagerly. 'Congratulations. These are good. *More* than good. But—no sign of that diary? The one you'd suspected Sheldon left at Wycherley before setting off on his last journey?'

'I couldn't find it, Alec. I couldn't damn well find it…' Lucas raked his hand through his hair. 'I've left Bentinck still looking. But unfortunately, I suspect I'm not the only one searching.'

Alec started. 'You mean—the French have got wind of it?'

'You and I know Wild Jack had begun to talk, for money. So it was, I'm afraid, inevitable.' And Lucas told Alec quickly about the attack on Verena above Ragg's Cove, of the bullet through his window. 'I've been shot at twice,' he grimaced. 'At least on the battlefield you know roughly which direction the bullets are coming from.'

Alec listened, his expression serious. 'Haven't you sometimes regretted leaving the army, Lucas? You could have stayed in uniform and still done intelligence work, as many of us do!'

'I thought about it, God knows. But Wellington asked me specifically if I would operate as a civilian. I'm a useful source as to what's going on in London, amongst the politicians and the foreign diplomats there. And, Alec—' Lucas's face suddenly darkened '—after what happened with Verena's father, I got used, I suppose, to leading a double life. But God help me, sometimes I just long for a straightforward battle.' He knocked back the last of his wine and looked around. 'Perhaps we'd better either join the ladies, or throw away a fistful of guineas in the gaming room, before people start to wonder what we're up to. After all—' he raised an eyebrow cynically '—both you and I have reputations to keep up.'

Alec grinned wickedly. 'Of course.' Then he was serious again. 'Lucas, my ship's going on to Portsmouth, but I'll leave my dispatches with you and find a vessel to take me back to Portugal, tonight if the tide's right, so I can get these to his lordship, as soon as possible…' He was searching through the maps again. 'One more thing. Have you ever come across anything about a place called Busaco?'

'No. Is it important?'

'It could be, yes. It's a nine-mile rocky ridge, just before the mountains drop down to Portugal's coastal plain, and Wellington is planning to draw the French up there after him. It will take him six to seven weeks to get there. Look out for anything about it, will you? He'll need any advantage he can get.'

Busaco. Busaco… 'Of course.'

Lucas was starting to get up, but Alec asked almost abruptly, 'Does Verena have any idea yet, Lucas? About her father?'

Lucas's expression was taut. 'No. She still sees him as a hero. That's how I want it to stay.'

Alec started to protest. 'You're being more than unfair on yourself, Lucas! Why the devil should *you* have to bear all this, when the fellow was—'

'Alec?'

'Yes?'

'Do me a favour and stow it, will you?'

Alec hesitated. Then he nodded. 'I wish you luck with her,' he said quietly.

Lucas's firm mouth twisted into a smile. 'My thanks. Now, back to the fray. Smarten yourself up, dear fellow.'

Alec grinned. 'Heiresses?'

'Most definitely. You've no objection to a French one, have you?'

'Not in the slightest,' breathed Alec. 'Lead on, my friend.'

As soon as they entered the drawing room, they were surrounded by a cluster of women, glittering in fine gowns and jewels. 'Gentlemen!' the Comtesse declared. 'You are breaking our hearts! How can our two most handsome guests so neglect the ladies?'

Lucas smiled. 'Comtesse.' And Alec's eyes widened as they were approached by even more exiled beauties. Lucas honoured his promise to partner the Comtesse, who was charming and pretty.

But suddenly, in the middle of the set, he was struck by a hammer blow.

Busaco. Alec had confided that Lord Wellington was planning to face the French there, in six to seven weeks' time. The name had seemed familiar, and now he remembered more. There were legends about Busaco. The steep hills there were said to have once contained mines, where, it was rumoured, explorers returning from the Americas centuries ago had hidden their gold. No treasure had ever been found; and the mine tunnels, if they ever existed, were lost beneath loose rocks and scrub. But—Wild Jack had explored that territory. And both Lucas's grandfather and Verena had told Lucas recently that Jack Sheldon had boasted of finding something of great value…

Had he found those long-lost mines of Busaco? Did he write about them in his missing diary?

Lord Wellington desperately needed a victory at Busaco. It could hang on something as simple as that. Those tunnels could be used to hide cannon and marksmen, and to launch an attack from nowhere on the vastly superior French as they climbed up from the valley towards the waiting British.

Tomorrow he would sail back to England; he would say nothing to Alec yet, about the lost mines. He might be wrong. The damned mines might be just another wild goose chase, an unnecessary distraction.

Back to England, and Wycherley.

The Comtesse de Brouet was flirting with him, using all her wiles; she was wasting her time, because Lucas was remembering Verena. He remembered that last kiss. Remembered her hands, shyly but ardently pulling him closer; her lovely face, flushed with passion; her full breasts and long, silken legs as she twined herself around him, breathing his name, as she let herself submit to the meaning of love, and love's ecstasy…

And he remembered, bitterly, that her father had been prepared to sell vital secrets to the enemy.

'I wish you luck with her,' Alec had said quietly.

And he thought now, with anguish, *I am going to need a damned deal more than luck.*

Chapter Fourteen

It was a hot September morning. Days of heavy rain had given way to sunshine and Verena was walking up to the village celebration on the Common with Izzy. Izzy was bursting with excitement, because that very afternoon she and Deb and Lady Frances were going at last to London.

They wanted Verena to go with them. She knew she *should* go with them.

But she held back, because… Because she still hoped Lucas would come back? But then what?

How could she ever ignore the warning her father had sent her?

Yes, Wycherley was safe. The compensation for the diverted stream that Lucas had told her the Earl owed her family had been settled, and the sum was beyond her expectations.

'This is all quite proper and correct, Miss Sheldon!' Mr Mayhew had assured her, kindly.

All of the Sheldon family's outstanding bills had been paid off, together with the mortgage on the house. With proper investment, the estate, with its farms and tenancies, would be able to run at a profit again. The Sheldons would be able to buy new furniture, new gowns, even rent a modest London house for the forthcoming Season…

Lucas had ensured that the Earl paid them this money.

And Verena wished she could have flung it all back in Lucas Conistone's face.

The heir of Stancliffe. Do not trust him. He is our enemy, her beloved father had written.

If she had read that warning earlier, what then?

She might not have been strong enough to refuse the sum that meant the saving of Wycherley, but she would have been strong enough to resist Lucas's endearments, and his sweet caresses…

Or would she?

Lucas had been away for a lot longer than the week he'd promised. Best for her if he did not come back at all.

As they climbed the sunlit path in their simple cotton frocks and bonnets, Izzy was still chattering about London. This was merely a preparatory trip to buy clothes and establish contacts, but Izzy was thrilled.

'It's so exciting, Verena, that we are no longer poor! Just imagine—once I'm eighteen in November I will be able to have my come-out, and attend wonderful parties, and balls! It's all thanks to Lucas, isn't it? And Mama says he was so *extremely* grateful to you, for tending him after he was injured, that he might even propose to you soon, darling Verena!'

Oh, no. Her foolish mother…

'Then she is talking nonsense,' Verena responded crisply. The sun was brilliant in a bright blue sky, the birds were singing, some late guelder roses sweetly scented the air. *And her heart was breaking.* She forced a smile. 'Stop making ridiculous plans for me, my dear,' she went on.

'I hope you've packed your bags for your journey this afternoon?'

'Oh, yes! I have checked everything a *hundred* times!'

They were going to Chichester tonight, to stay with Aunt Grace, then on to London by stage the following day.

Sometimes hope visited Verena fleetingly, and that was the hardest of all. *Perhaps her father was mistaken.* But so often she had felt that Lucas was not telling her the truth. There were too many unanswered questions. His abrupt resignation from the army. That terrible sword scar. His secrecy about his travels. His strange interrogation, when he'd first arrived, about her father and his diary. It was becoming clear to her that her father knew something about Lucas that Lucas did not wish to be revealed. Yes, he had helped them to get compensation from the Earl—but was that money somehow Lucas's price for her silence? Silence about what?

Lucas had gone from Wycherley so swiftly, leaving her with the words, *'When I return, I want you to say, "Lucas, I will marry you".'* He had not returned. And she had allowed him to all but seduce her. She'd been shameful and wanton; since then her father's message had awakened her to the harsh reality that Lucas was not what he seemed.

Bentinck, however, was still at Wycherley. Lucas had told her she needed protection—but from whom? Sinister Frenchmen, or from Lucas himself? She guessed that Bentinck was probably trailing her even now, keeping her in sight on the leafy path up to the Common.

'Come on, Verena, you slowcoach!' Izzy, hitching up her skirts in a most unladylike fashion, was practically running up the last section of the path. Verena quickened her step, forcing a smile.

The Common was dotted with trestle tables that groaned with food and pitchers of home-brewed ale. All the farmers' wives had contributed—there were loaves, cheeses, pickles and home-cured hams for the noontide feast—and Wycherley's cook, determined not to be outdone, had sent up baskets laden with her famous pork pies and sweet apple cakes. A fiddler was playing country jigs for the energetic ones to dance to, and a Punch-and-Judy man had all the children clustered, enraptured, around his brightly checked stall. It should have been the happiest scene in the world.

'Hurry, Verena, do!' Izzy was pulling her sister by the hand into the midst of the merrymakers. Verena followed, then stopped in amazement when everyone fell back into a circle around her and started to clap and cheer. Even the dancing had stopped. Old Tom was there, and Ned Goodhew, and all the men she'd defended from the militia down on the beach. Billy, in the end, had to step forwards and raise his tankard for silence.

'To our Miss Verena!' he declared. 'If she ain't the saviour of us all, then I dunno who is! Remember how she came down to Ragg's Cove and gave Colonel Harrap what for?'

There was another round of applause, and someone gave three cheers. Verena's heart was full. 'I assure you,' she said quietly, 'that I really did very little.' She hesitated. *Give credit where it's due.* 'Lord Conistone does, you know, have some influence with the Chichester magistrates.'

They all nodded and applauded again. Ned Goodhew piped up. 'We heard somethin' about Lord Conistone saving the whole estate, Miss Verena!'

Really, it was the Earl, she thought, the Earl who had paid them the compensation, but at Lucas's instigation, so she said, after hesitating, 'It is indeed true that he has helped us all. And no one can be happier than me that my family can continue to live at Wycherley as before.'

'Hurrah for Lord Conistone!' Billy raised his tankard

again. 'Will he be comin' here today, Miss Verena, so we can thank his lordship properly?'

She shook her head, and though she was still smiling, it was as if a shadow had passed across the sun. 'Not today, Billy. But I'll pass on your thanks when I do see him.' She turned to them all. 'Please, carry on enjoying yourselves!'

Then she wandered round with Izzy, feigning lightheartedness, trying out the hoop-la David had set up, then sitting on the sun-warmed grass with Izzy to laugh at the antics of Mr Punch.

But she thought of Lucas all the time.

Sometimes what had happened between them the night before he left seemed like a dream. In her bed at night she could not sleep, recalling his wonderful kisses, and those sweet, ecstasy-bestowing caresses that brought fresh colour to her cheeks every time she remembered them. *Do not trust him.*

It was almost noon and the sun was high when Captain Martin Bryant arrived, looking dapper in his scarlet uniform. He'd been making official reports in London, he told her, bowing low over her hand.

'Captain Bryant,' she said lightly. 'This is a wonderful occasion, don't you think?'

She suddenly noticed that Martin's eyes were brooding, his expression upset. 'Perhaps. But I've heard distressing news, Verena.'

'Really?'

'Yes. I heard that you've allowed yourself to become indebted to Conistone, of all people. I didn't realise you were so easily swayed by the lure of money!'

She gasped. But she kept her head high and said coolly, 'Captain Bryant, if you intend to insult me, then I warn you that I'll walk away from you this minute. Yes, we *have* received money; but it's from the Stancliffe estate, not from Lord Conistone, and it is money that was rightly owed to us. Having said all of that, it's really none of your business!'

'Oh, Verena,' he groaned, 'I meant no offence! But I still think you should treat Conistone with the utmost caution!'

'Easy enough,' she replied shortly, 'since I have not seen him for weeks.'

'But he will be back!' He was blocking her path. 'And I want to ask you—when he was last here, was he asking you, perhaps, about your father's private papers, his diary, even?'

Her heart began to thump.

Martin was going on, desperately, 'Conistone *has* asked you about your father's papers, hasn't he? Do you know *why* he had to hurry off?'

She was feeling rather overwhelmed now, with the heat and Martin's intense stare. 'I don't actually consider it any of my business.'

'But it is, because he's been deceiving you! I heard in London that he was sailing to the island of Jersey for a grand ball, where he—and his idle friend Stewart—were the very special guests of a wealthy French Countess!'

'Lord Conistone has his own life to lead,' she breathed.

'But he deceives everyone so thoroughly! My guess, Verena, is that as well as dallying with this Countess, he's making money out of the war with some kind of despicable profiteering, while others fight, and, yes, die for their country! How can you have anything to do with him?'

Her mouth was dry. *In Jersey, partying. Profiteering. A wealthy French Countess…* Oh, God. Was Lucas fluent in French as well as Portuguese endearments?

She replied steadily, 'I'm really not interested in gossip, Captain. And I'm leaving now—I have business back at the house. Please do not follow me.'

She turned and walked away, her head held high, though inside she was in a turmoil of bitter hurt. She could hear Martin coming after her. 'Verena, please! I just don't want you to be hurt by that arrogant wretch Conistone...'

Too late.

If she'd held a faint hope before today that her father's warning not to trust Lucas might be wrong, then that hope had now died a cruel death. Martin Bryant might be a fool in many ways, but he was doing his duty. He wasn't to know that his duty involved breaking her heart. She hurried on quickly down the path, knowing, of course, that Bentinck would be following her. Bentinck would have seen her encounter with Captain Bryant. Bentinck would report it...

I must keep busy. Wycherley is safe—I must not think about anything else.

Oh, Lucas.

Verena had worked out ways of keeping herself distracted. One method was to absorb herself with the household accounts in her father's study, and her head was aching with figures by the time she heard her sisters returning from the festivities up on the Common shortly after one. They called for her and she joined them with a forced smile; Pippa was there with her twins, and Izzy chattered away about the excitement on the Common that morning, and the even greater excitement of their forthcoming journey that afternoon.

Pippa's little boys were hungry and she turned to Verena. 'Be an angel and fetch them something, would you? Just something simple, love! Thinly sliced bread and butter, perhaps, and a little milk!'

It had been Cook's morning off, and she wasn't back yet. In the cool quiet of the kitchen, Verena busied herself putting on one of Cook's starched aprons, finding a fresh loaf and slicing it for the children. But her mind was still reeling.

In Jersey, partying. Profiteering. A French Countess... All this, on top of her father's dire warning. She rested her hands on the cool marble worktop and bowed her head in despair.

She thought she heard a horse arriving in the courtyard outside. Heard a man's low voice, talking to Turley. David, probably, come to join his family.

She pulled herself together and started buttering the bread. Noticing suddenly that she'd knocked some crumbs to the floor, she dropped to her knees and began to brush them up.

She heard light footsteps in the passageway outside, and Izzy's merry voice. 'Verena, haven't you got the bread and butter yet?'

Then Izzy came into the kitchen and pulled up at the sight of Verena on her knees with brush and dustpan in her hands. 'Verena, honestly, big sister, just look at you! What would Lucas think? You look like a housemaid in that apron, on your hands and knees, you foolish creature!'

There were more footsteps drawing near, heavier this time. Then a drawling male voice that made her blood race said, 'Lucas would think—how can a younger sister let her older sister do all these chores, without even offering to help?'

He was here. Lucas was here.

Chapter Fifteen

Verena got swiftly to her feet. The tall, broad-shouldered figure of Lord Lucas Conistone filled the doorway. There were dark shadows under his eyes and stubble on his chin. His black hair was ungroomed.

But he still sent her senses reeling. He looked every bit the handsome, noble rake. He looked—*dangerous.*

And wasn't he dangerous? Hadn't he stolen her heart, and broken it into a thousand pieces? *Why was he here?*

Izzy was blushing to the roots of her blonde hair. 'Oh, Lucas, Verena's always like this, always busy!'

Verena pushed the plate of buttered bread towards her sister. 'Here, Izzy. Take this through, will you?' She ran her hands through her hair, feeling quite sick. Began to tidy away the knife and the butter dish.

Izzy picked up the plate and gave Lucas a sunny smile. 'Of course. Sorry, Verena. I'm so glad you're back, Lucas! We're going to *London* this afternoon!' And she hurried out of the room with the bread and butter.

Lucas turned to Verena. She kept her face from him still, as she brushed some crumbs from the table.

He crossed the floor towards her, tall and magnificently male in his long grey riding coat. His suntanned features were emphasised by his thick dark hair; his muslin neckcloth lay in negligent folds. She remembered how he had kissed her, how he had caressed her. And the longing to be in his arms again throbbed helplessly through her.

He said, quietly, 'Are you going to London with them, Verena?'

'No. No, I'm staying here...' She was putting the loaf away, still not meeting his eyes.

But he was taking her hand, and his touch seared her. 'You should not let them treat you as they do.'

She snatched her hand away, the terrible heartache racking her. *Partying...a French Countess...* She swung round to face him. 'They're my family, Lucas. I do not mind.'

He met her eyes gravely. 'I'm sorry I was late for the celebration on the Common. I was—delayed. Are you very angry with me?' His dark grey gaze was burning into her. Verena felt utter despair. Her body's message was to let him hold her, let him love her...

You must not trust him.

She tilted her face to his defiantly. Saw the sudden, dangerous narrowing of his eyes. 'Lucas,' she breathed, 'when you were last here, you made me an offer you cannot possibly keep, and I cannot possibly accept.'

'I asked you to marry me,' he said levelly. 'I have every intention of keeping my word.'

Her breath caught in her throat. 'You felt—*forced* into offering for me.'

He ran his hand tiredly through his dark tousled hair. Suddenly she realised he looked as if he hadn't slept for days. He grated, 'No one forces me to do a damned thing. Why exactly was I forced into offering for you?'

'My—my behaviour that night in your room was shameful,' she whispered.

His narrowed eyes were bleak in the harsh structure of his face. 'Your behaviour was natural and exquisite. Tell me, Verena, tell me what has changed since I was last here.'

She knew her face was as pale as his. 'You went away. You said you were going to London, but you *didn't…*'

'Who told you that? And what else have you heard?' Lucas's voice rasped like gravel.

'Does it matter?' She was utterly shaken because *he had not denied it.* 'Lucas, you told me to trust you, but how can I, when you *will not tell me the truth*?' It was a last, desperate plea. She wanted to be wrong. She wanted to be in his arms. She wanted so much to be kissed by him, cherished by him, that it hurt.

He said, dangerously quiet, 'I have to lead my own life, Verena.'

She felt her heart was breaking. 'But if you just *told* everyone what you do, there wouldn't be these rumours, don't you see? About your—your…'

'My cowardice, you mean?'

'Lucas, I've never believed that, never!'

But he was white now around the mouth. Every muscle of his powerful body seemed charged with anger. He was a strong, tense, male animal towering above her, and then he was saying, in a cool voice, 'So the gossips have been at work. When we were last together, I was under the impression—forgive me—that in your eyes I could do no wrong. Now someone less gentlemanly than me might infer from your behaviour, on the night in question, that you were just possibly thinking of using me to save your home, your family and your much-talked-of tenants and villagers. Verena, the saviour of the people.'

Oh, dear God. He was accusing her of trying to entrap

him that night. He had the same opinion of her as his grandfather. Mortification flooded her cheeks and retreated, leaving her feeling sick to her stomach. *The heir of Stancliffe. Do not trust him.*

She had done far worse than that.

She had given her heart, her whole being, to him.

Verena managed to say, 'If you think that I intentionally deceived you, then I—I will somehow return the money to your grandfather as soon as I can.'

'Oh, don't be so ridiculously noble,' he cried. 'That sum means nothing to my grandfather. And I certainly won't let you ruin your family for the sake of your wretched pride.'

Verena could hardly speak. 'Lucas,' she whispered, 'I know—everyone knows—that your grandfather and my father had a terrible argument before he went away. Could you tell me—did *you* argue with my father also?'

For a moment he said nothing. His hooded grey eyes were almost black. She was more than ever aware of the concealed strength of mind and purpose that emanated from his powerful figure.

'Please,' he said. 'Verena, just trust me for a little longer, I beg you.' He spread out his finely shaped hands, a proud man, almost pleading with her.

But he had not answered her question. 'I cannot trust you, Lucas,' she breathed. 'I cannot.'

He nodded slowly, his broad chest rising and falling beneath his open greatcoat as he endeavoured to steady his ragged breathing. He was rubbing his upper arm absently where the bullet had caught him when he came to her rescue. The memory of that night, when he'd saved her from her attackers and kissed her so tenderly, seared her heart.

He said quietly, 'Can you just bring yourself to answer one last question? Before he left, did your father say anything to you about some old mines he'd discovered in Portugal? Did he show you maps? Believe me, I beg you, when I say I have your well-being in mind.'

Mines. Maps. This was exactly what Martin had warned her of. *'Conistone is making money out of the war,'* Martin had said bitterly, *'while others fight and, yes, die for their country...'*

Oh, God. Even now, Lucas was using her, exploiting the hold he still had over her, even though she knew now that she was nothing, less than nothing to him.

'I've told you,' she whispered. 'I've told you all along that I don't know of any maps, or the diary you keep asking me about! Lucas, if you have any regard for me at all, please leave me alone, please don't try to see me again...'

He stood very still. His eyes were hooded. Only a muscle clenching in his jaw betrayed the emotions sweeping through him. He said at last, almost sadly, 'You know, you could have *talked* to me, Verena, instead of listening to everything that was bad about me. Yes, I have enemies, but you could have tried to trust me as you used to, instead of believing every stupid rumour that pulled me down.'

But one of those warnings was from her own father. And how could she tell him that? She gazed up at him, white-faced. 'Lucas, I'm truly sorry, believe me, that everything's gone so wrong.'

'It doesn't really matter,' he said wearily. 'But I would count it as a great personal favour if you would refrain from talking about everything of a personal nature that has passed between us.'

'You must know it is hardly likely.' Her voice was low, because there was a great lump in her throat that threatened to choke her.

His hand reached out to cup her cheek gently. 'Never think ill of yourself for the time we shared together, will you, *minha querida*?' His voice was suddenly soft. And so, so tender... 'And Verena?'

'Yes?' Her emotions as she gazed up into his strong hard-boned face threatened to overwhelm her.

'Will you try not to think too harshly of me?'

'Oh, Lucas...'

'It's all right,' he was saying gently, 'it's all right.' The tears filled her eyes now, hot and bitter. Suddenly he was easing her into his arms and gentling the back of her head with his hand until her face was turned upwards to his. She could not move away. Those tears spilled freely down her cheeks. If her life had depended on it, she could not resist him. This man. *This man her father had said was her enemy.* Gently, very gently, he brushed her teardrops aside with his fingertips. Then he let his lips capture hers with a firm, dry warmth that made her heart hammer against her ribcage; and she was surrendering to him, and her hands were stealing up to twine round those powerful shoulders...

She snatched her hands back to her sides. *'No.'*

He stared down at her and this time his eyes were like cold, hard steel. 'Don't ever try to pretend,' he said in a quiet voice that sliced through her, 'that that kiss was my fault.'

She buried her face in her hands. *Oh, God.* No wonder he despised her.

He was already heading for the door, but he turned and said curtly, 'One last favour, Verena. I would like Bentinck to continue staying here with you.'

Her head jerked up at that. 'You are not serious, I hope!'

'Never more so. I won't impose myself on you, but you need Bentinck here, to safeguard you. And don't tell me you *are* safe. You remember as well as I the attack on the cliff path.'

The Frenchmen. It was true, they had targeted her, but… 'You still think—they might be nearby?'

'It's possible,' he answered harshly. 'No need to alarm your family. You can tell them Bentinck's here at my request, to supervise the workers who are going to start work here in the next week or so.'

She jumped. '*What* workers?'

'The ones I've hired to renovate Wycherley,' he answered simply. 'Your mother's already given her consent. Mr Mayhew has spoken to her.'

Her scatterbrained mother must have forgotten. Or—even more likely—decided not to mention it, in case Verena chided her for accepting charity again. 'Lucas—you have no right—'

'Don't worry,' he said tersely, 'your estate is paying their wages. As I said, the matter is agreed. And I will brook no argument. Because, you see, your father asked me to look after you.'

'My father…?' Now Verena was truly stunned. 'No! Impossible!'

He looked as if he was remembering something from a long time ago, and that memory was dark indeed. 'You must make your own mind up,' he said tiredly, 'whether or not to believe me. But the fact remains—I *did* promise your father I would look after you all. And now I will take my leave, since my presence is unwelcome. Goodbye, Verena.'

'Wait! You must tell me more—about my father…'

'I don't really think,' he replied, 'that there's anything more to be said. Do you?'

And he turned and walked away without looking back. Out of her life.

She wished she had never seen that letter, with its cruel,

cruel words. She wanted to run after Lucas and let him hold her again, kiss her again and never let her go.

But it was too late. She watched Lucas leave the house with despair in her heart. He was going—where?

What did it matter? One thing was certain. He was leaving her life for good.

Cook was back from her morning off. She came bustling into the kitchen, sweeping off her cloak. 'Now, how did they all enjoy my pies and cakes up on the Common? Did they all get eaten?'

Verena forced a bright smile and gave Cook the answer she dearly wanted. 'I was home by then. But Izzy told me yours were the first to go, Cook! Not a crumb left—everyone made straight for them!'

'As for that Bentinck,' went on Cook grimly as she crashed the pans around, 'he'll eat anything, he will. Is he leaving us soon, the black-haired misery?'

Verena knew very well that Bentinck and Cook had set up an unlikely friendship. Even Turley had warmed to him; Verena had overheard Bentinck telling Turley about a boxing match in which Bentinck had supposedly defeated the famed Cribb, and Verena suspected this had aroused Turley's reluctant admiration.

Verena said, 'I'm afraid Bentinck will be with us for a little while yet, Cook.' Then she realised that her mother was calling to her from the drawing room.

'Verena? Verena, my dear, is that you?' called Lady Frances. 'I can't think where you've been hiding, when you must know how very much we need you, we will be departing very soon… Now, did I hear that Lord Conistone has arrived, you sly puss? I do hope you've invited him to call again? Such a shame that we will not be here, but then again—' she almost winked '—it could be such an opportunity for you! You do know, don't you, that he's most kindly arranged for some labourers to start work on our house? Verena, dearest? Verena?'

'He had to go, Mama.'

'But I was sure he harboured intentions, my dear! *Marital* intentions! Even Pippa said so!'

Verena whirled round on her mother. 'There is nothing whatsoever between Lord Conistone and me! And you must *not* accept his every offer of help as if we were—incompetent *paupers*!'

Her mother's face fell. 'But I thought— He has paid you such special attention, my love!'

Verena drew a deep breath and touched her mother's hand. 'Calm yourself, Mama. We mean nothing to one another at all.'

Her mother pursed her lips and went off to complete her packing. Verena, who could stand no more, slipped away to her dear father's study, and sat by herself in the darkness.

She still loved Lucas—a love that was clearly impossible. But—why had he said that her father had told him to look after her?

It must be another lie.

Her family left at last, with all their luggage crammed into the old coach. Soon after that, it began to rain. The house was almost unbearably quiet apart from the steady drumming of the raindrops against the windows.

Impossible to go outside in this weather; equally impossible to do *nothing*, so she decided to continue with a task she'd begun a few days ago: sorting through the boxes containing her father's business papers that had been moved out of the north wing in spring when the rain came in through the roof.

She'd already worked methodically through two of

the boxes, which contained nothing but petty household records. Then she came to another.

And this box had been recently disturbed. Its lid had not been refitted tightly, and there were fingermarks all over the dust that lay on its surface.

Lifting the lid off, she found more documents. Picking up a slim wallet marked in her father's writing, she read: *Notes made on the route of the River Tagus; its source and progress through the Portuguese mountains, 1808.*

She opened the wallet. There was nothing inside.

Her heart was beating rather fast. It was probably nothing, she told herself. But—this box had been opened within the last few weeks, to judge by those fingermarks. Opened by whom?

Lucas had been asking her about maps, only this morning…

Suddenly she heard footsteps, together with the sound of someone whistling 'The British Grenadiers'. She swung round to see Bentinck standing in the doorway.

'Everything satisfactory up 'ere, ma'am?' His gaze had fastened already on the open box and the empty wallet in her hand.

This was the outside of enough. She stood briskly up to face him, pushing back a stray lock of her chestnut hair. 'Everything is *completely* satisfactory, thank you, Bentinck! Except—would you tell me if you have keys to this wing of the house?'

'I have, ma'am. 'Cos I might need them when the builders start work up here.'

'As a matter of fact,' said Verena crisply, 'you won't. And I would like you to return those keys to me immediately. In fact, I would like you to give me every single key you have that belongs to this house. And I would like you to leave Wycherley—*at once*.'

His jaw dropped. 'But Lord Conistone, he said—'

'I really don't give a fig what Lord Conistone said! I am in charge here and I would like you to go now, Bentinck. For good. Do you understand?'

He folded his arms across his chest stubbornly. 'Can't go till tomorrow, ma'am. Need to pack me things, make arrangements…'

She almost stamped her foot. She no longer believed there was a threat to her—only from Lucas. 'Tomorrow, then! And it will not be soon enough!'

She swept away from him towards the stairs, her colour high.

'Miss Verena!' Cook was calling her from downstairs. 'There you are, miss, I've been looking everywhere for you! There is a letter for you.'

Verena came downstairs to take it from her—and her heart stopped. The letter was sealed with a familiar crest.

It was from the Earl of Stancliffe.

She tore it open, and read: *Miss Sheldon. Though we have not met for some time, I would be obliged if you, and you only, would pay me a visit at Stancliffe Manor at your earliest convenience. Today, if possible.*

She stood there, stunned. She used to think the Earl was their enemy. But he had paid them so very generously for the stream; clearly he no longer suspected her of trying to entrap Lucas in marriage…

She did not notice Bentinck hurrying out to the group of labourers working on the south wall, speaking urgently to one of them, handing him a note in his own rough handwriting, then sending him galloping off on Bentinck's own sturdy bay cob.

Lucas Conistone had not gone far. He was down at the Royal George close by Framlington harbour, buying some of the locals a drink. They all knew Lord Conistone, and their awe of him steadily shrank as the second, then the third round of ale was added by the happy innkeeper to his lordship's account.

They'd not needed much encouragement to talk to his lordship about various sightings of suspicious strangers along this part of the coast. 'Boney's men,' they muttered darkly, 'spies everywhere, my lord!' Then the messenger sent by Bentinck arrived.

Lucas tore open the letter and read it, cursing under his breath.

The Earl has sent Miss Verena a letter. I opened it and sealed it again before she got it. He's invited her to visit, and she's going. I will follow her. Make haste yourself to Stancliffe, my lord.

Chapter Sixteen

Bentinck had caught up with Verena as she left the house, making her jump when he said, 'Maybe I should come with you on your walk, ma'am? It's getting late.'

'Nonsense, Bentinck! It's only four o'clock, it won't be dark for hours! Anyway, I told you you're dismissed!'

'Not till tomorrow,' he replied calmly.

'As far as I'm concerned,' returned Verena, 'your duties are over as from now!' She ordered him to go to the south meadow, telling him that some suspicious-looking characters had been reported there earlier. 'Possibly French spies,' she warned. That did the trick; it got him heading in completely the opposite direction, while she set off westwards to Stancliffe Manor.

Whenever they used to visit Stancliffe as children, Verena had hated how she and her sisters were told always to curtsy and be silent before the Earl, to speak only when spoken to. The last time she had been here was a little over two years ago, during her father's final summer in England. She'd known he was going to Portsmouth that very night on his travels again, so she'd walked across the fields to meet him and waited for him outside the big, forbidding house.

Usually her father and the Earl talked for hours about places they'd visited overseas, for the Earl too had voyaged abroad. But that last time, Verena had heard sharp voices drifting out from the open window of the Earl's study.

'You are a fool, Sheldon!' the Earl had exploded. 'You married a silly, empty-headed fool of a wife and you cannot expect me to bail you all out!'

Verena, listening white and shocked, could hear no more. When her father came out, they walked home in near silence. He just said, in a low voice, 'I have to go away again this one more time, Verena. But believe me, when I come home I will be rich and we will be beholden to no one!'

Suddenly, as she turned to take the footpath that led to Stancliffe Manor, she stopped.

Was she mistaken? Or did she remember that as her father set out to visit the Earl that last time, he'd carried his diary with him, the slim red leather-bound volume in which he'd recorded every detail of his travels? She'd assumed he had it with him when he died—that was why she'd always told Lucas she had no idea where it was.

But did he have it with him when he came *away* from Stancliffe?

She couldn't remember. All she remembered was the hurry he'd been in to get away. His bags had already been packed, and he had lost no time in heading straight for Portsmouth, to sail away that very night, for ever.

Now Stancliffe Manor was in view, at the end of a long, chestnut-lined driveway. The skies were growing leaden again and she quickened her step. Through the grounds ran a river, which had been dammed half a century ago to form a picturesque lake with several wooded islands connected by ornamental footbridges. On the largest island was a small pavilion, where, in summer, her father and the Earl used to sit and talk. It all made a sylvan scene when the sun shone down. But today, after the recent heavy rain, the lake, swollen by the brown waters of the river in full spate, looked stormy, threatening almost.

She looked back just once because she thought she'd heard a twig snap somewhere close to the path behind the tall chestnuts. She shivered. The wind was moaning down from the hills and it was starting to rain again. But she was almost at the house. Just as she started to climb the wide steps, the big door swung open, and a grey-haired man in a black, stained coat stepped out, frowning down at her.

'State your business!'

It was the Earl's steward, Rickmanby, with his twisted body and spiteful face. She and Pippa used to detest him and he always made it clear their dislike was returned.

'Good day, Rickmanby,' she replied evenly. 'I'm sure you remember me. I am Verena Sheldon, from Wycherley. The Earl sent for me.'

He made a great show of making up his mind as she stood outside in the cold rain that was now starting to fall heavily. At last he muttered, 'Ye'd best come in, then.'

And Verena, boiling at his rudeness, climbed the wide steps to enter the huge house that seemed every bit as daunting as it had in her childhood.

Rickmanby took her in silence to a vast, unlit room on the ground floor that held an odour of smoke and damp. He offered to light neither fire nor candles, nor did he suggest refreshment. 'I will tell the Earl you are here,' he said heavily and closed the big door, leaving her alone.

And the minutes went by.

This is ridiculous, she whispered to herself, after what

seemed an interminable time. I feel like a prisoner. If the Earl does not appear soon, I will simply leave.

But nature was conspiring against her also. Outside the rain poured down in a deluge. The sky was black, except for the lightning that seemed to crack it asunder with shafts of white light almost more frightening than the thunder.

Impossible to go home in this. Impossible, too, to imagine that Rickmanby would make her the offer of a carriage. Verena bit her lip and walked to and fro, to and fro. How much time had gone by? Half an hour? An hour? There was no clock in the room. Just rows of ancient, dusty books, and some old, tapestry-covered chairs that looked as if they would crumble were anyone to actually dare sit on them…

Suddenly she froze. For a door was opening, slowly, from the hallway. A white-haired man leaning on a stick appeared there in the half-light and took a step forwards. Then he rubbed one hand across his rheumy eyes. 'Verena,' he breathed. 'Verena Sheldon. Is it really you?'

Verena wanted to turn and run. Far away from this place of such dark memories. Far from this powerful, rich old man who had so cruelly slandered her.

But he had repented and helped them. She faced him steadfastly.

'I am indeed Verena Sheldon, my lord. I am Jack's oldest daughter and your goddaughter. You sent me a message, asking me to visit. And I've come, because despite our past differences, it was good of you to arrange the compensation for the stream…'

'The stream?' He was limping towards her, scowling. 'Compensation? What the deuce are you talking about, girl?'

Verena was quickly backing away. *Oh, no.* He didn't know a thing about it! Another of Lucas's tricks; yet another revelation of his incomprehensible determination to make them beholden to him…

She looked for the door, but the old Earl was blocking her way. Then suddenly he was putting his finger to his lips, nodding conspiratorially.

'I'll tell you why I asked you here. You and I must talk.' He dropped his voice even lower. 'About the gold.'

She realised she had been holding her breath. Now she let it out, but her heart was still racing violently. *Gold?*

'We will sit,' the Earl was muttering. 'We will talk.'

He was all outward calmness now, but she could not forget that earlier look of bitter cunning.

The Earl sat close by the fireplace. She seated herself reluctantly in a worn armchair opposite to him.

'Now, Miss Sheldon,' went on the Earl softly, 'you know and I know what your father found, don't we? And other people want to find it, but we have to stop them. They are all around us. They come quite openly now.'

Verena's heart was beating hard. Was he mad? She answered as steadily as she could, 'If my father discovered anything at all of value, my lord, then I do not know of it.'

My father must have talked to the Earl, as he did to me, about some rumour of treasure that came to nothing…

The Earl stood up. Banged his stick on the floor. 'You must know where it is! I want the gold! Half of it should be mine!'

She stood up also, clenching her hands. 'I've told you! I don't know what gold you're talking about!'

He stared at her. Then he shook his head, as if confused. 'They call it the hill of lost treasure,' he muttered. 'Where the gold from the Americas was hidden centuries ago, in the mines up there, high in a lost valley… He wanted my money to fund his search. I gave it to him. Then he told me that there *is* no gold, the liar, the thief!'

He was limping now, with the aid of his stick, over to the window where the storm could be seen in full play, with lightning forking across the thunderous grey sky and the rain sheeting down. He swung round to face her, jabbing his finger. 'He lied to me! But *I* have his diary!'

Her heart stopped.

Was this the diary that Lucas had wanted? Not at Wycherley, not taken by her poor father on his last-ever journey, but—*here*?

'His diary holds the secret!' the Earl rambled on. He looked carefully over his shoulder. 'There have been strange people round, asking for it. Even Lucas was asking. I know what he is up to. I know he wants the gold, too! But it's mine!'

Somehow Verena kept her voice steady. 'Where is this diary, my lord?'

'So many ask me that! So many!' He shook his head, clearly agitated. 'And I cannot make sense of his writing, you understand? But they killed your father for what he knew! Yes, killed him, do you hear?'

Verena stood there, stunned.

'Come!' the Earl instructed. He was hobbling towards the door that led out into the rain-drenched garden. 'Come, I will show you where it is!' He flung the door open. The cold air rushed in. 'And you will read it to me and tell me where Jack has hidden the gold!'

And he was gone, limping as fast as he could through the pouring rain across the lawns, his old coat flying out behind him.

Verena gasped as the rain blew into the room and the sound of thunder reverberated round outside. She went to tug desperately at the bell-pull. 'Rickmanby! Rickmanby!'

No answer. She ran out into the hallway, and called again, for anyone; still no one came. The big house seemed to moan and creak in the darkness of the storm.

They killed your father for what he knew...

The Earl had almost disappeared, running towards the woods as the rain lashed down. Wrapping her cloak around her, gasping at the cold and the rain, she ran after him, across the sodden lawns to the shrubbery, beyond which lay the lake, with its wooded islets, the largest of them with its little Gothic pavilion, where her father and the Earl used to sit talking for hour after hour.

She got to the first of the bridges and hesitated. The lake had risen yet further, brown and turbulent, swirling round the bridge's fragile stanchions. But she had to reach the Earl and guide him back to safety! She hurried across to the first islet. Then crossed another bridge, to the next, and the next...

The last one was the weakest. She took every step carefully, feeling the whole frail construction shudder beneath her as the flood waters continued to rise; but at last she was there, at the pavilion. She pushed open the door with its peeling blue paint. And he was inside, in the darkness, crouching in a corner, huddled over a slim leather case the size of a book, his hand over his eyes as lightning illuminated the interior.

'Jack!' he cried out. 'Is it you?'

Verena walked steadily towards him. 'Not Jack, my lord. It's me. Verena, Jack's daughter.'

'Ah, Verena!' He was weeping now. 'Jack betrayed me, so I stole it and hid it here. But I cannot read it... Please, will *you* tell me where the gold is?'

From the case he drew out a book bound in faded red

leather. She knew it, of course. Lucas had wanted this so badly he'd offered her money. *Some people would pay...*

Bentinck, nosing around. The ransacked boxes of papers.

This was her father's diary.

Thunder rumbled ominously outside. 'Soon,' Verena soothed, 'soon we will talk about the gold! But my lord, first you must come back to the house.' She held out her hand. 'Give me my father's diary. I will keep it safe for you.'

'No!'

'Then leave it here. We can come back for it when the storm has gone.'

'Only if you tell me about the gold!'

She hesitated. She hated lying, but— 'I will,' she said softly. 'I will, once we are safely back at the house.'

He let the book slip to the floor, then came slowly, suspiciously towards her, his eyes darting from side to side. She led him out through the door.

And saw, with a sick lurch of her heart, that the footbridge to the next islet was already under water. The handrails were still visible, but they were old and half-rotted. The wind and the floods were turning the lake into a raging seascape, with waves snarling and battering.

Suddenly the Earl staggered forwards, his white hair wild, his black clothes drenched, towards the half-submerged bridge. Verena flew after him.

'My lord! It's not safe—please *wait*—someone will come for us!' But he was already stepping onto the bridge, grasping the handrails.

Verena suppressed a cry and forced herself to stay where she was, for her added weight would be too much for that ancient structure. She watched in anguish, seeing that the Earl had just reached the next islet when a great surge of water swept over the narrow bridge and took away the last support. Pieces of old timber toppled into the stormy grey lake and rode away on the foam like driftwood.

She was alone on the island. The Earl's black-coated, white-haired figure had disappeared between the trees. She prayed that an instinctive sense of direction would somehow carry him back to the house. But would the Earl remember that she was stranded here? Would he tell the servants?

He would be rambling about Jack and the pavilion, perhaps even herself, but they would put his words down to an old, sick man's fevered imagination. Rickmanby would assume that Verena had left long ago for Wycherley.

No one would dream that she was marooned here, in this desolate place.

Stranded, on this shrine to adventurers.

They killed your father, for what he knew.

From Framlington harbour, Lucas had ridden like the wind to Stancliffe, knowing he should not have left her, not for an instant. Leaping from his horse, he'd marched to the door and pulled it open, to be met by Rickmanby.

'Where is she?' Lucas had rapped out. 'Where the hell is the girl?'

Rickmanby backed away. 'Dunno, my lord.'

'What about my grandfather? Do you at least know where *he* is, you fool?'

'Upstairs, my lord.' And Rickmanby had led the way up to the Earl's bedchamber, where a fire had been lit, and his grandfather, shaking with cold and soaked to the skin, was wrapped in a blanket. When he saw Lucas he cried out, again and again,

'It's there! You must save it for me!'

'What is there?' Lucas almost wanted to shake him.

'The secret of the gold! That swindler Jack Sheldon's gold!'

'What in hell…?'

'I couldn't read it,' the Earl quavered. 'I stole it from him, Lucas, but I couldn't read it, then the waters came…'

And Lucas Conistone realised, at last, what had happened to Jack Sheldon's diary.

As the lightning flashed across the sky, Verena could see that on the far side of the pavilion was a small wood-burning brazier, set beneath a chimney pipe. Beside it was a box of firewood. She had no way of lighting it. But she had—this. She swiftly picked up the leather-bound book and, sweeping her wet hair back from her face, she leafed carefully through the damp pages of her father's diary, almost holding her breath.

Each sheet was covered with not only words, but also sketches and maps. She read, in Portuguese, *Today, I held my first meeting with the one they call* O Estrangeiro. *He, too, wanted my maps—treasure indeed.*

O estrangeiro. Portuguese for foreigner. Treasure…

She frowned, then stiffened, her eyes flying to the door. For a moment she'd thought she heard someone calling her name. Then the sound was lost, muffled by the rain pounding on the roof, and a fresh peal of thunder. She went back to the book. *Then* O Estrangeiro *paid me the agreed sum, with a promise of more next time…*

There it was again. A man's voice, coming closer. 'Verena! Verena! Answer me, for God's sake!' She quickly jammed the diary back into its leather case and hid it under the mouldering cushions of the window seat. Then she hurried over to the door, her heart pounding.

Lucas. It was Lucas. Her breathing was quite ragged. *Do not trust him.*

Chapter Seventeen

As the moon pierced the scudding clouds, Verena had a clear view of Lucas Conistone's lithe, muscular figure. He wore no coat. His soaked white shirt was hanging open and loose, as he strode towards the pavilion with some sort of pack slung over his shoulder, and his long water-streaked hair clinging starkly to his cheekbones. The heavy rain was sluicing off his tight breeches and wet leather boots, and he looked more dangerously masculine than ever. She caught her breath at the sight of his wide shoulders, his long powerful thighs as he prowled towards the pavilion door, his jaw clenched, his grey eyes narrowed to iron slits. 'Verena!' he called again, in his deep, compelling voice. 'I know you're here!'

She opened the door wide, tilting her chin in defiance, determined to hide the fact that she was trembling with cold—yes, and fear. 'I'm here, Lucas,' she answered, attempting calm. 'I thought you were on your way back to London.'

The way he looked at her. She felt dreadfully vulnerable, dreadfully conscious of the way her own wet clothes clung to her. This man had gone to incredible lengths to find her father's diary. Had even tried to seduce her for it.

She must not let him know it was here.

He said curtly, 'Unfinished business called me back. I arrived at Stancliffe Manor to find my grandfather soaking wet and talking wildly about you, and the island. What in God's name were you thinking of, stranding yourself here in this wild weather?'

She went white. 'Do you think I actually intended all this?'

He said grimly, 'I can't imagine what the hell you were thinking, to be honest.'

And he clearly didn't want to give her a chance to explain.

Already he was ushering her back into the pavilion, swinging the oilskin bundle down from his shoulder. He looked swiftly around. 'I'd better see if I can get a fire going. It could be hours before the flood water subsides.'

She backed away in fresh panic. 'I will not stay here!' *With you. Alone.*

He gazed at her, rubbing his hand through his soaking hair. 'Really? What else do you intend? The main bridge is broken. I'm not a miracle worker. There's no way you can leave until the floods go down and help arrives. I sent a message to Wycherley to let your staff know that you were caught in the storm and are staying safe at Stancliffe.'

Safe? He towered above her, the epitome of masculinity in this confined space. *All alone with him. All night.* Safe? Dear Lord, anything but. Her throat was dry. She said defiantly, '*You* managed to get here!'

'I swam,' he rapped out.

'With *that*…?' She was looking at the heavy oilskin pack he was carrying.

'I brought a few necessities. I guessed we'd have to stay for the night.'

Guessed—or intended? Her heart hammered.

He'd slammed the door shut and lit a candle with tinder and flint he'd retrieved from his watertight pack. He was pulling other things out: a stoppered flask, candles and a bundle of clothes that he passed to her. There were also dry clothes for himself. Stripping off his wet shirt, affording her a breathtaking view of his broad back, he pulled on a fresh clean white shirt. She stood riveted, clutching the garments he'd handed her. *The way he moved. The way the candlelight flickered on the play of sinew and muscle as he eased the garment on.*

He turned round, catching her gaze. His shirt was still open, giving her this time a glimpse of rippling chest and ridged abdomen, where a sprinkling of dusky hairs arrowed down to the waistband of his tight-fitting wet breeches. *That terrible, all-too-recent sabre scar on his ribs...*

His brow lifted sardonically as he fastened a button and pointed to the garments meant for her. 'Something wrong with the clothes I brought you? Not the right colour?'

She realised she had been staring. She swallowed. 'This is intolerable! I don't— There's nowhere to get changed.'

'Well, you have a choice.' He was still buttoning his own shirt. 'Sit and shiver in your old clothes, or take a deep, deep breath and get changed in here. I promise on my honour—yes, I do still have some remnants of it—that I'll turn my back. I'll even shut my eyes if you want to be quite sure. And you'd better turn your back, too, because I'm about to remove my breeches.'

She gasped and whirled away from him, squeezing her own eyes tightly shut. Imagining—oh, Lord, imagining him peeling those soaked breeches from—from...

'All done,' he said cheerfully after a few moments. 'Now

it's your turn. I'm going to build up this fire; I'll whistle loudly, so I won't even *hear* you getting changed. When you've finished, you can clap your hands or mutter curses at me.'

He reached for the firewood, whistling a lively tune that she had a horrible feeling was a rather rude soldiers' ditty. Biting her lip, she got changed into a warm woollen gown of faded red, some stockings and a thick India shawl. Where had he got them? Better not to ask.

Just pretend this is normal, Verena. To be stranded for the night with the last person on earth you wanted to see.

Suddenly Lucas broke off his whistling to say, 'The Earl often used to come here with your father, I know. Deuce take it, this wood is damp… But why did my grandfather bring *you* here, Verena? What exactly were you doing here with him in the first place?'

She pulled the shawl tightly around her. 'Do you think I *intended* all this?' she asked fiercely. 'He asked me to come to Stancliffe Manor, then he ran out of the house and through the garden! I hurried after him and found him here, in the storm. He managed to return across the bridge, but it started to give way as he was crossing it. Does that answer your question?'

He stood, after throwing one last log on the fire. 'I suppose you realise you were mad to come out here after him, without letting anyone know?'

Resentment burned. 'I did call, for Rickmanby! And then I realised there wasn't time.'

He frowned down at her. 'You had no business coming here in the first place. I told you never to go *anywhere* without Bentinck.'

Her indignation overflowed. 'I detest that man!'

'Then you're a fool,' he said quietly, 'for I would trust him with my life.'

She closed her eyes briefly, saying nothing. He turned his attention back to spreading out to dry the wet clothes he'd peeled off.

The fire was starting at last to give out some warmth, but she sat as far as she could from it, huddled on a window seat in the big shawl. Her glance slid towards the cushions under which her father's diary lay, then away again. *O Estrangeiro.* Maps. Treasure. She didn't understand.

But she certainly understood that she was trapped on this island for the night, with an incredibly dangerous man. *You must forget his kisses. You must forget about his lovemaking. Your father would warn you he is playing some deep, dark game, and you must not be drawn in.*

Lucas said curtly, 'If you're worrying about your reputation, then there's no need. Bentinck knows I've come here for you, but he's telling them all at the house that I'm asleep in my old room.'

Her breath hitched in her throat. 'Is there anything you *don't* tell Bentinck, pray?'

'Very little,' he said flatly. 'And if you'd trusted him a fraction more, you wouldn't have ended up stranded *here*. He said you'd given him his notice today, back at Wycherley, but he followed you nevertheless. And aren't you glad he did? He lost you, of course, once you'd gone into the house. But he was able to alert me that you were somewhere in Stancliffe's grounds.'

She felt bewildered and rather sick. So Lucas had not been far away. She said, striving to keep her voice steady, 'Since you're here, you can perhaps explain something to me. I mentioned the compensation, for the stream, to your grandfather, Lucas. And he seemed to know nothing at all about it.'

He was stooping to attend to the fire again, still whistling softly. 'He has a poor memory,' he said. 'Everything was legal and above board, I assure you. The Wycherley estate was fully entitled to that compensation.'

She watched him from her window seat, the shawl around her shoulders. 'But who paid it? You, or him?'

He turned to her and spread out his hands. 'Does it exactly matter?'

'It matters to *my family*. You paid it. Didn't you?' Her voice shook with emotion now. 'You paid it all, your grandfather knew nothing... Why, Lucas? Why this constant, relentless interference? Why don't you just—*leave us alone*?'

He looked down at her in silence, his hands on his hips. After a moment he said politely, 'Should I go away again, Verena? I could always swim, you know, back across the lake, and leave you alone here—'

'No!'

She hadn't meant it to sound so emphatic. His mouth twisted. 'You mean you actually want my company?'

The thunder was rumbling further away now, but the wind was still moaning in the trees. The fire and the candles he'd lit made some things better, but other things worse. The shadows, for example, were playing tricks, flickering and leaping around the walls and domed ceiling of the pavilion. She remembered the stories she and Pippa had frightened each other with, as children. The servants used to say ghosts haunted Stancliffe's lakes by night...

She said stiffly, 'I wouldn't dream of putting you through the ordeal of having to swim across that lake again, Lord Conistone!'

'Mighty considerate of you,' he drawled. He pulled a chair across and sat astride it, his folded arms resting on its back so that he was facing her. She found herself rather unnervingly captivated by the golden skin revealed by the open neck of his shirt. 'Mind,' he continued, 'it would certainly add to the interesting speculation about my various—escapades. Rumours about midnight swimming feats would make a change from the gossip that usually surrounds me. Concerning parties. And drinking. And so forth.' He looked at her questioningly. 'Go on. Tell me exactly why I received such a frosty reception earlier at Wycherley. What have you heard about me, Miss Sheldon? Though I used to think you disdained society tattle…'

'I do!' she cried. 'I do! Though it's hard to ignore, when they say you've been to—oh, to the Channel Isles, with your idle friend Alec Stewart, attending some grand ball held by—by a French Countess!'

He was on his feet. For just one terrifying moment, as his lean body coiled as if for action, she was truly afraid of what he might do, because she had never seen such blazing anger in his eyes.

Then he said, almost quietly, 'Is that what you heard?'

She gazed up at him, white-faced. 'Is it true, Lucas?'

He shrugged. 'Perhaps it is. Perhaps it isn't.'

She bowed her head bitterly. 'And with an answer like that, you expect me to—*trust* you?'

'Sometimes the truth is—not so easily definable,' he said softly. 'Besides, I'm getting rather used to malicious whispers from ignorant fools.'

He turned to put more wood on the fire. The rain was beating down again on the wooden roof of the pavilion. She swung away from him, to look out through the windows at the cold, dark night. He'd not even troubled to deny where he'd been.

Yet she could not forget the night he had saved her, the night he got shot. Or that terrible scar, from a French sabre.

So many mysteries. Too many mysteries…

He was standing up now from the fire, which was at last giving out a glowing heat.

'There,' he said. 'Even you have to admit that at times I have my uses.'

She turned back to him, her arms clasped more tightly across her breasts. 'We would have managed!' she whispered rather desperately. 'If you hadn't come back into our lives, Lucas, my family would have managed! You are *everywhere*, you seem to know everything before it happens—oh, I wish I'd never met you!'

'Really?' he answered evenly. 'A few weeks ago, you were happy enough to share my bed. Had you forgotten?'

A gasp came to her lips. Her eyes were wide and desperate. *Forget?* Oh, Lord, the things she had let him do to her. The intense, exquisite, mind-searing pleasure he had bestowed…

Her heart was hammering. 'Lucas, you said—we were both agreed—that what happened that night was a terrible mistake! The wine I'd drunk…'

'Ah. The wine,' he said lightly. 'And there was I, thinking you were seriously considering my proposal of marriage. The straitlaced Miss Sheldon, undone by a glass of madeira.'

She jumped to her feet. 'No! Please, Lucas, don't mock!' *He was accusing her of being a lightskirt.* 'I was weak and foolish and I've acknowledged it, but we decided that you must not be forced into marriage to save my reputation!'

His hands were on her shoulders. 'Do you seriously think I could be *forced* into marriage?'

Looking down at her, his dark gaze searing her, he began to subtly knead her tender skin through her gown with his strong fingers, sending shivers of raging desire all through her. Reminding her of the way she had arched beneath his intimate caresses, had risen to sublime ecstasy at the touch of his knowing hands…

She closed her eyes. She was shaking.

'Verena,' he murmured, 'do you think all marriages should be for love?'

His enticing breath was warm on her cheek. She could not move. *You must resist him. You must…* Somehow she said steadily, 'I'm not at all sure that I believe in love. From what I've seen, love can only hurt you.'

'What a world-weary matron you are, Miss Sheldon,' he sighed lightly. 'How old are you? Ah, yes, all of twenty-two. And sensibly turning your back on the frivolities of youth…' He let her go at last, and turned to look round. 'Dare I suggest some wine now, to lighten your despair? Since you find yourself in such—distasteful company?'

He reached for the flask and held it in front of her. *The strait-laced Miss Sheldon, undone by a glass of madeira.*

'No, thank you!' She shook her head tightly.

'Then I'll drink it alone,' he said, taking a deep swig before putting the bottle down and looking around. 'Time now, I think, to consider our sleeping arrangements…'

The room lurched. 'I—I don't *need* to sleep!'

He looked at her, his head on one side, his eyes narrowed. 'You look ready to faint on your feet.' He started to pick out some cushions from the window seat; for a moment her heart thudded with fear, but he went nowhere near the hiding place and she relaxed.

He laid the cushions in a corner on the floor. 'I'm sorry I can't do better, but you should be reasonably comfortable there.'

Verena whispered, 'What about you?'

'I'll stay awake for a while. Keep the fire in, and the local ghosts out, so to speak.'

He *knew* about her childish fears. She nodded,

temporarily unable to speak. Somehow she felt so—safe with him, yet his very presence was a threat. Yes, he'd swum through flood waters, to come to her rescue—but could he somehow know her father's diary was here? If he was after it, *why*? And why didn't he just say so?

The physical longing to be once more in his arms tore through her. But—she had to remember her father's warning. Martin Bryant's warning. She couldn't afford to trust this man again, ever. The cost of a betrayal, this time, would be too high.

Her heart aching sorely, she settled on the cushions upon the floor, with the shawl to cover her. He was sitting on a bench, staring into the fire, his curling black hair still wet, his hard-boned face bleak. *I think about the war all the time*, he'd once told her. Were his thoughts ravaged by guilt, at not being there? Was he remembering past battles? Fallen comrades?

Her eyes rested again on the cushions beneath which she'd hidden the diary in its case. Could it possibly be true what the old Earl had said? That someone had actually killed her father for what he knew?

Her mind full of warring emotions, she closed her eyes and slept, exhausted.

Chapter Eighteen

Lucas Conistone watched the shadows from the fire play on Verena's face. How beautiful she looked as she lay there sleeping. How wildly he had longed, on the instant of his arrival here, to gather her in his arms and peel those wet clothes from her lovely, slender form; kiss her sweet lips, her breasts, and teach her how sublime love between a man and a woman could really be…

Damnation.

His arousal still burned darkly. He hated his lies to her. Hated not being able to tell her everything. She was lovely, brave and innocent—until he, Lucas Conistone, had started to take away that innocence. Deliberately.

She didn't realise so many things.

She didn't realise, for instance, that as she got changed earlier she'd been reflected—many times—in the windows of this octagonal room, which in the blackness of the surrounding night acted like mirrors. He'd tried his best not to look. But, damn it, he was only flesh and blood, and even with his back to her, he couldn't help but glimpse a slender thigh, a delicate shoulder, even one rounded, pink-tipped breast…

It had taken all Lucas's considerable will-power not to jump on her then and there. Just the thought of it made him hard and hot for her. He wanted to sweep her to the ground and make ardent, delicious love to her. He wanted to kiss her into oblivion and protect her from her enemies. From the world.

It was quite damnable that, thanks to his grandfather, it had to be Verena of all people leading him here to what he had been seeking for so long. What would she say, when she found out the truth? Lucas could not bear the thought of her suffering. Of her being in danger, because of her father's past. There was, as he'd decided earlier, only one sure way to protect her.

Marriage. She had to become his wife.

Lucas looked outside. The rain had stopped at last. Verena was soundly asleep, her face tender and trusting as a child's. He gazed down at her. *I'm sorry, Verena.* Then he moved across the room, towards those cushions to which her eyes had wandered so often. *Too often.*

Verena dreamed a horrifying dream. The wind was howling and the rain was lashing at her cheeks and hair. At first she thought she was standing on the narrow bridge to the island, but then in her dream the lake had turned into the sea, and she was on board a ship with Lucas; the ship had struck a rock and was sinking fast.

In her dream Lucas was trying to call out to her as the stormy surf churned around them, then Verena realised that Lucas himself was in danger, for an unidentified dark figure was standing over him with a knife. She was struggling to get to Lucas across the wildly tilting deck to warn him, but the mainsail was in tatters, and she couldn't see him any more, and great black waves were pouring across the deck…

'Lucas, don't die!' she cried out. 'Please, please don't die!'

Then she saw that the man holding that knife over Lucas was—her father.

She woke, crying out Lucas's name, only to realise he was kneeling at her side and holding her in his strong arms, soothing her. 'You were having a bad dream. But it's all right, *querida*. Everything's all right.'

She shuddered. 'I dreamed there was a storm, at sea…'

'Hush, Verena.' His arms around her were warm and comforting.

'But—someone was trying to kill you, Lucas! I was trying to get to you, but I was too late…'

'Oh, my dear.' He was cradling her in his arms now. 'For so long, you have carried such a weight on your shoulders. You have been so utterly brave!'

His fingers were gently tracing the line of her throat. She tried to pull away from him, suddenly realising what was happening. To her. To them both. 'Lucas…'

'It's all right,' he murmured. 'I'm here. I'm safe. I'm with you…' His mouth twisted a little. 'At least, I *think* that's all right—but—do you?'

His fingertip had found its way to her lips. That warm, dry touch on the delicate skin of her mouth sent great tremors juddering through her body. She found her arms slipping around his shoulders. Somehow he was tilting her chin, lifting her face to his, and he was kissing her cheek, then bending to kiss her throat, causing her to arch back her head so he could roam freely with his lips across the delicate skin of her neck and shoulders, making her tremble with delight…

Then he was kissing her mouth. She realised there was nothing she wanted more on this earth than for Lucas to kiss her.

She felt herself warming. Melting. Memories flooded back, of the time he had kissed her before. Of the way she had sworn never to let him kiss her again. Her brain remembered her vow of resistance, but her body did not. Besides, now his tongue was probing her lips and exploring, so sweetly; his hand was caressing her breasts, finding one delicate peak and teasing it between finger and thumb, until it was tight and hot—a caress so firm, so insistent, that her whole being was throbbing in time to the deliberate movement of his fingertips, while at the same time his tongue was thrusting into her mouth and retreating lingeringly, then delving again, deep, and slow, and firm…

She was trembling wildly. He released her from his kiss, but only to stroke back her wild and wanton hair from her face. His molten grey eyes were gazing down at her in the shimmering half-light from the fire. Verena's heart was hammering. Dear Lord. How, how could she tell herself she must not trust him, when her entire being yearned to be at one with him?

Perhaps her father was wrong. The cruel, treacherous hope began to snake its way into her desire-hazed mind. After all, hadn't Lucas done all he could to help them? Hadn't he saved Wycherley? Perhaps her father had mistakenly surmised that Lucas hated them all as much as the Earl did…

Impossible. *Impossible.*

His hands were sliding round her back this time, caressing her, sending darts of flame along her body. Behind him, she could see, through the small window, that the moon was out again, dancing behind wild clouds, its light casting Lucas's handsome face into harsh relief, and glittering on that thick mane of midnight-black hair, the straight brow, the clear eyes and starkly moulded jaw and cheekbones.

'Ah, Verena. If I asked you to marry me again now,' he was murmuring huskily, 'what would be your answer, I wonder?'

His mouth was about to cover hers again. She put her hands on the hard wall of his chest, resisting him. She must end it, she must. She said, trembling, 'This is impossible. I am no one in your world. You would lose everything if you courted me.'

'You've never given me a chance to say whether I thought you were worth the loss,' he whispered. His lips touched her throat. 'Everything I've done, I do for you. I think of you when I'm far away, *meu amor.* You are my dream of a better life.'

He kissed her again and she surrendered. Willingly she gave him her mouth, her tongue twining with his. His hands had deliberately parted her gown; this time he was running his palms flatly over both her breasts until her nipples were hard, jutting peaks of desire. Her hips were lifting, grinding instinctively against his; she could feel, as his heavily muscled thighs pressed against hers, the hardness of his aroused manhood through the taut cloth of his breeches…

Then he bent his head suddenly, to lick and curl with his tongue round one scarlet nipple, sucking and drawing it between his teeth. Her moan of pleasure became a sharp gasp as her body was seized by a violent shuddering of delight. Of ardent longing.

'Everything,' he was repeating huskily. 'Everything, for you…'

Still gazing at her, he stood up and began to unbutton his shirt. His magnificent, muscular torso gleamed in the firelight as he shrugged the shirt off. The outline of his proud erection was all too evident beneath the fabric of his skintight breeches.

Her throat was dry, her pulse racing. A primitive instinct seemed to take possession of her whole body, snaking wantonly over each nerve-ending and stirring her flesh into pulsating life. Now he was down at her side again, kneeling on the cushions, his thumb brushing her swollen mouth, running down her throat, to her breasts. Her hands flew to cover them, the twin stiffened peaks humiliating evidence of her reaction to him. He caught them and held them away, his iron strength tempered by gentleness. He breathed, 'They're beautiful. You are beautiful.'

He must have made love to so many exquisite women, she told herself. *He must have said these things so many times to so many others.*

Even now his eyes were dark, unfathomable. Yet, as he took her hand and lifted it to his lips to kiss it, the shafts of longing rippled through her body, again and again. She gasped as the dark heat pooled at her abdomen and lower, realised his fingers had slipped down to caress the apex of her thighs. She heard a soft moan—*oh, Lord, her own*—as he parted the delicate folds of skin and began to stroke with his forefinger, up and down, seeking and revelling in the silky moistness there.

Her hips arched suddenly, wanting him, finding him; her hands were clasped round his strong shoulders, clenching on firm, warm male muscle. *'Lucas…'*

'Hush,' he was saying softly between kisses, 'hush, you are beautiful, so beautiful…'

He was dealing with his own garments now, reaching to the fastening of his breeches, and the colour flooded her face as he drew her close and she felt the lengthy silken heat of him tense and quiver against her stomach. *The strength.*

The power. The desire there. For her. Then he was kissing her again, savouring her lush mouth with his tongue.

She wanted him. Her body was a whirlpool of passion, of desire; and this man was at the heart of her longing. 'Tell me,' she whispered huskily. 'Tell me how to give *you* pleasure, Lucas, as you give pleasure to me…'

'Kiss me,' he breathed. She did, flickering and darting with her tongue inside his mouth, tasting the silken flesh there.

'Ah, Verena—' He guided her hand down to his hard shaft and she gasped as her fingertips explored the hot, pulsing flesh.

Now he was cradling her slender hips, lifting them, and she could see, in the flickering half-light, the core of his masculinity poised to enter her. She dug her fingers into his iron-hard arms as he lowered himself gradually and she felt the engorged head of his manhood probing at the very heart of her femininity. She felt the tightness, as her most secret place sought to accommodate him, then the hard, pulsing surge. Her cry of surprise, and wonder, rose involuntarily; and then came the beginnings of the most exquisite pleasure as he supported his upper body's weight on his arms and began to move, gazing down at her, all the time.

'Verena. Beautiful one. I'm not hurting you, am I?' he whispered.

'No. Oh, no.' Instinctively she lifted her hips, already delighting in this most intimate of caresses. He bowed his head and kissed her, his tongue plunging sensually to match the thrust of his manhood. She welcomed every touch ardently.

She had not dreamed it would be like this. Power. Fulfilment. Love…

His strokes deepened, lengthened, intensified in their

strength. She was crying out his name, raking his back with her fingers, as she spiralled into the exquisite sensations that were taking her to unknown heights and, incredibly, keeping her there. His virile manhood stroked her, fulfilled her, while his lips roved her throat, her breasts. And he urged her beyond pleasure to a place where she had never been. Never dreamed existed. Her world exploded into splinters of shattering delight.

Then he was joining her. Thrusting harder yet, lifting her, crushing her to him. '*Verena.*' At last he was spending himself within her, convulsing again and again, while she gloried in, was sated in, the pleasure of possessing. Of being possessed.

Afterwards he drew her close in his arms, and cradled her until she slept.

She woke with a start, in the grey light of dawn. And, in broken fragments, it all started coming back to her. Dear God. She closed her eyes against the remembered images tumbling through her mind. She'd been wanton, primitive, abandoned. And had adored every minute of it.

A slight sound had her eyes flying wide open again, and she sat up, holding the shawl against her naked breasts as Lucas came in through the door, carrying wood for the fire, which still glowed softly. In the cold light of dawn, he looked even more handsome. He stopped and smiled at her; she almost swooned with desire. He was dressed in his breeches and boots, with a soft grey kersey waistcoat over his white shirt that emphasised his broad shoulders and narrow hips. His thick black hair curled to the nape of his neck. His lean cheeks and jaw were stubbled with the beginnings of a beard. His eyes, despite that smile, were hooded. Questioning.

Everything I've done, I do for you. He'd spoken words

of love. Yet he looked everything that was powerful, male, dangerous.

Her father—he must have been wrong! He *must* have been mistaken, because Lucas had asked her, again, to marry him.

Lucas went to put down the firewood. She held herself tense, waiting.

'Did you sleep well?' His enquiry was full of tenderness.

Sleep well? Yes, she had, and that was the worst of it. She had slept in his arms all night. She had willingly surrendered to him—everything.

And she would do again, she realised. If he took her in his arms now, and kissed her, she would do the same again.

'Look at me,' he said. His voice was still soft, but it was a command none the less.

Lowering his formidable frame to her side, he reached for her and drew her into his arms. He was all muscle and sinew, and broad-shouldered grace; she remembered—too well—how it felt to have his arms enfolding her, the touch of his lips on her mouth, on her…*everywhere.*

He said, 'Verena. I rather think that rescue is on the way.'

'Oh, *no.*' She jumped to her feet.

'There's time enough, *querida.*' He pulled her down again and kissed her, cupping her face and stroking it with his fingers before easing his grasp a little and gazing down into her eyes.

'That's better. Panic will get us nowhere.' He soothed her tousled hair back from her temples, his eyes still dark and unreadable.

'Lucas. About last night,' she whispered. 'You must not

feel any obligation.' Struggling free, she started to pull on her clothes.

His eyes blackened further. He, too, stood up, towering over her. 'Nevertheless, it happened and we must deal with it.'

'But it should *not* have happened! It was a mistake!'

His face tightened. 'On whose part?'

'Mine! Both of ours!' She was buttoning up her gown. 'Who is coming? Is it Bentinck?'

Lucas was padding over to the window. 'Indeed. Bentinck's brought the flat-bottomed boat they use for moving timber from the islands. And I'm afraid it looks as if he's brought half the servants' quarters.'

Verena hurried swiftly to his side, her trembling fingers smoothing down her bodice. Out there, indeed, she saw a boat, rowed by two burly menservants and steered by Bentinck. At his side was Rickmanby's gaunt form.

She whirled back to Lucas. 'We can tell them the truth. That I was stranded here after following your grandfather. That you came simply to rescue me. We can appeal to their discretion.'

He shook his head, his strong jaw tightening. 'Discretion? I'm not sure that's a word that exists in a servant's vocabulary. And is that really what you want? Oh, Verena. Are you so determined to have nothing to do with me, even though you practically begged me to make love to you last night?'

Her cheeks blazed with colour at that. It was true. Even now, he could have taken her like a street slut. She still wanted him so badly that her whole body throbbed with anguish. 'You will not humiliate me!' she breathed. 'You will not!'

They were coming closer now—Bentinck, Rickmanby,

the two other men. Bentinck was leading the way, scowling as usual.

Lucas went out to meet him. She pulled her shawl tighter as she heard Bentinck saying, in his rough way, 'Sorry, milord. I'd have come by myself if I could, but the old Earl's been rambling to everyone about the girl being stuck on the island…'

Lucas commanded, 'Wait here, Bentinck, will you?'

'Aye, milord.'

And Lucas came back in to where Verena waited, shivering with tension. 'Well?' he said quietly. 'There's only one thing for it, Verena. I know I've asked before, and you've refused. But now I think even you have to agree that there's no other option. Marry me.'

Chapter Nineteen

Three hours later she was back at Wycherley Hall. Pippa and David were there, looking anxious.

'Turley told us you went to Stancliffe Manor and were caught in the storm!' Pippa exclaimed. 'But, Verena, *why*—?'

Verena drew a deep breath. 'Pippa, Lord Conistone has asked me to marry him.'

Pippa's mouth was opening in exclamation; David took his wife's hand warningly. Verena went on, 'But he has to go away again, on business, and we will not make an official announcement until we can tell Mama, in London, together. So please say nothing to anyone as yet…'

Pippa considered this quietly for a few moments before saying, 'Are you quite sure, my dear?'

Verena looked at her favourite sister steadily. She could not confide her terrible doubts even to Pippa. 'I *want* to be sure. So very much.'

David Parker, smiling broadly, urged his wife, 'Wish her joy, Pippa!' He gave Verena a quick hug. 'I always said there was something between the two of you! Something good! I always said Conistone was a sound man, beneath that idle veneer! Come, Pippa, let's celebrate—sherry at the least, even though it is scarcely noon!'

And Pippa, too, was cheering up. 'Izzy will be over the moon at having a viscount for a brother-in-law,' she observed, 'and oh, my, Mama will faint with joy. Deb will be jealous to death—but don't let any of them spoil this for you, sister mine!'

David had already gone to fetch glasses for a toast; Pippa hugged her close. 'I really am very happy for you,' Pippa whispered. 'And truth to tell, just a tiny bit jealous myself, for he truly is every woman's dream!'

Verena joined them in their elation, for she could not tell even David and Pippa all her doubts, her fears. True, they had been caught in a compromising situation. But Lucas could have bought or charmed his way out of it. He was no fool, to be trapped into a lifetime's commitment by a moment's indiscretion.

It was she, Verena, who'd been the fool. More than a fool, she'd been a slut. Dear God, she'd been powerless to prevent what happened. And, much worse, she had not even *wanted* to prevent what happened… She shut her eyes. Just the memory of his lean, hard-muscled body making slow love to her was enough to set her pulse racing again, her breasts tingling anew.

Shameless. Utterly shameless. *Oh, Lucas.*

She longed to believe in him. She longed for her father to be wrong.

'No need for desperate measures, Lucas,' she had managed to say calmly earlier as he'd arranged to send her back to Wycherley in his grandfather's gig. 'No need for haste. I'll explain to them all that you came to rescue me, that's all!'

'On the contrary,' he'd drawled, 'there's every need for haste.' His grey eyes were steel-hard as they assessed her. 'Servants talk. You have your family and your sisters to consider. All right, so perhaps you, with your good name sullied—as it will be if you don't marry me—might crawl away and live in the country. They certainly will not wish to do so. You must agree to a betrothal, and soon, or the Sheldon family's reputation will be ruined.'

If she were sure of this man and of his love, then marriage to him would be the most wonderful thing in the world. But how could she be sure?

Oh, Father. If only I could talk to you one last time.

'Yesterday,' Lucas went on, 'I saw my attorney. He has a letter for you, to be opened if I don't return.'

She felt her breath catch in her throat. 'If you don't return? From where?'

'I have to go away again soon. In fact, I have to leave tonight. I have urgent business. And I want to make quite, quite sure you're provided for.'

At first she was speechless. Then she whispered, 'You are always leaving me. Behaving—inexplicably. Yet you plead with me to trust you. Sometimes, I feel as if my life and my future are merely your playthings…'

His eyes were dark. Hooded. 'Some day,' he said quietly, 'some day very soon I will be able to explain. Some day soon I will want your answer.'

She nodded, her throat aching. 'You—you will wish to speak to my mother before the engagement is announced.'

'Of course.' He took her hand and kissed it. 'Meanwhile—I need your trust, Verena. I need your love.'

The gig had brought her from Stancliffe back to Wycherley, and already she yearned to hear his husky soft drawl.

To see his lazy smile, his dancing grey eyes. The longing for him was almost a physical pain. But so many of her questions were unanswered.

It was a relief to get away from Pippa and David and their congratulations and reach the sanctuary of her own room. To have the chance to address, at last, one of the issues that troubled her so.

Back on the island, when Lucas had gone out to speak to the newly arrived Bentinck, she'd quickly retrieved her father's diary in its slim case from its hiding place in the pavilion and concealed it beneath her cloak. Surely, surely, *this* would contain the answers to at least some of her questions!

Now she eased the leather case open, uneasily aware of something she'd scarcely acknowledged at the time. It felt—too light.

And there was a reason for that.

The diary was not there.

She had to keep going. Even though her world was shattered into tiny pieces around her, she had to keep going. Pippa and David had left, and she was alone in the house except for the servants, until she had a visitor later that day. Captain Martin Bryant.

She did not want to see Captain Bryant. But unfortunately Turley had already told him that she was here.

'Please show him to the parlour then, Turley,' she said tightly. 'I will be there in a moment.'

Martin Bryant was pacing up and down the room when she entered. 'Captain,' she said, 'what brings you here?' She was praying he hadn't heard some rumour about her night with Lucas. She'd told Pippa and David to say nothing, but servants' gossip flew like the wind…

His fists were clenched. 'I heard you've seen Lucas Conistone again, Miss Sheldon! At Stancliffe!'

Oh, no. What else had he heard? Her chin jerked upwards. 'That is hardly your business, Captain Bryant!'

His pale blue eyes betrayed agitation. 'I'm afraid it's my *official* business, Miss Sheldon! I've asked you this before—but has Conistone been asking you about a diary of your father's, some kind of record of his travels in the Peninsula?'

The diary again. The room rocked around her. Her hand flew to her mouth, then dropped again.

'I knew it!' he exclaimed bitterly. 'He has, hasn't he? You denied it earlier, but I was certain that brute Conistone would be worming his way in here to a purpose, *using* you… Verena, your father's diary is vitally important!'

Certainly it was important to Lucas. He had seduced her for it. Suddenly, full of unspeakable dread, she remembered what the old Earl had said. *They killed your father for what he knew.*

She whispered, 'What is in my father's diary? Please, Martin, I must know.'

He'd been striding to and fro in agitation. Now he stopped and faced her. 'You must have heard, Verena, that Lord Wellington is marching towards Lisbon across the Portuguese mountains.'

She nodded, clasping her hands together. 'I have read in the newspaper that possession of Lisbon is vital, yes.'

'The French are in pursuit. They have twice Wellington's men, twice his armaments! Wellington is relying,' went on Martin harshly, 'on moving faster than the French across the difficult terrain. He needs maps. And no one has ever explored and charted those mountains as your father did!'

She sat down, her heart thudding sickeningly. 'So people really are after his papers.'

'His diary of the year before last, to be precise,' cut in Martin. 'And I'll ask you again—has Conistone pestered you for this diary? I warn you, Conistone will sacrifice anyone, and anything, to get it! You must tell me where that diary is; it is bringing you into incredible danger!'

She jumped to her feet again. 'If I was in danger because of that diary, then so was Lucas! He tried to protect me! He was shot at, twice!'

'Perhaps,' said Martin silkily, 'they were trying to silence him. He's not making a very good job of things, after all.'

'They?'

'His French comrades.'

The room was spinning around her. Martin had hinted at this weeks ago; she had taken no heed. 'Captain Bryant, you're not saying—that Lucas is working for the French?'

'Who else would he work for, after he left the army in such disgrace?'

Her hand went to her throat. 'But—why?'

'Not for money, certainly,' said Martin bitterly. 'He has no need of *that*. But—he won't have forgotten the insults that flew around after he left the army. He's a coward, Verena. And this betrayal of an entire campaign is the horribly twisted revenge of an extremely clever man whose life has gone utterly wrong. You'd have thought Lucas Conistone had everything, wouldn't you? Money, looks, title… But beneath it all he's bitter as hell and full of hatred. I guess that he's promised to take your father's diary to the French in Portugal—indeed, I've been told he's on his way there now. Thank God he hasn't found it.'

But he had. The nausea rose in her throat till she could barely stand. 'You say—he's on his way to Portugal?'

'He's set off for Portsmouth, yes.'

With the diary.

She said tightly, 'If you really believe that he is a traitor, why not report it?'

He shrugged. 'He has powerful friends, so I need proof, Verena, extremely good proof. And if I challenged him alone I'd be a dead man. But—perhaps I should not be telling you all this!' He walked over to the window, then swung round to face her again, his face quite desperate. 'After all—you've as good as sold yourself to him, haven't you?'

Had he heard about the secret betrothal? Her night with him on the island? The colour burned in her cheeks. 'Martin, I've sold myself to no one! That is an abominable lie!'

'Is it? Is it?' He spread out his hands, palms upwards. 'Everyone knows that he's lavishing money on your family—*why*? Verena, I love you! I can't offer you what Lucas can. But I can offer you a loyal and a brave heart!'

Suddenly he whirled round to face the door, hearing what Verena did. The sound of heavy footsteps outside, and the familiar whistling of 'The British Grenadiers'.

She hurried to the door. 'Bentinck! What are you doing in this part of the house?'

Bentinck had stayed, on Lucas's precise instructions. She had known better than to argue. 'Looking for you, ma'am,' he said. 'Some parcels 'ave just arrived by carrier; fabric for curtains and other such fancy things, I b'lieve. Will you come and sign for them? The carrier's out in the yard.'

'Yes. I'll make my own way there.' Still he didn't move. She said sharply, 'Well? What are you waiting here for?'

'To make sure everything's all right, ma'am. That's all.'

He was Lucas's spy. And she'd had enough of him.

'I can manage perfectly well without you, Bentinck, I assure you!'

For a moment Bentinck looked inclined to stand his ground. 'Lord Conistone, he said—'

She ushered him out into the hallway, shutting the door on Captain Bryant. 'Bentinck,' she announced, 'I'm leaving Wycherley later today, to join my mother and sisters in London. You will leave also. And definitely—most definitely—not in my company! You've no need at all to fear for my safety—I'll be far better chaperoned in London than I am here, I assure you!'

'Even so—'

'If I don't see you leaving this house within the hour, Bentinck, I will have you arrested for trespass. Is that clear?'

He bowed his head. 'Quite clear, ma'am.' His face was wooden. 'Would you put that in writing, ma'am, for his lordship?'

Pale with fury, she hurried to the study, scribbled a note and thrust it at him.

'Thank you, ma'am, obliged, I'm sure!' And he walked slowly away.

Drawing her hand wearily across her eyes, Verena went back to Martin Bryant.

'You must go,' she said icily. She held the door open and he picked up his hat, still hesitating.

'Conistone is more than a coward, Verena. He's a damned traitor! I'll carry on doing what I can, to find proof of it. But for God's sake have nothing more to do with him, and if you *do* find this diary of your father's, let me know, will you? Believe me, I'll make very sure that Lord Wellington gets it!'

He left, hurrying out to where his horse was tethered.

Verena went to sign for the curtain fabrics; then, as the carrier's cart rumbled off, she simply stood there, alone.

Had Lucas really gone to the extremity of *seducing* her to get her father's diary? Did Lucas truly intend to deliver it to the French, as Martin Bryant said? She pressed her hands to her temples.

Perhaps Lucas had taken it because it was dangerous for her, Verena, to have in her possession! After all, he *must* care for her! He had asked her twice, now, to marry him…

Hope was crushed by a new and dire thought. Marriage would prevent her testifying against him if he was accused of treason. For no wife could give evidence against her husband in court.

She felt sick to her stomach. But she had to be strong. She had to get the diary back. She had to confront Lucas with what she knew, and get him to tell her the truth.

But could she really face the truth?

She went inside to change her clothes. From her window she saw Bentinck riding away. She sat there, in the utter stillness, her mind conjuring up a thousand scenarios, her heart shattering into a thousand pieces. Then she prepared to leave Wycherley herself—and not for London.

Chapter Twenty

6:00 p.m.—Portsmouth

The din of sailors' shouts and women crying farewells to loved ones filled the crowded quayside. Verena gazed around at all the vessels, all the people, in Portsmouth's bustling harbour. She'd ridden here alone, as quickly as she could.

She had to find Lucas before he sailed for Portugal and get the diary back.

Would he be on a naval ship? Or would he be taking an ordinary passage on one of the many small vessels that carried troops and ammunition out to Lisbon for the British army?

'He's a coward,' Martin had said scornfully. 'And this betrayal is the revenge of a man whose life has gone utterly wrong.'

Still so hard to believe...

Squaring her slender shoulders, she pushed her way along the harbour, asking the same question again and again, 'Is there a ship sailing for Lisbon tonight?'

Often her request was greeted with raucous laughter. 'Going there yourself, are you, darling? Got a man in the army? Or has some randy buck got you in trouble and is doing his best to run away from you?'

People clearly wondered what she, a young, respectably dressed lady, was doing here on her own. Most of the women here on this crowded dockside were from the town, come to say tearful goodbyes to the sailors, or the scarlet-jacketed infantry bound for the Peninsula. And there were, of course, the whores. A giggling group of them paraded past her now, the skirts of their tawdry gowns blowing in the strong sea breeze, their faces painted, their bosoms outthrust.

And as dusk gathered, even Verena's indomitable spirit was starting to falter. *Perhaps he's already sailed. Perhaps Martin was wrong and he's leaving from one of the other ports. I am an utter fool.* She would have to ride home again, to Wycherley. It would take a while for her to be missed, because of course Bentinck had left, and she'd explained to Cook that she was visiting a friend and might stay overnight. She'd also left a sealed note for Pippa. Just in case.

She had to confront Lucas and get the diary back. Her father never gave up, and neither would she. Her fingers fastened instinctively round the small package she had in her pocket, of her father's letters to her. She'd brought them as a talisman, to inspire her with the courage her father had always told her she possessed.

Stubbornly she continued to push her way through the crowds, asking and asking if any ships were due to leave for Lisbon.

And suddenly, she got an answer. A man in a shabby tricorne hat, with the wind-roughened complexion of a seafarer, listened to her with interest. 'There's the *Goldfinch*, m'dear. Sailing as soon as the tide turns.' He pointed along the quayside to where a down-at-heel brig was being loaded with provisions. 'Got someone to say goodbye to, have you?' He grinned. 'A lover's farewell?'

Goodbye, and so much more! She gave a coy smile. 'Indeed, I have a great deal to say to this particular gentleman! Can you tell me, sir, where I will find the *Goldfinch*'s captain?'

He tipped his dirty hat. 'Right before you. Captain Jed Brooks at your service—*ma'am*. And who are you so eager to see?'

She hesitated. She did not like the look of Captain Brooks. She glanced at the *Goldfinch*—would Lucas really travel on such an untidy wreck of a ship?

If what you dread is true, then this is exactly the kind of vessel he would choose.

She said, 'His name is Conistone. Lucas Conistone…'

He looked down a grubby list he'd pulled from his pocket. 'We're carrying marines in case of trouble from the Frenchies and a few business gents from England; we've a Wilkins, a Patterson… But Conistone? No. No one of that name.'

'My thanks,' she said quickly to Captain Jed Brooks. 'I'll try elsewhere.'

He touched his hat, regarding her lasciviously a moment longer. 'Good luck with your quest, missy! And I only hope your man appreciates the trouble you've gone to, to say farewell to him!' He went off chuckling, pushing his way through the crowds on the wharf to his ship.

At a distance, Verena watched as Captain Brooks swaggered up the gangplank. The *Goldfinch* was heaving with activity. Sailors were swarming up the rigging. Deckhands, swearing lustily, were hauling supplies on board. A troop of twenty marines were lined up on the foc'sle deck, watching the crowds on the harbourside and whistling at the girls.

She was just about to turn and leave when she glimpsed a figure on the deck of the *Goldfinch*. Almost instantly he was hidden again, by the soldiers crowding the guard rail, and she gasped in disappointment. But she was so sure she had recognised the proud bearing, the aristocratic features, the slightly overlong black hair that singled out Lord Lucas Conistone!

She hurried up the gangplank, pushing her way past the busy sailors. She had seen him near the bridge. But now there was no sign. She must have been mistaken. Slowly she made her way back towards the gangplank.

Then suddenly two of the sailors barred her way. Two pairs of tattooed, brawny arms pinioned her. She could smell their sweat. 'Women below deck!' One of them grinned.

She tried to throw them off. 'Take your hands off me!'

'You'd prefer one of the army lads to us, would you, darling? Never fear, you'll get your pick of them all soon enough, my lovely!'

She kicked and struggled. She shouted for help. But they almost lifted her along the deck and thrust her down a hatchway into a large but airless space below the ship's foredeck, that was lit by a single filthy lantern hanging from an overhead beam. Some coarsely dressed women were already huddled in the far corner, playing cards and swigging gin. She caught her breath. *Oh, no...*

She turned desperately to the sailor who still grasped her arm. 'You must listen to me. This is a mistake.'

He eyed her with appreciation. 'Your mistake then, not ours, sweetheart,' he shrugged. 'Don't worry. We'll be nine, ten days a-sailin' to Lisbon, dependin' on the weather. Long enough to get used to having the time of your life!'

He climbed back up the ladder like a monkey, and the hatch slammed down. The other women turned to gaze at her. Their faces were bright with rouge, their clothes gaudy and revealing. 'Evenin'!' called out one of them as she dealt a pack of cards. 'Come to join us in a game of rummy, darlin', have yer? Or are you too bloody stuck-up?'

She could hear the straining of timber, the rasping of windlasses up above as the ship started to move. Dear God, this was a shipful of whores. Camp followers. Being sent to supply the men of Wellington's army with—a necessary comfort, as it was explained in polite circles… She ran back to the ladder and banged desperately on the hatch. 'I've no intention of sailing on this ship. I demand to speak to the Captain. You must let me out!'

Her voice faded. Up on the deck, she could hear men roaring orders. The ship juddered and strained as the wind caught her rigging and the waves embraced her creaking hull.

They had set sail.

The hatch remained closed, and the women below laughed and laughed. 'Make the most of it, missy! You're in for a treat on this voyage.'

Lisbon. Ten days' sailing, at least. She must have been utterly wrong, thinking she saw Lucas here. *You fool, Verena.* Pippa and the servants at Wycherley would be distracted with worry. She *must* speak to the Captain and explain! Surely he would help her to transfer to another British ship, heading back for Portsmouth…

And why should the Captain do that? At sea, his word was law and she didn't have much hope for the law of Captain Jed Brooks. Best, perhaps, terrible though it seemed, to stay hidden down here. At least there was room enough for her to keep to herself, while the whores played cards or combed one another's hair.

The first night she had been wretchedly seasick, but by the morning she was more used to the ship's rolling motion. They were brought food—miserable food, but it was enough to keep her alive—and no one seemed inclined to trouble her. Sometimes, when the light of the lantern was good enough, she was even able to bring out her father's letters to read. They were the only comfort she had.

For the whores on the ship, it was business as usual. As the days and nights went by, she grew to know the routine. Every evening the sailors would come down to bring up whores for the marines and officers, two or three at a time. The women would return later, jingling their money, and Verena would try to shut her ears to the coarseness of their talk.

One night a sailor came down alone, and led one of the whores close, too close to the corner that Verena had made her temporary home. In the lantern light she glimpsed him fondling the woman's dark-tipped, heavy breasts, heard him coupling with her roughly.

Verena buried her head in her hands, trying to ignore the sailor's growls of delight.

She stayed in her corner, coming out only for food and to relieve herself at what they called the heads. She slept when she could, wrapped in one of the coarse blankets they'd been thrown. Most of the other women ignored her—she was not competing for attention, and was therefore no threat. Though one of the younger ones, Annie, actually befriended her, and talked to her sorrowfully about her grim upbringing in Portsmouth and how this journey was almost a relief from the rough streets.

Verena thought, *When we get to Lisbon, I will find someone to help me. Lisbon, they say, is still held by the British; I will find someone in command and get back to England...*

She looked often at her father's maps, remembering what she'd read in the newspapers about the British army marching across the mountains to reach Lisbon. Could Lucas really be a traitor? Could he?

On what must have been the eighth day, everything changed.

The hatch opened, and a sailor climbed down. 'Right!' he was yelling. 'Six of you little beauties wanted up in the captain's cabin. He's havin' a bit of a party, him and his friends, and they need some choice female company!'

Several of the women had already jumped to their feet, patting their hair and pulling their gowns low to display their full breasts.

'Steady on!' grinned the sailor. 'Only six, mind! And none of the old hags! You two'll do, and you—' He was jabbing his finger at Annie and two of the younger whores. 'And the pair of you, aye, the gigglers, and—' His gaze suddenly fell on Verena. A broad grin spread across his pockmarked features. 'How about *you*, now? Yes, you with the chestnut hair. You look like a dainty thing.'

She was desperate. 'No. This is all a terrible mistake—'

Annie stepped in front of her, trying to protect her. 'You leave her alone. She ain't used to it…' But it was in vain.

'Come along,' the sailor said softly. He was wagging his finger. 'Captain's orders. You're all of you little ladies in for a treat.'

Her thoughts roved wildly as she was herded with the others up the ladder and along the deck to the Captain's cabin. *I will explain to Captain Brooks who I am. I will threaten him with the law…* She swallowed. If she made trouble, he could have her thrown overboard. No one would ever know—because no one knew she was here. Oh, what a fool she had been.

The sailor in charge, gripping her arm so tightly that he bruised her skin, kicked open the door to the Captain's cabin.

Captain Brooks and his companions were sitting round the table. The lingering smell of hot rich food indicated that they'd just eaten, and the stench of tobacco and wine in this fusty, low-ceilinged apartment was suffocating. Verena swayed on her feet. Annie put a steadying arm around her. 'Chin up, now, dearie,' she whispered. 'With luck you'll get a kind one. And any rate, it's easier than having to service a dozen of the brutes down below.'

They were all pushed further into the cabin. There were six men, sitting round the table. The Captain. A couple of passengers, two marine officers…and *Lucas*.

Chapter Twenty-One

Lord Lucas Conistone was leaning back in his chair, his arms folded across his chest. He was wearing a faded black coat over a shabby striped-silk waistcoat, and his necktie was undone. A rakish air clung to him; his dark hair was dishevelled, and his eyes hooded.

Verena, speechless, saw his expressionless glance flicker lazily across the new arrivals. He must have seen her! But—

'Devil take it, Brooks, they look a mighty dull bunch,' Lucas drawled. 'If that's your idea of entertainment, I'll pass.' He reached for the port bottle and refilled his glass.

Just over a week ago, she had been cradled in this man's arms. Just over a week ago, he had made powerful, passionate love to her and had asked her to marry him.

And now he was travelling to Portugal, on this foul ship. With her father's diary, which was wanted by both French and English…

Captain Brooks, flushed with wine, thumped his fist on the table. 'You'll pass, you say? No, by God, you don't get out of this so easily, Mr Patterson! You're to—' he broke off, hiccupping '—you're to choose a wench to keep you warm and cosy in that cabin of yours!'

Mr Patterson. Lucas was travelling under an assumed name. If she'd had any lingering hope, it was gone. Lucas was going to Portugal—to sell her father's diary to the French.

She must have shuddered in her anguish, for the woman next to her whispered in her ear, 'Never fear, girl. Most of them are so drunk they'll be snoring within minutes. Though there's one handsome feller there—' she indicated Lucas wistfully '—whom I'd take into my bed for free any time.'

Lucas, still seated, was stretching his arms before concealing a half-yawn. His eyes flickered over her once and she saw a familiar gleam in his iron-grey pupils. The woman was right. He was devastatingly attractive. Every part of him emanated strength, sensuality and utter ruthlessness.

And now—what would he do now, what would Captain Brooks do, if she exposed Lucas for who he was? Nothing, probably, except laugh at her. Why should they believe a single word she said?

Nothing that could happen to her now would be worse than the knowledge that Lucas was a traitor. Dear God. *Keep calm. Keep calm.* She kept her head high, though she felt sick with despair.

Captain Brooks was clearly drunk. 'Never say you men don't have everything you want sailing on board my *Goldfinch*,' he chuckled. 'But some things come extra. Now, at this stage of the voyage, I reckon you're all more than ready for some entertainment—and I'd wager there's more than one of you men interested in that little chestnut-haired wench with the gold-brown eyes!' His ugly gaze fastened on Verena. 'Come, gentlemen, what am I bid for her?'

'Reckon she looks a mite fancy to be in the trade,' muttered one of his companions.

'Ah,' said Captain Brooks. 'Perhaps so, Mr Wilkins, but that means there'll be a bit of fight left in her, and surely you'd enjoy knocking it out of her and giving her the ride of her life…'

'I'll put down a guinea for her,' said a burly-looking marine officer, his cheeks flushed with wine as he leered at Verena.

'Thank you, Lieutenant Devenish,' appoved Brooks. 'One guinea on the table for her, gentlemen! What about you, Mr Patterson? You're a man fond of buying fancy goods, I'm sure!'

Lucas said—nothing. Devenish licked his lips. But then another officer, a swarthy man who reeked of sweat, thumped down some coins. 'Two guineas for the chestnut-haired filly!'

'Ah!' Captain Brooks looked delighted. 'We have a race on, gents. Any advance? Mr. Wilkins?'

'I'd be throwing money away,' grunted Wilkins. He was gazing at Annie. 'I'll bid three shilling for the lively red-head there. Any advances?'

There were none, so Wilkins led Annie out of the cabin by the wrist, already pressing wet kisses on her and fumbling for her breasts. Lieutenant Devenish shoved more coins towards the Captain. 'Three guineas.' Grinning, he got up and staggered towards Verena. 'I think you're mine, sweetheart.'

She flinched, shuddering. *'Never…'*

Then Lucas unfolded his arms lazily. The muscles of his face scarcely moving, he drawled, 'She's not yours yet, Devenish. I'll bid four guineas for her.'

Brooks shouted with delight. Devenish's jaw dropped. 'Devil take it, Patterson—four guineas?'

'Exactly so.' Lucas counted the coins on to the table with his long, lean fingers. There was a stunned silence. Lucas drank more port and leaned back carelessly in his chair, linking his hands behind his head.

Lieutenant Devenish looked bullishly at Lucas. 'Five, then, for the chestnut-haired jade!'

'Six,' said Lucas steadily.

There were gasps of amazement.

'Come now,' said the Captain, leaning across the table amiably to pat Lucas on the shoulder, 'Why don't you and Devenish share her, eh, Mr Patterson? While the rest of us watch? Three guineas each—now, wouldn't that be capital sport?'

Verena felt her legs giving way. *No.* She would throw herself over the side, rather than that.

Lucas was saying flatly, 'Six guineas for her in privacy, Captain. Or when we reach port I'll drop a hint in an appropriate ear that you're planning to carry contraband goods back to England.'

'You wouldn't damn well dare…'

'Try me. And don't think to get rid of me on the way. Remember, Brooks, I'm expected in Portugal by friends who'd have you shot if anything happened to me on board your ship.'

Were those friends French spies? Verena's thoughts ran riot. Meanwhile Captain Jed Brooks had visibly whitened.

'Very well,' he muttered. 'Very well… Any higher offers? Lieutenant Devenish? No? Then she's all yours, Mr Patterson. Let us drink to your very good health, Mr Patterson, before you go to take your pleasure with the slut.' He gathered up Lucas's coins, then poured more port into all their glasses and managed a shaky laugh. He drank deeply, but Lucas shoved his drink aside. Then, looking at Devenish and the Captain with cold scorn, he stood up.

She'd forgotten how tall he was. How broad-shouldered. How magnificently male. For the first time he looked at her properly and she tilted her head in an effort to meet his gaze defiantly.

'You lucky cow,' whispered one of the waiting women to her. 'I'd give it 'im for free, as often as he damn well liked.'

Verena clenched her fists. He was walking slowly towards her. Claiming her. This was intolerable. She whispered, through gritted teeth, 'I will not go anywhere with you, Lucas! I will tell them who—'

For one brief moment she was aware of his grey eyes blazing; then he clamped her to him and crushed her mouth under his. And all rational thought was obliterated as he fastened his lips over hers in a kiss that drew the soul from her body. For seconds—minutes—there was nothing else in her world but this man, his strength, the taste of him, as she became caught up in the meaningful possession imposed by his mouth.

Every intimacy they'd ever shared was in that kiss. Her treacherous body ached for more. Her breasts longed for the caress of those firm, strong palms. Her womb was a throb of longing.

By the time he released her, she could barely stand. He hissed in her ear, *'Leave this to me. Or we're both dead.'*

She wrenched herself away and tried to slap him, but he gripped her arm to lead her from the cabin, bowing his head almost politely to the Captain and the others. 'Gentlemen. Wish me joy. You will observe that I'm set to have an entertaining night.'

They raised their glasses, laughing, envious. The women looked on wistfully.

Lucas got her outside and slammed the door so they were alone. He seized both of her shoulders and almost shook her.

'You little fool. What in hell are you doing here?' The skin round his mouth was white with anger.

She tilted her chin, her eyes flashing also, though she was exhausted and sick at heart to find all her worst fears come true. 'I did not *intend* to sail on this foul ship!'

Disbelief etched creases around his eyes. 'Then what—how—?'

'I came to Portsmouth to find you, Lucas, before you sailed!' She tugged herself free from him and put her hands on her hips. 'You stole my father's diary. And I want it back!'

His grey eyes became almost black. 'So you knew about it.'

'Of course I did. And now I know you are nothing but a *traitor*!'

He stared at her. Incredulous. Then without further speech he hauled her along the galleyway and opened the door to a tiny cabin that was more like a cupboard. Slamming and bolting the door behind them, he swiftly lit the lantern. She trembled at the force in his every move.

'I will scream! I tell you, I will shout for help, Lucas, if you so much as lay a finger on me!'

He let out a harsh laugh. 'And who in hell do you think will come to your rescue? Captain bloody Brooks? Or that man Devenish? Do you know what he'd have put you through? Do you?'

'I—I would have told the Captain who I am!' This time her voice shook a little.

'Do you think he would give a damn?' scoffed Lucas. 'My God, Brooks is notorious. He has trouble getting it up himself, so he likes to get his friends—on this occasion,

Devenish—to try out a girl while he watches… You were lucky I was there. What the devil do you think you're playing at?'

She swallowed, hard. 'Lucas, I want my father's diary.'

His eyes never left hers as slowly he drew the small leather-bound volume from a deep pocket inside his coat. She took it, clutched it tightly and said, in a low voice, 'Was it really necessary to seduce me for this?'

He was breathing harshly. 'Seduction? That night in the pavilion? My dear, I rather thought we were *both* willing participants.'

She raised her hand to strike him for that, but he caught her roughly again by the shoulders. 'Verena. Do you have any idea *why* I took it?'

He was holding her tight. Too tight. Yet his fingertips seemed almost to be caressing her through the fabric of her gown. His hooded grey eyes were burning into her. *And, dear Lord, she wanted nothing more than to be enfolded in his strong arms…*

But she could not trust him ever again, and felt as if she wanted to die.

Yet she met his gaze steadfastly. She owed this to herself and to her father. '*Why?* It's because my father's diary contains information of great value to both sides in this war, Lucas! I think you were after it from the moment you came to Wycherley. That was why you insisted on helping my family. Why you were intent on—seducing me…'

'Verena,' he breathed, 'what in hell do you think I intended to do with it?'

She flinched at his scorn, but tossed her hair back and looked him straight in the eye. 'Since you used every possible deceit to obtain it, what do you *imagine* I think? How can your intentions be honourable, Lucas? How can they be *loyal*?'

He said, with menacing quiet, 'I think that someone has been putting a great deal of rubbish into your head. Do you seriously think that—I'm a traitor?'

'How can I know *what* to think?' she cried. 'Those Frenchmen, who attacked me on the cliff path that day you came to Wycherley—they were after me for what my father knew, weren't they?'

He said harshly, 'I believe so, yes. And I also—unless I've got this completely wrong—remember that they tried to kill me when I came to your rescue.'

She caught her breath. 'They cannot have realised who you were and what you were up to—'

'Neither the hell do you.'

She tossed her head. 'Then tell me. Try to explain why you are travelling under a false name—*Mr Patterson*!'

He leaned one shoulder against the cabin door. Folded his arms across his chest and crossed his strong, booted legs. Only then did he say, in his familiar, chilling drawl, 'I'm taking your father's diary to Lord Wellington. This was the first ship I could find. The matter is urgent—and secret.'

She whitened.

He went on, 'Your father's diary contains vital information. Plans and maps describing the difficult route Wellington must use to get his army back to the safety of Lisbon before winter sets in. The French want Wild Jack's maps and diary too.'

'But—why didn't you tell me this, that night in the pavilion?' Her world was spinning around. Oh, his kisses. His tender lovemaking. 'Why the *secrecy*, Lucas? How could you expect me to trust you, when you were never honest with me? How can I help myself believing that *everything* was—and is still—a lie?'

Lucas Conistone wanted to pull her into his arms. He

wanted to protect her from what was to come. He had never rebuked himself more bitterly. He should have told her the truth in the island pavilion. He should have told her on the day of that damned furniture sale.

But—how could he have told her what was in that diary? How could he tell her now? Her world was built on her love for her father—who had tried to betray his country.

As Lucas had feared, the diary made clear—if you could understand the Portuguese dialect, and the code names for his contacts, which the Earl never could—that Jack Sheldon was starting to sell information to the French.

It contained records of two years of Jack's journeying across the unmapped and wild terrain of Portugal's uplands. Records that could be vital in Wellington's desperate bid to outwit the French in the race for Lisbon. Records of his meetings with the man known as *O Estrangeiro*—'The Foreigner'—who was a notorious French spy.

Thank God Verena had not had the chance to read it.

'My father,' she was saying bitterly, 'my poor, dear father, if only he had realised the value of what he had! He could have helped Lord Wellington…'

When Lucas had seen her being hauled into the *Goldfinch*'s stuffy cabin, he'd felt real despair. He'd wanted to jump to his feet and drive his fist into Brooks's lecherous face.

He felt despair again, now. He'd been desperate to protect her from knowing what her father had tried to do. Ironically, it was his own grandfather who'd thwarted Jack's treachery—by hiding away that diary for the last two years, while Wellington's spies—chief among them Lucas Conistone—searched for Jack Sheldon's corpse, which lay lost and rotting in a remote river bed.

They'd all thought the vital diary was with Jack to the end. They were all wrong.

'Yes,' Lucas repeated tiredly, 'he could have helped Lord Wellington. Verena, as soon as we touch land, I'm putting you on the next ship home. You'll be safe for the remainder of this journey, I promise you that. Though I won't trouble you again with my actual presence.'

She bit her lip. 'Lucas, I—'

He cut her off. 'I think we've said enough, don't you?' He walked to the door. 'Oh, and by the way, Bentinck's on board.'

'Bentinck?'

'He told me you dismissed him, telling him you were going to your family in London. So he rode to Portsmouth, to join me. A good job you wrote that note, or I'd have had his hide. Didn't I once tell you to trust him with your life?'

Her eyes were wide and anguished. 'How could I trust him—or you—when you told me so little?'

He bowed his head. 'You're right, of course,' he acknowledged quietly. 'Now, get some rest.'

He went, closing the door behind him. When all he really wanted to do was take her in his arms and kiss her doubts away and make love to her all night long. He'd hoped to marry her. And then some day he'd intended to tell her the bitter truth, softening his words with love.

But if he explained everything *now*, it would mean the destruction of her entire world, and she would hate him for it. *Even more than she did already.*

Verena lay on the narrow bunk alone, utterly tormented by dark thoughts.

Do not trust the heir of Stancliffe, her father had written. Why?

The jagged rolling of the ship set all her questions tumbling anew in her mind. Why hadn't Lucas told her earlier that he worked in secret for Lord Wellington?

Because he felt he couldn't trust her? Or because he was *still* lying to her about something, even now?

At last she must have slept, but she was woken by the even wilder motion of the ship as it ploughed through heavy seas, and she realised she was feeling sick. Also, she could hear voices, just outside the tiny cabin's door. Two men were talking softly. Lucas and Bentinck. Bentinck, who had set off for Portsmouth from Wycherley only a brief while before *she* did, to join his master…

'Have you told her the truth, milord?' Bentinck's rough voice. 'Because if you ask me it's damned well time you did!'

'I've told her quite enough.' Lucas's voice. Cold, forbidding. 'And she's sleeping. I won't have her put through any more, do you hear me?'

'But she has to know some time about that father of hers!'

Verena got to her feet sharply, reaching to the wall for support, because the ship was rolling violently now, and her stomach clenched with seasickness.

'Bentinck,' Lucas was saying in a soft voice, 'if you breathe a single word to her about her father, I'll kill you with my bare hands, I swear.'

'But it ain't fair, milord! Not just! And one of these days she'll find out all right that her sainted pa was trying to sell information to the damned Frenchies! Dealing with that vicious spy of old Boney's that they called The Foreigner, whom you, milord, put an end to six months ago, though you nearly got yourself killed when he stuck his sabre in your ribs…'

For a moment the world stood still around Verena. Then her head began to spin horribly round and round.

Then O Estrangeiro *paid me the agreed sum, with a promise of more next time.*

The diary. The crucial diary. Her father's words: *Some day soon, Verena, I'm going to make us all rich…*

By betraying his country? No. She let out a low cry. No, it could not be true, it couldn't…

As the floor of her cabin rocked with the increasing swell of the sea, she struggled across to the door and flung it open. Lucas was remonstrating with Bentinck, his handsome face stark, almost haggard in the dim glow of the ship's lantern. He snapped round to face her, breathing, *'Verena.'*

'Lucas. Lucas, tell me it isn't true. Tell me that this is a foul, foul lie!'

Lucas shot a look at his companion and said evenly, 'Bentinck, I think I really am going to have to kill you for this.'

Bentinck glanced with dismay at Verena. Said stubbornly, 'You do just that, milord. But she'd have found out soon enough about her pa! She ought to know that if it weren't for *you*, the whole blasted world would know about Jack Sheldon's doings!'

The wind howled above them. The waves could be heard beating in fury now against the side of the rolling ship. 'Bentinck, shut up,' said Lucas. 'Verena, go back into your cabin. I'll be with you shortly—' He broke off as the ship juddered violently to one side. Verena flung out a hand to save herself from falling; felt the nausea rising in her stomach.

'No,' she whispered, 'I won't go back into that cabin, not until you explain everything, Lucas!'

Bentinck, obstinate as a mule, was saying, 'Well, ma'am,

I would 'ave told you it from the start, but milord Conistone wouldn't, to save your feelings, and a fool he is too, not to 'ave let you know your father was bargaining with them Frogs! Yes, and your pa knew Lord Conistone was on to him! Lord Conistone only resigned from the army all quiet-like to be one of Wellington's top spies, pretendin' to be a gentleman of fashion, so he'd hear everything and see everything and no one would know! A real hero, is milord, just as much as any of them swaggering cavalry gents who go strutting around town with all their medals a-glitterin'. And Lord Conistone insisted that you should never be told about your pa, though I argued and argued with him!'

Her father's letter swam before her eyes. *Do not trust him. He is our enemy.*

Her father wrote that to her because Lucas knew about his meetings with *O Estrangeiro.* And Lucas guessed that those meetings would be recorded in his diary, in which her father so foolishly wrote everything…

She gazed up at him, white-faced.

'If you *still* don't believe his lordship,' Bentinck was saying belligerently, 'then just ask to see his letters from Lord Wellington! Lord Conistone's spared you, ma'am, 'cos he thought, firstly, that you'd be in peril if you knew about Wild Jack's doings—'

'Those Frenchmen at Ragg's Cove,' Verena said faintly.

'Exactly! And secondly,' went on Bentinck, 'because milord thought it would break your heart to hear the truth about your pa. But I said you was bound to find out sooner or later, and I was right!'

It all made terrible and perfect sense. She looked from one to the other, agonised. Remembered her father's increasing desperation over their monetary woes, then his optimism. His brittle excitement on his last visit home. 'I've found a way to make us all rich, Verena!'

Yes. By selling his maps to the French. By then, both French and English were after his diary. But the Earl had got it first.

Lucas and Bentinck were waiting for her reaction. For her to—say something. What did one do in such circumstances? she thought numbly. What course of action would Miss Bonamy recommend for a young woman, alone on board a rough sailing ship, who'd just been told her father was a traitor to his country?

A huge spasm of grief filled her entire being.

The matter was taken out of her hands when a great wave caught the ship and heaved it sideways, knocking her off balance. She was aware of Lucas lunging towards her, to save her… *'Verena!'*

Too late. She caught her head against a low beam, and felt a bruising pain, followed by almost merciful blackness.

Chapter Twenty-Two

Verena woke to find her left temple throbbing as if it had been hit with a hammer. The nausea gathered again. Realising she was back on the bunk in Lucas's cabin, she twisted sideways and started to retch helplessly.

Everything was still swaying and rattling wildly. But someone was there, holding out a basin for her. She heard Lucas Conistone's voice, saying gently, 'My poor girl. We're riding a westerly storm, I'm afraid. But we're almost through the worst.'

She finished being sick at last and hauled herself up, her head swimming. He held out a tin mug to her of lukewarm tea, sweetened with sugar. She drank it thirstily. He took the mug back, then bathed her face very carefully with a cloth wrung out in a ewer of water set on the cabin floor.

Meanwhile, she remembered everything. *Lucas is a British agent. And my father was—a traitor.* She felt weak, and wretched, and sick with humiliation.

She suddenly realised that she was dressed only in her thin white chemise. Someone had removed her gown.

She burned with renewed shame. 'Where is my…?'

'You were sick all over it,' he said. 'I've brought another one for you.'

She nodded, tight-lipped. Then realised it was a flimsy garment made of pale pink muslin. Short-sleeved. Extremely low-necked. Bedecked with tawdry lace and frayed scarlet ribbons.

It must belong to one of those women.

'Better than nothing,' Lucas drawled. 'Isn't it? It has to cover you fractionally more than that—undergarment you're wearing.'

The colour started to rise in her cheeks. She got too quickly to her feet, staggering involuntarily as the ship rolled.

'Sit down,' he said almost sharply. 'Don't be a fool. I'll finish washing you before you put it on.'

He sat down beside her on the bunk, planting the ewer of water firmly between his booted legs and dipping the cloth into it. Then he squeezed it out and drifted its cool dampness over her face and temples. Down her neck. Featherlight. Tantalising. Cold… Her nipples puckered, standing out through the silk of her chemise. She crossed her hands over her breasts in acute embarrassment.

He drew them gently apart. 'No need to be ashamed.'

She drew a deep breath. 'On the contrary. You must despise me.'

He stopped his stroking. 'Why would I do that?'

'Because of my father…'

'*Querida*, that is nothing to do with you,' he breathed softly.

She turned her head to face him, agonised. 'Oh, Lucas. Why didn't you tell me the truth about him earlier?'

He sat back, rubbing one hand across his temple. The question that haunted him also. 'I knew that you loved your father deeply, Verena. I did not want to destroy that love.

Even if you believed me, about your father, I thought you would have hated me because I knew the truth.' His voice became harder. 'As I expect you do now.'

She was silent. Utterly wretched. His very nearness, his tender strength, made the heat rise up from deep within her, and suffused her whole body with incredible longing.

'Lucas, I saw his diary,' she whispered at last. 'In the pavilion. I read about his—meetings.'

He paid me the agreed sum, with a promise of more next time.

Lucas had gone very still. 'You'd seen it…'

'I'd seen it, but I didn't understand—until now—what it all meant. I should have guessed, I should have known. My father had promised he would make us rich. How else, but by selling information to the French?' Her voice failed; she took a deep breath then went on, 'I saw the evidence with my own eyes, that night in the pavilion, but I refused to believe it. My own father…'

'He loved you,' Lucas said almost urgently. 'Always remember that. To the end, he loved you.'

He was dipping the cloth again in the water, stroking her arms, her hands. His head was bowed in concentration as he sat at her side, his dark lashes softening his harsh cheekbones with shadow. The ship still swayed, but less wildly now.

'The scar,' she said suddenly, 'across your ribs, Lucas; Dr Pilkington said it was done by a French sabre, but I didn't realise…'

'That was *O Estrangeiro*'s doing,' he said. 'An encounter in Portugal, earlier this year.'

'Dr Pilkington said you could have died from that wound!'

'Nonsense. I fought them off.'

'They?'

'The French spy known as The Foreigner had two friends with him. They were—inept. Now they are dead.'

He wasn't looking at her. Only concentrating on wiping, soothing. She saw his wide shoulders flex and contract beneath the white lawn shirt he wore, saw the strong muscles of his forearms, where his sleeves were rolled up, saw the skin brown from the sun, the light dusting of sunbleached hairs, the steady movements of his lean fingers. Somehow his tenderness served only to emphasise his incredible strength. His utter masculinity.

How she treasured these moments of not having to think. Of just being able to gaze at his intent profile, noting how the shadow of a beard darkened the hard planes of his high cheekbones, his sculpted jaw.

Despair wrenched at her heart anew. *Time to start facing reality, Verena.* How could he feel anything but scorn for her now?

She said at last, 'Lucas.' He stopped what he was doing. 'Lucas, I loved my father.'

'Do you think I don't know that?' he said quietly.

'Why—' her voice broke '—why did he do it?'

He cupped her chin in his hands and tilted her face, very gently, to meet his. 'He was a desperate man, Verena!' Lucas's eyes burned into hers, tender and concerned. 'As you must have known, he lived for his travels, his adventures, but eventually he must have realised he had neglected Wycherley, culpably so.'

Verena nodded wretchedly. 'He didn't even realise your grandfather had diverted that stream for his corn mill.'

'Exactly. My grandfather was utterly wrong to do it, of course, but a good landowner should have known, instantly… Your father realised the estate was failing. But while on his travels, I think he truly believed, at first, that he'd found the mythical place in the Portuguese hills where ancient treasure was supposed to be hidden. And he tried to sell that secret to my grandfather. My grandfather paid for a share in the treasure, but by then your father had realised the legend of gold was a lie.' Lucas hesitated. 'By then your father also knew, I'm afraid, that he had something else that could be of great value in a time of war. The details of unmapped routes across the mountains of Spain and Portugal.' Lucas took her hand and held it. 'Verena, your father saw my grandfather on his last visit home two years ago; and they argued—didn't they?—badly, over the diary, over the so-called treasure. Your father was in a great hurry to get back to Portugal to meet his French paymasters. He probably didn't realise until he was on board ship that my grandfather had substituted the diary with a blank one. By then it was too late for your father to return. For he knew that all his dark secrets would be betrayed by what was in that diary.'

Verena breathed, 'Yet it lay in that pavilion, forgotten, because the Earl could not read it!' She pressed her palms to her cheeks. 'Until the Earl led *me* there, in hopes that I would translate the secret of the non-existent gold!'

'And I guessed it was there and found it while you slept. I was hoping desperately, Verena, for *your* sake, that you didn't know of its existence.'

Her eyes were wide again with distress. 'I'd looked at it only briefly. I'd seen, and wondered, about his meeting with *O Estrangeiro*. But then I tried to hide the diary again, because I knew you wanted it—and—my father warned me not to trust you, Lucas.'

His voice was sharp. 'When?'

'It was in one of his letters. Sent after he left England, for the last time. Only I didn't discover it until you went away. And when you came back, on the day of the Fair…'

'Hush' He took her hands. 'Dear God, I understand it all now. Your coldness. Your *fear* of me...'

'I thought, you see, that you'd been enjoying yourself. On the island of Jersey.' She was shaking her head. 'Really, you were probably in *danger*...'

'I was meeting Alec there. He's no wastrel, but one of Wellington's top couriers.'

She nodded, biting her lip. 'Of course...'

'And you see now why I couldn't tell you everything?' His eyes were bleak, his face haggard. 'I was in a hellish situation, but I never dreamed you would be put through such a terrible ordeal. If I could turn back time, I would, believe me.'

He might as well say it—he regretted *everything*. He had said nothing at all about what else had happened in the pavilion, how they had made passionate love. It had all been a ruse, to distract her, so he could get the diary. Even his offer of marriage had been made in desperation, to get it, and himself, away from her.

Oh, Verena, you are going to need all your courage now.

She withdrew her hands firmly from him, and tried to shrug. She even ventured a faint smile. 'I fear my behaviour has been an object lesson in how not to conduct oneself in a crisis,' she said as steadily as she could. 'I'm sorry, Lucas. You must rue the day indeed that you ever met the Sheldon family. Is there anywhere else on this cursed ship where I can spend the rest of the journey?'

Even as she rose, bracing herself against the pain in her heart, his fingers suddenly closed over her slender shoulders and he swung her round to face him. He said, in his low, rich voice that seared her soul, 'How do you think that I feel about my grandfather? Do you think I'm proud of *him*, a man who would put the ordinary people back into a state of serfdom if he could and would sell his soul for yet more riches? Listen to me, Verena. We make our own destiny. You are not your father. You are honest and brave and true. Any fault in this is mine. I cursed myself a thousand times for my errors in handling this. A thousand times I thought, *I should have told her. I should have told her.*'

'Lucas.' Her voice was very quiet. 'Did you seduce me to get the diary? Did you have—orders to seduce me?'

He was silent, his gaze raking her. Then he said, 'There have been moments when I would have flung that diary to the bottom of the ocean, Verena, if I could only have your love. And—' his eyes flickered dangerously '—in case you hadn't noticed—nobody orders me to do a damn thing.'

The ship gave a violent roll. With a half-sigh, half-groan of longing—*'Verena'*—he gathered her in his arms and clasped her to him on the narrow bunk. And the storm that raged outside was nothing to the storm of passion that raged within her heart.

She realised she was hungry for him. Famished for him. Needed him as a lost traveller in the desert needs water. She flung her arms around him, clasping his head so her fingers trailed in his thick hair; she lifted her mouth to his, tasting him with her tongue, exploring, delighting when his own firm, beautiful lips captured hers in turn and returned, doublefold, the passion.

Every part of her remembered and wanted to renew the intimate contact they'd previously shared. As the peaks of her breasts rubbed against his hard-muscled chest, the longing for him to cup them, to caress them, was almost a pain. Sensing it, he ripped aside her chemise and lowered his head to lave their crests with his tongue, while she clasped and unclasped her fingers, raking them over the supple curves of his wide, sinewy back. 'Lucas,' she said in a husky voice, 'Lucas, you have my love. You have always had it.'

He lifted his head from her bosom, his eyes brooding, almost black with passion. *'Meu amor...'*

He was on his feet. At first, she thought he was leaving her. But then, smiling darkly, he was shedding his boots and waistcoat, then stripping off his shirt and breeches, leaving them on the floor.

He came slowly towards her. She caught her breath at the sheer male magnificence of him. The strength and fine moulded curves of his chest and powerful thighs. The lean beauty of his waist and hips. His manhood was quivering with taut passion as it thrust outwards. She felt the liquid heat pooling in her womb.

She wanted this man, so very much. And incredibly he still wanted *her.*

His iron-grey eyes smouldering, he lowered himself beside her on the narrow bunk and gathered her in his arms, holding her close, covering her face with kisses. His strong, hair-roughened legs twined with her own silken ones. She felt the throb of his shaft against her abdomen; she snuggled against him so his chest caressed her breasts.

She was arching towards him, hungry for more intimate contact. But he held back. He lifted his head above hers, his eyes dark in the lantern's light, and whispered,

'There are some things I must say to you. I meant every kiss, every word of passion I've ever offered to you, Verena. I want to marry you.'

The intensity of his voice almost scorched her. 'Lucas. Lucas, are you sure? My family—my father...'

'You are not your father.' He kissed her again, tenderly cherishing her lips.

Her heart was full. This was where she needed to be; in his arms, as the storm surged around the ship. Feeling, close against her body, the smooth strength of his shoulders, his lean hips; the roughness of his strongly-moulded thighs. The heat and silken power of his erection against her stomach.

He was kissing her again. This time his tongue was sliding between her lips, beginning a slow, insistent intrusion that caused her womb to throb in primitive echo. Her legs slid apart. She gasped as his strong fingers stroked up her slender thighs and began to caress the moist folds of her sex, finding the swollen peak that was the centre of all her desire.

She arched her hips against his hand almost violently. 'Lucas—'

'Patience, sweetheart. Time enough.'

Trailing his lips down her throat, he took the peak of one breast in his mouth, licking and caressing its stiffness. At the same time, she could feel the silken blunt tip of his manhood nudging against her with increasing pressure. She cried out again in pure need and opened to him, clasping him tight as he entered her in one smooth, blissful thrust. Breathing his name, she clasped her arms and legs around his virile body and bared her flushed face for his kisses.

'Verena—' It was almost a growl, from the pit of his being. He used his powerful arms to support his weight as his mouth found hers. Their tongues twined and, as he began to thrust, she matched his every move. Her whole body was centred on the power and strength of his manhood driving primitively, deeply within her, bringing her nearer and nearer to exquisite extremity. She clenched herself around him, holding herself quite still for a single breathtaking moment.

Then she was over the edge.

She was crying out, again and again, as the sheer, wondrous waves of pleasure cascaded through her, and ecstasy exploded in every sensitised nerve ending of her body. He was with her, riding her, deep within her until she felt him, too, explode, spilling his seed. He lay shuddering, sweat-sheened, against her.

Afterwards he drew her very close, pulling her on to her side, facing him. He kissed her damp skin, her throat, her lips, almost with reverence, letting his fingers trail down the soft curve of her cheek and throat. 'Oh, Verena. I was so afraid of you knowing the truth. Of losing you.'

'I understand it all now,' she told him softly. 'Everything you did was to save me from knowing that my father was a traitor. You've done so much for me, Lucas. But why?'

'Because I love you. Surely I've convinced you of that?' He kissed her with tenderness. 'I wanted—no, I *needed* your love in return.'

And she'd given it. So freely.

Then he kissed her again, sweet and long, and held her close, until she slept in his arms. And he wondered, his thoughts dark again, how in God's name was he going to tell her—everything else?

Chapter Twenty-Three

Some hours later, Lucas Conistone eased himself away from Verena very carefully and got dressed again.

He left her sleeping in the tiny cabin, lulled by the now-gentle motion of the waves, and went out on deck as dawn was breaking. Lucas knew this coast well. Yesterday they had rounded the north-west cape of Spain, and now to the south-east he could see the twinkling harbour lights of Oporto and the Portuguese coast in the distance.

Captain Brooks, the grey morning light starkly revealing a complexion raddled by drink and debauchery, was strutting towards him, grinning. Lucas had longed to knock the living daylights out of him since first boarding his ship. But he'd needed this passage to Portugal, couldn't delay the delivery of the vital information he'd got.

'We'll be in sight of Lisbon in less than two days, Mr Patterson,' said Jed Brooks. He still stank of port. 'Worth the six guineas, was she, the little wench with chestnut hair? Damned fiery, I should think, beneath that demure exterior. I'd wager she danced a merry jig for you as you shafted her—had her squealing for more, did you?'

The ship rolled suddenly. Lucas, pretending to miss his footing, deliberately lurched sideways to jab the man forcefully in the guts with his elbow. As Brooks doubled over with pain, Lucas lifted one eyebrow in feigned apology. 'So very sorry,' he drawled. 'Not got my sea legs yet, Captain.'

Captain Brooks was still swearing softly and clutching his arms over his belly. 'Aye, well, Mr Patterson,' he muttered, 'you'll be glad when we get to Lisbon, eh? We all will. Then I'll be off back to good old England.'

'Indeed,' said Lucas politely. 'I hope you have a—fruitful voyage home, Captain. Profitable, I mean.'

Captain Brooks's colour deepened. 'I appreciate your good wishes, sir! It's been a pleasure having you aboard, gentry like you. And not a word now, to the Customs men, eh, about the fine brandy I'll be taking back to Portsmouth?' He mopped his brow with a dirty rag of a handkerchief and gave an ugly wink.

Lucas, his long coat trailing half-open in the breeze, leaned his back against the guard rail, folded his muscular arms across his chest and smiled, though his hooded eyes were still dangerous. 'Not a word,' he echoed lightly, 'as long as you put me, the girl I bought last night and my servant off at Oporto. You see, Lisbon doesn't quite suit me after all.'

The Captain scowled. 'Oporto be damned. Lisbon's my destination!'

'A pity, Captain. I must say I expected you to be more—accommodating.' Lucas slipped back his coat further, to reveal the two gleaming pistols thrust into his belt.

'By God, sir, are you trying to threaten me?'

Lucas raised his eyebrows in mock innocence. Suddenly Bentinck appeared, too, and in his bulky hand was an equally fierce-looking blunderbuss. 'Everything all fit and fancy, Mr Patterson—sir?'

'Everything's fit and fancy,' answered Lucas. 'Captain Brooks has kindly agreed to set us down at Oporto.'

Bentinck grinned. 'That's very generous of 'im, Mr Patterson, ain't it now?'

Captain Brooks strode away, angrily muttering under his breath.

Lucas watched him go, frowning. Bentinck hovered; his master, unhelpful, turned to rest his arms silently on the guardrail, gazing at the long grey line of the distant coast. Bentinck coughed. No response.

Bentinck said, 'Oporto?'

'It will save days in my travelling time. I must get inland to Lord Wellington and the army as a matter of urgency.'

'And the girl?'

'She can take a ship for England from Oporto—with *you*, Bentinck—and be back there safely considerably earlier than if she went on to Lisbon.'

'Very well, milord. Now, I know you'll be crucifyin' yourself, what with her learning the truth about her father—'

Lucas turned to him, his eyes hooded. 'Thanks to you, if you remember.'

'Yes, but it was about time she knew it an' all, milord,' Bentinck softly exploded, 'instead of blamin' you for the whole buffle-headed mess!'

Lucas was silent a moment. 'She loved him, Bentinck.'

Bentinck pulled down the corners of his mouth in a fierce scowl. 'He didn't deserve her love, that's for sure. But she's accepted the truth from you? That he was goin' to sell the British army out to the Frenchies?'

'I didn't put it quite as crudely as that. Her world has been overturned. But she's accepted it as the truth, yes.'

'And the rest of it, milord? What did she say when you told her everything else?' Bentinck pushed on remorselessly. 'The very worst of it?'

Lucas was gazing out to sea again, his fine lips firmly pressed together.

Bentinck swore aloud. 'You *haven't* told her, have you? Beg pardon, milord, but you do realise there'll be all hell to pay when she does find out?'

Lucas turned on him. Though his face was still calm, his eyes darkened to the opaque steely grey that signalled danger. 'Then I very much hope that *you* won't be the one to tell her, Bentinck.'

'Of course not, milord!' Bentinck said indignantly. 'What do you take me for, some kind of snitch? But I'm blowed if—'

Lucas cut in. 'Since our obliging Captain will shortly be taking his ship into Oporto,' he said softly, 'it's time for us to get ready. And—Bentinck—kindly leave Miss Sheldon to me, will you?'

Oporto amazed Verena, with its colour and bustle. There was little sign here of the war that raged across Europe, as the native Portuguese went about their daily business of fishing and trading around this busy harbour where the River Douro flowed into the sea.

But Lucas warned her, as they alighted from the *Goldfinch*'s boat, that French spies could be anywhere, and that the small British presence here might soon have to be pulled out. For all military resources, he explained, were being concentrated on the race for the much more important city of Lisbon, nearly two hundred miles to the south.

Lucas left her briefly with Bentinck while he went to see the British military attaché. When he returned, he sent

Bentinck off to secure Verena a suitable passage home and quietly told her the news.

'So far Wellington is ahead of the French. But before the final push for Lisbon, he intends to make a stand in the hills above Coimbra, to slow down the enemy pursuit. He's planned his route, and this resistance, for months, Verena; his victory very much depends on knowing the terrain.'

She concentrated on every word. Trying hard, for this last hour with him, not to think how she would miss this man: his sweet and tender kisses, his powerful, breathtaking lovemaking.

The time they'd spent together in that cabin would be for ever etched on her heart. She could finally be sure that this brave and honourable man loved her.

Yet every moment with him was still clouded by the knowledge of what her father had tried to do.

Now, she said, 'So my father's maps, Lucas, and those descriptions, in his diary…'

'Will be vital,' he assured her gravely. 'No one mapped this country as well as your father did. I'm getting the diary to Lord Wellington as soon as possible.'

And going once more into danger. But it was all part of who he was, how he lived. And she loved him all the more for it.

She must show courage too. She voiced now the thoughts she'd had earlier, as she waited for him, with Bentinck.

'Lucas, couldn't the British army come down here, to Oporto? Why go all the way to Lisbon?'

'Because Lisbon is Portugal's capital and its heart. It has a vital harbour, and all of it is at this moment being fortified to withstand a long French siege. Wellington knows he'll draw the French army after him, but it's intentional. Alongside our Portuguese allies, he can hold the city indefinitely, because he can get reinforcements and supplies by sea. From there his army can march out again, to retake first Portugal, then Spain. A few months ago, Napoleon looked set to conquer all of Europe, Britain included; but Wellington is the one man who can stop him.'

And her father would have betrayed all of Wellington's army, and his own country...

'Lucas,' she whispered, 'how many people know about my father?'

'Very few,' he assured her. 'Like me, they are men who work in secret. They will say nothing.' He put a finger under her chin and tilted up her head so her eyes met his. 'You must always remember your father was a desperate man, his mind twisted by his misfortunes. Now Bentinck will be back very soon. Are you ready to go, *querida*?'

He was glad to see that some colour had returned to her cheeks. 'Only because I have to,' she whispered. She put her arms around his waist and laid her cheek against his chest, then looked up into his ardent, handsome face. So dear to her. So precious. 'Lucas. I can only hope some day to be worthy of *your* love. *Your* trust.'

'You have proved yourself so already,' he interrupted her, and kissed her sweetly, lingeringly. 'Come. It's time to take you to your ship.'

Bentinck, by some miracle, had found a merchant ship sailing for Portsmouth on the afternoon tide. He and Lucas briefly discussed the details, then Bentinck tactfully withdrew.

'No Captain Brooks, I trust?' She said it lightly to Lucas, but a shiver rippled through her.

'No Captain Brooks.' Lucas looked down at her, smiling. 'Bentinck informs me there are quite a few respectable passengers aboard this one. You will travel in relative comfort.'

'I would rather travel aboard a complete wreck of a ship,

if you were there to share my cabin,' she said softly. 'I will miss you, Lucas.'

'And I you. I will be back soon. And then…' he took her hand and pressed it to his lips '…we will be married.'

'At the Wycherley church!' she said suddenly, her face alight. 'Oh, I can see it now! With all the villagers there, and simple flowers from the fields and hedgerows—there will be dancing on the green—'

'And you will be my harvest bride.' He kissed her tenderly. 'My amber-eyed harvest maiden.'

Verena stood a moment, looking her last on the scenic city of Oporto and at the steep and hilly country beyond it, which Lucas would shortly be ascending. 'Do you know, Lucas, where you'll find Lord Wellington?'

'Roughly, yes. The attaché told me he's going to make a stand with his army on the ridge of Busaco.'

She nodded. 'Busaco.' The name sounded somehow familiar.

'Have you heard of it?' His expression was suddenly intent.

'Isn't it mentioned in my father's diary?'

'No. I've read it from cover to cover.'

'Then I must have imagined it. I'm sorry.'

He sighed a little, then took her hand and brushed it with his lips. 'No matter. No matter at all. Come, *meu amor.* There is your ship.'

Though the vessel would not be sailing for two hours, she was allowed to board, and she knew Lucas must be eager to set off. She smiled back, though she hated, now, being parted from him for a moment. 'I will think of you all the time,' she breathed. 'Goodbye, Lucas.'

He took her hands. 'I love you,' he whispered. 'Always remember that.' Then he tipped her face up towards his and bent to kiss her.

The touch of his lips against hers was sweet beyond bearing. Suddenly she flung her arms around his neck, drinking in the male strength of him, the warmth of his hard body against hers. 'Lucas! Come back safely!' she whispered desperately.

Then Bentinck was behind them, clearing his throat with unaccustomed tact, ready to escort her onto the ship back to England. To reality. Pippa and the servants—they would be half-crazy with worry. At least she could rely on Pippa to have the good sense not to have told her mother in London… She watched Lucas until he was out of sight.

Busaco.

Surely she'd come across that name recently? But she could not remember where. She turned to walk sadly towards the gangplank of the Portsmouth-bound ship, with Bentinck following behind. She had a small cabin to herself, but until the ship sailed she preferred to remain on deck, gazing at the hills while the sailors prepared for embarkation, thinking of Lucas making his way up there…

She pulled up with a start. Busaco. Her hand went to her pocket. *Her father's last letters.*

She scoured each scrawled missive until she found the one she wanted. The letter with the map. The close-set writing, the detailed drawings…

She whirled round and called for Bentinck, who was hovering close by. She said, 'There is to be no getting rid of you, is there, Mr Bentinck?'

'None at all, ma'am,' he replied pleasantly. 'For which I do offer hearty apologies, I'm sure!'

'No need to apologise at all,' she answered in a thoughtful tone. 'It is I who should apologise to *you*, for not trusting you. Now. Tell me about this place called Busaco to which your master is heading. *Quickly.*'

Chapter Twenty-Four

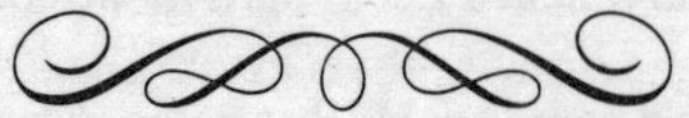

Three days later—Busaco, Portugal

The place known as Busaco was a nine-mile ridge of rocky hillside, rising to nearly two thousand feet in places, and falling away vertiginously to pine and cedar forests on one side and the coastal plain on the other.

This was where Lord Wellington had decided, months ago, to stop and face the French army during the inevitable race to Lisbon. And he had relied on his scouts and intelligencers to help him achieve victory.

'This war in the Peninsula is going to be won by whoever has the best knowledge of this upland terrain,' he'd once said to Lucas. 'We've got to out-think and out-plan the French at every step. I need maps, Conistone. I need you and your men to gather intelligence about every inch of ground from Lisbon all the way to Madrid.'

So Lucas, in the October of 1808, had resigned his commission, and agreed to be Wellington's spy; outwardly a civilian, outwardly unconnected with the war, but secretly gleaning vital information not only in enemy terrain, but also in the lofty drawing rooms of Europe.

And the irony was that Lucas had been chosen because of Verena's father.

When he was a boy, Lucas had listened avidly as Jack Sheldon talked to the Earl about his travels in Spain and Portugal. When Jack realised Lucas was interested, he taught him Portuguese, and some Spanish also; often Lucas had pored over Jack's maps of wild and unexplored places, while Jack vividly described every detail.

Then the Earl and Jack had had their bitter falling-out and Jack had stormed off on his travels again, never to return. Deep in financial trouble, he'd started negotiating in secret with the French, who, anticipating a long struggle against the English forces in the Peninsula, were desperate to get hold of everything he'd written, every detail of his explorations.

And so, just a few days ago, Lucas, on board the *Goldfinch*, had been forced to tell Verena that her father was a traitor.

The trouble was that she still didn't know everything. And Lucas's problem now was, when to tell her? When the devil should he tell her it all?

Lucas rubbed his eyes wearily. Just now he had even more pressing matters on his mind.

The lost mines of Busaco were said, by the locals, to be part of an ancient network driven centuries ago into the hills; no one had found them, despite the rumours of South American gold hidden there by the returning *conquistadores*. When Lord Wellington, poring over his own maps months ago, had decided Busaco ridge would be the ideal vantage point to make a stand against the French army in the autumn, it was assumed that the stories of the mines were nothing but a myth.

But then Lucas, puzzling over Jack Sheldon's boasts to both Verena and the Earl, began to wonder, *What if Sheldon really had found those long-lost mines?*

Easy to consider the task impossible, for the steep escarpment below the ridge was covered with loose scree and thorny scrub, and lower down trees grew thickly, their roots tangled amongst the rocks. But Lucas found that the whispers of gold persisted—whispers that Jack Sheldon had found those tunnels and recorded their whereabouts for himself. Yet though Lucas spent long nights on the *Goldfinch*, poring over Wild Jack's diary by the light of a guttering candle, he could find no reference to Busaco or its lost tunnels.

And here, at Busaco, the French were expected daily.

'They'll outnumber us massively,' Alec Stewart, who was already here, had said to Lucas. 'Fortunately their intelligence is much poorer than ours.' He grinned. 'Especially as your enterprising Portuguese companion—what was his name, Miguel?—fobbed off the French scouts with some fake maps, which sent their generals all over the mountains on their way here.'

Lucas gave an answering smile. 'I hope the French paid him well.' Inwardly he saluted his diminutive friend: *Obrigado, Miguel. My thanks.*

'No doubt they did.' Alec's face became serious again. 'But those lost tunnels—if only we'd found them, Lucas! We could have hidden men and cannon. And the French, as they marched up the valley, wouldn't even have known where the attack was coming from!'

As if he didn't know. As if he'd needed reminding.

Here Lucas still went by the name of Patterson, a scout of Wellington's. While Alec wore his smart captain's uniform, Lucas wore old civilian clothes and looked like a barbarian, or so Alec cheerfully told him. Here only Alec,

Lord Wellington and a few close friends among the senior officers knew who he really was.

'We have to give the French a mighty big surprise if we're to win enough of a victory to get ourselves to Lisbon in time,' Wellington had confided to him last night. 'Conistone, you're my man for tactics, you know this territory like the back of your hand…'

All except for the mines. Where the hell were Wild Jack's maps of Busaco?

Lucas had risked all to find them. He'd risked, and nearly lost, the woman he loved. But those crucial maps seemed not to exist.

There was no rebuke from Wellington. The great general just said, in his curt way, 'Perhaps those damned mines never existed. We'll find another way to take the Frogs by surprise.'

Wellington had ranged his troops all along and behind the ridge, so that most of them would be hidden from view when the French marched up the valley tomorrow. And still Lucas hadn't given up. With Alec's steady help, he got all the soldiers who could be spared to clamber round the lower slopes, searching.

But it seemed that any mine entrances had long since been hidden by dense furze and thorn, ancient tree roots and areas of loose shale that were for ever sliding down the mountainside. If the tunnels had ever existed, they now looked lost for ever.

As the sun began to set, Lucas's aide, who had prepared a camp fire, was trying to press food on him: some horse meat, boiled in a stew; days-old bread; rough Portuguese wine. Lucas had little appetite.

Then he heard voices. *Familiar* voices. He turned his head sharply, and got to his feet. No. Surely not.

There was the barked challenge of a sentry, and, in response, a belligerent male voice. An *unmistakeable* voice. In the name of God…

'Now, there ain't no use trying to stop me, however flash your pistols! We ain't climbed up all this way from Oporto to be told Mr Patterson ain't allowed no visitors, you hear? You step back, my man, or I'll plant you such a facer as you won't wake till old Boney's been chased all the way back to Paris!'

Bentinck. What the hell…? As long as he was alone. As long as…

Lucas thrust aside his dish and got to his feet, striding across to the scene of the altercation. 'What in damnation are you doing here, Bentinck? I told you to see that Verena sailed home on that ship!'

Bentinck swung round to him, his face a picture. 'I'll be blowed if that wasn't my intention, Mr Patterson! But what you *didn't* say was wot I was to do if the lady upped sticks and decided she wasn't goin' home after all, but was travellin' all the way up *here*! On this mule that I'll swear is as stubborn as her!' He jabbed his finger towards the wiry-looking mule whose reins he grasped; and to the woman in a cloak who was sliding quickly from the mule's saddle to step forwards, her hood falling back from her glorious chestnut hair as she lifted her head to him, almost defiantly.

'Please don't be angry with Bentinck, Mr Patterson!' said Verena quickly. 'It's not his fault I'm here; it's mine, because you see I absolutely insisted that he bring me to see you!'

A crowd of soldiers had gathered round, their jaws dropping at the sight of her. At her—yes, devil take it, at her sheer *beauty.* Lucas's heart thudded. She might have struggled on muleback up here—an arduous journey if ever there was one—but, deuce take it, she was as cool, as fresh, as lovely as if she were appearing at a top-lofty London ball, and as tempting…

All the way up, from Oporto! Three days traversing steep tracks—even the goddamned mule must have had to be practically hauled up some of the most treacherous and narrow parts of the path.

He couldn't believe it.

Yet—she was here. And seeing her revived all the love—and, be honest, all the *lust*—Lucas always felt in her presence. He wanted nothing more than to crush her in his arms and make love to her. But here they were, about to face a huge French army, and by this time tomorrow, half of them at least might well be dead, the rest embarked on a long, arduous retreat to Lisbon while fighting a desperate rearguard action…

He said, curtly because he was afraid for her, 'Oh, Verena. Your reasons for coming here had better be good.'

She did not flinch. She lifted her lovely wide amber eyes to him and said honestly, 'I think they are. You see—Mr Patterson—I think I can help your General Wellington win tomorrow's battle.' She drew closer and dropped her voice. 'I've found my father's plans, of the ancient mountain-mines of Busaco.'

He guided her quickly over to his makeshift camp, where they would have some privacy. He offered her some of the rough army wine, and Verena told him swiftly what she'd remembered when he left her in Oporto. 'When you mentioned the place, *Busaco*,' she told him, 'I knew that I had heard or seen the name somewhere before.' She was reaching into her pocket. 'Here.' She held out some folded sheets of paper. 'This map, and these sketches, were drawn on the back of a letter to me from my father. They refer to the old mine shafts at Busaco…'

At that point her lovely face clouded and Lucas knew she was thinking of her father, was still trying to reconcile herself to his treachery. But she pressed on steadily. 'Because I knew *you* were making for the ridge of Busaco, to meet Lord Wellington, I had no alternative but to ride to you up here.'

'Your sense of duty to the fore as ever, Miss Sheldon,' he teased gently. 'So you—*persuaded* Bentinck to escort you?'

She pulled a slight face. 'I as good as forced poor Bentinck, yes. Unfair of me. I said, if he didn't come with me, I'd find you by myself. He was not very pleased, and the climb was a little—difficult. But—Lucas, I hope I did right?'

'Difficult!' He chuckled at her understatement. 'You have done very well indeed. You are brave and wonderful, and, *minha querida*, I love you more than I can say.'

He got his aide to bring her hot soup and a blanket. She chided him for fussing over her, but the temperature was dropping sharply as night approached and the moon, silvery and full, rose above them. He'd set her by the fire, building it up while she talked. The pages of Jack's letter were spread out between them, but his eyes never left her face.

'Verena,' Lucas confirmed softly, 'these plans could mean the difference between victory and defeat tomorrow.'

'As important as that?' she breathed.

'As important as that.' But he saw the shadows that still clouded her lovely face, and said gently, 'I'm sorry. This must be painful for you.'

She shook her head defiantly. 'Bentinck has been more than kind. He warned me…' she swallowed on the lump in her throat '…not to use my father's name, in case—in case anybody *knew*.'

His heart missed a beat. Indeed.

'But, Lucas, I keep telling myself,' she said, steadfastly gazing up at him, 'that whatever my father did, he did for his family. What he tried to do was wrong. Terrible. *But he still loved us.*'

He put his arms round her and kissed her with great tenderness. 'I understand everything. You must stop reproaching yourself. You have done your duty—*more* than your duty.'

Letting her go reluctantly, he picked up the letter that mapped the tunnels of Busaco. 'And now I must go now to his lordship. There is still just time. If we can find these old mine entrances, *tonight*, we can get men with rifles, perhaps cannon even, into these hideouts. But your part in this is done. Now you must let Bentinck take you to the safety of the old convent, half a mile back on the Oporto road, which is Wellington's staff headquarters. And then, tomorrow, you can head for home.'

'No!' she protested. 'No, you don't understand! You *need* me, Lucas, to interpret these maps!'

'I can read Portuguese.'

'But the notes he's written on them are in the old dialect that my father learned from his mother, Lucia—look, do you see?' She pointed her finger at the page. 'He has written everything down: where the old tunnels are, in relation to the ridge and the convent; their width, their height, and where they lead to, back within the hillside… I can understand, I know the dialect, he taught it to me, but do *you*?'

'No,' said Lucas simply. 'I don't.'

Chapter Twenty-Five

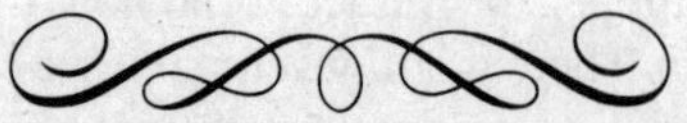

And so it was that Verena ended up combing the mountainside at night, with Lucas and the sappers, and with two gunners-in-chief also, searching for the mine entrances by the light of the moon.

Alec was with them all the time. His face was racked with tiredness, but his optimism never failed. She felt hot with shame when she remembered how she had branded him a wastrel and a rake.

Some of the tunnels marked on the map had been hopelessly blocked by falls of shale, and would require hours of digging, hours they couldn't spare. But others were more easily accessible, and Lucas ordered men to swiftly clear these of fallen stones and undergrowth. Then the cannon were heaved in by the gunners, and some of the army's most expert riflemen, all done as swiftly, as silently as possible. The passage of the big guns was muffled by the armfuls of heather thrown under their wheels; the men were ordered to communicate quietly, in case French scouts were already moving up the valley in advance of their army. The soldiers were supplied with ammunition, food and water for twenty-four hours. Then the furze bushes were pulled across to conceal the entrances.

As they climbed back up to the camp, Verena, white with tiredness yet determined not to rest, saw Wellington talking to his commanders. She gazed, rapt, at this famous general, who with his gift for leadership and his tactical genius was slowly turning the tide of the war. He was not tall, but his figure, distinctive in his grey cloak and cocked hat, commanded respect wherever he went.

'We need to take the French utterly by surprise tomorrow,' she heard him warning his commanders. 'We must inflict as much damage as possible on their guns and supply wagons, so we've got a head start in what is, I fear, going to be a most damnably hellish race for the safety of Lisbon—'

Then suddenly Lord Wellington broke off. He'd spotted Verena, who stood between Lucas and Bentinck.

She shrank back. *What if he knew about her father?*

But if anything his face grew less harsh. 'So you, young lady, are the saviour who brought us this valuable knowledge, are you?' he said in a gentler voice. 'You have done well, ma'am. Exceedingly well.'

That, as Bentinck told her later, was praise indeed. Lucas was smiling down at her and nodding. She hoped he was thinking, as she was, *This, at least, has gone some way towards righting my father's wrong.*

Lucas persuaded her to take some sleep before her journey, and obediently she wrapped herself up in blankets near the embers of the fire. She slept, though he stayed awake. Alert.

At the first light of dawn, as the pennants of the approaching French glinted sporadically two miles away through the thin valley mist, he said to her, 'Now, Verena, you leave. Understood? No arguments.'

'But, Lucas—' She could hear the steady thud of the enemy's drums. Her heart constricted in fear for the lives of all these men. For him.

He kissed her softly. A caress, a promise, made by his lips brushing hers, his arms enfolding her, his harsh, unshaven cheek pressed with the utmost gentleness against her delicate skin. 'I will see you down in Coimbra.' A smile softened his features. 'From there we will travel home. Together.'

With the ominous drums of the advancing French still echoing in her ears, with the same stubborn mule to ride sidesaddle on, she and Bentinck made the journey south to Coimbra, only a few miles away.

By the time they got there, she was weary and saddlesore. Her heart tightened with apprehension when she realised that Coimbra was in a state of sheer panic. Its Portuguese inhabitants were convinced, in spite of everything the small British force there could do, that Wellington's army was about to be defeated, and that the French monsters would be on them at any minute, to massacre them in revenge for siding with the British.

Peasants from the stony hillsides, lost children, nuns from rural convents, Portuguese gentlemen and their wives—all had crowded into Coimbra, loudly clamouring for protection. Bentinck, somehow—a miracle worker, she was beginning to believe—managed to find her a small room in a little backstreet hotel where several respectable English travellers were staying.

Verena found it impossible to do nothing except sit there and wait; so she offered herself as a translator to the commander of the British troops, helping to interpret the news brought in by the various Portuguese scouts; while Bentinck, his expression by now one of weary resignation, acted as her unofficial chaperon. And thus she—and he—were amongst the first to hear the report of the battle to be known as Busaco. Fast riders galloped into Coimbra late that day. The huge French army under Massena had marched up the valley alongside the long, steep ridge and straight into the trap. Massena's men did not understand where so much gunfire was coming from, or how such a small English army could pin them down.

'The hillside itself has opened to shelter the English!' the French were heard to cry in disbelief. They had been forced to flee in disarray. The British had managed to capture some of their vital supply wagons and were already on the march; heading first to Coimbra, and after that, Lisbon.

Bentinck was grinning from ear to ear. 'That'll show 'em!' He even gave Verena a little hug.

Verena breathed, 'So the French are defeated?'

Bentinck hesitated. 'Not exactly. There's still far more of them, and they'll be after the British just as soon as they've got over their fright and pulled themselves together. But Lord Wellington, he knows what he's doing, he'll get to Lisbon before them! And—' his face brightened '—Lord Conistone will be here in no time, you'll see! He'll be lookin' forward to a good meal and a hot bath. And somewhat pleasanter company than wot 'e's been getting lately!'

She was beginning to hope that the impediments which had continually hindered their love were almost overcome. She held to her heart the knowledge that Lucas had forgiven her, firstly for doubting him, and secondly for her father's treachery. *'That was none of your doing, Verena!'* Lucas had reminded her forcefully. She hurried back to the little hotel and her first floor bedchamber, a sanctuary from the pandemonium of the city's streets.

Now all she had to do was wait. And soon afterwards she heard horses. Heard the servants running outside, calling, 'English. English soldiers are here…'

Lucas? Her heart began to thump.

She checked herself briefly in the looking-glass. The gown she'd bought in Oporto had been worn to shreds by her travelling, so she'd managed to purchase a new dress in one of Coimbra's almost-empty shops. The shade of emerald green, vividly adorned with embroidery, suited her colouring well, and the shopkeeper had pulled out, from under the counter, a lovely gold shawl. 'Take it, *minha senhora*! It matches your golden eyes; you will look beautiful tonight for *o seu marido*, your husband, yes?'

Tonight. Surely before they left for home, as he'd promised, he would spend tonight with her, here! She would bathe the dust and dirt from his body and rub oils into his aching muscles. Would kiss away his bruises, until he forgot the battle in the flame of mutual passion…

Verena, you are becoming little better than a whore! she rebuked herself. But she was smiling as she whispered the words. She felt her own body respond with tumultuous desires at the thought of his need for her. She would answer and return her lover's passion a hundredfold.

She could hear voices—Englishmen's voices—outside. Bentinck would have found him, told him she was here… With a secret smile, she went tiptoeing out on to her balcony that overlooked a tiled and paved courtyard full of scented flowers, where fountains played. And her heart leaped, because Lucas was indeed there.

He looked travel-worn. His long coat and boots were covered with dust; his thick black hair curled roughly past his collar. But even so he looked so handsome, so desirable, that her heart raced almost painfully with longing. And she was glad to see that Alec was safely there also. She was about to call out to them, to tell them she was here—but then she paused, frowning. Something was wrong.

They should have been relaxed, joyful even, for Lord Wellington had gained a crucial victory. But Lucas looked sombre. Even—angry. Alec was remonstrating with him, gesticulating in his usual flamboyant manner.

'In God's name, Lucas, haven't you told her *everything* yet?' Alec was exclaiming. 'About the whole damnable business?'

They were talking about her. Verena.

Lucas was saying tightly, 'I told her as much as she needed to know, Alec. That her father wanted to sell information to the French. I don't see that she needs to know any more. I'll go and speak to her soon, but first I've got dispatches for the commander here.'

'See the commander by all means,' declared Alec. 'But when you come back—you must tell her it all! And I'll tell you why! Because some day someone else will tell her, you idiot! That it was actually *you* who pursued her father through the mountains, thinking he had that damned diary. Pursued him to his death!'

If she hadn't been leaning against the balustrade of the balcony, she would have fallen. Her whole body started to tremble.

Oh, dear God. The old Earl's words rang like a funeral bell in her head. 'They killed your father for what he knew...'

Somehow she got back into the coolness of her room and pressed her hands to her face. Lucas was a secret agent. A spy. His task had been to pursue her father and get that diary from him before he could sell it to the enemy. That, she already knew. But what she *hadn't* realised was that then—then, of course, Lucas's final duty would be to kill him.

Lucas's grandfather had the diary, all the time. But Lucas had not known that as he chased after the traitor Jack Sheldon.

Dizzily she remembered hearing the news of her father's death. *Fell into a raging mountain river... Was swept away downstream...* The news had been a terrible shock, but not as great as the one she felt rocking her heart and soul at this moment. She dragged breath after breath into her lungs, as if just to exist was an effort.

'Your father loved you,' Lucas had said to her on board the *Goldfinch*. 'Always remember that. To the end, he loved you.'

How could Lucas have known that, unless he was *actually there*?

The enormity of it crushed her soul.

No wonder Bentinck had warned her not to use her full name as they'd climbed up to the army at Busaco. Not only would Lucas's comrades know Jack Sheldon was a spy, they'd also know that Lucas had killed her father in retribution.

Even if it was a righteous execution, she could not live with Lucas, day after day, and wonder, *Was my father afraid? Did he plead with Lucas for his life?*

Her stomach clenched until she felt nauseous. Now, at last, she understood all of Lucas's hesitancy, his reluctance to declare himself fully. Although he loved her—yes, she believed that now, and the knowledge was cruel indeed—he must have known, as Alec had just so brutally pointed out to him, that some day, she was bound to find out.

She could not marry the man who had killed her father. *Oh, Verena. This is going to take all your courage.*

Gathering up her few possessions, she made fresh plans and set her face to a new life. Without Lucas.

It had been such a beautiful, impossible dream.

It took the impatient Lucas Conistone much longer than he'd thought to give his report to the British commander of the small force here in Coimbra, then make his way back to the hotel—only to learn that Verena had gone.

Bentinck defended himself hotly. 'One moment she was here in the hotel, milord, happy as a lark 'cos the battle's been won. Next—she's upped and vanished!'

'She can't have vanished. She must be here, somewhere!' Lucas paced the hotel room in a state of mounting rage and dread.

Not fair, he reminded himself bleakly, to round on Bentinck. Even Bentinck couldn't be with her every minute of the day. Alec hovered anxiously in the background as Lucas demanded, '*When* did she go, Bentinck? You must at least know that roughly!'

Bentinck pursed his lips. 'Must've been around the time you and Captain Stewart arrived, or near enough, milord.'

'So we just missed her… Damn it all! Find her, will you? There are all kinds of ruffians around… *Find her!*'

Lucas secured the aid of some soldiers; with them and Alec he scoured every narrow street. But it was Bentinck who was first with some news.

'Think I've got something, milord,' he panted. 'I heard that an English wine merchant and his wife were heading back to England today. They had a carriage booked to take them to the coast.'

'And?' Lucas was brittle with impatience; Alec at his side was also listening anxiously.

'They took someone else with them in their carriage,'

explained Bentinck, 'a young lady with chestnut-coloured hair. Her name, they say, was Miss Lucia…'

Verena's grandmother's name. Lucas was wild-eyed. 'To England… Where were they sailing from?'

'No one's sure, milord. The carriage left an hour ago.'

Alec muttered, 'There's something else you ought to know, Lucas old fellow. A French spy's been locked up in the Coimbra gaol, and now the British army's almost here, he's started offering information in the hope of saving his skin. He appears to know a little about Wild Jack, and he says some French agents actually went over to England a few months ago, thinking they might find something useful at Jack's home. Wycherley.'

As he had suspected. 'Go on,' breathed Lucas.

'Well, there's an English soldier involved,' Alec went on. 'A captain, who was captured at Talavera and let out of a French prison camp after swearing he'd be able to track down Jack Sheldon's precious diary…'

Lucas swore aloud.

'What, Lucas?' Alec looked distraught. 'You look as though you've seen a ghost, man!'

Lucas breathed, 'I know who it is, Alec. And oh, God, oh, God, I should have realised it, a long time ago…'

He was already on his way as he spoke, striding towards the stables, Bentinck hard on his heels. Alec, too, was chasing after him.

'Lucas! Where, dear fellow, are you going?'

Lucas called back over his shoulder, 'To get my horse. To find a ship to England. Even if it's captained by that damned Jed Brooks!'

But even as he ran, he was thinking in anguish: Why had she left so suddenly? *Why?*

Chapter Twenty-Six

Wycherley

It was a fine October afternoon. Verena had been home for nearly a fortnight now, and Pippa was a daily visitor, though Izzy, Deb and Lady Frances were still in London, and blithely unaware that Verena had ever been away.

Verena had returned from Portugal on a packet ship in the company of kind Mr Cameron, a wine merchant, and his wife, who'd been staying at the little hotel in Coimbra while they made arrangements for their journey home. She'd hurried to knock on the door of their room as soon as that dreadful conversation she'd overheard in the courtyard had sunk in.

'Mr Cameron,' she said swiftly, 'I remember you saying that you and your wife are travelling to the coast and sailing for Portsmouth tonight. May I ask you a very great favour? Might I travel with you?'

'Of course, my dear Miss Sheldon!' agreed Mr Cameron. 'But may my wife and I be permitted to ask—why the urgency?'

'Something has happened—that I did not expect,' she whispered. She tilted her chin stubbornly. *She would not cry.* 'I must go home. And—I would so much value the protection of your company.'

Every hour, every minute of that voyage, she imagined Lucas finding her room empty. Frantically searching the hotel. The entire town.

She'd had enough of lies and rumours. Of having her hopes raised, then so devastatingly shattered.

And so at last she reached Wycherley, where David and Pippa, summoned by Turley, rode over immediately from their farm to see her.

'Verena, we didn't realise you'd gone at first!' explained Pippa, after tearful hugs and kisses. 'Because the day after Mama and the girls left for London, we had to leave suddenly ourselves, for Oxfordshire, where David's father was taken ill! We sent you a note to explain, but of course you would not ever have *received* it.'

'What about Cook? And Turley?'

'They both assumed you'd gone to London to join Mama, and when we got back two days ago, so did I, until I found the note you'd left me, mysteriously saying you would be back soon! Then we were almost out of our minds with worry!'

'I'm so sorry,' said Verena quietly. 'Pippa, can I rest a little before I tell you it all?'

'Of course!' Pippa hugged her tightly. 'As long as you're *all right*.'

So Verena had scarcely been missed. That at least was a huge relief. 'Quite all right. Really.' Verena hugged her sister back.

Could she ever tell Pippa about Lucas? It was unthinkable at the moment; the hurt was too recent, too raw. And as for their father—she would never say anything. Why should her dear sister also have to suffer the terrible knowledge of their father's hidden past?

'David and I did wonder,' Pippa confided, as she poured them both tea, 'if perhaps you'd run away with Lord Conistone, seeing as you are secretly betrothed. An elopement, my dear! We were quite excited!'

Close. Too close. Verena tried to smile, and said lightly, 'I'm afraid we are no longer engaged to be married, Pippa. Secretly or otherwise.'

'Oh!' Pippa had been stunned. 'Oh, I'm so very sorry.'

Two days after her return home, Verena had wandered down the path towards the sea at Ragg's Cove and gazed out. *Lucas had killed her father.* If only he'd told her from the very start, she agonised. But when? And how? How could such dreadful news ever be broken gently?

She breathed in the clear sea air. At least Wycherley was safe. She would find her own, small happinesses here. And the stabbingly painful memories of her love for Lucas would fade in time—wouldn't they?

She only wished she could believe it.

Verena went into Framlington the next day and was looking for birthday gifts for Pippa's twins, who would soon be one, when someone riding by called out her name.

It was Captain Martin Bryant.

The last time she'd seen him, he'd done his best to poison her mind against Lucas, to tell her even that he might be working for the French.

And now Martin Bryant pulled his horse up and saluted her. 'Verena! They said you'd been to London!'

As good an alibi as any other. Gazing up at Captain Bryant, she said coldly, 'I've been away, yes. But, as you see, I'm home.'

She wanted to move on, but he seemed not to notice her

coldness. 'I'm rejoining my old division in Portugal soon,' he told her eagerly. 'May I call on you later today?'

Her first impulse was to refuse, but then she thought, *No.* She had one last piece of business with Martin Bryant. Without giving any secrets away, she had to tell him how utterly wrong he had been to speak so maliciously about Lucas.

'You may,' she said, with a calmness she did not feel. 'I will be at home from five.'

By the time he arrived, the October dusk was settling. She realised Martin was restless…nervous, even. After Cook had brought in the tea tray, he would not sit, but paced to and fro in front of the fire, before swinging round to face her and stammering out hotly, 'Verena. I must speak to you about a matter that's been on my mind ever since our meeting today!'

'And I, too,' she said crisply, 'need to speak to *you*, Captain Bryant. You spoke to me some weeks ago about Lord Lucas Conistone.'

'Ah, yes,' he said, shrugging. His pale blue eyes first kept darting to the door, then to the window. 'Yes, perhaps I was wrong about Conistone, but there's something else.' His eyes were fixed on her now. 'Verena, it's about your father.'

Oh, no. 'Even less,' she responded quickly, 'do I want to talk about *him*.'

'But this is something you must know! Please—if you'll just step outside with me, so we are alone…' He pointed to the door which led directly out into the garden.

She hesitated, her heart thudding. Did Martin *know* her father had turned traitor? She was absolutely terrified of her family learning the bitter truth.

He had already opened the door and reluctantly she

followed him a little way outside. 'Very well, Captain Bryant,' she said tightly. 'For a few moments only...'

'Just come further into the garden, away from the servants,' he urged. 'I have really important news and I don't want anyone else to hear it!'

If this was about her father, neither did she. She followed him towards a thick copse of fir trees, a sombre spot, where the last of the dying daylight could not penetrate. And heavy raindrops were starting to fall. She suddenly imagined she heard a low whispering, somewhere in the undergrowth.

Her heart started to race. She could not help but remember that night in July when she'd gone down to the cove and those Frenchmen had tried to abduct her. She felt very cold. And they had already gone further from the house than she'd intended.

'This is quite far enough, Captain Bryant,' she declared, starting to turn. 'In fact, I think I should go back in, for it's starting to rain—'

That was when he leaped on her. And—there were two others, coming swiftly from the shadows of the trees. She started to cry out, but Martin's hand was clamped across her mouth and one of his companions pinned her arms behind her back. She couldn't breathe. Her senses were starting to reel, but still she fought.

The two men cursed her in French. Martin Bryant looked like one demented as he ordered them to hold her tight. He had a piece of rope in his hands. She struggled with the last of her strength.

'You,' she cried to Martin. 'And the French—*you* are working for them...'

'We wanted your father's diary,' he grated out. 'That damned Lucas Conistone got it, instead. And now—we want Conistone.'

In the rain that was falling steadily now, he started

wrapping the rope around her wrists. That was when the full horror dawned. They were going to use her to lure Lucas into a trap. She was feeling sick, but she shook her head in defiance. 'No. You've got it all wrong. Lucas is in Portugal!'

A malicious smile twisted Martin Bryant's face. 'But, you see, he's not. I got news yesterday that he's on his way back to England.'

Her heart hammered. 'That may be so! But what makes you think he'd trouble himself to come here to Wycherley?'

'He will,' said Martin Bryant. 'Because I'll let him know that you are my prisoner. Conistone escaped my pistol before, but he won't this time.'

'You—*shot* him?'

He glanced at her quickly. 'At Wycherley, yes.'

The broken window...

Her hands were tied securely and the two Frenchmen were already manhandling her in the near darkness along the steep path that led down to Ragg's Cove. It could be hours before anyone realised she was missing.

She tried again, twisting her head to see Martin as he followed grimly behind. 'If Lucas does come, he will bring help!'

'I'll tell him to come alone.'

No good despairing. No good screaming for help. No one could hear and these men would just silence her by tying something round her mouth, or worse. She must think how to help Lucas, who might soon be charging headfirst into danger on her account.

'Martin,' she breathed as they dragged her down the path to the beach, '*why*?'

The bitter look in his pale blue eyes frightened her. 'Believe me, I had good reason, Verena. It was the only way I could get out of that hellhole of a French prison after Talavera. It was the price of my life. Why should others, like Lucas Conistone and his friends, live in the lap of luxury when people like me were marching across barren mountains eating wretched army food and being shot to pieces?'

Verena thought of Busaco. Of the danger and hardship that Lucas endured willingly. That terrible sabre scar… She whispered, 'You're wrong, so very wrong! Lucas has given up so much to serve his country!'

'Rubbish,' said Martin shortly. 'He plays games, your secret hero. And unlike the ordinary soldiers, he's free to sail back to the life of a wealthy man, with his friends of the Prince's set, abandoning himself to the decadent parties, the beautiful women.'

'You're lying,' she said bitterly. 'You've *always* lied about him!'

But if he heard her, he did not respond. They were nearly down at the shore now. Her captors' shoes were crunching on shingle. In the darkness she saw the gleam of a rowing boat, anchored twenty yards or so from the sea's edge. With the rope still tugging rawly at her wrists, Verena turned to him defiantly.

'After this, Martin? What's next for you, after this?'

After betraying your country? She was thinking desperately. She guessed they would take her to some isolated spot, keep her prisoner until Lucas came after her, and then they would ambush him. Kill him…

Martin's eyes were wild. 'What's next? Why, I will be rewarded, of course! And I thought you'd marry me if I had money, Verena!'

She exclaimed, 'Are you mad?'

'Why not? The French have promised me gold to capture or kill Conistone—enough gold to give me—and you—the chance of a better life! I can offer you so much, Verena! I—I care for you so much!'

Dear God. He was out of his mind. Forcing herself to breathe steadily, she lifted her eyes to him, wide, pleading. 'Untie me, Martin. Please.' She made a huge endeavour to soften her voice. 'Look—my wrists are bleeding. If you truly care for me, as you say, you cannot want me to suffer. And—if you are *kind* to me…'

She let the hint of a promise slip into her voice. She despised herself for it, but she had no other weapon. The two Frenchmen had gone wading into the sea to haul the boat nearer. Martin lurched towards her, the light of hope in his pale eyes.

'*Kind* to you? Are you saying that there's a chance, Verena? That you could really feel something for me?'

He was mad, she realised in complete despair, to think she could feel anything but contempt for him. Though her heart was hammering, she managed to murmur softly, 'Martin, we all make mistakes, don't we? Please, free me from these ropes, if you have the regard for me that you claim…'

He was breathing hard. 'I can't let you go free. But I can loosen them a little.'

'Then do that. *Please*. It's hurting so much!'

'I don't want you in pain, Verena! Never that!' He started working at the knot, loosening her bindings.

'Thank you,' she breathed. 'Thank you, Martin…'

One of the Frenchmen hauling in the boat was calling to him. Martin hesitated, then hurried down to the water's edge.

Instantly Verena fought furiously with her bonds. In relaxing the knot, he'd made it possible—just—for her to work her hands free, though the coarse rope tore into her skin.

Now Martin was coming back, his hand outstretched. 'Verena, you're to come on the boat now, they're taking you to—'

She swung her freed fists up together, hammering them forcefully into his face and clawing at him with her fingernails. He staggered back, the marks of her fingers livid on his cheek. Then she ran. She heard Martin screaming her name, lurching after her, stumbling in the dark. *Aim for the rocks ahead of you. You must climb up through a narrow cleft, then left a foot or two, to the next ledge. Now up again, to the right…*

When she and Pippa were children they used to play games in this secluded cove, pretending they were smugglers. She prayed she could remember the way. The rain had stopped, but the rocks were still slippery. *A steep climb up to the next gap in the rock.* She was on the cliff face now, her skirts impeding her. *Handholds here to the left, and up, up towards the top…* Not far to go. Not far. Her breath was coming in short, ragged gasps.

She could hear Martin clambering after her, roaring out her name. She was growing tired and was almost at the cliff top when she lost her footing. She recovered herself, just in time, but she jarred her left wrist badly, and felt the splinters of pain tearing up through her arm like a jagged knife.

Martin was after her still, cursing. Somehow she dragged herself on, up towards the cliff top, her lungs on fire. Pain and exhaustion muffled her senses. She must be going mad herself, because she could hear the sound of drums; at first she thought herself back at Busaco, listening to the faint but ominous approach of the mighty army of the French.

Then she realised. *The procession.* She'd forgotten. It was the start of the festivities, for St Luke's fair! Her father had long ago given the villagers permission to walk through

Wycherley's land, along the cliff path on the night before the October fair. And they were coming now, with drums and fiddlers, all the locals like Billy and old Tom, and Ned Sawrey and their wives and families. She could see the faint glow of their many lanterns, hear the laughter of excited children…

It was all so happy and normal that she wanted to weep. And all she had to do was get to them. But she could hear rocks tumbling close behind her. Her palms were torn and bleeding. As she heaved herself up the last few feet of the crumbling cliff face, she had to use both hands, and her senses reeled as new and agonising pain tore through her left wrist.

And Martin was getting closer, his voice harsh as he gasped out, 'You deceived me, bitch! I'll kill you! I've got a gun!'

Chapter Twenty-Seven

Lucas had found a ship to take him to Portsmouth, and Alec Stewart insisted on travelling with him. 'I need to report to the Navy Board in Portsmouth,' Alec declared, 'and then I'll be able to lend a hand. No arguing, Lucas.'

They both knew that Verena could well be in trouble. They both knew speed was essential. But off Ushant a heavy storm rolled up from the Bay of Biscay and their ship had to seek shelter. Lucas, burning with frustration, had no choice but to accept the delay.

He thought all the time of Verena. Why had she flown Coimbra so suddenly? What in God's name had she heard? He was desperate with anxiety by the time the little ship at last reached Portsmouth, where Alec promised, 'I'll follow you, Lucas. I'll be on my way to Wycherley just as soon as I've got my business here sorted.'

Lucas galloped the ten miles to Wycherley in the rain.

Verena was not in the house. Turley said, bewildered, as Lucas strode from room to room calling her name, 'I don't understand, my lord! She was with Captain Bryant in the parlour, taking tea less than half an hour ago…'

With Bryant. God in heaven…

It was then that Lucas noticed the door to the garden was still ajar. He charged out into the darkness, roaring her name, with Turley close behind. Lucas turned to him and almost shook him. 'She's in danger, man. We need everyone we can get to search for her, do you understand?'

Turley's brow was furrowed with worry. 'Of course. But everyone's at the procession, my lord.'

'What procession?'

'It's the eve of St Luke's fair. They were starting off down in Framlington, an hour or so ago. You ride and find them, they'll help for sure! Oh, Miss Verena, if anything should happen to her…'

And so Lucas saddled up again in search of the torchlit procession of villagers, and found them closer than he'd dared hope, just above Ragg's Cove. Billy and Ned were leading the way; the beating of the drums suddenly stopped as he sprang off his sweat-sheened horse to confront them. They gathered round and shook their heads in dismay at his question. 'Miss Verena's gone from the house and no one knows where? No, Lord Conistone! We've not seen 'er! But we can get a search party together right now, if you want, my lord!'

It was then that he heard someone calling his name. So faintly, but it was a voice he would know anywhere. 'Hush!' he cried. Then he called louder, *'Verena!'*

The procession had already ground to a halt. Now the music was stilled and the chatter, too.

'Lucas…' The voice again.

Lucas swung round, gazing towards the cliff. Then he threw his horse's reins at someone, grabbed a lantern and was running, running for its edge. And he could see her, just a few feet from safety, clinging in the darkness to the crumbling rock face as stones and dust rattled down the steep drop below.

'Lucas!' she called again.

'Verena.' Quickly he assessed the situation. 'We'll get you safely up. *Hold on...*'

Then he saw Martin Bryant, about ten feet below her, pressed into a crevice on the cliff face, aiming his pistol.

Lucas was reaching for his own gun, but before he could shoot, something heavy went hurtling down past his shoulder. Bryant juddered with shock, let out a great cry and toppled backwards into the darkness.

'Nothin' like a good lump of rock, Lord Conistone,' said Billy grimly. 'And my aim is always spot on. Now, the main thing is to get Miss Verena up to safety.'

Ned was already running to them with a rope; Lucas tied one end swiftly round his own waist, and while Ned and Billy held the free end secure he lowered himself to where Verena still clung and grasped her tightly.

'Oh, Lucas.' She felt fragile to him, and infinitely precious as she wrapped her arms round his waist and breathed his name.

'My love,' he whispered, pressing his cheek against hers. 'Thank God you're safe.' He called up to Billy, 'Pull away!'

By the time he got her to the top of the cliff and rested her on the sea-turf there, her eyes were closed. He knelt and lifted her hands to examine the scratches that covered her palms; she let out a low cry at that and her eyes opened wide.

'Damn,' he swore softly. He saw that her wrist was badly swollen.

He turned. The villagers hovered close by, anxious, silent. Still cradling her, he called to Billy and Matt to bring him his horse. 'She's hurt. I'm going to take her, now, to the doctor's house.'

'No, Lucas!' she argued. She was trying to sit up. 'You must get Martin Bryant!'

Lucas doubted Bryant would have survived his fall. As well for him if he didn't. 'I think Martin Bryant's taken care of,' he said softly.

'But the others—'

'What others?'

'There were two Frenchmen, down at the shore, with a boat. Be careful—they're armed…'

'Not for much longer,' Lucas answered grimly. 'Alec will be here shortly, and he'll get them in. Right now I'm concerned about *you*. You've hurt your wrist.'

'Oh, that.' She tried to shrug and smile. 'It's just bruised…'

'Bruised! My brave, foolish, beautiful girl, it looks to me very much as if it's broken. The doctor must attend to it.'

'Such a fuss,' she said faintly. And then, half to herself, 'Miss Bonamy would advise that a lady should never draw attention to her ailments.'

'Miss Bonamy be damned,' Lucas Conistone said with considerable force. 'Billy! Ned! Pass Miss Sheldon up to me, will you?'

He mounted his big horse first, then the careful hands of Billy and the others lifted her up, so he could settle her sideways in front of him. He clasped her tightly with his left hand round her waist, the reins in his right. The warmth of her, the sweet scent of her skin and her clouds of tumbling hair, ravished his senses. The thought of the terrible danger she'd been in tore at him as if someone had stabbed his heart.

He wanted her. And not just physically—though, damn

it, even now the nearness of her, the sweet pressure of her body against his thighs and loins, was setting his lust surging again—but he wanted her at his side, as his life's companion. She was brave, she was sweet, she was utterly endearing. Who else but Verena Sheldon would have chased him to Portsmouth, endured the company of a shipful of whores, then dragged Bentinck up to Busaco ridge to deliver that vital map?

She was more precious than anything to him. He had gambled all to gain her trust, her love. He'd thought she had come to terms so bravely with the dreadful news that her father was a traitor.

Yet something, in Coimbra, had made her run from him.

But she had called out his name, there on the cliff face. She had turned to him in her moment of need. And now, nestling into him with a little sigh, it was as if she *knew* she belonged in his arms... Damn it all, was there still hope?

When Verena opened her eyes she realised that Lucas was steadily guiding his horse along the road down to Framlington and she was cradled against his strong, warm body. Feeling his heart beating steadily was enough to make her pain seem as nothing. Above her the black sky wheeled and the stars shone brightly.

'All right, *querida*?' he murmured.

'Thank you, I am,' she whispered. The endearment, from him, sounded so right. So true. She'd thought that Martin Bryant would end her life with his pistol. No one else but Lucas could have been here, at the very place, the very moment, to save her...

Yet he had killed her father.

She could not bear to know the details. Not yet. But her heart ached for what could never be.

She lifted her head to see him frowning, his austere profile silvered in the moonlight.

'I'm a fool,' he was saying bitterly as they drew closer to the village. 'I should have guessed about Bryant much earlier. It must have been he who lit that fire on the cliff to guide in the French who attacked you…'

Of course. 'And it was Martin who shot at you through the window, wasn't it, Lucas?'

He glanced at her sharply. 'You knew about that?'

'He told me. Tonight. He said, "Conistone escaped my pistol before, but he won't this time." Oh, Lucas…' she drew a ragged breath '…you should have told me about *everything*.'

He said tersely, 'And you should have been honest with *me*, Verena. Why in God's name did you leave Coimbra?'

She felt her throat tighten. He sounded angry. Anguished. How could she say to him now, when he had yet again risked his own life for hers, *'Lucas, I know that you killed my father?'*

She answered very quietly, 'Maybe I felt I'd done what I needed to do. Paid my father's debts.'

'Oh, Verena.' He was cradling her strongly, tenderly, using just one hand on the reins. 'You've paid in full and more. Why punish yourself so?'

She shook her head, speechless. Her wrist was starting to ache badly again. Yet his tender arm around her caused ten times more pain than any physical hurt.

Lucas seemed about to say something else. Then— 'We will talk later,' he said curtly.

Yes. Later. And she must put an end to any lingering hope.

Paid in full and more? Perhaps. Yet she had made such dreadful mistakes along the way. She had misjudged Lucas again and again, assuming him lazy and indolent. Believing Deb's false accusations about him. Thinking he had set Bentinck to spy on her when really Bentinck was her protector.

Misjudgements could be corrected. But the final hurdle was insurmountable. Yes, she believed he *did* love her, in his way; but how could marriage ever work, when every time he looked at her, he would be reminded of her father, his treachery and his death?

Her heart surged with almost unbearable emotion. Yes, it was all almost over. But—and she lifted her chin in defiance—no one could take away the love she'd felt for him. Still felt for him. She would never love anyone else. Lucas Conistone was incomparable.

That was her tragedy; the memory of his love would also be her inner joy, in the years to come. She closed her eyes, clenching her teeth, because now the pain in her wrist was white-hot, consuming all her thoughts, and only his strong grasp was keeping her from succumbing to it.

It was Dr Pilkington's spinster sister Maude who answered the door. Maude quickly summoned her brother, and he looked suitably startled to find Lord Conistone there, carrying Verena in his arms.

'We need your services, Doctor,' Lucas said quickly. 'Miss Sheldon met with an accident.'

Dr Pilkington sized up the situation swiftly, and if he wanted to ask more, hid it well. 'St Luke's Eve celebrations, I take it, my lord Conistone?'

He drew Lucas aside and spoke briefly with him, while Maude kindly ushered Verena through to his consulting room and lit candles. There Dr Pilkington soon joined her and gently examined her wrist. 'My dear Miss Sheldon, it looks as if you've broken it! No, perhaps it's just a bad sprain…'

'I fell, you see. So stupid of me,' she murmured.

'Hmm.' His voice expressed mild but significant doubt. Gentle though the doctor was, the pain still sliced through her as he applied a cold compress and went to search for bandages. 'Good of Lord Conistone to bring you in,' he went on as he worked. 'He was just telling me he must leave for London tonight, some important business; but he wanted to see that you were all right first. He works for the government, doesn't he? Rather dangerous stuff, I believe.'

'You know!'

'I guessed. That sabre scar, amongst other things. Thought I'd better keep it quiet, eh?'

He was binding her wrist now, with the utmost care, then called to Maude, who brought hot, sweet tea laced with laudanum drops. Verena took only a sip. She was in torment, both physical and mental, but laudanum was not the answer. The door was open and briefly she saw Lucas outside, pacing the hallway, his hands clasped behind his back, his dark head bowed.

She wanted to call out to him. *Lucas. My love, please forgive me, for everything. Take care of yourself. And remember that wherever you go, you take my heart with you.*

She woke in the night. The room was dark except for a single candle glowing in a corner. She saw Maude sitting in a chair with some embroidery lying in her lap, snoring gently.

Verena's wrist, still tightly bandaged, seemed to ache a little less, but her heart, she felt, would never mend.

Lucas would have gone by now. Martin Bryant would be

dead or captured. Her father's maps had saved the British army at Busaco, and now it was over. She closed her eyes and felt tears pricking at her lids.

Stupid, stupid to cry. Verena Sheldon was not supposed to cry. Verena Sheldon was the sensible one, the pillar of her family. It was only because she was tired still, and because of the pain…

She must have slept a little again, but she opened her eyes quickly, because she thought she'd heard footsteps, and quiet voices.

Maude had gone. The door was open.

'How are you feeling?'

A drawling male voice. Lucas's voice. He stood in the doorway, his tall frame dominating the small room, his handsome face etched into planes of light and dark by the candlelight.

She blinked. Confused. 'But Dr Pilkington told me you were going to London—'

'I decided London can wait a while.'

She caught her breath. *Implying that he would rather be here?* No. Impossible.

He strolled closer, soft-footed as a cat. But she knew that softness was deceptive, because he was a leader of men. A killer of men.

'Did you—find Captain Bryant?'

'He died in his fall from the cliff, Verena. Alec arrived very soon afterwards, and with the help of some of the villagers he rounded up Bryant's French friends and escorted them to Chichester gaol.' He sat by her side, pulling up Maude's empty chair. 'I asked you how you were.'

She managed a faint smile. 'A sprained wrist—it's nothing, I assure you! But Lucas, you should have gone to London, I'll be quite all right now.'

A shadow of anger crossed his face. '*Leave* you? In God's name, why?' He clenched his fists. 'You are ignoring the fact that I asked you to be my wife! Damn it all, Verena, what if I refuse to let you go?'

She swallowed hard on the ache in her throat. *I never knew love could hurt so much.* 'Lucas, I know that you feel bound by duty. But I understand that you cannot possibly marry me.'

'Why ever not?'

'Because of my father!'

He rasped, 'Your father, Verena, was led by foolishness and greed to *attempt* to become a traitor, and you have more than made up for his folly—'

She broke in quietly, 'I know that you killed him, Lucas.'

He was on his feet. He sat down again. He drew one hand across his brow. 'Tell me. Tell me how you know that.'

Her throat was dry, her wrist throbbing. 'I—I overheard you and Alec talking, down in the courtyard, when you came for me at Coimbra…'

His eyes were dark. Hooded. *That damned conversation with Alec in the courtyard of the inn where she was staying.* She must have been somewhere near. Hell and damnation…

'Dear God,' he said softly. His eyes burned into hers. He said at last, slowly and deliberately, 'I did not kill your father.'

'But Alec said—'

He got up suddenly again from his chair and this time paced the room, running his hand distractedly through his hair. 'I was responsible for his death, yes. But—*I did not kill him.*' He swung round on her. 'Hell. I had better tell you everything.'

He sat down again, tense. 'That autumn, when I was

home on leave, I knew nothing about what your father was up to, Verena, I swear. But—when Lord Wellington asked me to resign, and to work in secret for him, in England, as well as the Peninsula—I was told about your father.'

She nodded mutely, feeling a black hole of despair opening up within her.

Lucas went on tersely, 'We knew, I'm afraid, that your father was negotiating to sell vital information to the French. We knew that he kept a diary, crammed with records and maps of his travels. We could not let the French get it. That winter we chased your father into the mountains on the Spanish border and caught him at the edge of a deep gorge. He could go no further. He said, "Look after her for me, will you, Lucas? Tell her I did it for Wycherley. For all of them." Then he said, "For God's sake, look after Verena..."'

Lucas let his voice trail away. Verena gazed at him, white as a sheet.

Lucas went on, in a low voice, 'I told him that if he would come back with me, and hand over his diary and all his papers to the British, there might be hope for him. And your father hesitated, Verena! I'd swear he hesitated! He was clutching something wrapped in oilskin, and I guessed it was his diary. But then—' and here Lucas rubbed his fingers across his temples '—some of our soldiers came rushing up. He just repeated the words, "Look after her," and stepped backwards—to his death. The river at the bottom of the gorge swept him away. He chose his own end, Verena.' Lucas sighed and leaned back. 'And his very last thoughts were of you.'

The silence lay heavily between them. Verena said at last, in what was little more than a whisper, 'And he did not have the diary anyway.'

'No. At least, not the one we wanted, the old one; my grandfather had that. Your father's body was found earlier this year, Verena, and he was buried in the mountains he loved.' He was gazing at her with dark, ravaged eyes. 'You will think I should have told you all this from the beginning. But you see, I guessed you already hated me. You'd answered none of my letters, and I thought you would hate me even more if you realised I was there at your father's death. Yes, I wanted that diary for Wellington, but I still loved you. I never stopped loving you.'

He drew a deep breath. 'We know the truth now. The diary Jack Sheldon had been holding was one he'd started afresh, only weeks before. My grandfather had tricked him. And my grandfather had hidden the diary we wanted, though, frustrated and half-mad, he'd been unable to read it. Whereas you, Verena, possessed what turned out to be the most important of all your father's possessions—the map of the mines at Busaco.'

Verena closed her eyes, imagining her father's desperation before he jumped to his death. *Oh, Papa. Why...*

Lucas eased his chair back from her side and said quietly, 'I will leave you in peace now, to sleep. I just wanted you to know the truth. All of it.'

The anguish tore through her very soul. Yet again, she had misjudged this man. And surely this time he would never forgive her.

'You must go, Lucas,' she said steadily, swallowing on the burning ache in her throat. 'The doctor told me you have urgent business in London.'

He was standing up. 'It's true, I'm afraid I can't postpone my journey any longer. Alec tells me Bryant's French friends have begun to reveal vital information about a network of enemy spies here in England, and I must report it.'

She nodded. 'I understand.'

Afterwards, when he'd gone, she lay awake; and the

pain in her bound wrist was nowhere near as great as the pain in her heart. This, surely, was the end. *Oh, Lucas.* Oh, my love.

Chapter Twenty-Eight

Wycherley Hall had never been a busier or happier place, for Izzy was having her eighteenth birthday party here tonight, and almost a hundred guests had arrived already. But Viscount Conistone, whom her mother had invited along with his friend Alec Stewart, had not replied to the invitation. Lucas was living the high life with the Prince's set, people said.

Verena knew the truth about Lucas Conistone now and she felt privileged for knowing it. She had been busy for the last week from dawn till dusk, organising everything; though just sometimes she would stop, for no reason, in whatever she was doing, remembering Lucas. Thinking she heard his soft, drawling voice. Thinking she saw him striding towards her, a glad smile on his handsome face.

The nights were the hardest. She would lie awake, afraid of sleep, because sometimes she dreamed he was there, holding her in his arms. And to wake from those dreams was agony.

Though it was mid-November, the day had been full of sunshine. All afternoon the villagers had brought presents for Izzy, and been offered copious refreshment. And now the Sheldons' friends and relatives were still pouring in for the evening's party.

Then Verena suddenly saw a familiar figure—'Alec!'—and her heart skipped a beat, but as he came striding towards her, smiling, she saw he was alone. Verena forced her disappointment aside to greet him warmly and only later asked him if he had news of Lucas, putting her question politely, as if she and Lucas were but distant acquaintances.

'He's busy,' Alec replied equally lightly, 'busy as ever, my dear Miss Sheldon!'

So—he was going to tell her nothing.

'And Portugal?' she asked, quickly changing the subject. 'I heard that Lord Wellington and his army reached Lisbon successfully.'

'They did,' he told her earnestly. 'Wellington won the race for Lisbon, which has been turned into a mighty fortress by the British; and there his lordship can prepare his troops for a fresh offensive against the enemy come the new year.'

She thought, *The victory at Busaco helped make all this possible. And my father's papers played their part. I played my part...*

Small compensation for waking every morning with a cold, empty hollow where her heart should be.

Suddenly she heard her mother.

'Captain Stewart?' Lady Frances's voice was coming piercingly nearer as she swept towards them and pulled up in a rustle of silks and lace. 'My dear Captain Stewart, I do trust you are enjoying our *petite assemblée*?'

Her mother was still practising her French phrases for London; next week, they returned there. Alec bowed low over her hand. 'Most thoroughly, Lady Sheldon; charming feathers in your hair, by the way; excellent to see you in such blooming health! You look as young as your lovely daughters!'

Lady Frances tapped his hand with her fan. 'Dear boy,' she crooned, 'you're such a tease! *Such* exciting times—I knew everything would come right for us! Oh, my darling Deb, my darling Izzy—next spring one of them will doubtless make the match of the Season!'

She was eyeing up Alec, speculatively; Alec, laughing, promised to dance with each of them. 'But Verena first!' he insisted.

Verena, her wrist quite healed, gladly allowed him to lead her towards the set, and said, with a smile lurking at the corners of her mouth, 'I fear my mother is in matchmaking mode.'

'Then I, my dear Miss Sheldon, am of no use to her whatsoever!' He shook his head. 'Quite done up, as they say—quite done up!'

'You will have to find yourself an heiress,' said Verena softly. 'A very kind, lovely heiress. Alec, I'm so sorry I misjudged you.'

His eyes danced. 'You thought me a wastrel and a rake—' he smiled '—which meant my ruse was working. Made it easier for Lucas, you see, if he was seen mixing with a layabout like me… As to that heiress, I think I'd prefer to find true love. But that is rare indeed.'

Indeed. She hesitated, then said, 'You told me Lucas is busy. I suppose he is at present in London or Lisbon or some other faraway place?'

'Lucas is a law unto himself, so it's no use quizzing me, dear Miss Sheldon. I will only say something wrong and get myself in a pickle! He asked you to trust him, didn't he?'

'Yes! But—'

'Then do so,' said Alec Stewart firmly and whirled her into the dance.

Supper was served next, and Verena knew she should mingle. Should share the general happiness. But—she couldn't. Just for once, she could not pretend.

She shrugged on a cloak, and slipped out into the garden to watch the moonlight glimmering over the dark, sparkling sea.

She had resolved to put Lucas Conistone from her mind, but it was no good. The terrible ache in her heart whenever she thought of him was as great as ever. She put her hands to her face. He would not come near her again, ever. She had misjudged him too often, and too badly…

Suddenly she thought she heard slow, steady footsteps, coming towards her from the house. She whirled round, her pulse racing.

A man stood, his imposing figure etched silver by the moonlight. His ebony hair gleamed softly, curling around the familiar hard, strong profile. The whiteness of his shirt made the darkness of his exquisitely fitted riding coat all the more striking; the soft fabric clung as if moulded to his wide shoulders, skimming past his lean torso and powerful legs.

Lucas. Here. His grey eyes were hooded, his expression unreadable.

She forced herself into calmness as he walked towards her. 'My lord. We were not expecting you…'

'Weren't you? Your mother invited me.'

He was very close now. Verena's heart was thumping against her ribs. 'Poor Mama,' she attempted to say lightly. 'She doesn't give up, does she?'

His eyes captured hers. Dark, intense, the iron grey

gleaming with gold. 'Neither do I, Miss Sheldon,' he said softly.

She clasped her hands together, struggling to make the small talk that she usually found so easy. Easy with anyone but Lucas. 'I hear from Alec—' *Alec must have known Lucas was on his way here!* '—that you've been busy.'

'Yes,' he said. 'I've been back to Lisbon, where Wellington's defences are holding well.'

'Alex told me a little of it—I'm so very glad.'

'And my lord Wellington asked me about the heroine of Busaco, so I told him about your wrist. He told me—practically ordered me—to leave my duties and come home to see you.' He was drawing closer. She saw the lines of tension, and fatigue, etched around his eyes, but his expression was full of warmth. And something else. Longing? Yearning? She could not begin to hope; it was too painful. But…

He took her hand and kissed it gently.

'Verena,' he said huskily, 'I tried to listen to what you said. I tried to accept that we should be apart. But I had to come to you just one more time, to tell you how I feel.'

Her pulse began to race. 'I understand, Lucas. I know you can never forget, about my father…'

'You are not your father.' He shook his dark head slightly. 'Verena, I never stopped caring for you, ever.'

Never stopped caring. She could hardly breathe. Her heart squeezed tight as if clamped in a vice.

'But,' he went on in the same low, rich voice that drove fresh shafts of anguish through her, 'I was so desperately afraid that you would hate me, if you knew everything.'

She drew a deep breath. Her throat was aching; somehow she managed to speak steadily. 'Of course.' She lifted her gaze to meet his—*this might be the last time you are alone with him, you must be calm, you must be strong*... 'And I realise,' she went on, 'it's not just my father. Lucas. I'm afraid I have made so many incredibly foolish mistakes—'

'No more than I, Verena. And yours were only out of loyalty to your family.' A muscle at the corner of his mouth clenched. 'Who, except for Pippa, do not deserve you in the slightest. And neither do I.'

He was turning away again, his face in shadow. She braced herself.

This is the moment. He is going to tell me that in spite of everything, we must say goodbye. I must not let him know how just seeing him again is tearing me into pieces...

He was reaching into the deep pocket of his greatcoat, then turning back to her and smiling. And in his strong, lean hand was—a small box of morocco leather.

He said, in that husky voice that she had grown to love so dearly, 'Verena. My darling. I'm hoping you will forgive me: for the times I've let you down, the times I've not been here when you needed me... Verena, I need your love, so very much.'

She gazed at him, her eyes wide with questions. He nodded. 'Please. Open it.'

In it was a ring, a spectacular diamond encircled by emeralds. He put it on her finger, and drew her into his arms, his lips caressing her forehead with a tender kiss. 'It's known as the Stancliffe diamond,' he whispered. 'A pretentious name. But I want you to accept it as my bride-to-be.'

Her pulse was racing. In shock. And—hope; yes, she dared, at last, to hope. 'Lucas...'

He was gazing deep into her eyes. 'It's not good enough for you, but I offer it with my whole heart. Verena, I love you. Your sense of honour; your selflessness; your love for Wycherley and its people; your loyalty, even to your father...

Listen to me, *meu amor.* I want you with me. Always. If I have to go away again, I want to know that you will be here, waiting for me. Will you marry me? Can you learn, perhaps, to love me?'

'Oh,' she said quietly, 'I have loved you for years. So very much, Lucas.'

His eyes were dark with the promise of passion as he lowered his mouth and brushed his lips against her own, letting his fingers tenderly stroke her cheek. With the tip of his tongue he caressed the soft fullness of her lower lip, and sensation spiralled in her as she opened to him, tasting his sweetness. The kiss was long and incandescent with mutual desire.

He drew away reluctantly. Murmured huskily, 'Oh. And by the way, Miss Sheldon—did I tell you how incredibly *beautiful* you are?'

She gazed up at him, her heart full, her eyes shimmering with love. 'If it means another kiss like that,' she breathed, 'then, Lucas, you can tell me again and again.'

And Verena felt that her own private heaven was finally attainable.

Epilogue

March 1811—London

The meeting in the War Office had gone on into the early hours. Lord Lucas Conistone, escaping at last, took deep breaths of the crisp night air and drank in the sounds and scents of London by night. Overhead the sky was for once clear of the city's smoke, and, seeing a lone bright star, he remembered the velvety nights in the mountains of the Peninsula, with a million stars overhead. Remembered too the rolling downs of Hampshire at midnight, where the air would be headily scented with spring gorse, and early primroses, and the sea…

Soon, he would be riding westwards. Heading home. His travels, for now, were over.

Yesterday morning he'd returned from Lisbon bearing dispatches. Since then he'd been closeted with the King's chief ministers, and Lucas had been able to tell them, personally, the news: that Wellington's strategy of wintering safely in Lisbon, after luring a large French army into pursuit, had succeeded beyond their wildest expectations.

The French had endured a terrible winter of starvation and disease while trying to besiege the British force, and in early March the enemy had to turn round and make the exhausting march back to the frontier through the barren hills, harried all the way by the Portuguese. All in all, the French had lost twenty-five thousand men.

Lord Liverpool, Secretary for War, whom Lucas knew had valiantly struggled against his government colleagues to get more men and supplies for Wellington's vital campaign, had barely been able to conceal his delight, and relief. 'What next, Conistone?'

'Lord Wellington is preparing, my lord, to move out from Lisbon to secure all of Portugal, then aim for the French-held Spanish border fortresses by the summer,' Lucas replied.

'And, by God, he'll take them too!' Lord Liverpool was jubilant. 'We'll have Bonaparte on the run! Appreciate all your efforts, Conistone. And Wellington wrote to me you had more than a little to do with the success of that vital encounter at Busaco last September—is it true?'

Lucas did not answer straight away. Lord Liverpool was to tell a colleague afterwards that he seemed—abstracted. But finally, Lucas said, 'The real credit lies with someone who prefers to remain anonymous, my lord.' And a smile lifted the corner of his mouth.

Lord Liverpool patted his shoulder. 'Well, thank the fellow heartily when next you see him, will you? Now, we'd better let you go, Conistone. You've had a lot to deal with since your grandfather died.'

The old Earl had passed away in December. Lucas, the new Earl, had been torn between his duties to the great estate and his role as Wellington's aide—but Verena had told him to fulfil his commitment to the army by travelling to Portugal just one more time.

'Lord Wellington needs you,' she told him softly. 'It will take him time to find a replacement for you.'

'Won't you miss me, *minha querida*?'

'I'll miss you every minute of every day, Lucas,' she said in her quiet, tender voice. 'But you must do your duty, as you always have.'

They'd been married in the Wycherley church, just as she'd wished, on a sunny late November day, and she'd looked exquisite, her amber eyes luminous with happiness. As the great drawing room of Stancliffe Manor rang with music from the orchestra, Verena danced every dance—with Lucas. The Earl, though his health was failing, was present throughout, enjoying this happy occasion, his animosity towards the Sheldons forgotten. He died peacefully in his bed, a few days later.

There was much to do to set the house and the estate to rights. Before Lucas left for Lisbon in late December, with the frost crisping the ground, he had asked Verena if she wished to spend the next few weeks in London with her mother and sisters while he was away, so she could enjoy their company and the shops and theatres. But she'd said, no, there would be time enough for all that when he was home again for good.

Alec was waiting outside the War Office for him, with a horse. The plan was that Lucas stay at Alec's house in Bedford Street for what remained of the night, then set off for Hampshire at first light.

'So that's the end of your travels for now?' queried Alec lightly.

'For a while.' Lucas, swinging easily astride the big horse, grinned at him, his teeth white in the darkness. 'After all, I've got my reputation as a man of leisure to keep up.'

'And an earldom to look after,' Alec reminded him. 'So

you'll not be serving as Lord Wellington's secret agent again?'

'Did I say that, Alec?'

Alec sighed. 'There'll be the devil to pay if Verena thinks you plan to go off adventuring again!'

'Not in the near future,' declared Lucas. He couldn't wait to get home to Verena. 'How's your latest heiress, Alec? Is a betrothal in the offing?'

Alec shook his head ruefully. 'Her father was a cotton trader, so she's rich as Croesus—but alas, Lucas, the tongue on her! I'm sailing back to Portugal on Monday, and I tell you, the cannons of the French will be a welcome relief after the perils of London's marriage mart!'

They rode on together through the quiet streets, chatting amiably until they got to Bedford Street. Alec's groom was waiting to take the horses; and Lucas, who'd often stayed here before, bade Alec goodnight and headed up to the guest room.

He started to undress, flinging off his coat, his cravat, his shirt. Eyeing the pristine, lonely bed with distaste.

Only one more night alone. Tomorrow, he'd be with Verena.

He had his back to the door and was pulling off his boots, when he heard a soft knock. Heard the door opening.

Lucas sighed. Alec's manservant was attentive, but really, he thought, this was too much…

He swung round. 'I've already said I do not require anything else tonight.'

A husky female voice whispered, 'Not even me?'

His eyes widened. 'What the—?'

Verena was there. She was dressed—if you could call it dressed, he thought in amazement—in a light cream muslin concoction that teased and tantalised. She was smiling at him as she softly sidled into the room and closed the door.

'I should have waited,' she breathed. 'Darling Lucas, I know I should have waited in Hampshire, but then I thought, *why wait any longer*?'

Lucas was laughing, a low, delicious sound as he drew his wife into his arms. 'Alec. I'll tear a strip off him.'

'You won't, will you?' She was smiling back, almost mischievously. 'Once, my lord Conistone, you paid six guineas for me.'

'On board the *Goldfinch*…'

'Exactly. And I merely want to prove to you that you'd made a good bargain, you see!'

He gave a shout of laughter, then, 'Expensive,' he murmured, '*vastly* expensive, let me see…' He pulled her into his arms with a low growl, burying his face in the loose abundance of her hair, and she melted gladly, so gladly into his embrace.

Just for a moment earlier, waiting for his and Alec's return, Verena had thought, *Lucas will be tired, he might be dismayed to see me here. He has such important business to deal with, such important people to see…*

But—no. He was still her adored Lucas. He was swinging her up into his arms as if she weighed nothing; laughing, she clasped her hands round his naked shoulders, her heart racing so wildly, so erotically at the silken feel of those muscles rippling beneath taut skin that she felt almost faint.

'So long, my lord,' she murmured. 'It's been so long.'

'You need wait no longer,' he murmured ardently. He was laying her, ever so gently, on the bed. And then he was pressing kisses to her throat, to her neck, as he quickly loosened the ribbons that held her ridiculous gown together, his fingers grazing her breasts, which ached and stiffened for more. Then he was thrusting off his breeches and moving lower, his tongue tracing a hot line down to her abdomen. She gasped because he was parting her thighs, kissing her sweetly at that tiny nub of pleasure, his tongue probing intimately until she dragged her hands through his thick dark hair and groaned aloud her need.

His own desire was pulsing heavily. Lithely he moved his sleek, strong body up the bed, and she clung to him, murmuring his name, declaring her passionate love as she kissed his chest, his shoulders, his hands.

'There was I thinking you would be waiting at home, my lady,' he murmured teasingly, letting his fingers play with the taut peaks of her nipples. 'Sound asleep in your solitary bed and safely out of mischief…'

'And aren't you glad I'm not?' she breathed, ravenously running her hands along the strong, smooth contours of his shoulders.

Lucas's blood was roaring through his veins. At his groin his erection throbbed, hot and heavy; he was so hard for her that he ached. He bent to kiss her breasts, flicking his tongue back and forth over her nipples; his shaft pressed hard against her belly, and she was moving, writhing against him, letting her silken legs open to the force of his powerful thighs.

'Lucas,' she whispered, her eyes molten with need. 'Please…'

It was a moan of acute desire, answering the desire that surged so relentlessly, like a tide, through every sinew of his body. Verena arched herself up towards him, and he covered her swollen mouth with his, thrusting deep with his tongue. And, taking his weight on his shoulders, he poised himself above her and penetrated her deeply, deliciously. '*Verena.*'

She clung to him in rapture. And he held her there, for

long moments of bliss; held her on a knife-edge of sublime sensation as he slowly, deeply pleasured her, until, with a moan, he lost himself in those sweet depths, was plunging faster and faster; and then there was nothing in the whole world but the two of them. Verena, crying out his name, soared to a pinnacle of pleasure so all-consuming that if she had not been clinging to Lucas, she feared she would have been swept away to oblivion.

In the silent house, somewhere, a clock chimed two. But Lucas, holding her tightly, did not want to sleep yet. Not now this woman who was the centre of his world was back in his arms.

And it seemed she felt the same, for she nestled close to him with a little sigh of contentment, her clouds of hair like a rich curtain across his chest and shoulders. She breathed, 'Tell me. Tell me all your news, my love.'

So he told her, making light of all the hardships and dangers. But she knew. She knew what this man had been through, out of honour, out of duty. Her heart filled with emotion as she listened to his terse account of the long siege of Lisbon. She knew, as she stroked his tired face, that as Wellington's aide Mr Patterson he'd done his utmost for his country, and more.

When he'd finished, he gathered her in his arms so her cheek was cushioned by his shoulder and murmured, 'Now tell me about home.'

Gladly, she told him the things she knew he'd want to hear. How the Wycherley and Stancliffe estates were prospering, and how the villagers had drunk to his health on New Year's Eve.

'And how are you finding life as the grand Lady Stancliffe, my love?' He touched the tip of her nose teasingly.

'Oh, I fulfil my duties exceedingly well!' she declared archly. Then she laughed, and proceeded to tell him how she'd helped David with the birthing of a foal one night in February, and how she'd only last week made a dozen huge Simnel cakes with Pippa and Cook ready for Eastertide. 'And in short,' she concluded, 'I carry on just as before. Mama is quite appalled!'

'And I am delighted,' he told her softly, kissing her forehead, her eyelids, her lips.

This was more than lust—this was true love. Fulfilment. Happiness. Home was wherever Verena was.

At first Verena had been anxious that Stancliffe Manor would be shadowed for her, by painful memories. But then she realised that with Lucas at her side, everything was different. It had also been decided that David and Pippa and their growing family—Pippa was expecting another baby—would move from their farm into Wycherley Hall, for Lady Sheldon, Izzy and Deb much preferred London.

'Deb and dear Izzy,' Verena informed Lucas as she nestled closer in his arms, 'have so many suitors, Lucas, that Mama is near to fainting for joy at every ball they attend!'

'Are you quite sure you, too, don't want to enjoy a month or two of London parties, like your sisters, and order endless new gowns?'

She pretended to shudder. 'Oh, *absolutely* sure!'

He gave a sigh. 'I know. You want to get back in time for the spring sowings, is that it?' he teased.

'Naturally.' She laughed, taking his hands in hers, caressing those long fine fingers, then looked up at him from under downcast lashes, almost shyly. 'Lucas, I just want to be with *you*. Home is wherever you are.'

He enfolded her in his arms and kissed her. 'I love you so much, Verena. You'll have to get used to hearing that, again and again. You won't grow tired of it, will you?'

'Never,' she said, laying her head contentedly against

his chest and feeling his strong, steady heartbeat. 'Never, Lucas, my love.'

She curled against him with a little sigh.

Home was indeed being in this man's arms. The candle had gone out, leaving the room in darkness, but she knew that, at long last, the brightest of futures beckoned, for both of them.

* * * * *

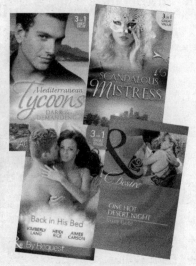

MILLS & BOON®

Why not subscribe?

Never miss a title and save money too!

Here's what's available to you if you join the exclusive **Mills & Boon Book Club** today:

- ✦ *Titles up to a month ahead of the shops*
- ✦ *Amazing discounts*
- ✦ *Free P&P*
- ✦ *Earn Bonus Book points that can be redeemed against other titles and gifts*
- ✦ *Choose from monthly or pre-paid plans*

Still want more?

Well, if you join today we'll even give you ***50% OFF your first parcel!***

So visit **www.millsandboon.co.uk/subs or call Customer Relations on 020 8288 2888** to be a part of this exclusive Book Club!

SUBS_2014

City & County Libraries
WITHDRAWN